ECHO

Scandinavian Stories About Girls

Edited by Ia Dübois and Katherine Hanson

WOMEN IN TRANSLATION
SEATTLE

Publication of this book was made possible with the support of the Danish Literature Information Centre, the Finnish Literature Information Centre, Norwegian Literature Abroad and the Swedish Institute.

Cover painting: Ellen Thesleff: *Echo, 1891*. Private collection Espoo, Finland. Photographer: Central Art Archives/ Antti Kuivalainen. Used with the permission of the Finnish National Gallery.

Cover design: Clare Conrad
Typesetting and text design: Alison Rogalsky

Library of Congress Cataloging-in-Publication Data

ECHO : Scandinavian stories about girls / edited by Ia Dübois and Katherine Hanson.
    p. cm.
ISBN 1-879679-14-0 (alk. paper)
1. Girls—Literary collections. 2. Girls—Scandinavia—Literary collections.
3. Women authors, Scandinavian—Biography.
I. Dübois, Ia. II. Hanson, Katherine, 1946–
PT7092.E5 E24 2000   839'4—dc21   99-055211

Women in Translation
523 N. 84th Street
Seattle, Washington 98103
wit@scn.org
http://www.drizzle.com/~wit/

First edition, April, 2000
Printed in the United States

Acknowledgments

Compiling an anthology is a broad undertaking involving advice, assistance and collaboration from many. We are indebted to the Danish Literature Information Centre, the Finnish Literature Information Centre, Norwegian Literature Abroad and the Swedish Institute for financial support and help in obtaining permissions. To our colleagues and friends who have offered useful suggestions and comments along the way, Lotta Gavel Adams, Roger Holmström, Christine Ingebritsen, Sirkku Latomaa, Michael Schick, and Marianne Stølen, a thousand thanks! Many of the translations in this volume are new and we would like to acknowledge and express our gratitude to the translators—without the careful and creative work of the translators, there would be no anthology. A book is first known by its cover and we are deeply appreciative of the fine cover and text design done by Clare Conrad and Alison Rogalsky respectively. And finally, our most heartfelt thanks to our editor, Barbara Wilson, who has been a constant source of good cheer, invaluable assistance on every aspect of this project, and soothing tea!

SCANDINAVIA

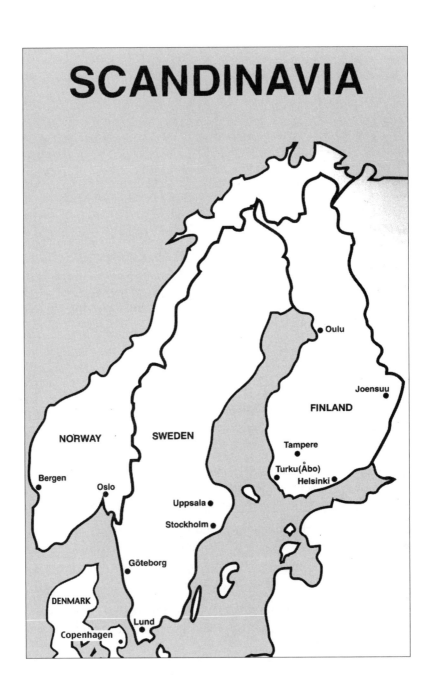

Oulu

Joensuu

FINLAND

NORWAY

SWEDEN

Tampere

Turku(Åbo)

Helsinki

Bergen

Oslo

Uppsala

Stockholm

Göteborg

DENMARK

Lund

Copenhagen

Contents

Introduction

Pippi Longstocking, the red-headed girl with striped stockings, big shoes and a love of adventure burst onto the world scene in the 1950s. But Astrid Lindgren's Pippi was neither the first nor the last strong young female character created by a Scandinavian author. As the fiction and prose excerpts in this collection attest, the tradition of writing for and about children is long-standing in the Nordic countries. From the nineteenth century to contemporary times, writers have delighted in telling stories about adventuresome, creative, bold and thoughtful girls.

That these relatively small countries on Europe's northern edge should have produced such a vibrant literature for and about young people tells us something about the status children enjoy in Scandinavian society. Scandinavians are oriented toward home and family, and children are the focal point. The people of the Nordic countries enjoy one of the shortest working days among the developed nations and all employees are entitled to lengthy paid vacations. For parents with children this means time together. And then there is the matter of parental leave: when a child is born the mother is granted a year's paid maternity leave, and the father is also encouraged to apply for a paternity leave of one month.

One may well wonder how provisions so favorable to the well-being of children and women managed to become law, and part of the explanation undoubtedly lies in the make-up of the governments; for many years women have played an important role in Scandinavian politics. The parliaments of the various countries have long had a high percentage of female representatives. Iceland elected its first woman president, Vigdís Finnbogadottir, in 1980 (she served as President until 1996) and Norway its first female prime minister, Gro Harlem Brundtland, in 1981. During the years Gro Harlem Brundtland was head of the Norwegian government, she appointed many women to her cabinet, a practice which continued after she stepped down as Prime Minister in 1996. In the fall of 1999, as this book is going to print, all four candidates for President of the Republic of Finland are women! The presence of so many women in their country's legislatures and top government positions raises yet another interesting question: what have been the formative influences on the women of Scandinavia, inspiring them to participate and lead in the public sphere on the one hand, and to honor and protect their private lives, as mothers and homemakers, on the other?

Among the many factors influencing a girl's development are the stories she hears and reads. Stories can stimulate the imagination and encourage creative thinking, and they can subtly, or not so subtly, suggest roles the child might pursue later on in life. Stories about girls who are demure and submissive and whose games involve little or no physical activity encourage girls to assume a passive role, while stories about girls who are curious and active might have a very different effect. Girls brought up on tales whose heroines are spunky and adventuresome are likely to inherit some of those qualities and to enter adulthood with a well-defined sense of their own potential and entitlement. What kind of stories did the mature women in the Scandinavian countries read when they were girls? And what are the stories their daughters and granddaughters are reading today?

Echo is an anthology of stories about girls and girlhood. The authors, all women, represent four countries and four languages— Denmark, Finland, Norway and Sweden—and the selections span two centuries—the oldest author was born in 1813, the youngest in 1957. Some of the stories were written with children or young readers in mind, while others were composed from a child's point of view for an older audience. There are stories that are purely fictional, excerpts from memoirs, and chapters from semi-autobiographical novels. The selections in this anthology range widely through different time periods and settings, and yet they are linked together by a common thread: each selection contains a story, or a fragment of a story, about growing up female.

Scandinavian society has undergone dramatic changes in the course of these two centuries. Until the end of the nineteenth century Scandinavia was a rural society; the majority of the population made their living farming and fishing. Most people did not own their land and were living at subsistence level, so when, around 1850, rumors of rich farmland and limitless opportunities in the New World started spreading through Scandinavia, the dream of America led hundreds of thousands to leave their homeland. Today, at the end of the twentieth century, the Scandinavian countries are among the most developed and affluent nations in the world and have themselves become lands of opportunity for people from around the world. The once homogeneous societies of Denmark, Finland, Norway and Sweden are becoming multicultural. People from many countries, many different cultural and ethnic backgrounds, are living and working and raising families in Scandinavia. We have included stories from three of the oldest minority groups—Sámi, Rom and Jewish—and only regret we were unable to represent more of the cultural diversity that enriches contemporary society.

The ages of the girls depicted in this collection range roughly from five to fifteen. The youngest are starting to develop an identity separate from their parents, and they are filled with questions about the world and God and how they will fit in. The oldest are on the verge of sexual maturity and are coming to grips with questions and confused feelings related to changes taking place in their bodies. And in

between are stories of nine and ten-year-olds who are forming relationships with their peers at school and at play.

The female protagonists in these stories matured at different ages
depending on when they lived and the circumstances of their lives. A
hundred years ago, when times were hard, children had to assume
heavy work loads at an early age and so a twelve-year-old might seem
responsible and grown up beyond her years. Sexuality, on the other
hand, seems not to exist in stories from the nineteenth century. It is
true that girls reached sexual maturity at a later age then than now,
but we must also take into consideration that female sexuality was not
considered an appropriate topic for literature at that time.

Choosing the stories was our first task as editors and this was a
delightful voyage of discovery as we read books from the different
countries and language groups, written from the mid-nineteenth century to the end of the twentieth in a variety of genre. In making our
selections we strove for balance and representation, at the same time
as we agreed to only include those selections we were enthusiastic
about! In working with the material we have become aware of motifs
and themes extending across generations, national boundaries and
ethnic groups. We discovered that many of the stories are richly lay-
ered with multiple themes and that the links connecting the stories
run on many different levels. Every reader will relate to a story in her
own way—that is the beauty and wonder of reading—still, a discus-
sion of some of the lines crisscrossing the stories you are about to
explore may prove to be a useful guide.

Echo opens and closes with stories about naming, an act that can,
as we read, have a direct influence on a person's identity and how she
perceives herself. Six-year-old Josephine, in the story by Maria Gripe,
chooses her own name to replace a name she doesn't feel is *her*. And
she insists upon calling her father a name that she herself has chosen.
The girl child in "My Soul Is Troubled by Conflicting Names" chooses
a name from the two names she received at birth, one from her father, the other from her mother. At the time she made her choice,
when she started school, she perceived the different destinies each

name held out for her and so she was, in effect, making a life choice. The significance of a name is again central to one of the episodes in the excerpt from Camilla Collett's memoir. Also in Collett's story the girl has been christened by her father, an event that marked the beginning of a life journey that did not follow the traditional course laid out for women at the time. The authors of these naming stories, Maria Gripe, Hagar Olsson, Camilla Collett, represent different countries, different generations, different centuries even.

Rejection of the traditional female role is a theme common to many of the stories in this volume. Inger Johanne, the pen name of author Dikken Zwilgmeyer and the heroine of her own stories, ignored all rules of feminine modesty when she made her debut in 1890. In a Prologue to her second book Inger Johanne writes about all the praise her first book received in the newspapers. Whenever a review appeared, she took the newspaper and read it out loud to her friends: "I usually stood on a fence or a rock, and when I was done reading, I waved the newspaper in the air and shouted hurray." Because critics have said she has talent, she has decided she no longer wants to be a dairymaid when she grows up—"now I would most like to be an author." Irrepressibly curious and energetic, Inger Johanne thinks she'd like to be an engineer in "Søren Bricklayer's Piglets." She realizes being a girl makes this impossible, but still, if her brother, Karsten, were to become an engineer, she could work in his office and tell him what to do, "Because Karsten never has any new ideas, but I do."

Inger Johanne's initiative and can-do attitude bring to mind Pippi Longstocking, another free spirit who exudes optimism and enthusiasm. Astrid Lindgren is represented in *Echo* with a character from one of her more recent works, Ronia, the daughter of a robber chieftain. Ronia lives in the forest and is as physically daring and active as any girl in literature, but her character possesses a seriousness and depth, and she struggles with a more subtle form of female rebellion—going against the wishes of a dearly beloved father.

"The Child Who Loved Roads" by Cora Sandel is a realistic yet poetic account of a nineteenth century girl's resistance to the confining role young women were expected to assume when they were too old to act like little girls. The story's protagonist vows she will never wear long skirts and sit in parlors embroidering or crocheting. She longs to run down country roads, be in open spaces, give her imagination free rein on the hills, "a place in life where freedom had no boundaries." In her memoir from childhood, *Early Spring*, Tove Ditlevsen relates her earliest memories of her mother's animated accounts of life *before* marriage. She perceives that marriage and children marked the end of her mother's happiness and she imagines quite a different life for herself, one devoted to reading and learning and poetry. Like the girl in "The Child Who Loved Roads," she yearns for the freedom to develop her mind and be creative.

Experiences at school figure prominently in several stories in this collection. Scandinavian women born during the nineteenth or early twentieth century describe school as a liberating, sometimes exhilerating experience. In *Stepping Lightly* Agnes Henningsen writes about her childhood on a Danish country manor where she and her sisters received tutoring from governesses. At age fifteen she was sent to a boarding school and she was thrilled to be in a classroom with other girls her own age for the first time in her life. Girls with whom she could form friendships and against whom she could compete. When, after two years, she completed her studies, she went out into the world "with a belief in her own abilities."

A half century earlier, Camilla Collett was more critical of how her schooling prepared her for life. In her memoir, *During the Long Nights*, she recalls the years spent at a finishing school which, she complains, prepared the girls for "the life of a cloister." This is not the true purpose of a school, which should rather prepare girls "to make your way in the world afterwards. You should learn to know yourself and your talents and powers and whether they are equal to the battles that will inevitably come." In spite of its curriculum, the school did provide Camilla with an opportunity to grow and develop through her friendship with one of the other students. How she won this friendship is related in "The Hunger Trial."

Teachers can be important mentors for girls both through the skills and knowledge they impart and through their example. Both Agnes Henningsen and Tove Ditlevsen describe the positive influence of a teacher, but the most striking account of a teacher capturing the imagination of a pupil is Moa Martinson's "The New Teacher." For Mia the new teacher represents a kind of woman she had never before imagined. "For the first time in my life I noticed a woman," she relates. A recognition that not only opens her eyes to female destinies different from her mother's, but also to the woman taking shape within herself.

Many of the stories in *Echo* have a school setting, but not all school experiences are positive. For the outsider school can be a cruel and hostile environment as we see in the poignant account of the little Sámi girl in *Kátjá* by Ellen Marie Vars. Leah, in the story by Susanne Levin, manages to escape the taunts of her classmates, largely because she has learned to separate the Jewish world of her home and family from the Swedish world of her school. Being different means being denied acceptance.

The theme of the outsider is also treated in Katarine Taikon's story about Katitzi who is reunited with her Gypsy family, but one needn't belong to an ethnic minority to feel excluded and lonely. Hannafia, the heroine of Irmelin Sandman Lilius' story, has just moved to a new place where nothing is familiar and no one wants to be her friend. In a tale that is more fantastic than realistic, Sandman Lilius demonstrates how the source of overcoming psychological difficulties lies within the child's own imagination. Seeking—and finding—creative solutions to serious problems is exemplified in a good many stories in this volume. In addition to those already discussed are pieces by Selma Lagerlöf, Tove Jansson and Suzanne Osten.

Coping with problems is never easy, in real life or in fiction, but it can help to have role models and a story can be a wonderful way to find one. Ti in Suzanne Osten's *The Girl, the Mother and the Garbage* lives alone with her schizophrenic mother. She loves her mother's stories and doesn't really mind her eccentric notions about clothes and head scarves. But when her mother's actions test even her child's sense of reality, Ti knows it's up to her to get them both back on track. In "Red Reflections" by Torborg Nedreaas, six-year-old Herdis is stunned when her mother announces she is moving out to start a new life with another man. Herdis feels the pain intensely, but the story's final sentence is a sign she will weather the storm. *Truth or Consequence* by Annika Thor takes up the confusion and hurt experienced by all girls in their early teens when alliances and friendships can shift overnight. Nora is faced with a tough decision—whether to follow her conscience or go along with the demands of her girl friends. And she learns an important lesson about loyalty and integrity.

Scandinavian literature for children and young people has historically had a strong ethical component. Examples include the many lessons in Hans Christian Andersen's tales, and the ethic of work and responsibility in *The Wonderful Adventures of Nils* by Selma Lagerlöf. There are ample illustrations of this in *Echo* as well, though perhaps nowhere as winningly as in "Kulla-Gulla." In the 1940s and '50s Martha Sandwall-Bergström wrote a series of books about Kulla-Gulla, a young farm worker who maintains her integrity, optimism and compassion through all manner of adversity.

Kulla-Gulla is a heroine of almost mythic proportion. She resides in rural Sweden at some undefined time in the past when common folk were poor. She has no mother or father and her status of orphan makes her many accomplishments seem all the more remarkable. She shoulders responsibilities beyond her years and somehow finds the physical stamina and strength of character to stay the course. She is respectful and courteous toward her superiors and yet possesses dignity and confidence and looks her teacher or foreman in the eye when she ventures to disagree. Kulla-Gulla is a model of honesty, hard work and fair play, values that have shaped and continue to shape Scandinavian society.

While the stories in *Echo* do indeed have serious content, there is also a good measure of lightheartedness and fun. "Søren Bricklayer's Piglets" with Inger Johanne is a high spirited story of children at play and the girls in Laila Stien's "Here I Come!" are an animated bunch of ten year olds who go straight from school to the ski slopes. In "Raffle Tickets" and "Sixth Grade Girls Learn to Cook Cod" Tove Nilsen and Gerd Brantenberg capture girls being girls at their funniest and most endearing.

There are also wonderfully slow and gentle narratives about long summer vacations spent in the countryside. Three of these accounts have been written by three of Scandinavia's best-known authors, Tove Jansson, Selma Lagerlöf and Sigrid Undset, and are based on the authors' memories of their own childhood vacations. A fourth, "Grandma in the Painting Room" by Dea Trier Mørch, is an episode from a summer three grandchildren spent with their grandparents.

Grandparents, especially grandmothers, have a strong and reassuring presence in the lives of several girls in this collection, and it seems appropriate to conclude with a note on those mentors who are oldest. The bond that stretches across generations is a very special one. In the story by Dea Trier Mørch, Grandma is an artist and her painting room holds an irresistible attraction to the children, but in this piece she is at her most creative as a storyteller. She tells the story of her life to a granddaughter who is moved and thrilled by this tale. Moved by the events in her grandmother's life, thrilled by the knowledge that she is somehow part of her grandma's story. Stories are how we record our lives, our joys, our sorrows, our accomplishments. They are a part of ourselves we can share, a legacy we can pass on, to instruct, to entertain, to inspire.

Katherine Hanson and Ia Dübois

ECHO

⟨ℜ *Maria Gripe*

Swedish children's author Maria Gripe (1923–) has long been recognized as one of Scandinavia's most popular writers of books for children. With poetic sensitivity she tells stories of everyday girls and boys with everyday problems, and always from the child's perspective. Gripe's light touch manages to illuminate her young characters' curiosity, independence and interest in who they are and where they come from.

Naming oneself can be an act of utmost importance, especially if the name you were born with doesn't suit you at all. In choosing a new name, one begins to tell a story. In the selection below, taken from *Josephine,* a six-year-old girl renames herself, and the story begins . . .

Josephine

Actually, her name isn't Josephine, and it isn't Joandersson, either.

Her name is Anna Grå.

It's rather a lovely name, if it happens to suit you. But she feels too small for it. To be called Ann Gray—because that's what the name means in Swedish—is rather like wearing shoes that are too big. You keep walking right out of them. So you have to put them away in the cupboard until they fit.

You can do that with names, too, if they won't keep step. At least that's what she's done.

She taught herself to write Anna Grå. Then she wrote it on the bottom of a cardboard box in capital letters, put the lid on, and hid it away at the back of her cupboard.

So, there's Anna Grå, waiting for her to grow up enough to *be* Anna Grå.

Meanwhile, she has to have another name. That shouldn't be hard. There are heaps to choose from.

Her first name must be as unusual as possible. Lots of people can share her last name.

Absolutely no one in the village is called *Josephine*. But most of them are called Johansson or Andersson. If you put these two to-gether, you get Joandersson, so that twice as many people share that name.

Josephine Joandersson is a nice jolly name, a name to make any-one happy.

Josephine is one person and no one else: Joandersson means thou-sands and thousands of people.

And that's just as it should be!

She wants to be called Josephine Joandersson.

So much for Anna Grå. She's been forgotten.

Mandy cooks the meals at the vicarage, where Josephine lives. She's an important person. Sometimes, as she stirs the contents of her steaming saucepans or kneads her dough, she has the strangest things to tell, mostly about the World and Man.

Sometimes she talks about how big the world is, and how small people are. And she describes man's littleness on our huge earth in long words.

Josephine listens to her every time with the same awe and delight.

It's not easy to understand what Mandy means. After all, anyone can see that Mandy isn't particularly small. In fact, she's the biggest person at the vicarage. Mandy's arms and hands are the largest Josephine has ever seen. And yet Mandy assures her that on this earth she's only a tiny midge, a defenseless little insect, a dot.

Josephine can't take her eyes off Mandy. She's round like a dot, that's true; but she certainly isn't a small dot. And Josephine can't imagine anyone less defenseless than Mandy.

Her voice isn't gnatlike, either, and that's a fact. No voice in the vicarage makes itself heard more loudly.

Yes, Mandy is certainly full of riddles!

At other times she sighs and says that the world is getting smaller and smaller. This often happens as she flips through the newspapers.

"Is it shrinking, then?" asks Josephine.

"Yes, indeed," says Mandy. "It's shrinking a bit every day."

"Like my blue jumper in the wash?"

"Exactly."

That sounds terrible. Josephine's jumper has got so small, she can't wear it any more. Is this what's going to happen to the whole world?

"Can we grow out of it, Mandy?" asks Josephine.

"Out of what?"

"The world. Is it getting too small for us?"

"Yes," says Mandy. "You're getting to be as wise as a prophet, Miss Josephine."

Mandy loses herself in the newspaper. But now Josephine is really worried.

"What'll we do, then?" she asks, pulling the paper away from Mandy. "If there isn't enough room for us?"

Mandy's spectacles slide down to the tip of her nose. She gives Josephine a reassuring look.

"No danger of that," she says. "Because, you see, Josephine, we're getting smaller too."

Wide-eyed, Josephine stares at Mandy's huge bulk.

"Are you shrinking, too, Mandy?"

"Of course. You see, Miss Josephine, the world is just a tiny star among all the other little stars in the sky. And all of us are only little specks of dust. One fine day we may fly off to the moon, who knows. . . . "

So Mandy and Josephine chat in the kitchen of the vicarage; and to Josephine it becomes clearer and clearer that it's a very strange world she's living in.

It's hard to be sure of anything.

For example, everyone says the world is as round as a ball—while anyone can see for himself that it's flat.

But, big or little, flat or round, one thing is sure: it's *old*.

The church is old, too: so old, no one knows who built it.

"And it's no use worrying about that," says Mandy. "Old churches like these, no one builds them. They just grow up by themselves. Look at the roof! Doesn't it look as if it'd grown straight up out of the earth?"

Yes, it really does.

The church is just across the road. Beside it stands a wooden bell tower with two bells that ring out ponderously, making the air quiver and roll in waves. It has been ringing like that for hundreds and hundreds of years. And when the sky is blue, the sound goes straight up, flying like a swallow. But when the sky is gray, then the sound becomes heavy and groans, like thunder over the forest.

Josephine isn't scared of the church bells. She is used to them. She has heard them ever since she was born.

Behind the church lies a field. There are bells there, too, but they're tiny little flowers and ring so quietly you can hardly hear them—though Josephine says she has. The field is called Bell Meadow. And there everything is new: the flowers and the grass are new each year.

Otherwise everything is as old as can be. The linden trees in the avenue and the oak in the paddock. The oak is terribly old and has a hole in it.

And the vicarage is old, too, of course. . . .

The bed she sleeps in, the chair she's sitting on, the sofa and the chest of drawers in Josephine's room, all of them are old.

And Mandy. Isn't she sometimes called *Old* Mandy?

Josephine has six brothers and sisters. But they're grown up and don't live at the vicarage any more, except Agneta, who is going to be married soon.

If one didn't know they were her brothers and sisters, one would take them for ordinary uncles and aunts, Josephine thinks, they are so big. Josephine herself is six, seven this winter.

She is quite small for her age: no one believes she is going to start school this autumn. But she is!

She has to start school; after all, she is an aunt! And was, even *before* she was born!

How would it look if a couple of her nephews were going to school—and not she, their aunt?

Papa-Father is the church's vicar.

He has lived for many years, Josephine knows. She doesn't know exactly *how* many; not a hundred, certainly, but far more than she can count. That doesn't matter, though, because his years don't make him old.

Sometimes he pretends to be old, particularly with Josephine. Like the time when he came and wanted her to call him Father, instead of Papa.

"You are so little, and have such an old Papa," he said, and made himself seem old and serious.

Josephine just laughed, but he was stubborn. She *must* say Father, he said. He looked tall and slim: his face moved about high above Josephine's. When she said Father, it was as if his face rose slowly to an even greater height, so that she could never reach it again.

Then she hit on the idea of calling him Papa-Father, and he agreed.

To say Papa-Father is like holding a balloon. Papa is the string and Father the balloon. If she weren't allowed to say Papa before Father, it would feel as if she had let go of the string and let the balloon fly straight up into the sky.

This would be particularly dangerous with Papa-Father, who is a clergyman and thinks a lot about heaven.

Mostly he is not to be disturbed. The two big brown doors to his room are almost always closed. And no one is allowed to open them. Anyway, she can't. The door handles are big and heavy; you can hang your whole weight on them and still they won't open. Though that's something she doesn't do any more—only when she was little.

But the doors remind her of Papa-Father. It makes you feel safe just to stand there, knowing he's inside.

There he sits, writing his sermon. "Sermon" is what his Big Talk in church on Sunday is called. He talks all by himself, and no one is allowed to interrupt—no one, because he's talking about Old Man God.

Everyone knows who Old Man God is. He's the oldest person on earth and in heaven. He's older than anything else that exists, because he was there first and made everything, all by himself. In his pictures, too, he looks old and tired. Josephine has a picture of him, in a book she was given by Papa-Father. He's a fine old fellow with white hair and a beard. Josephine calls him Old Man God.

But Old Man God's son—you can't help feeling sorry for him. He grew so quickly, he was almost never small—just a baby for a little while. But then presto, he grew up and got into all sorts of trouble. He never had time to play, it all went so quickly. In the end he flew up to heaven—just like a balloon without a string.

Sometimes Josephine wonders about her own brothers and sisters. Did growing up happen to them just as quickly? Poor things— maybe they never had time to play either?

And what will happen to her? She wants to go on playing and playing . . . .

Excerpted from *Josephine.* Translated from the Swedish by Paul Britten Austin.

ᏁᏞ *Tove Jansson*

In her popular books about the Moomin family, author and illustrator Tove Jansson (1914–) has created an entire world unto itself. The geography of this mythical world bears a striking resemblance to the forests and coastal islands of Jansson's native Finland, but the inhabitants are a droll assortment of fanciful characters. The early books about Moomintroll, Moominmamma and Moomin-pappa were written for children, but in her later tales from Moominvalley, Jansson clearly has an adult audience in mind.

Tove Jansson wrote stories about her own childhood in *Sculptor's Daughter*, the book from which "The Golden Calf" has been taken. Jansson grew up in an artistic home—her mother was a painter and her father a sculptor—and as the story below demonstrates, she took a creative approach to life already as a child. Here as in the Moomin books the seemingly simple narrative, a recollection of summers in the country with grandparents and cousins, contains a richly symbolic text.

The Golden Calf

Grandfather was a clergyman and used to preach to the King. Once, before his children and his children's children and his children's children's children covered the face of the earth, Grandfather came to a long field which was surrounded by forests and hills so that it looked like Paradise. At one end it opened out into a bay for his descendants to bathe in.

Then Grandfather thought, here will I dwell and multiply, for verily this is the Land of Canaan.

Then Grandfather and Grandmother built a big two-story house with a sloping roof and lots of rooms and steps and terraces and a huge veranda and placed plain wooden furniture everywhere inside and outside the house and when it was ready Grandfather began to plant things until the field became a Garden of Eden where he walked around in his big black beard. All he had to do was to point at a plant and it was blessed and grew until it groaned under its own weight.

The whole house was overgrown with honeysuckle and Virginia creeper and walls of small rambler roses grew round the veranda. Inside these walls Grandmother sat in a pale gray silk dress and brought up her children. There were so many bees and bumble bees flying around her that it sounded like soft organ music, and in the daytime it was sunny and at night it rained and in the rock garden there lived an angel who wasn't to be disturbed.

She was still there when Mummy and I went out to live in the West Room, which also had white furniture and peaceful pictures but no sculpture.

I was a grandchild. Karin was another grandchild but her hair curled naturally and she had very big eyes. We played The Children of Israel together in the field.

God lived on the hill above the rock garden and there was a forbidden cart up there. At sunset he spread out like a mist over the house and the field. He could make himself quite small and creep in everywhere in order to see what one was doing and sometimes he was only a great big eye. Moreover, he looked just like Grandfather.

We raised our voices in the wilderness and were continually disobedient because God so likes to forgive sinners. God forbade us to gather manna under the laburnum tree but we did all the same. Then he sent worms up from the earth to eat up the manna. But we went on being disobedient and we still raised our voices.

All the time we expected him to get so angry that he would show himself. The very idea was tremendous. We could think of nothing but God. We sacrificed to him, we gave him blueberries and crab apples and flowers and milk and sometimes we made a small burnt-offering. We sang for him and we prayed to him to give us a sign that he was interested in what we were doing.

One morning Karin said that the sign had come to her. He had sent a yellow bunting into her room and it had perched on the picture of Jesus Walking on the Waters and nodded its head three times.

"Verily, verily I say unto you," Karin said, "many are called but few are chosen."

She put on a white dress and went round all day with roses in her hair and sang hymns and carried on in a very affected way. She was more beautiful than ever and I hated her. *My* window had been open too. *I* had a picture of the Guardian Angel at the Abyss on my wall. I had burnt as many burnt-offerings and picked even more blueberries for him. And as for raising my voice in the wilderness I had been just as disobedient as she in order to get divine forgiveness.

At morning prayers on the veranda Karin looked as though Grandfather was preaching only to her. She nodded her head slowly with a thoughtful look on her face. She clasped her hands long before the Lord's Prayer. She sang with great emphasis and kept her eyes on the ceiling. After that business of the yellow bunting God belonged to her.

We didn't speak to each other and I stopped raising my voice in the wilderness and sacrificing and was so jealous that I felt sick.

One day Karin lined up all the cousins in the field, even the ones who couldn't talk yet, and held a Bible class for them.

It was then that I made the golden calf.

When Grandfather was young and was planting like mad he put a circle of spruce trees at the bottom of the field because he wanted a little arbor to have his afternoon tea in. The spruce trees grew and grew until they were huge and black and their branches got all tangled up with each other. It was quite dark inside the arbor and all the needles fell off and lay on the ground because they never got enough sunshine. Nobody wanted to have tea there any longer but preferred to sit under the laburnum or on the veranda.

I made my golden calf in the arbor because it was a pagan place and a circle is always a good setting for sculpture.

It was very difficult to get the legs to stay upright but in the end they did and I nailed them to the base just to make sure. Sometimes I stood still, listening for the first rumble of the wrath of God. But so far he had said nothing. His great eye just looked right down into the arbor through the hole between the tops of the spruce trees. At last I had got him to show some interest.

The head of the calf turned out very well. I used tin cans and rags and bits of a muff and tied the lot together with string. If you stood a little way away and screwed up your eyes the calf really did shine like gold in the darkness, particularly round its nose.

I became more and more interested in it and began to think more and more about the calf and less and less about God. It was a very good golden calf. Finally I put a circle of stones round it and collected dry twigs for a burnt-offering.

Only when the burnt-offering was ready to light did I begin to feel afraid again and I stood completely still and listened.

God kept completely quiet. Perhaps he was waiting for me to take out the matches. He wanted to see if I really would do something so awful as to sacrifice to the golden calf and, even worse, dance in front of it afterwards. Then he would come down from his hill in a cloud of lightning and wrath and show that he knew that I existed. Then Karin could keep her old yellow bunting and her prayers and her blueberries!

I stood there and listened and listened and the silence grew and grew until it was overpowering. Everything was listening. It was late in the afternoon and the light coming through the trees made the branches look red. The golden calf looked at me and waited and my legs began to feel weak. I started to walk backwards towards the gap between the trees, looking at the calf all the time, and as it became lighter and warmer I thought that I should have signed my name on the base.

Grandmother was standing outside the arbor and she was wearing her lovely gray silk dress and her parting was as straight as an angel's.

"What have you been playing at in there?" she said, and walked straight past me. She stood in front of the golden calf and looked at it and smiled. She put her arm around me and absent-mindedly pressed me against the gray silk and said: "Look what you've made! A little lamb. God's little lamb!"

Then she let go of me and walked slowly down the field.

I stayed where I was and my eyes began to smart and the bottom fell out of everything and God went back to his hill again and calmed down. She hadn't even noticed that it was a calf! A lamb! Good grief! It didn't look one little bit like a lamb, nowhere near it!

I stared and stared at my calf. And what Grandmother had said seemed to have taken all the gold away from it and the legs were wrong and the head was wrong, everything about it was wrong and if it looked like anything at all perhaps it was a lamb. It wasn't any good. It wasn't sculpture at all.

I went to the junk room and sat there for a long time and thought. I found a sack. I put it on and then went out into the field and shuffled around in front of Karin on bent knees with my hair hanging over my eyes.

"Whatever are you doing?" Karin asked.

Then I answered, "Verily, verily I say unto you, I am a great sinner."

"Really?" said Karin. I could see that she was impressed.

Then everything was as usual again, and we lay under the laburnum tree and whispered together about God. Grandfather walked up and down making everything grow and the angel was still there in the rock garden as if nothing had happened at all.

Story from *Bildhuggarens dotter.* Translated from the Swedish by Kingsley Hart.

Ⓠ *Tove Ditlevsen*

Tove Ditlevsen (1917–1976) grew up in a working class neighborhood in Copenhagen in the 1920s and '30s. As a child she felt drawn to reading and the mystery of words and her dream was to become a poet and meet people who would understand her. Ditlevsen pursued her dream and became one of Denmark's most popular poets. She also wrote prose fiction and authored three autobiographical books; the first two, *Childhood* and *Youth,* have been published in English translation under the title *Early Spring.* Two chapters from *Early Spring* have been excerpted below.

Ditlevsen does not remember childhood as secure and idyllic. The times were hard for working class families—they shared cramped living quarters, had to stretch what little money they had, and constantly worried that unemployment would strike them next. These are not conditions that encourage children to be children. In the selection below Ditlevsen relates that the grownups couldn't stand "the song in my heart or the garlands of words in my soul." She recalls a childhood that seemed detached from her inner world, painful memories which she has transformed into a language that is full of beauty and strength.

Early Spring

Childhood is long and narrow like a coffin, and you can't get out of it on your own. It's there all the time and everyone can see it just as clearly as you can see Pretty Ludvig's harelip. It's the same with him as with Pretty Lili, who's so ugly you can't imagine she ever had a mother. Everything that is ugly or unfortunate is called beautiful, and no one knows why. You can't get out of childhood, and it clings to you like a bad smell. You notice it in other children—each childhood has its own smell. You don't recognize your own and sometimes you're afraid that it's worse than others'. You're standing talking to another girl whose childhood smells of coal and ashes, and suddenly she takes a step back because she has noticed the terrible stink of your childhood. On the sly, you observe the adults whose childhood lies inside them, torn and full of holes like a used and moth-eaten rug no one thinks about anymore or has any use for. You can't tell by looking at them that they've had a childhood, and you don't dare ask how they managed to make it through without their faces getting deeply scarred and marked by it. You suspect that they've used some secret shortcut and donned their adult form many years ahead of time. They did it one day when they were home alone and their childhood lay like three bands of iron around their heart, like Iron Hans in Grimms' fairy tale, whose bands broke only when his master was freed. But if you don't know such a shortcut, childhood must be endured and trudged through hour by hour, through an absolutely interminable number of years. Only death can free you from it, so you think a lot about death, and picture it as a white-robed, friendly angel who some night will kiss your eyelids so that they never will open again. I always think that when I'm grown-up my mother will finally like me the way she likes Edvin now. Because my childhood irritates her just as much as it irritates me, and we are only happy together whenever she suddenly forgets about its existence. Then she talks to me the way she talks to her friends or to Aunt Rosalia, and I'm very careful to make my answers so short that she won't suddenly remember I'm only a child. I let go of her hand and keep a slight distance between us so she won't be able to smell my childhood, either. It almost always happens when I go shopping with her on Istedgade. She tells me how much fun she had as a young girl. She went out dancing every night and was never off the dance floor. "I had a new boyfriend every night," she says and laughs loudly, "but that had to stop when I met Ditlev." That's my father and otherwise she always calls him "Father," just as he calls her "Mother" or "Mutter." I get the impression there was a time when she was happy and different, but that it all came to an abrupt end when she met Ditlev. When she talks about him it's as if he's someone other than my father, a dark spirit who crushes and destroys everything that is beautiful and light and lively. And I wish that this Ditlev had never come into her life. When she gets to his name, she usually catches sight of my childhood and looks at it angrily and threateningly, while the dark rim around her blue iris grows even darker. This childhood then shivers with fear and despairingly tries to slip away on tiptoe, but it's still far too little and can't be discarded yet for several hundred years.

People with such a visible, flagrant childhood both inside and out are called children, and you can treat them any way you like because there's nothing to fear from them. They have no weapons and no masks unless they are very cunning. I am that kind of cunning child, and my mask is stupidity, which I'm always careful not to let anyone tear away from me. I let my mouth fall open a little and make my eyes completely blank, as if they're always just staring off into the blue. Whenever it starts singing inside me, I'm especially careful not to let my mask show any holes. None of the grownups can stand the song in my heart or the garlands of words in my soul. But they know about them because bits seep out of me through a secret channel I don't recognize and therefore can't stop up. "You're not putting on airs?" they say, suspiciously, and I assure them that it wouldn't even occur to me to put on airs. In school they ask, "What are you thinking about? What was the last sentence I said?" But they never really see through me. Only the children in the courtyard or in the street do. "You're going around playing dumb," a big girl says menacingly and comes up close to me, "but you're not dumb at all." Then she starts to cross-examine me, and a lot of other girls gather silently around me, forming a circle I can't slip through until I've proved I really am stupid. At last it seems clear to them after all of my idiotic replies, and reluctantly they make a little hole in the circle so I can just squeeze through and escape to safety. "Because you shouldn't pretend to be something you're not," one of them yells after me, moralistic and admonishing.

Childhood is dark and it's always moaning like a little animal that's locked in a cellar and forgotten. It comes out of your throat like your breath in the cold, and sometimes it's too little, other times too big. It never fits exactly. It's only when it has been cast off that you can look at it calmly and talk about it like an illness you've survived. Most grownups say that they've had a happy childhood and maybe they really believe it themselves, but I don't think so. I think they've just managed to forget it. My mother didn't have a happy childhood, and it's not as hidden away in her as it is in other people. She tells me how terrible it was when her father had the D.T.'s and they all had to stand holding up the wall so that it wouldn't fall on him. When I say that I feel sorry for him, she yells, "Sorry! It was his own fault, the drunken pig! He drank a whole bottle of schnapps every day, and in spite of everything, things were a lot better for us when he finally pulled himself together and hanged himself." She also says, "He murdered my five little brothers. He took them out of the cradle and crushed their heads against the wall." Once I ask my Aunt Rosalia, who is mother's sister, whether this is true, and she says, "Of course it's not true. They just died. Our father was an unhappy person, but your mother was only four years old when he died. She has inherited Granny's hatred of him." Granny is their mother, and even though she's old now, I can imagine that her soul can hold a lot of hatred. Granny lives on the island of Amager. Her hair is completely white and she's always dressed in black. Just as with my father and mother, I may only address her in an indirect way, which makes all conversations very difficult and full of repetitions. She makes the sign of the cross before she cuts the bread, and whenever she clips her fingernails, she burns the clippings in the stove. I ask her why she does this, but she says that she doesn't know. It was something her mother did. Like all grownups, she doesn't like it when children ask about something, so she gives short answers. Wherever you turn, you run up against your childhood and hurt yourself because it's sharp-edged and hard, and stops only when it has torn you completely apart. It seems that everyone has their own and each is totally different. My brother's childhood is very noisy, for example, while mine is quiet and furtive and watchful. No one likes it and no one has any use for it. Suddenly it's much too tall and I can look into my mother's eyes when we both get up. "You grow while you're asleep," she says. Then I try to stay awake at night, but sleep overpowers me and in the morning I feel quite dizzy looking down at my feet, the distance has grown so great. "You big cow," the boys on the street yell after me, and if it keeps on like this, I'll have to go to Stormogulen where all the giants grow. Now childhood hurts. It's called growing pains and doesn't stop until you're twenty. That's what Edvin says, who knows everything—about the world and society, too—like my father, who takes him along to political meetings; my mother thinks it will end in both of them being arrested by the police. They don't listen when she says things like that because she knows as little about politics as I do. She also says that my father can't find work because he's a socialist and belongs to the union, and that Stauning, whose picture my father has hung up on the wall next to the sailor's wife, will lead us into trouble one day. I like Stauning, whom I've seen and heard many times in Fælled Park. I like him because his long beard waves so gaily in the wind and because he says "comrades" to the workers even though he's Prime Minister and could allow himself to be more stuck-up. When it comes to politics, I think my mother is wrong, but no one is interested in what girls think or don't think about such things.

One day my childhood smells of blood, and I can't avoid noticing and knowing it. "Now you can have children," says my mother. "It's much too soon, you're not even thirteen yet." I know how you have children because I sleep with my parents, and in other ways you can't help knowing it, either. But even so, somehow I still don't understand, and I imagine that at any time I can wake up with a little child beside me. Her name will be Baby Maria, because it will be a girl. I don't like boys and I'm not allowed to play with them, either. Edvin is the only one I love and admire, and he's the only one I can imagine myself marrying. But you can't marry your brother and even if you could, he wouldn't have me. He's said that often enough. Everyone loves my brother, and I often think his childhood suits him better than mine suits me. He has a custom-made childhood that expands in tune with his growth, while mine is made for a completely different girl. Whenever I think such thoughts, my mask becomes even more stupid, because you can't talk to anyone about these kinds of things, and I always dream about meeting some mysterious person who will listen to me and understand me. I know from books that such people exist, but you can't find any of them on my childhood street.

CR

I've started middle school and with that the world has begun to widen. I was allowed to continue because my parents have figured out I still won't be much more than fourteen when I finish school, and since they're giving Edvin training, I shouldn't be left out. At the same time, I've finally gotten permission to use the public library on Valdemarsgade, which has a section with children's books. My mother thinks that I'll get even stranger from reading books that are written for adults; and my father, who doesn't agree, doesn't say anything since I come under my mother's authority and in crucial matters he doesn't dare go against world order. So for the first time I set foot in a library, and I'm speechless with confusion at seeing so many books collected in one place. The children's librarian is named Helga Mollerup, and she's known and loved by many children in the neighborhood because whenever there's no heat or light at home, they're allowed to sit in the reading room right up until the library closes at five o'clock in the evening. They do their homework there or leaf through books, and Miss Mollerup throws them out only if they start getting noisy, because it's supposed to be completely quiet, like in a church. She asks me how old I am and finds books she thinks are right for a ten-year-old. She is tall and slim and pretty, with dark, lively eyes. Her hands are big and beautiful and I regard them with a certain respect, because it's said that she can slap harder than any man. She's dressed like my teacher, Miss Klausen, in a rather long, smooth skirt and a blouse with a low white collar at the neck. But, unlike Miss Klausen, she doesn't seem to suffer from an insurmountable aversion to children—on the contrary. I'm placed at a table with a children's book in front of me, the title and author of which I've fortunately forgotten. I read, "'Father, Diana has had puppies.' With these words, a slender young girl fifteen years old came storming into the room, where, in addition to the councilman, there were. . . " etc. Page after page. I don't have it in me to read it. It fills me with sadness and unbearable boredom. I can't understand how language—that delicate and sensitive instrument—can be so terribly mistreated, or how such monstrous sentences can find their way into a book that gets into the library where a clever and attractive woman like Miss Mollerup actually recommends it to defenseless children to read. For now, however, I can't express these thoughts, so I have to be content with saying that the books are boring and that I would rather have something by Zacharias Nielsen or Vilhelm Bergsøe. But Miss Mollerup says that children's books are exciting if you just have patience enough to keep reading until the plot gets going. Only when I stubbornly insist on having access to the shelves with the adult books does she give in, astonished, and offer to get some books for me if I'll tell her which ones, since I can't go in there myself. "One by Victor Hugo," I say. "It's pronounced Ügó," she says, smiling, and pats me on the head. It doesn't embarrass me that she corrects my pronunciation, but when I come home with *Les Misérables* and my father says approvingly, "Victor Hugo—yes, he's good!" I say didactically and self-importantly, "It's pronounced Ügó." "I don't give a damn how it's pronounced," he says calmly. "All those kinds of names should be said the way they're spelled. Anything else is just showing off." It's never any use to come home and tell my parents anything people said who don't live on our street. Once when the school dentist requested that I ask my mother to buy me a toothbrush and I was dumb enough to mention it at home, my mother snapped, "You can tell her that she can darn well buy you a toothbrush herself!" But whenever she has a toothache, she first goes around suffering for about a week, while the whole house echoes with her miserable moaning. Then, out on the landing, she asks the advice of another woman, who recommends that she pour schnapps on a wad of cotton and hold it against the infected tooth, which she spends several more days doing, with no results. Only then does she get all dressed up in her finest and venture out to Vesterbrogade, where our doctor lives. He takes his pincers and pulls out the tooth and then she has peace for a while. A dentist never comes into the picture.

In the middle school the girls are better dressed and less sniveling than in the primary school. None of them has lice or a harelip, either. My father says that now I'll be going to school with children of people who are "better off," but that that's no reason for me to look down on my own home. That's true enough. The children's fathers are mostly skilled workers, and I make my father into a "machinist," which I think sounds better than stoker. The richest girl in the class has a father who owns a barbershop on Gasværksvej. Her name is Edith Schnoor and she lisps from sheer self-importance. Our classroom teacher is named Miss Mathiassen, a small, lively woman who seems to enjoy teaching. Together with Miss Klausen, Miss Mollerup, and the principal at the old school (the one who resembled a witch), she gives me the distinct impression that women can only have influence in the working world if they're completely flat-chested. My mother is an exception; otherwise all the housewives at home on my street have enormous busts that they consciously thrust out as they walk. I wonder why that is. Miss Mathiassen is the only female teacher we have. She's discovered that I like poetry, and it doesn't work to play dumb with her. I save that for the subjects that don't interest me—but there are lots of those. I only like Danish and English. Our English teacher is named Damsgaard, and he can be terribly short-tempered. Then he pounds the table and says, "Upon my word, I'll teach you!" He uses this mild oath so often that before long he's known exclusively as "Upon my word." One time he reads aloud a sentence that's supposed to be especially difficult, and he asks me to repeat it. It goes like this: "In reply to your inquiry I can particularly recommend you the boarding house at eleven Woburn Place. Some of my friends stayed there last winter and spoke highly about it." He praises my correct pronunciation, and that's the reason I can never forget that idiotic sentence.

All the girls in my class have poetry albums, and after I've nagged my mother long enough, I get one too. It's brown and it says "Poetry" on the outside in gold letters. I let some of the girls write the usual verses in it, and in between I put in some of my own poems with the date and my name underneath so that posterity will have no doubt that I was a child genius. I hide it in one of the dresser drawers in the bedroom under a stack of towels and dishcloths, where I think it will be relatively safe from profane eyes. But one evening Edvin and I are home alone because my parents are out playing cards with my aunt and uncle. Otherwise Edvin is usually out in the evening, but he's been too tired for that since he started his apprenticeship. It's a bad workplace, he says, and he often begs my father to let him find a different one. When that does no good, he starts shouting and says that he'll run off to sea and leave home and much more. Then my father shouts, too, and then when my mother interferes in the fight and takes Edvin's side, there's an uproar in the living room that almost drowns out the racket downstairs at Rapunzel's. It's Edvin's fault that nearly every evening now all peace in the living room is destroyed, and sometimes I wish that he'd follow through with his threats and leave. Now he sits sulking and withdrawn, leafing through *Social-Demokraten*, while only the ticking clock on the wall breaks the silence. I'm doing my homework, but the silence between us oppresses me. He stares at me with his dark, thoughtful eyes that are suddenly just as melancholy as my father's. Then he says, "Aren't you going to bed soon, damn it? You can never be alone in this damn house!" "You can go into the bedroom, you know," I answer, hurt. "I bloody well will, too," he mumbles, grabbing the newspaper and going out. He slams the door hard after him. A little while later, to my surprise and uneasiness, I hear a burst of laughter from in there. What can be so funny? I go inside and stiffen with horror. Edvin is sitting on my mother's bed with my poor album in his hand. He's completely doubled up with laughter. Bright red in the face with shame, I take a step toward him and put out my hand. "Give me that book," I say and stamp my foot. "You have no right to take it!" "Oh God," he gasps and doubles up with laughter, "this is hilarious. You're really full of lies. Listen to this!" Then, interrupted by fits of laughter, he reads:

Do you remember that time we sailed
along the still, clear stream?
The moon was mirrored in the sea.

Everything was like a lovely dream.
Suddenly you lay the oar to rest,
and let the boat go still.
You said nothing, but my dear—
the passion in your gaze did thrill.

You took me in your arms so strong.
Lovingly you kissed me.
Never, never will I forget
that hour spent with thee.

"Oh no! Ha ha ha!" He falls back and keeps on laughing, and the tears stream from my eyes. "I hate you," I yell, stamping my foot powerlessly. "I hate you, I hate you! I wish you'd drown in a marl pit!" With those last words, I'm just about to rush out the door, when Edvin's insane laughter takes on a new, disturbing sound. I turn around in the doorway and look at him lying on his stomach across my mother's striped comforter with his face hidden in the crook of one arm. My precious book has fallen to the floor. He sobs inconsolably and uncontrollably, and I am horrified. Hesitantly, I approach the bed, but I don't dare touch him. That's something we've never done. I dry my own tears with the sleeve of my dress and say, "I didn't mean it, Edvin, the part about the marl pit. I . . . I don't even know what it is." He keeps sobbing without answering and suddenly turns over and gives me a hopeless look. "I hate them, the boss and the assistants," he says. "They . . . beat me . . . all day and I'll never learn to paint cars. I'm just sent out to get beer for all of them. I hate Father because I can't change workplaces. And when you come home, you can never be alone. There's not one damn corner where you can have anything for yourself." I look down at my poetry album and say, "I can't have anything for myself, either, you know—and neither can Father or Mother. They're not even alone when they . . . when they. . . . " He looks at me, surprised, and finally stops crying. "No," he says sadly. "Jesus, I've never thought about that." He gets up, regretting, of course, that his sister has seen him in a moment of weakness. "Well," he says in a tough voice, "it probably all gets better when you move away from home." I agree with him about that. Then I go out and count the eggs in the pantry. I take two and move the rest around so it looks like there are more of them. "I'm going to mix us an egg schnapps," I yell toward the living room and start the preparations. At that moment, I like Edvin much better than in all the years when he was distant and wonderful, handsome and cheerful. It wasn't really human that he never seemed to feel bad about anything.

Excerpted from *Barndom.* Translated from the Danish by Tiina Nunnally.

◌ Irmelin Sandman Lilius

Irmelin Sandman Lilius (1936–) is the Finnish author of over forty books for both children and adults. Beginning in 1967, with *Bonadea*, the core of Sandman Lilius' authorship has been the fictional coastal town of Tulavall and its colorful gallery of citizens. "The Cave" is taken from the short story collection *The Sea of Barbidel*.

In "The Cave," as in much of her fiction, Sandman Lilius uses fantastic elements to illustrate psychological action. Hannafia Alle, the story's protagonist, is new to Tulavall, and faces the usual challenges of making her way in a strange place. Her large family is too busy to pay her much attention, and the local girls won't have anything to do with her because she is an outsider. While walking alone in the forest one day, an unusual movement in a mountainside cave opening catches her eye. When Hannafia returns to investigate it with her big brother Albin, they are drawn into a fantastical—and perilous—realm deep inside the mountain.

The Cave

Sometimes the ship *Southwest* took on passengers, but not often, since there were only enough sleeping berths for the crew. But once, during Michaelmas in September, the whole Alle family came on board.

The crew brought the Alles from Långhals Sound in Snappertuna to Tulavall. Papa Alle had been a tenant farmer in Grålleborg, and it had been a struggle, so he wanted to see if life would be easier in town. He had gotten a job at the Tulavall Sawmill, and he thought the older boys might be able to find work there, too.

Besides the four older boys, there were two younger ones, and four girls. Mama Alle was sitting to leeward with her back to the cabin wall, holding the youngest child in her arms. It was sunny and warm for that time of year, and she said that as far as she was concerned the voyage could be a long one.

Tuspuru Schando was preparing food.

He was sitting down, scrubbing potatoes in a metal basin, when one of the little Alle girls appeared in the doorway and said, "Let me do that."

Tuspuru let her do it. Her hands were small, but she was fast. When she was done, she asked, "What can I do now?"

He couldn't think of anything else for her to do.

"Can I stay in here with you?" she asked.

"Is it because you want to look at me?" he asked. He was used to children wanting to look at him because he was a foreigner, with brown skin and black hair.

"No," she said. "Well, yes," she added and blushed. "Of course I like looking at you, too . . . But . . ."

"Is it because you're afraid?" Tuspuru asked.

She nodded with tears in her eyes. "I didn't want to leave, but I couldn't stay behind by myself."

"Aren't the others afraid, too?" Tuspuru asked.

"I don't know. Maybe Albin, but he pretends not to be." She nodded towards the second oldest Alle boy, who stood leaning against the rail.

"What's your name?" Tuspuru asked.

"Hannafia."

He didn't know what to say to comfort and encourage her, but he gave her a handful of raisins.

"Are you allowed to take raisins out of the cupboard just like that?" she asked.

"I'm the cook on this trip," he said. "I'm in charge of the food."

Hannafia hid the raisins in her apron pocket. "How old are you?" she asked.

"Old enough. If you ever come to my island in the Pirean Sea everyone will want to look at you because you have such pretty hair."

She pressed her hands against her silvery-blond head. "But we all have hair like this," she said.

"My little sisters would like to play with you," he said.

Her own little sisters only played with each other. They were sitting on the deck next to Mother Alle, singing:

Gone are the days of my childhood
If only its innocence remained—

They arrived in Tulavall in the darkness of late evening. Papa Alle's cousin met them with a horse and cart. Everyone was tired and the younger children were crying. Tuspuru said to Hannafia, "Next time we put into port here I'll come visit you. Where will you be living?"

"In Old Man's Lane, up towards Guardian Mountain," she said. "In the Ram's old hut."

A few days later she was sitting on the steps to the Ram's old hut, trying to feel what it was like to call it home. She felt only emptiness.

Her sisters were playing in the yard and singing:

A young man thinks of springtime alone
while the gray-haired man
longs to turn another stone.

Two girls came walking down from the corner of Gullkronagatan. Hannafia knew them well enough to know that their names were Gull-Maj and Janette, and that they didn't want to play with her. Gull-Maj was carrying a doll under each arm, while Janette was pushing a doll in a carriage. She was having trouble with the carriage which had lost a wheel. When they walked past Hannafia, she heard them calling each other "my dear Countess" and "my sweet Baroness." They pranced by, casting sidelong glances at Hannafia. Gull-Maj was wearing the prettiest brooch Hannafia had ever seen. It was a golden flower with four petals inside painted in pastel shades: light red, light yellow, light green and light blue, with a brilliant red glittering stone at its center. Janette didn't have a brooch, but she wore a silver cross around her neck.

They wandered up the hill to where the houses ended and the woods began, then turned and slowly wandered back again.

"Why are you just walking back and forth?" Hannafia asked them.

"No one," Janette said haughtily, "goes up into the forest."

"That's not a real forest," Hannafia said, remembering the way the Long Neck Woods back home stretched out for miles and miles.

"You don't know anything about our forest because you already had shoes on your feet when you came here," Janette said.

Hannafia watched them walk away. When they disappeared around the corner, she stood up and started walking towards the mountain.

She came to a place where the ground sloped downwards into a wooded ravine. Hannafia followed the slope and entered the shadow of the mountain. No houses or people were in sight. "It's almost like at home in the Long Neck Woods here," she said to herself. "But only almost." There was a crack between the part that felt like home and the part that didn't, and out of that crack seeped an icy cold stream of air.

She forced herself to walk farther.

Higher up the mountainside she spotted a cave.

The house was empty when she got home. The afternoon was warm, and she sat down on the steps again. After a while Albin came home, with his hands in his pockets and his cap pushed to the back of his head. He sat down next to her. He was sucking on a piece of toffee. She was looking down but could feel his eyes on her. After a while he asked, "What's wrong with you?"

Hannafia kept looking down. She could feel him watching her still, and she shrugged her shoulders slightly.

Then he took the toffee out of his mouth and put it in hers. She was so surprised and grateful that she started to cry. He whistled a tune and waited. When she could speak again she asked, "What does it mean when someone says you already had shoes on your feet when you came here?"

"That you weren't born here," he said.

"If you aren't born in a place— is that place unfriendly to you?"

she asked. "So you feel scared?"

"What do you mean? Has someone been teasing you? Was it those girls again?"

"I saw . . . something. . . Up there. But back home I never got scared. I mean, do you get scared more easily when you move someplace new?"

He scratched his neck and sighed. "Maybe," he said.

"Why aren't you at the saw mill?" she asked. "Aren't you supposed to be there until six o'clock?"

"The boiler broke," he said. "Now tell me what you saw."

"There was a cave, not a very big one, it was smaller than a fireplace, and I saw something move in there."

"A rabbit? A bird?"

"No, like a veil, at first it looked like a veil."

"A swarm of mosquitoes," he said, and laughed.

"No," she said.

He looked at her and then he said, "Show me. We'll go together and see if it's something you need to be scared of."

"You are nice," she said.

"Well, we have to come up with something to do while we wait for supper," he answered.

They stood together in the shadow of the mountain, and Hannafia pointed. He laughed, but then became serious all at once.

"What is it?" Hannafia asked.

"Shh!"

She looked anxiously at his face, and then up towards the cave again.

A woman was standing in the opening. Her hair was gray, but otherwise she looked young. Her clothes were long and wide and dark gray. Her clothes and her eyes gleamed, and she was smiling.

Albin started climbing up the cliff towards the woman.

Hannafia was scared, but not in the same way as before. She

climbed after Albin as fast as she could. She clutched his pants leg and whispered, "Be careful!"

He ignored her.

When he got up into the cave the woman slipped away from him, into the mountain, and he followed. Hannafia grabbed his shirt and was pulled along. The mountain opened, expanded, and then shut itself around them again. They were standing on rock and the air was cool and moist, but it wasn't dark because the woman's hair and clothing shone, and her eyes glistened like silver.

"Welcome," she greeted them.

Albin was watching the woman, and Hannafia was watching Albin. His expression was mild and wondering; she'd never seen him look that way before. Again, she whispered, "Be careful!"

"Why should he be careful?" the woman asked.

Hannafia was so frightened that her head was spinning, and she said the first thing that came to mind. "Well, Granny has told us about people being lured into the mountains. She says to look out for them, because there's always something they want from you."

"I want you to like me," the woman said.

"I like you," Albin said.

"I don't!" said Hannafia.

"How can I make you like me?" the woman asked. "Do you want jewelry?"

Hannafia noticed that the woman was wearing a crown of silver leaves and a necklace of radiant drops, and rings on her fingers. Sparks shimmered in the dark material of her skirt when she moved.

"No," Hannafia said.

"Do you want dolls?" asked the woman.

Hannafia shut her eyes and shook her head. "If we were at home in the Long Neck Mountains, maybe...." she started to say, but didn't know how to finish.

"There is no difference," said the woman.

"She doesn't understand," said Albin, and his voice was friendly and distant and calm; his voice sounded far over Hannafia's head, many many years over her head.

She whispered, *"You're* the one who doesn't understand . . . We're captives of the mountain now and we won't get out until we have beards down to our toes. . . . "

The lady of the mountain simply said, "My kingdom."

She led them into the mountain, down long passageways. The walls of the mountain shimmered with the colors of stone: gray and black-gray and white-gray and red. Albin followed her, smiling, taking long strides, while Hannafia trotted at his heels.

They walked through rock caverns and rooms and came to a black lake that the lady of the mountain called the Windless Lake. "Rock and water are first and eternal," she said. She fell to her knees by the lake and blew across its surface. She did that every time she came by, she explained, so the lake wouldn't be entirely without waves. When the ripples of her breath had run away into the darkness, there was a movement, and a big fish rose towards them. It was dingy and pale. It opened and shut its mouth, fanned its fins, and then sank into the depths again.

The lady of the mountain led them through a ravine full of beautiful sounds. Hannafia believed it was captives of the mountain plucking on strings, but it was only water dripping out of a crack in long silver threads: tink! and clink! and trill and srill. The lady of the mountain said, "That's the source of the water that the people in Tulavall call the Tisla stream."

Later they emerged from a narrow passageway and entered a hall as big as a church. "We must be very quiet," said the lady of the mountain, "because this is where the dragon lives that's feeding on my mountain. It's my enemy," she added.

She lifted her arm, and the children saw that the walls and the ceiling of the hall were streaked; the veins were not just gray, black, white or red; they did not merely mirror and refract light but were luminous in themselves. The widest streak swelled and shifted, and became the dragon. It shone brighter and brighter. It arched its back like a cat, and stretched down a paw with long claws.

Hannafia's heart hammered. Her sweaty hands reached for Albin. "Let's hurry back into that little passage!" she wanted to cry out, but all she managed to do was tremble.

Albin turned towards the lady of the mountain and asked, "Shall I kill the dragon for you?"

"You can't," Hannafia whimpered.

Suddenly the dragon was loose and rushing towards the children. Albin pulled a bundle of matches from his pocket. He lit the entire bundle and threw it into the dragon's jaws. They heard a bang, and then a violent blow tumbled the children to the ground. The hall filled with glowing flakes and the air smelled burnt. The dragon was gone. The flakes fell gently, diminished, and died out. The hall grew darker, but the radiance from the lady of the mountain remained.

"Never before has there been a fire in my mountain!" she said.

Albin smiled at her. Together they walked away through the hall, but Hannafia stayed behind. She heard a whimpering noise and had to see where it came from.

A dragon baby had crept out of the rock behind her. It sniffed the burnt air and started to weep. It gazed at Hannafia with bright tears flowing from its eyes. It wasn't any bigger than a kitten. Hannafia picked it up. It was soft as silk and rubbed its head against her fingers. It rolled up in her hand and stopped crying.

Albin turned around and called out to her. He was impatient, and when he saw what she was carrying he became angry. "That's an enemy!" he said.

"It's not *my* enemy," Hannafia said. "It's small and lonely."

Albin grabbed her arm. He looked fierce and nasty, like a stranger, and she cried in a quivery voice, "You're the worst of all my big brothers!"

She hid the little dragon in her apron, and Albin hesitated. He asked the lady of the mountain, "Do they grow quickly, these dragons?"

"No," she said, "they grow slowly."

Then Albin relented and said, "I'll come back and kill it for you later, when it's grown."

He and the lady of the mountain continued walking, and Hannafia followed them, holding the dragon baby in her arms.

Later, much later, they came to a ravine. Out of the ravine's darkness they heard a murmuring sound. Spanning the ravine was a bridge resembling a moonbeam more than anything else. It became visible when the light from the lady of the mountain fell across it. She walked out onto the bridge, and Albin followed. His shadow spread itself out behind him, concealing the bridge from Hannafia. Her feet felt for the bridge, but they met only darkness and empty air.

Then the dragon child stirred. It stretched its head out and it, too, started to shine. The bridge reappeared, and Hannafia ran across it.

She trotted after the other two.

They walked past cliffs streaked with veins that looked like all sorts of different things.

They entered a cavern so vast that they couldn't see to the end of it. It felt just like being outdoors at night. There was a sort of moonshine there, but they couldn't see any moon. They felt a fresh breeze and heard a roaring sound, as if from a beach. There were crevices that they had to watch out for. After they had walked for a while, they heard a humming sound coming from the ground. The humming grew into a song, a deep voiced song.

"Is that the captives of the mountain singing?" Hannafia asked.

"No," the lady of the mountain answered. "It's my memories."

And later, much later, they came to another cavern. The lady of the mountain slowed her steps and said, "Here we must be quiet."

In the distance, perched on a cliff, they spotted a shining black bird. It was bigger than a person, and looked like an eagle, but not exactly the same, because its skull was just like the head of an old bald man. Its beak was very big, and its eyes were big and black.

It had been sitting with its back towards them, but when they came in, it slowly turned and eyed them.

"I have to walk through here occasionally," said the lady of the mountain.

"Shall I kill it for you?" Albin asked.

She didn't answer. She merely smiled and started walking faster. Albin hung back, his eyes held by the giant bird's gaze. He fumbled in his pockets. The lady of the mountain stepped into the shelter of a passageway leading into the cliff. Hannafia couldn't decide whether to seek refuge with her, or to stay with her brother. The bird lifted its wings, filling the air with whispers.

Albin dug up a lump of cobbler's pitch from his pocket and hurled it at the bird's head.

The bird snatched up the lump and swallowed it.

Albin pulled out a piece of chewing tobacco and threw it. But he had gotten scared: his aim was so poor that the tobacco plug would have missed its mark if the bird hadn't shot its head forward to seize it.

"Come on!" Hannafia hissed, reaching for Albin.

Suddenly the bird rose and spread its wings, and at last Albin fled. He grabbed Hannafia's hand as he ran past and pulled her into the passageway where the lady of the mountain stood waiting.

Still later they came to a cavern filled with strange shadows. The lady of the mountain gave Albin a sidelong glance and started to walk very fast.

"There must be something dangerous here, too," Hannafia whispered.

As she spoke, the shadows grew dark and dense, and started rushing towards them. They looked like dogs. Albin was terrified of large dogs. He stopped, and Hannafia tugged at him. The dogs were coming at them from all directions. Albin dug in his pockets for something to throw at them, but came up empty-handed.

Then he grabbed at the dragon baby, shouting, "Throw it!"

"No!" Hannafia shrieked, stretching the dragon as far from Albin's reach as she could.

The dragon baby shone like a lantern. The dogs thickened to a teeming eddy around them, but they didn't step inside the dragon baby's circle of light.

"Come on!" Hannafia said.

But the fear had settled in Albin's legs, and he couldn't move.

"Come help me!" Hannafia shouted to the lady of the mountain. "I know you can do magic. Make it so I have the strength to carry him!" At once Albin turned into a stone, small enough to hold in her hand.

"Now get me out of here!" Hannafia shouted

The lady of the mountain glided away along the cliff, and a stripe of daylight appeared where she had been standing.

Hannafia held the dragon baby in one hand and Albin in the other. She started walking towards the ribbon of light, and it grew wider with each step she took. Behind her the lady of the mountain began to weep.

"What are you crying about?" Hannafia asked crossly. "You have rock and water, and they are first and eternal," she said, echoing the lady of the mountain's own words.

There was no answer, but the weeping became more bitter.

Hannafia stood still. Ever since they had left the cottage in the Long Neck Woods she, too, had been crying. Deep down inside herself she had quietly wept.

"We can't stay here, you must understand that," she snapped. "But you can come out with me. If you can. Make it so you can."

Hannafia had been prepared to come out of the mountain as an old, old woman, into a world where no one knew her, and the thought had frightened her.

But when she found herself standing in the evening sun below

Edvin the wheelwright's farm, just where Gullkrona Lane joins the main road to the north, Gull-Maj and Janette were the first people she saw, and they looked the same as before. They were standing there with their dolls and doll carriage, and Janette was making nasty faces.

Gull-Maj asked, "What are you going to do with those?"

Hannafia looked down. She had three stones in her apron: the dragon baby, Albin and the lady of the mountain. "Play with them, of course," she replied.

She walked up Gullkrona Hill with her stones and continued up along Old Man's Lane. She sat down on her front steps and lined up the stones beside her.

Mother had come home. She had a fire burning in the stove and the porridge pot was on. Hannafia's little sisters were playing around the corner, singing:

Though the road seems long and steep
and a sigh closes each day
if release you wish to reap
you must walk each step of its way.

"What are you going to do with those?" Albin asked. He was sitting beside her on the steps. He touched the stone that was the lady of the mountain and the stone that was the dragon baby.

"Play," Hannafia answered.

The clock in the town hall tower struck six.

It wasn't until some time in October that the ship *Southwest* returned to Tulavall. Tuspuru Schando sought out Hannafia as he had promised. "How are things?" he asked.

When she had told him everything that had happened and explained that everything was okay now, and showed him the stones which she kept under a bush since she didn't think they'd like to be kept indoors, he said: "It could be true what she said, your lady of the mountain, that rock and water are eternal. But even things that aren't eternal come back again."

"Like what?" Hannafia asked.

"People," Tuspuru said. "And boats and ships."

Short story from *Barbidels Hav*. Translated from the Swedish by Anna Sonnerup.

@ Astrid Lindgren

For many of us, the names Astrid Lindgren (1907–) and Pippi Longstocking are
inseparable. Together they have been two of Sweden's most successful ambassa-
dors in the twentieth century. When Pippi arrived on the scene in the 1940s, she
challenged the notion of what books for children ought to be and how female
protagonists ought to act. Happily living outside the realm of adult authority,
Pippi is curious and fun loving, and she possesses superhuman strength—an
undeniable advantage for a child in a world ruled by adults! Pippi literally took
the world by storm and today Lindgren's books about Pippi have been translated into over fifty languages.

The selection below has been excerpted from *Ronia, the Robber's Daughter*.
Ronia shares many of Pippi's qualities, but where Pippi is a fantastic character,
the eternal child, Ronia is a realistic and complex character who experiences all
the emotion and pain of growing up.

The novel is set in a fairy-tale-like forest where Ronia lives with her mother
and father, Lovis and Matt. Ronia's father is the leader of a band of robbers, but
Matt and his band are not the only robbers in the forest. The rival robber
chieftain's name is Borka and he and Matt are sworn enemies. This does not
concern Ronia much until one day, deep in the forest, she meets Borka's son,
Birk. They become the closest of companions, but their happiness is marred by
their fathers' hostility and feuding. Ronia, who has never questioned her father's
wisdom, nor her love for him, is deeply troubled by his actions and by a way of
life that can lead to such cruelty and heartache.

Ronia, The Robber's Daughter

Ronia wanted to go home. Thanks to a couple of bad-tempered old
robber chieftains, it was no fun staying in the woods any more.

That day, like all other days, she and Birk separated long before
the Wolf's Neck and far from all robber tracks. They knew where
Matt usually came riding home and where Borka's paths ran, yet they
were always worried that someone might see them together.

Ronia let Birk go ahead.

"I'll see you tomorrow," he said, and off he ran.

Ronia delayed for a time, watching the fox cubs jumping and

playing. They were a joy to see, but Ronia felt no joy, and she wondered glumly if things could ever be as they had been before. Perhaps she would never again rejoice in the forest as she once had.

Then she turned toward home. When she reached the Wolf's Neck, she found Jep and Little-Snip on guard. They seemed merrier than usual.

"Hurry home and see what's happened," Jep said.

Ronia was curious. "It must be something pleasant—I can tell from your faces."

"Oh, yes, you're right there," said Little-Snip with a grin. "Go and see for yourself."

Ronia began to run. She could certainly do with something pleasant.

Soon she was outside the closed door of the stone hall and could hear Matt laughing inside, a great ringing laugh that warmed her and took away all her worry. And now she wanted to find out what made him laugh so. She ran eagerly into the stone hall. As soon as Matt caught sight of her, he rushed forward and threw his arms around her. He lifted her high in the air and swung her around, quite carried away.

"Ronia darling," he shouted, "you were right! There need be no bloodshed. Now Borka will go to blazes faster than his first belch after breakfast, believe me!"

"How so?" asked Ronia.

Matt pointed. "Look there! Look who I've just caught with my own hands!"

The stone hall was full of excited robbers jumping around and making a noise, so at first Ronia could not see what Matt was pointing at.

"You see, Ronia darling, I have only to say to Borka, 'Are you staying or going? Do you want your snake fry back or not?'"

Then she saw Birk. There he was, lying in a corner, bound hand and foot, with blood on his forehead and desperation in his eyes, and around him Matt's robbers leaped, whooping and yelling.

"Hey there, little Borkason, when are you going home to your father?"

Ronia gave a shriek, and tears of rage spurted from her eyes.

"You can't do that!" She started to beat Matt wherever she could reach with balled fists. "You beast, you can't do that!"

Matt dropped her with a thud; there was no more laughter now. He was pale with fury.

"What's that my daughter says I can't do?" he asked menacingly.

"I'll tell you," shrieked Ronia. "You can go robbing all the money and goods and rubbish you want, but you can't rob people, because if you do I don't want to be your daughter any more!"

"Who's talking about people?" said Matt, his voice unrecognizable. "I've caught a snake fry, a louse, a little thieving hound, and I'm going to get my father's fortress cleaned out at last. Then you can be my daughter or not just as you choose."

"Beast!" shrieked Ronia.

Noodle-Pete moved between them, beginning to be frightened. Never before had he seen Matt's face so stony and terrible, and it scared him.

"That's no way to talk to your father," said Noodle-Pete, taking Ronia by the arm. But she threw him off.

"Beast!" she shrieked again.

Matt seemed not to hear her. It was as if she no longer existed for him.

"Fooloks," he said, in the same terrifying voice, "go up to Hell's Cap and send a message to Borka. Tell him I want to see him there as soon as the sun rises tomorrow morning. It would be safer for him to come, tell him that!"

Lovis stood listening in silence. She drew her eyebrows together, but said nothing. Finally she went over and looked at Birk, and when she saw the wound on his forehead she fetched her crock of healing herb juices. She was about to wash the wound when Matt bellowed, "Don't you lay a hand on the snake fry!"

"Snake fry or no," said Lovis, "this wound must be washed!"

And washed it was.

Then Matt advanced. He took hold of her and flung her across the floor. If Knott had not caught her, she would have slid straight into a bedpost.

But Lovis would never let anyone get away with that. And since Matt was not within striking distance, she dealt Knott a resounding blow. That was all the thanks he got for not letting her collide with the bedpost.

"Out, every man jack of you," screamed Lovis. "I'm sick of all of you. You never do anything but make trouble. Do you hear me, Matt? Get out of here!"

Matt gave her a black look. It would have scared anyone else, but not Lovis. She stood there, her arms folded, watching him march out of the stone hall, followed by all his robbers. But over his shoulder lay Birk, his copper hair hanging limply.

"You beast, Matt!" Ronia shrieked again, before the heavy door shut behind him.

Matt did not lie in his usual bed beside Lovis that night, and where he slept Lovis did not know.

"And I don't care, either," she said. "Now I can lie lengthwise and crosswise in this bed if I choose."

But she could not sleep. She could hear her child crying desperately, and her child would not accept any comforting. It was a night Ronia had to go through alone. She lay awake a long time, hating her father until she felt her heart contract with pain. But it is difficult to hate someone whom you have loved so much all your life, and that was why this was the heaviest of nights for Ronia.

At last she fell asleep, but she woke up as soon as light began to dawn. The sun would be rising soon, and by then she must be at Hell's Cap to see what happened there. Lovis tried to stop her, but Ronia was not to be stopped. She went, and Lovis followed her silently.

And there they stood, as they had once stood before, each on his own side of Hell's Gap, Matt and Borka with their robbers. Undis was there, too, and Ronia could hear her screams and curses a long way off. It was Matt she was cursing so fiercely that the air sizzled. But Matt was not going to be insulted for long.

"Can you make your woman be quiet, Borka?" he said. "It would be best for you to hear what I have to say."

Ronia had placed herself directly behind him so that he would not see her. She herself heard and saw more than she could bear. At Matt's side stood Birk, no longer tied hand and foot, but with a rope around his neck, and Matt was holding the rope in his hand as if he were leading a dog.

"You're a hard man, Matt," said Borka. "And a vile man. I can understand that you want me out of here. But to use my child to get what you want is vile!"

"I didn't ask what you thought about me," said Matt. "What I want to know is how soon you're going to get out."

Borka was so angry that words were choked in his throat. He stood in silence for a long time, but at last he said, "First I have to find a place where we can settle down out of danger, and that may be difficult. But if you give me back my son, you have my word that we will be gone before the summer is over."

"Good," said Matt. "Then you have my word that you will get your son back before the summer is over."

"I meant I want him now," said Borka.

"And I meant that you shan't have him," said Matt. "But we have dungeons in Matt's Fort. He will not want for a roof over his head, so let that be a comfort to you if it happens to be a rainy summer."

Ronia caught her breath. Her father had thought it out so cruelly. Borka must leave now, at once; otherwise Birk would be locked up in a dungeon until the end of summer. But he would not be able to live there that long, Ronia knew. He would die, and she would no longer have a brother.

She would not have a father she could love, either. That hurt too. She wanted to punish Matt for that, and because she could no longer be his daughter, oh, how she wanted him to suffer as she herself was suffering, and how grimly she yearned to destroy everything for him and bring all his plans to naught!

And suddenly she knew—knew what she was going to do. Once,

long ago, she had done it, and in a rage that time, too, but not as beside herself as she was now. Almost as if in a fever, she took a run and flew across Hell's Gap. Matt saw her in mid-leap, and a cry burst from him, the kind of cry wild animals utter in their death agony, and the blood in his robbers turned to ice, for they had heard nothing like it before. And then they saw Ronia, his Ronia, on the other side of the abyss, with his enemy. Nothing worse could possibly have happened—and nothing so incomprehensible.

It was incomprehensible to the Borka robbers too. They stared at Ronia as if a wild harpy had unexpectedly landed in their midst.

Borka was equally confounded, but he recovered his wits quickly. Something had happened that changed everything; he could see that. Here was Matt's wild harpy of a daughter helping him out of the jam he was in. Why she should do anything so senseless he had no idea, but he hastened to put a rope around her neck and laughed to himself as he did it.

Then he shouted to Matt, "We have dungeons underground on this side too. Your daughter will not want for a roof over her head, either, if it happens to be a rainy summer. Comfort yourself with that thought, Matt!"

But Matt was beyond all comfort. Like a wounded bear he stood there, rocking his massive body as if to subdue some unbearable torment. Ronia wept as she watched him. He had dropped the rope that held Birk prisoner, but Birk still stood there, pale and crushed, looking across Hell's Gap at Ronia.

Then Undis stepped up to her and gave her a slap. "Yes, cry! I'd do the same if I had a beast like that for a father!"

But Borka told Undis to hold her tongue. She was not to interfere, he said.

Ronia herself had called Matt a beast, yet now she wished she could comfort him for what she had done to him that had made him suffer so terribly.

Lovis, too, wanted to help him, as always when he was in need. She was standing beside him now, but he did not even notice. He noticed nothing. Just now he was alone in the world.

Then Borka called to him. "Do you hear, Matt? Are you going to give me back my son or not?"

But Matt just stood there, rocking, and did not answer.

Then Borka shouted, "Are you going to give me back my son or not?"

Matt woke up at last. "Certainly I am," he said indifferently. "When you like."

"When I like is now," said Borka. "Not when summer is over, but *now!*"

Matt nodded. "When you like, as I said."

It was as if it no longer concerned him. But Borka said with a grin, "And at the same time you will get back your child. Fair exchange is no robbery—you know that, you scoundrel!"

"I have no child," said Matt.

Borka's happy grin faded. "What do you mean by that? Is this some new mischief you're brewing?"

"Come and get your son," said Matt. "But you can't give me back my child, for I have none."

"But I have," screamed Lovis in a voice that lifted the crows from the battlements. "And I want my child back, understand, Borka! Now!"

Then she fixed her eyes on Matt. "Even if that child's father has gone as crazy as they come."

Matt turned and walked away with heavy footsteps.

Matt was not to be seen in the stone hall for the next few days, nor was he at the Wolf's Neck when the children were exchanged. Lovis was there instead to receive her daughter. She was supported by Fooloks and Jep, and they had Birk with them. Borka and Undis were waiting with their robbers beyond the Wolf's Neck, and Undis, full of anger and triumph, burst out as soon as she saw Lovis. "That child-robber Matt—I can well understand he's too ashamed to show his face!"

Lovis was too proud to answer. She drew Ronia to her and was about to move away without a word. She had thought a lot about the reason her daughter had put herself in Borka's hands, but at this meeting she was beginning to see something. They were looking at each other, Ronia and Birk, as if they were alone at the Wolf's Neck and in the world. Yes, no one could help seeing that these two had a bond between them.

Undis noticed at once, and she did not like what she saw. She caught hold of Birk fiercely.

"What is there between you?"

"She is my sister," said Birk. "And she saved my life."

Ronia leaned against Lovis and cried. "Just as Birk saved mine," she muttered.

But Borka was turning scarlet with anger.

"Has my son been going behind my back and keeping company with my enemy's offspring?"

"She is my sister," said Birk again, looking at Ronia.

"Sister!" shouted Undis. "Oh, yes, we know what that will mean in a year or two!"

She seized Birk and tried to pull him away.

"Don't touch me," said Birk. "I'll go by myself, and I won't have your hands on me."

He turned and went, and there came a cry of misery from Ronia. "Birk!"

But he had gone.

When Lovis was alone with Ronia, she wanted to ask a few questions, but she had no chance.

"Don't talk to me," Ronia said.

So Lovis left her in peace, and they walked home in silence.

Excerpted from *Ronia Rövardotter.* Translated from the Swedish by Patricia Crampton.

❧ Cora Sandel

Cora Sandel (1880–1974) is best known for her trilogy about Alberta, a teenage girl living in a small coastal town in Northern Norway who longs to experience the world beyond. Alberta's determination to break away from a stifling environment and pursue her dream of becoming an artist is rewarded at the end of the first novel. In the second book she travels to Paris where new challenges await her. By the end of the third novel, she has found her literary voice.

The girl child in the story below is Alberta's soul mate. Like Alberta, she comes alive when she is out on the roads, alone. The timespan of the story is indefinite—we don't know exactly how old the child is or how much time lapses, but it's clear that she grows and matures. And in the process the road takes on new dimensions, fulfilling its promise of "unknown possibilities" around every bend.

The Child Who Loved Roads

Most of all she loved roads with the solitary track of a horse down the middle and with grass between the wheel ruts. Narrow old roads with lots of bends and nobody else around and here and there perhaps a piece of straw, fallen from a load of hay. On these roads the child became springy, light as air. She was filled with happiness at breaking free, at existing. Behind every bend waited unknown possibilities, however many times you'd gone down the road. You could make them up yourself if nothing else.

Down the highway she walked, dragging her feet in dust and gravel. Dust and gravel were among the bad things in life. You got tired, hot, heavy, longed to be picked up and carried.

Then suddenly the narrow old road was there, and the child began to run, leaping high with happiness.

She hadn't been so tired after all, the grownups said. There's a lot grownups don't understand. You have to give up on explaining anything to them and take them as they are, an inconvenience, for the most part. No one should grow up. No, children should stay children and rule the whole world. Everything would be more fun and better then.

46

Early on the child learned that it was best to be alone on the road. A good ways in front of the others anyway. Only then did you come to know the road as it really was, with its marks of wheels and horses' hooves, its small, stubborn stones sticking up, its shifting lights and shadows. Only then did you come to know the fringes of the road, warm from sun and greenness, plump and furry with chervil and lady's mantle—altogether a strange and wonderful world unto itself, where you could wander free as you pleased, and everything was good, safe, and just the way you wanted it.

At least it was in the summer. In winter the road was something else entirely. In the twilight of a snow-gray day your legs could turn to lead, everything was so sad. You never seemed to get any further; there was always a long ways to go. The middle of the road was brown and ugly, like rice pudding with cinnamon on it, a dish that grew in her mouth and that she couldn't stand. People and trees stood out black and sorrowful against the white. You did have the sledding hill, the field with deep snow for rolling on, the courtyard for building forts and caves, the skis without real bindings. For small children shouldn't have real bindings, the grownups said; they could break their legs falling. In the twilight everything was merely sad, and nothing about it could compare to the roads in summer.

To be let loose on them, without a jacket, without a hat, bare, that was life the way it should be. Only one thing compared to it, the hills at the big farm, where she was often a guest.

There were paths bordered with heather and crowberry leading up to views over the blue fjord and to a light, never-still breeze that tickled your scalp. White stone protruded from the heather and the path. At the bottom of the hill you found wild strawberries, higher up blueberries, not just a few either, and bilberries. On top lay the crowberries in patches like large carpets.

The child could pass hours lying on her stomach near a bush stuffing herself, and at the same time thinking of all sorts of things. She possessed an active imagination, seldom longed for company and could sometimes fly into a rage if she got it.

"You're so contrary," said the grownups. "Can't you be nice and sweet like the others, just a little? You should be thankful any one wants to be with you," they said.

"It won't be easy for you when you're older," they also said.

The child forgot it as soon as it was said. She ran off to the road or paths and remembered nothing of anything so unreasonable, so completely ridiculous.

One road went from the house on the big farm, went along the garden where huge old red currant bushes hung over the picket fence, casually offering their magnificence; the road went across fields, bordered by thin young trees, made a leap over a hill and swung two times like an S before it wandered out in the world and became one with the boring highway.

The child's own road, newly taken possession of summer after summer. Here no one came running after you, here you could wander without company. Nothing could happen but the right things. If anyone came driving or riding it was uncles, aunts or the farm boy. They saw you from a long distance, they stopped; if they came by wagon you got a ride to the farm.

Here and there on the hills were where the stories came into being, short ones and long ones. If it didn't look like they were living up to their promise, you just stopped and started a new one.

A place in life where freedom had no boundaries. Very different from what grownups meant when they said, "in this life," or "in this world," and sighed. They also said, "in this difficult life." As if to make things as nasty as possible.

Being together with someone—that was sometimes fun and sometimes not at all. You couldn't explain why or why not; it was all tied up with everything you were pretending, things you'd never think of talking to grownups about. On the contrary, you held tightly to it, like someone insisting on something wrong they've done. Maybe it was "wrong;" maybe it was one of those things that ought to be "rooted out of you." Or at best to laugh about a little, to whisper over your head.

"Constructive" it wasn't, in any case. They were always talking about the necessity of doing "constructive things."

It could be fun, when Alette came, Letta. She was a redhead, freckled, full of laughter, easy to get along with. At her house, on the neighboring farm, was a chest in the loft, full of old-fashioned clothes. Dresses in wonderful light colors, flounce after flounce on the wide tarlatan skirts, a name that was far prettier than, for example, blue cotton cambric. A man's suit, yellow knee breeches and a green coat with gold buttons, an unbelievable costume that didn't look like anything the uncles wore. A folding parasol, a whole collection of odd hats. To dress up in all that, strut around in it, stumble in the long skirts, mimic the grownups and make them laugh where they sat on the garden steps, was fun enough for a while. But it was nothing to base a life on.

For that you could only use the roads, the paths and the hills.

Grownup, well, you probably had to turn into one. Everyone did; you couldn't avoid it.

But like some of them? Definitely not.

In the first place the child was going to run her whole life, never do anything so boring as walk slowly and deliberately. In the second and third place. . . .

The grown-ups didn't have much that was worthwhile. It was true they got everything they wanted, could buy themselves things they wanted and go to bed when they felt like it, eat things at the table that children didn't get—all the best things, in short. They could command and destroy, give canings and presents. But they got long skirts or trousers to wear and then they *walked. Just* walked. You had to wonder if it had something to do with what was called Confirmation, if there wasn't something about it that injured their legs. There probably was, since they hid them and walked. They *couldn't* run any longer. Even though—you saw them dance; you saw them play "Bachelor Seeks a Mate" and "Last Pair Out."

Maybe it was their minds something was wrong with?

Everything truly fun disappeared from their lives, and they let it happen. None of them rebelled. On the contrary, they grew conceited about their sad transformation. Was there anything so conceited as the big girls when they got long skirts and put up their hair!

They walked, they sat and embroidered, sat and wrote, sat and chatted, knitted, crocheted. Walked and sat, sat and walked. Stupid, they were so stupid!

Trailing skirts were dangerous. She'd have to watch out, when the time came. Run away maybe.

At home, in the city street, were the mean boys.

Really big boys, the kind that were practically uncles, were often nice. They were the ones who organized the big circus in the empty lot, with trapeze artists, clowns and tickets that the grownups bought in complete seriousness: parquet circle, first class, second class. A ringmaster in a tuxedo went around the circus ring and cracked his long whip at the horses doing tricks. A true circus, so to speak, except that the horses consisted of two boys under a blanket that sometimes sagged in the middle. But that was easy to overlook.

The big boys arranged competition races in the winter, saw to it that you got new skis and real bindings; they were pillars of support. One of them once got up and lambasted his sister, who had tattled on him. A bunch of lies, made-up, shameful, that you just had to sit there and take, for you didn't get anywhere saying it wasn't true.

They were pillars all the same.

But there was a half-grown kind, a mean kind, that made such a racket. They ran back and forth with wooden bats in their hands and the balls shot between them like bullets. In the winter they threw hard snowballs, and if anyone had put up an especially fine fort anywhere, they came rushing down in a crowd and stormed it, left it destroyed. Sometimes they threatened you with a beating. For no reason, just to threaten. The child was deathly afraid of them, took any roundabout way she could to avoid them; she would rather be too late for dinner.

Sometimes she *had* to come through enemy lines to get home. With her heart in her throat, with her head bowed as if in a storm, she sneaked sideways along the walls of the houses. The taunts rained down.

One day a boy of that sort came after the child, grabbed her arm squeezed it hard and said, "You know what you are? Do you?"

No answer.

"You're just a girl. Go home where you belong."

Hard as a whip the words struck the child. Just a girl—*just*. . . . From that moment she had a heavy burden to bear, one of the heaviest, the feeling of being something inferior, of being born that way, beyond help.

With such a burden on your back the world becomes a different place for you. Your sense of yourself begins to change.

But the roads remained an even bigger consolation than before. On them even "just a girl" felt easy, free and secure.

The child was one of those who feels sorry. For skinny horses and horses who got the whip, for cats who looked homeless, for children who were smaller than she was and who didn't have mittens in winter, for people who just looked poor, and for drunken men.

Why she was so sorry for drunken men was never clear. They'd drunk hard liquor; they could have left it alone. They were their own worst enemies, the grown-ups explained; if things went so badly for them it was their own fault.

In the child's eyes they were nothing but helpless. They tumbled here and there; sometimes they fell down and remained lying there—the constable came and roughly dragged them off. Sorry for them, she was sorry for them; they couldn't help it, they couldn't help it for anything, however they'd come to be that way. They were like little children who can't walk on their own and do things wrong because they don't know any better.

The child cried herself to sleep at times on account of the drunkards. And on account of the horses, cats and poor people. Once you're like that, you don't have it easy. The cats she could have taken home if it hadn't been for the grownups. She wasn't allowed. As if one cat more or less mattered. You were powerless, in this as in everything.

On the summertime roads you forgot your troubles. If you met a poorly clad person you usually knew who they were, where they lived, that they had nicer clothes at home that they saved for Sundays. The horses you met were rounded, comfortable, easy-going. They waved their long tails up over thick haunches and grazed by the roadside as soon as they got a chance. The cats rubbed against your legs, purring loudly. Farm cats who belonged somewhere and were just out for a walk.

However, you hardly ever met anyone, neither people nor animals. That was wonderful; it became more and more wonderful as the child grew older. She had a steadily stronger desire to keep making up stories in her head. There was no place that they came so readily as along a two-wheeled track with grass in between. Or up on the hill where the breeze brushed your scalp.

Time passed. The child ran, long braid flapping, on the roads.

If she was overtaken by the grown-ups, she heard, "You're too old now to be running like that. Soon you'll be wearing long skirts, remember. A young lady walks, she holds herself nicely, thinks about how she places her feet. Then she can't rush away like you do."

The child ran even faster than before. To get out of earshot, out of range as much as possible. Her legs had grown long; they were an advantage when she took to her heels. The braid swung, the lengthened skirt swung. The child thought—one day I won't turn around when they call, I won't wait for anyone. That might be sooner than they suspect. The roads lead much farther than I realized; they lead out into the world, away from all of them.

When she stopped, she looked around with new eyes, seeing not only the roadsides any longer, but the horizons. Behind them lay what she longed for, craved: freedom.

But one of the big boys, the kind that were practically uncles, suddenly popped up out of nowhere. He was Letta's cousin, had passed exams, was called a university student.

You didn't see much of him. Letta said he was stupid and conceited, a self-important fellow who kept to his room or with the grownups. He himself was definitely not that old, said Letta, who remembered him in short pants, remembered that he stole apples at someone's and got a caning for it at home. That wasn't so very long ago; she'd been ten years old, on a visit to his parents. Now she was thirteen, almost fourteen.

He had a strange effect on the child; he upset her from the first moment in a way that was both painful and good. It was impossible to think of him when he was nearby and could turn up; you can't think when you're blushing in confusion. But out on the roads he crept into her thoughts to the extent that she couldn't get him out again; he took up residence there, inserted himself in the middle of an on-going story, which had to be completely changed. There was no other recourse.

The story came to be about him. He became the main character, along with herself. In spite of the fact that she didn't really know how he looked; she never quite risked looking at him. And in spite of the fact that he wore long trousers, walked, and consequently belonged to the poor fool category.

It was inexplicable, and she felt it as slightly shameful, a defeat. The child grew fiery red with embarrassment if he so much as made an appearance. As the misfortune was written on her face, it was necessary to avoid Letta and her family, to keep to the roads as never before.

You could be in Letta's garden and still be unseen.

Letta followed, full of suggestions; she wanted them to get dressed up like summers before, make fun of the cousin, who was sitting on the steps with the grownups—mimic him.

"He doesn't interest me."

"You think he interests me? That's why we can tease him a little, can't we?"

"I'm not interested in teasing such a disgusting person," announced the child, marveling at her own words.

"Come anyway, though."

"No."

"Why not?"

"Because I don't want to, that's why."

But it was a terribly empty feeling, when Letta gave up and walked away. Just to talk about him was a new and remarkable experience, was something she yearned for, wanted and had to do.

The child was beginning to walk on the roads. Slowly even. She stood still for long moments at a time. For nothing, to fuss with the tie on her braid, to curl the end of the braid around her fingers, to scrape her toe in the gravel, stare out in space. She sat down in the grass by the roadside, trailed her hand searchingly around between the lady's mantle and avens, did it over and over.

Finally her hand had found something, a four-leafed clover. Thoughtfully the child walked on with it, holding it carefully between two fingers.

"Well now, finally you're acting like a big girl," said one of the aunts, pleased. "Not a minute too soon. Good thing we don't have to nag you anymore. Good thing there's still a little hem to let out in your dress. Next week we'll get Johanna the seamstress."

Hardly was it said than the child set off at full speed, in defiance, in panic.

Without her having noticed or understood it, she had allowed something to happen, something frightening, something detestable. Something that made them happy. But nothing should make them happy. For then they'd be getting you where they wanted you, a prisoner, some kind of invalid.

The child didn't hear the despairing sigh of a deeply worried grownup. That would have made her relieved and calm. Instead she only felt torn by life's contradictions, bewildered and confused by them.

One day the cousin left; he was simply gone. Letta said, "Who cares, he was conceited and engaged." Secretly, of course, but it had come out that he went around with a photograph and pressed flower in his wallet, and that he used to meet the postman far down the highway. Letta's father had taken him into the office, talked with him for a long time, pointed out what a serious thing an engagement is, nothing for a green new graduate. Green, that was probably a good description of him. Anyway, his fiancée's father was nothing but a shoemaker, said Letta. She thought the cousin's parents had been alerted.

"Imagine, engaged. Him!"

The child stood there and felt something strange in her face, felt herself grow pale. Not red at any rate, because then you got hot. This was a cold feeling.

"Well, good-bye," she said.

"Didn't you come to stay?"

The child had already gone, was out on the road, the good old road with the two curves like an S, with thin young trees along it and grass between the wheel tracks. Here was the same sense of escape as always; here you could run, not only in fantasy, but also free from all shame, everything deceitful that was out after you. And that was over now.

For it was over right away. In a short, painful moment—as when a tooth is pulled out.

Follow the road, never become what they call grown-up, never what they call old, two degrading conditions that made people stupid, ugly, boring. Stay how you are now, light as a feather, never tired, never out of breath. It came down to being careful, not just for lengthened skirts, but also for anything like this.

For a moment the child stopped, fished out of her pocket a dried four-leaf clover, tore it in pieces and let the wind take the bits.

And then she ran on, over the farmyard, right up the path to the hill where the fresh breeze blew.

Story from *Barnet som elsket veier.* Translated from the Norwegian by Barbara Wilson.

⟨𝒳 Dikken Zwilgmeyer

Dikken Zwilgmeyer (1853–1913) and her unconventional character, Inger Johanne, have inspired and delighted Norwegian children since 1890. That was the year *We Children* was published, the first in what became a series of books authored by "Inger Johanne. 13 years old." By keeping her name off the title page, Dikken Zwilgmeyer made it very clear that this was a new voice in Norwegian children's literature: the child's voice.

And Inger Johanne had no pretensions about being a well-mannered little girl! She was too full of energy and curiosity and ideas to be bothered with acting like a young lady. Inger Johanne's inventiveness sometimes got her into trouble, as in the following story taken from *Karsten and I*, but never for long. For she could win anyone over with her spunk and cheerful disposition and, not surprisingly, she became a role model for authors and children alike.

Søren Bricklayer's Piglets

Oh, I can't stand rainy weather! Especially during the summer. Maybe you like the kind of horrid pouring rain that goes on for days in the middle of wonderful summer, so that the gooseberries rain down from the trees and all that's left of those big magnificent strawberries you've been eyeing for days in eager anticipation is a soft, wet blob?

Not to mention the roses. Only the pistil remains—half-rotten rose petals lie strewn all over the wet soil, and mignonettes and tansies and daisies are flat on the ground, quite muddy and limp.

Our old house on the hill is the most wonderful house in town, no doubt about it, but in rainy weather it can be a little wet up there. All the water that gathers on the heath behind the house runs down over us, you see. It courses and flows in streams and tiny waterfalls down over the rocks through moss and heather, carrying with it all the soil in our vegetable patch, where there was little enough to begin with, and gouging deep trenches down across our big hill taking everything but the shiny, washed stones. After it's been raining steadily for several days, Father always has to bring in new dirt for the hill to make it look a little better.

As tiresome as it is on those rainy days, Karsten and I have loads of fun afterwards, when it's rained buckets for a few days and the heath is overflowing with water. Karsten and I build water works, you see. We make dams, sluices and waterfalls—you can imagine how much fun it is! Massa and Mina can't understand how I can think that kind of thing is fun, now that I'm thirteen years old. They make fun of me and gossip about me at school and to the boys, but I don't care a bit about that. Of course my feet do get terribly wet, along with the hem of my dress and a good portion of my sleeves, so I have to sneak up the back steps to change clothes so Mother won't see me. But it sure is fun.

Sometimes we start making trenches way up on the heath and build up the walls with sod and heather and moss to make the water run where we want it to. Karsten carries rocks, straining and sweating, bareheaded, his face as red as a beet, and I build walls and give orders. Because I'm the engineer, you see.

It would be an awful lot of fun to be an engineer when you grow up. I'm a little girl, so unfortunately I can't, but Karsten could be an engineer and I could work in his office and be the one who'd run the whole show—just like I do up here on the heath. Because Karsten never has any new ideas, but I do.

A ways down the heath is our basin that all the trenches empty into. It's in an absolutely fantastic location, right above the steepest cliff on the heath and down in a large hollow. You only need to build a levee on one side, but that must be extra solid. For sometimes we have over two feet of water in the basin and then it could easily overflow.

Then the big moment arrives when the water is released. Karsten and I each have a pole and quick as a flash we rip open the dam and the water plunges over the cliff! The yellowish bog water that we have channeled down all the way from the top of the heath leaps out in a single gush—it thunders and crashes and sprays like a real waterfall. The only problem is that it's over so fast. Because even if the basin is really full, the water empties out in five minutes. So we always make sure we release the waterfall when someone is watching. It doesn't really matter who it is, even if it's only Even Stoneworker's children. We must at least have one spectator and until we do we don't start the waterfall, you see.

Right below the cliff and a little to one side is Søren Bricklayer's house. Our field borders on his farm. When we start the waterfall, all the water flows into our field right in back of the big walnut tree. The waterfall had always followed that course and it never occurred to me that the water would flow in a different direction than it always had.

But listen to this.

It had rained nonstop for eleven days, right at the beginning of summer vacation. I think it's always like that, but in any case Karsten and I were bored stiff. Karsten did go out in the rain and sailed bark boats in the brewing vat that was out in the yard full of water, but I outgrew that kind of amusement many years ago, of course. Sitting and reading books in the middle of summer is pointless. At least I don't think it's any fun, so to be perfectly frank, I was bored.

But finally one day the sun came out.

It glittered and shone and dripped, and the rain glistened across the grassy fields, on fences and slopes of scree; there wasn't a cleft or crevice on the heath that didn't have water trickling down it.

What a waterfall there could be today!

"Karsten, Karsten, do you want to make a waterfall?"

Out of desperate boredom Karsten had rigged up a swing in the attic the previous evening, and now I saw his face through the dusty, green windowpanes up in the attic. A minute later he was down in the yard and both of us took off for the heath. Our only tool is an old trough that we use for bailing when we need to.

What a glorious summer day it was up on the heath! The sun was sparkling on the wet, purple heather tops, on the leaves of the lingon-berry and blueberry bushes, and on large, swaying ferns beaded with drops of water. But Karsten and I had plenty to do besides looking at how beautiful it was. Because today we were going to build Niagara

Falls. There was more than enough water.

My, how Karsten and I worked that morning. We made a completely new trench so there was a huge run-off into the basin. And the basin itself had to be widened and improved—it got so full it was on the verge of overflowing. Karsten plopped in twice and got wet way above his knees. Goodness, how we laughed!

There were still places where we had to stuff a little tuft of moss or shift a rock around so the basin would be really really watertight. Finally we were ready.

But then there wasn't a single person in sight who could admire the waterfall. And we didn't want all our effort to go for naught. Karsten wanted to release the waterfall, but I didn't, and we were about to start a quarrel when fortunately Thora Heja came trudging along down below. Thora Heja is an old mountain woman who makes a living by drowning kittens and chopping the heads off chickens for people.

"Where are you going, Thora Heja?" I shouted.

"Oh, I'm going down to execute two of the sexton's roosters," Thora cried up to us.

"Wait a minute and you'll see Niagara."

"Whaat?"

"Wait a minute and you'll see something really neat."

Karsten and I each grabbed a pole and burst the dam with lightening speed. I'm not really sure how it happened, but we somehow dislodged some big rocks we usually never touched and at that the entire waterfall took off in quite another direction, roaring and foaming—it was deafening and absolutely magnificent.

"Hurray!" Karsten and I shouted.

But in the midst of the roar of the waterfall the piercing squeal of a pig came up from the field below. The waterfall thundered and the pig squealed louder and louder. It never occurred to me there was any connection between the pig squeals and our waterfall. We couldn't see anything down in the field from up where we were standing, though I did think that Thora Heja was acting very strangely. Because instead of standing quietly and admiring our waterfall as we expected she would, she started screaming and shouting and pointing and waving her arms; finally she started to run, slogging through the wet grass until she was right below the heath, screaming and shouting without end. More and more voices were coming up from down below and they were all shouting at the same time, but the waterfall kept roaring because there was, as I said, an awful lot of water in the basin that day. And all of this took place during a much shorter time than it's taken me to describe it, of course. I heard Søren Bricklayer's angry voice down there.

"Shall this kind of thing be permitted . . . they're going to pay for this . . . even if it were. . . . "

A suspicion suddenly took hold of me. "Karsten, something must have gone wrong with the waterfall."

"I'll run down and see."

"No, are you crazy? Don't go—can't you hear how angry Søren Bricklayer is?"

The big basin had emptied completely; now the water was a slow, little trickle. Søren Bricklayer walked out into the field so he could look up at us. He's a skinny old man in white bricklayer clothes with a terribly pointed chin. His face was as red as a boiled lobster and he waved his arms and screamed, "Well, it's a good thing I have witnesses. You bratty kids—sending a torrent of water right down on people. You'll pay for this—you'll pay—two piglets are dead and it's nip and tuck with the others—if there's never been a lawsuit before, there will be now, for such injustice. . . . I'm going to your father and report you immediately."

And Søren Bricklayer took off in a terrible hurry up the hill and up to Father's office.

Karsten and I looked at each other for a minute.

I had a fleeting thought that it would be best to run away immediately.

"Where shall we go?" said Karsten. "Shall we hide up on the heath all day?"

"No, it's probably better to go down and best that we go right away—we have to defend ourselves against Søren Bricklayer."

"Yes, maybe he'll say that we aimed the waterfall at his pig on purpose."

Father was standing on the steps and Søren Bricklayer was down in the yard. How he was carrying on! He wrung his hands, cried and threatened.

Father had a wrinkle between his eyes and that always meant he was angry.

"What is this? Have you killed two of Søren Sørensen's piglets?"

"Our waterfall came down on his pigpen instead of the field," Karsten whimpered.

"Explain how this happened," Father said to me. And I explained everything in detail. It was a good thing we came down from the heath after all!

"Here's ten crowns for the piglets, Sørensen," Father said, "and that settles the matter between us."

But it wasn't quite settled for Karsten and me, because I had to break my piggy bank and pay Father back for the piglets. I'd been saving money since Christmas so there were over seven crowns in it—oh, it's disgusting that piglets tolerate so little. And I was sent to the room in the attic and had to sit there all afternoon just because of that waterfall.

Karsten got a spanking and had to empty his piggy bank too, but there wasn't more than fifteen *øre* in it. Because Karsten always picks the money out of the slit on his piggy bank after he's dropped it in.

That was definitely the last time in my life I'd make a waterfall!

Excerpted from *Karsten og jeg*. Translated from the Norwegian by Katherine Hanson.

⑥ Karin Michaëlis

At the end of a very productive writing career, Karen Michaëlis (1872–1950) collaborated on a book of reminiscences that was published in New York in 1946 under the title *Little Troll.* The book opens with stories from her childhood in the small Danish town of Randers and continues with narratives about events and people in her adult life. The story below, "Aunt Sophy Dies," is taken from *Little Troll.*

The thirteen-year-old narrator imagines herself standing on the threshold of her adult life. Her eyes to the future, she longs to strike out on her own. But when drama suddenly breaks loose around her, she experiences just how strong her ties to family are and what valuable mentors her grandmother and great aunt have been.

Aunt Sophy Dies

I was thirteen years old and had my own room in the attic. Through my dormer window I had a view of hundreds of red roofs, as alike as a crowd of people and as different. Those red roofs were my world, my garden full of red flowers, warmed by the sun, watered by the dew and the rain, always brilliant in new tints. When I got to be twenty years old, I was going to write a book full of poems about my red roofs.

In my attic room I lived through love adventures, now triumphant, now despairing, all created by my imagination. Sometimes I was struck by the embarrassing thought that I was just like Aunt Lina, who would embrace the grandfather clock and cry, "My beloved Otto!"

It was all the same to me, as to her, whether or not "he" loved me. It was enough that I loved "him"—unto death, or perhaps even longer. On that foundation I built castles, cathedrals, pyramids of imperishable beauty. All vanished in the blue, like the lovely soap bubbles I still blew out over the red roofs, in spite of my thirteen years.

School bored me to tears, as it had from the first day. I admired some of my school fellows, and feared a few. As I could not take teasing,

I was an easy target for anyone who found me out.

I yearned to grow up and do what I pleased without asking anyone's permission, to undergo every experience that life could offer, the worst with the best.

One summer night I was awakened by Father. He was standing half-dressed by my bed. "Get up and dress quickly," he said in a strange, solemn voice. "The town is burning."

Wide awake, I jumped out of bed and fumbled for stockings and shoes. "The town is burning!" Never had words stirred such a sweet and yet sad feeling in my heart. For a moment I imagined our house surrounded by flames. In a little while the roof would collapse and I would be trapped. It was a proud thought, especially if I went to my death "without moving a muscle."

I was a coward about physical pain, so I liked to think myself superheroic. But my dream of a heroic death did not last. The next moment I remembered all that I had planned for my future—the books I meant to write, the pictures I was to paint, the music I would compose, music that already sang in my blood; the journeys all around the world, the adventures, the dangers. No, it wouldn't do to miss all that. I must hurry and save my life.

Outside a sweeping wind whipped the flames about, the shadow dance on my walls grew wilder and wilder. My teeth began to chatter, as they always did when I was excited. The little rattling sound they made sounded in my eardrums like the hooves of galloping horses. I was sublimely exalted and extremely frightened. If I had been asked at that moment to thrust my hand into the flames, I should have done it without hesitation. I understood now how Nero could rejoice when Rome was burning. Rome was his city. Randers was mine. My city, my city—Aunt Sophy's. . . .

Aunt Sophy!

How could I have forgotten? Aunt Sophy had been ill for some days and had to have absolute quiet. But this evening Aunt Lina had come to get Mother, and when we went to bed Mother had not come back. . . .

I leaned out of the window. Neither Grandmother's house, nor the rest of Palace Square could be seen for a waving mass of flames. I heard a seething, crackling noise. And in the apple-green sky of dawn, partly visible behind and above fire and smoke, whirled black objects of undefinable shape, like wild strange birds. . . .

Aunt Sophy . . .

Mother called. "Goodness, child, why don't you come?"

Mother was still wearing her hat and coat, so she must have just returned. "How is Aunt Sophy?" I asked quickly. Mother's return could only mean that Aunt Sophy was better. In that case it was all right to enjoy the fire.

My brother, Hans, two years older than I, was leaning out of one of the open windows; my sister Alma, two years younger than I, sat in the frame of the other, hugging her doll. Father stood beside her. People were shouting on the stairs, running back and forth and slamming doors. I heard voices from everywhere, "The town is burning! The town is burning!"

Finally I realized what Mother had said, "Aunt Sophy is dying!"

Mother's eyes were swollen, her lips trembled. Aunt Sophy was also her aunt, her father's sister.

Father put his arms around her. "Well . . . well—none of us can know that. Perhaps she will get over it. We'll see—we'll see." He did his best to comfort her, but it was difficult because she did not cry. She only stared into space, muttering, "She is dying—dying—" She did not even seem to notice that Allen, my three-year-old brother, whom we all adored, was awake and calling to her pitifully.

Mother stood up, to go back to Aunt Sophy. Father pointed to the weather vane across the street. "The wind is turning east," he said. "Neither you nor I can be sure that the fire won't spread to our house. Your place is here with the children."

Mother stayed. But she went around as if in a trance, constantly seeming to listen for something beyond her hearing.

I was torn in two. Part of me was in torment because Aunt Sophy, the center of my life since I could remember, was slipping away forever. Another part of me was intoxicated, wild, madly excited by the consciousness of all that those words meant: "The town is burning!"

My parents had left the room. I ran down to the street. People were running around frantically with meaningless objects clutched in their hands—empty bird cages, chickens with their wings tied together, mouse traps, old brooms, pots and pans, clocks, oil paintings. Now and then a couple of panic-stricken horses with trailing reins dashed through the crowds. People wept aloud and prayed as they ran. A man sat on some steps writing in a notebook. A woman nursed her child on the sidewalk. In the wavering lights and shadows the faces looked distorted, as though seen through warped glass. Perhaps it was all a dream. Perhaps Randers was not burning at all. A town did not catch fire like a piece of paper too near a match. It was a dream.

I saw some lively, fat hogs with flabby teats. They could have come from only one place, the sties north of the town. What were they doing here? And goats with their kids, and many, many cows. Some of the cows were wild-eyed, blind with terror. They bumped against walls, into wagons. Some of them tumbled halfway down the steps of a basement. Many were frightfully mutilated, their blood flowing from open gashes, their bodies covered with raw burns.

A voice near me said that one of the big stock farms was in flames and that the animals had been set free only with great difficulty.

A wall came down with a thundering crash. Men and beasts leaped aside. Coal-black clouds shot high into the air. Parts of some machinery showered down. Tocsins sounded from St. Martin's Church, the hospital church, and the Catholic church. The noise grew. It bored into me like someone drilling a hole in my back.

For a few seconds there was a pause in the din. Then the lull was broken by a new, distant, clanging, reverberating sound coming quickly nearer. Everyone pressed back against the houses, to let a huge, unfamiliar fire brigade go by—engines, ladders, hose, all much grander than any we had ever seen. People murmured in awe, "Those are the engines from Århus!" One man trying to seem wiser than the others sniffed contemptuously, "Århus! Pooh! Anybody can see that they are the engines from Hamburg!"

From Hamburg! From Germany! From abroad! But then all Europe, perhaps the whole world, knew that Randers, *my town,* was in flames! I hoped fervently that the engines were from Hamburg. That would make the fire more glamorous.

But hardly had the procession passed when I remembered Aunt Sophy. . . .

It was broad daylight. The sun was rising above the roofs. How long had I roamed about, seeking adventure, inhaling smoke and misery? I felt like seizing something huge and heavy and hurling it against the sky, smashing its peaceful blue as if it were thin glass.

I began to run. Nothing must keep me from seeing Aunt Sophy, not the Lord Himself, if He really existed.

I fought my way with my fists to the entrance of Palace Square. There policemen, firemen and soldiers had stretched a cordon so tight that only the firemen were allowed to go through. I tried to force my way in, and bit the hand of the fireman who stopped me. In return, I got a resounding box on the ear. I turned and tried to make my way past the gardens at the rear.

Outside the fisherwomen's well house there was a howling, shrieking mob of half-naked men, women and children who had dragged most of the furniture out of their houses and were shouting for the firemen to come. Across the road in the lumberyard all the piles of wood were ablaze. In the midst of them stood the highest chimney of the town. I had watched when it was being built. Now I heard the chimney would fall, and it would cause great damage.

Unexpectedly my nose realized that the women in the well house were frying eels. At once I felt a hunger so great that it made me faint. At the same time I was ashamed of being "common" enough to think of fried eel when Aunt Sophy was dying. Ordinarily the path behind the gardens was clean and dry, even after rain. Now it was a quagmire. Here also the crowd was as dense as on "free Saturday," when the farmers came to town after the harvest to buy things and enjoy themselves.

A shout grew loud in the troubled air. "The fire has spread to the other side of the spring!" In fact, the fire burned everywhere. The

tocsins went on warning people; as if there could be one human being near or far who did not know that the town was in flames.

I squirmed in and out of the crowds until I reached Grandmother's
garden. When I was near enough to look through the fence, I saw that
Father's pride, the rosebushes, were broken and trampled. Along the
narrow, bark-strewn paths, with their low boxwood borders, flowed
a thick brown fluid, as though spilt from giant pots. Fire hoses wound
in and out everywhere. The fruit trees were blackened, their branches
broken, their birds' nests fallen to the ground. Firemen in yellow oil-
skins and hoods were crawling over Grandmother's high red roof.
From both sides the hoses played on the house. The water streamed
down the windows.

Beside the garden, separated from it by a narrow path, stood the
engine factory, ablaze. At that moment one of the boilers burst. Wheels
and rings whirled high in the air and crashed to the ground. The heat
was intense. I felt my hair, to see if it had caught fire.

Water wagons barred the gate to the garden; close by, hissing like a
mad cat, stood the steam engine. But I was bound to get in.

I took the fence in one jump. My dress caught and ripped on the
spiked picket.

I was in the garden, walking through the slough. A fireman called
to me. I ignored him. He tried to stop me, but I tore myself away. I
was driven by passion, gratitude, reverence and, above all, by the in-
describable tenderness which Aunt Sophy had awakened in me, a deep
response that would go with her to the grave.

When I reached the kitchen with its red brick floor, everything
was wrong. The two pails of water were missing, the floor was dirty,
even the ashes from the old-fashioned stove seemed to have been scattered all over the place.

Then I heard a sound that pierced the very marrow of my bones. I
had heard the sound once three years before. I had never mentioned
it to anyone, but had borne it like an open wound. Sanko, our dog,
had died on a cold winter night in our dark attic. I had been with
him. Three years had passed since then, yet it seemed to me that I still

need only put out my hand to touch the trembling, gasping animal.

I had kept what I felt to myself. So the memory had gone deeper and deeper, and become increasingly painful. Sanko died not only on that night long ago, he died again and again in my heart—until this minute when Aunt Sophy's death rattle shook my body as well as my soul. She, the best person on earth, the one I could spare least. . . .

A couple of firemen stamped through the kitchen, shouting and laughing, and slammed down the two water pails.

The door opened. Grandmother stood in the opening, tall and erect. This was the way she must have looked when she was younger and still more beautiful. Her black eyes flashed. "In there an old woman is fighting with death," she said. She made a commanding gesture. "Let no unnecessary noise disturb her last moments!"

"The chief has given orders," stammered one of the men. "The house is in danger—we have to . . ."

Grandmother waved them aside. "You heard what I said!" The men no longer existed for her.

She noticed me. Turning to the door, she pushed me gently into the other room and gently closed the door. She laid her finger on her lips. I did not move. She sank down in the armchair beside the stove. Over her head hung a picture of Voltaire. I was struck by the strong resemblance between his superior, benignly smiling face and Aunt Sophy's.

Usually a high, three-paneled screen covered with faded French wallpaper hid Aunt Sophy's bed, hid the straw mattress, the thick, homespun linen sheets and the coarse, woolen comforter. But on this day the three panels of the screen were folded together. The bed lay exposed in all its poverty. The pillow was not even covered with a white case. Where the sheet had been pulled awry by Aunt Sophy's tossing body, I caught a glimpse of a hard striped pillow, covered with horsehair cloth.

In this ascetic bed lay a strange and terrifying Aunt Sophy. Her face seemed shriveled into a tangle of wrinkles. Perspiration ran down her forehead, over her pale, sunken cheeks, into the hollows of her moving jaws. Her hands had always resembled a map of the world, the veins forming rivers with strange names. Now they looked as if they were full of swollen worms, writhing over the naked bones.

Where was her lovely, peaceful smile? Where her illuminating wisdom, her deep firm calm?

She lay there, in the burning town where the tocsins tolled and called. She lay there, groaning and gasping, her eyes protruding in nameless terror. Terror of what? She was the only perfect human being I had ever known. . . .

Now and then she looked about, as if seeing something she had lost or forgotten and must have at any price. Suddenly, with a strength inconceivable in her emaciated body, she sat up, folded her hands, and began in a high, singing voice: *"Our Father, Who art in Heaven . . . "*

She got no further. Her lips moved. But she had forgotten the words.

Her impotent anguish was more than I could bear. I threw myself on the floor before her bed and screamed the Lord's Prayer to help her. The sound did not reach her consciousness. She no longer heard any human voice.

After a short exhausted silence, she began again, whispering, imploring, desperate. "No—no! Not St. Helena! Great, powerful, merciful God—not St. Helena! Take my life! Take my soul! But save him—let him return to Corsica—or to Elba—to the pine woods of Corsica . . . "

She went on, now trying to remember the Lord's Prayer, now entreating the Lord to spare Napoleon. Now and then she fell back, silent, gasping.

Grandmother went to the bed and laid her hand on Aunt Sophy's forehead. "Rest in peace, dear! Rest in peace! You have earned it well!"

Aunt Sophy heard nothing. But abruptly she pushed Grandmother aside and rose higher and higher until slowly she stood up, swaying back and forth. She cried in agony, "I know—I know—I am the greatest sinner that ever lived! But now I'm asking for mercy—do you hear? I'm asking mercy for the greatest sinner that ever lived!"

She collapsed in Grandmother's arms. For a while it looked as though her struggles had ended. But she began again about Napoleon, Elba and St. Helena.

Grandmother remembered I was there. She looked at me and said quietly, "Go home, child. This is not for you!"

I did not answer. I could not move.

The door was torn open. The fire chief saluted Grandmother and remained silent a moment, as if expecting her to speak to him. He gave a sign to the men standing behind him in the kitchen. "Allow me," he said to Grandmother, "to send for a stretcher. I cannot guarantee your safety here for more than an hour at the most. The wind is changing."

Grandmother turned toward him. "The Lord has protected us through many hours and years, good and bad. I cannot believe that He will fail us now. My sister-in-law can have only a few minutes left. Let her die here, where she lived, where she was born . . . "

The fire chief hesitated. "But the responsibility," he said. "The responsibility . . . "

Grandmother seemed to grow taller. And suddenly it came to me whom she resembled. It was a figure I had seen in a picture, one of Michelangelo's sibyls, in the Sistine Chapel. Grandmother motioned the fire chief to go.

"The responsibility is in His hands. Let it remain there!"

I did not see Aunt Sophy again.

How I got back home and into my own bed in the attic I do not know. When I opened my eyes again, I saw the glimmering of the fire and the shadows of rising and falling flames on the white walls. The room was hot, but inside I was trembling and as cold as ice.

The fire lasted three days and three nights.

Excerpted from *Little Troll* (in collaboration with Lenore Sorsby).

ᐯ Katarina Taikon

Katarina Taikon (1932–95) was the first Swedish Gypsy, or *Rom,* to write about her people for children. Many readers had their first insights in the *Romani* culture and traditions through her series of books about Katitzi, a young *Rom* girl and her family.

The history of the *Rom* has been marked, in Sweden as elsewhere, by persecution and lack of civil rights. In the twentieth century, some *Rom* families began to assimilate into Swedish society and to leave their nomadic lifestyle. Other families have immigrated from Finland and Central Europe to Sweden. These newcomers often keep their traditional way of life and dress, which sets them apart from the *gajo,* or non-*Rom* population, and which often causes them to be stigmatized and excluded.

Brought up in the *gajo* culture in a boarding school after her mother's death, Katitzi has not understood the prejudice against her. In this excerpt Katitzi meets her siblings for the first time and begins to ask questions about the *Rom* culture she knows little of.

Katitzi

Katitzi felt that the trip would never end; they drove and drove. Finally she couldn't keep quiet any longer and asked, "Won't we be there soon, Papa?"

"Yes, it's only a few miles now."

Katitzi wondered why her father was so silent. He hadn't said a word during the whole trip. Maybe he doesn't like bringing me home, Katitzi thought.

"Were you happy at the school?" he asked suddenly.

"Oh yes, everyone was nice to me, but most of all Miss Kvist, of course."

"Weren't you ever homesick?"

"Yes, once in a while for the circus people, but of course they didn't let me go back there. Papa, do I have many sisters and brothers?"

"You have four sisters and two brothers."

"Where do we live and why don't we have a laundry room?"

"What are you talking about? Laundry room, what do you mean by that?"

"Well, Miss Kvist said that my sister had to borrow a big kettle to wash her clothes, and then she said that we don't have a laundry room. Is that true, Papa?"

"We don't have a laundry room, that's true. You see, we don't have a real house to live in, and it is a bit difficult to have a laundry room in tents and trailers."

"Why don't we live in a real house, Papa? Why do we live in tents and trailers—are we poor?"

"Well, we aren't really poor, but you have to understand, or maybe you're too small to understand, that we can't live in a house. People don't want us in houses."

"But Papa, why not? Are you mean?"

"Katitzi, you must listen and try to understand what I'm telling you. We are Gyspies."

"What, are you saying we're Gyspies too now? That's something ugly, I know that, because Ruttan at the orphanage called me a Gyspy and said we were riff raff."

"Katitzi, it's not ugly to be a Gyspy, but people are afraid of us, you see, because they think we are bad. They don't know us, and they don't dare to be around us."

"That's silly, Papa. If they don't know us, then they can't be afraid of us."

"One would think so, but that's the way it is anyway."

"Where do Gyspies come from, Papa?"

"A long time ago, about a thousand years ago, they came from India."

"Why did they come here? Are you from India too, Papa?"

"No, I'm not, and why the Gyspies came to Sweden, I don't know, but maybe it was so that they would have a better life."

"Papa, am I a Gyspy too?"

"Yes you are, but we don't call ourselves Gyspies. Gypsy is a name that others have come up with. We call ourselves *Rom* and that means human being."

"*Rom,* that sounds so funny, what kind of language is that?"

"That is our own language and that's called *Romany,* and it's spoken all over the world by all Gyspies. Look! Over there is our camp, down there at the edge of the forest. Can you see it?"

Katitzi looked. There were a lot of tents and they shone in all colors. It almost looked like a rainbow. In the middle of the field was a big barrel with smoke coming out of it.

"Is that where we live, Papa?"

"Yes, for the time being. What you see is our amusement park and the big girl you see is your sister. You can ask her about anything else you want to know. She knows almost everything."

"Don't I have a mother, Papa?"

"Your mother died when you were very small, but you have someone else you can call Mama now. But you need to keep out of her way as much as possible, because she is sickly and not very fond of children. And Katitzi, remember to always obey her, even if you feel that she is unfair once in a while."

Katitzi looked thoughtful, but didn't say anything. She wondered why her new mother would be unfair and why her father wouldn't object, but soon she forgot all of that. A whole bunch of kids came rushing up to her.

"Hi, Papa! Have you brought Katitzi home?"

"She's so pretty," said a girl in a long red skirt.

"Who's that?" asked Katitzi.

"I'm Paulina. Don't you remember me?"

"There now, it's not so strange that she doesn't remember you—she was so little when we sent her away. But you are three years older, so of course you remember Katitzi. You can help her get settled now. I think she should change clothes."

A tall woman was walking towards them. She had gray hair and looked very stern.

"Well, well, she is here now," the lady said and continued, "Hurry up and change. Find some clothes for her, Paulina. Take some of Rosa's old ones."

"No, I want my own clothes and nobody else's," Katitzi said.

"You listen to me now. I'm the one in charge here."

Paulina quickly took Katitzi's hand and off they ran.

"Please Katitzi, you must obey her and you must never talk back to her. She gets really angry then. And you have to call her Mama."

"Is that my new Mama, the lady who looked so angry? I'll never call her Mama, I'm quite sure of that."

"But promise not to talk back to her, because then there will be trouble. Come on, I'll show you where you are going to live. You and I live in this little tent. We get to live there the whole summer, but in the fall we must move in with the others in the big tent."

"Rosa! Rosa! Where are you? You must help me to find some clothes that will fit Katitzi."

"Well, let's see what we can do. Oh, it's so nice to have you back home again, Katitzi," Rosa said. "But what can I give you to wear? I'm so much taller than you are, but there must be something."

Rosa started to rummage through a bundle, pulling out one dress after another. But all of them were too big for Katitzi.

"We have to take this one. It's the smallest and if we take one of Paul's belts and pull it tight, it'll stay up."

Just then a young man walked across the field. It was Katitzi's brother Paul and he was fifteen years old.

"Well, well, Katitzi has finally come home. It's good to have the family together again. Rosa, don't forget to rosin the dance floor right tonight. You did a bad job yesterday. See you later—I'm going to check on the instruments."

"Paulina, what's rotsin?"

"It's called rosin, not rotsin, and it means that you sprinkle something on the dance floor and then you spread it out over the whole floor so that it gets slippery. That makes it easier for people to dance. We can help Rosa later, and then you can see how it's done."

Katitzi had put her new clothes on and she didn't recognize herself any longer. She was wearing a long dress that dragged along the ground and around her waist Rosa had tied one of Paul's belts so Katitzi wouldn't stumble and fall.

"What am I going to put on my feet?"

"You don't need anything on your feet in the summer. It's good for feet to be without shoes," said Paulina.

"But I can't go around without shoes. What about when it gets cold?" said Katitzi, looking very surprised. She wondered where she had landed.

"Silly you, of course you'll get shoes in the winter. Papa will make a pair for you then. What's in the bag, Katitzi?"

"Do you want to see? It's my beautiful doll that I got from the circus people. She can close her eyes and say Mama."

"Hide her right away! The lady is coming," said Paulina looking scared.

"What are you hiding behind your back?" Katitzi's new mother asked.

"It's my doll."

"Give it to me so I can have a look! Oh my, this is much too nice for you to play with in the camp. I'll put it away."

Then she took the doll and marched away with determined steps. Katitzi was close to tears.

"Why did she take my doll? I never get to play with it. First Miss Larsson took it and now this lady takes it."

"Please Katitzi, don't be sad. Tomorrow I'll make a doll for you that nobody will take away, I promise. And tomorrow I'll show you all the fun things in the forest. I'm so glad you've come home—you can't imagine how lonely I've been. Rosa is much too big to play with me and she doesn't have time either because she has to work all the time."

"But don't you play with the little kids?"

"Sometimes, but they're so little and the lady doesn't like it if I play with them."

"Are they the lady's children? Aren't they our sisters and brothers?"

"Well, you see, after Papa married this lady, he had them with her. Their names are Nila and Rosita and the little one is Lennart. They are our half sisters and half brother."

"How silly, half sisters and brothers! They're either our sisters and brothers or they aren't. Nobody can be half."

Paulina didn't know what to answer, but she said: "You'll understand this better when you get older."

"Why is there smoke coming out of that barrel, Paulina?"

"Don't say Paulina, say Lena, it's easier, but don't ever call me Kalle, because then I get so angry there's no telling what I'd do."

"Why would I call you Kalle? Are you crazy? You're not a boy."

"The lady calls me Kalle. She says I act like a boy and that's why she's cut off my hair too."

"Geez, she's crazy. What if she does that to me too? If she does, I'm telling Papa."

"No, I don't think she'll do that, because you're supposed to become a dancer and then you have to have long hair."

"What did you say? What am I supposed to become?"

"A dancer, you heard me."

"Yes, I heard you, but I don't know how to dance."

"Maybe you don't right now, but you'll learn. You see, everyone has to help out here in camp. If you listen you can hear Paul practicing on the accordion—he has to. Rosa plays the drums even though she wanted to learn to play the violin. But she didn't get to, because Papa plays that."

"I don't get it. Drums, accordion, violin, me dancing. What on earth are you talking about?"

"We have an amusement park, you see, and we all have to help out if we want to make any money. Papa, Rosa and Paul play their instruments. You see the dance floor over there—that's where people dance, and for them to dance, they have to have music."

"But what do you do, Lena? Are you one of those dancers you say I'm going to be?"

"No, Papa said that I'm not cut out for that, so I have to stand in the Guess a Number booth instead."

"Guess a Number, what's that? Can you explain it to me? You think I'm stupid maybe, but I don't know what it is."

"Well, there are a lot of pieces on a table and under some of the pieces there's a number. If someone points to the right piece, one with a number under it, then they win something."

"Do you get to point sometime?" asked Katitzi, who thought being at an amusement park was starting to sound exciting.

"No, why should I point? People are supposed to do that so we get money. Every time they point it costs twenty-five *öre*. We have other booths too. We have a shooting range that's run by a man Papa knows. He's *gajo*."

"What did you say he is?"

"*Gajo*. That's right, you have forgotten *Romany*. *Gajo* means he isn't *Rom*. Other people call us Gypsies, but we call ourselves *Rom*."

"I think I'm beginning to catch on. It'll take a long time before I understand everything, but it will come. What else is there in the amusement park, Lena?"

"We have One-armed Bandits, Go Fish, Ring Toss and then the carousel, of course."

"Do we have a carousel? Why didn't you say so right away? I love riding the carousel. You do get to ride on that, don't you?"

"Sometimes, when I have time and Papa lets me. I like to ride the carousel too, but we have to help out, so I can't just go off and ride the carousel—who would take care of my customers then?"

"Lena, I'm going to ride on the carousel—you can make a note of that."

"No I can't, because I can't write, so there. But maybe you can ride tonight, because this is your first day at home and you probably won't have to help out tonight."

"But I can't stay up late. I have to go to bed at seven o'clock."

"And who decides that, do you think? Katitzi, you aren't with the circus people now and you aren't at the orphanage either. Papa and the lady decide here and we have to obey. But sometimes we have a lot of fun and your sister Rosa is never mean. She never spanks us, so you don't have to be afraid of her. Come on Katitzi, they're calling for us to come and eat. After that we have to change, because we open at seven tonight and everything has to be ready then. We have to sweep the field."

"Sweep the field? Do we sweep it with a broom?"

"Yes, we do, but with a big broom. We have a lot of brooms and everyone helps."

"The lady too?" Katitzi asked a bit suspiciously.

"No, not the lady," Lena said. "She's rather sickly, they say, so she doesn't help with anything."

"But she must take care of her kids?"

"No, she doesn't. Rosa does that. But come on, let's go eat."

The two sisters trundled away hand in hand. Katitzi really looked funny. She looked as if she would stumble in her long skirt at any moment, but she tried to walk with as much dignity as possible, because she didn't want to fall and have Lena laugh at her.

In a big tent they had set up dinner on the floor. An oilcloth had been spread out and a big kettle had been placed in the middle.

Katitzi's father dished up soup for everyone. Katitzi and Lena got one bowl that they had to share. Katitzi wrinkled her nose, but Lena gave her a warning glance. Katitzi thought to herself, "There's a lot I don't know, but I'll probably get used to it."

❧

Katitzi started getting used to her new life, but there were many things that felt strange. In the orphanage she had had her own bed, but here she was forced to share a bed with her sister Lena. She thought the bed clothes were strange, but rather warm and nice. They had featherbeds, one they slept on, the other they covered themselves with. She thought the food was strange too. Never porridge and gruel like she'd had before, but strongly spiced food. Mostly soup with many vegetables, sometimes also chicken.

She was slowly getting used to the fact that she and Lena and her big sister Rosa, who was thirteen years old, had to work so much. That the lady who was her new mother never did any work, but only lay around reading and eating sweets—well, that was probably as it should be. But Katitzi couldn't get over how unfair it was that the lady was always screaming at her and pulled her hair whenever she could grab it. She often asked Rosa why the lady did this, but Rosa just said that she shouldn't feel bad, because things would surely get better when Katitzi got older.

But Katitzi thought that when she got older she would move into a beautiful house and she wouldn't let the lady come with her.

One day Katitzi's father and the lady had driven off in the red car. Paul had told the others that their father would try to find another place where they could live and set up their amusement park. It was nearly fall and the weather had turned rather cold. Katitzi and Lena could feel the cold on their feet and they wondered when their father would make shoes for them. They didn't dare ask him, because he seemed so sad, as if he were burdened with many worries.

On this day they had gotten strict orders to watch the other children and see to it that nothing happened to them. The smallest boy, Lennart, was only five months old and he was lying in a laundry basket in the little trailer where the children's father and the lady slept at night.

Rosa was washing clothes down at the lake as usual and Paul had gone to the village to see if there was some work for him. He was a very good tinsmith and could make copper pots nice and shiny, so down at the bakery they had promised Paul that he could repair and take care of their kettles.

Lena had gone to the forest to collect pine cones and Katitzi was alone at home with the three little kids.

All of a sudden she saw smoke pouring out of the little window of the trailer. She dropped everything and rushed over, but when she came to the door she shrank back, for the whole trailer was full of smoke and in the little basket Lennart was screaming his head off.

Katitzi was really scared and didn't know what to do. "I'd better run to the farm for help," she thought. But then she saw that the curtain had caught fire and knew she didn't have time to run for help. Katitzi's little sisters stood outside crying, one louder than the other. Katitzi's heart was beating so hard that she thought the whole camp would hear it. "Please Miss Kvist, help me," she thought and then Katitzi rushed inside the trailer. She coughed when the smoke got into her throat and she could hardly see her hand in front of her; her eyes smarted as if they were on fire. First she tore the curtain down and then she pulled the baby out of his basket as fast as she could. She threw the curtain on the ground with one hand and set the boy down with the other, and then she ran back into the trailer to see if anything else was burning. One of her father's featherbeds had caught fire and Katitzi took another featherbed and smothered the fire with it. She got blisters all over her hands, but she didn't feel anything right then. She was just glad she had managed to put the fire out. Lena had smelled the fire and now she came running. Rosa came too. They were horrified and now the tears started rolling down Katitzi's cheeks. "What if our little brother had been killed by the fire," she said.

"Little Katitzi, you've been wonderful," Rosa said, "but how could this have happened?"

Meanwhile Lena had gone inside the trailer to find out how the fire had started. A petroleum stove was the cause of the fire. It had exploded, the petroleum had caught fire and the fire had spread.

"We better hurry and get everything clean before they come home," said Rosa. "Katitzi, what happened to your eyebrows? They are completely singed. And look at your hands. Good Lord, you've burned them! Come, let's put some bandages on them."

"No, we have to clean up the trailer first," Katitzi said. "What if they came home now and saw that we'd had a fire—then it will be my fault because I didn't watch things."

"Don't you worry about that. I'll take care of this and God help whoever tries to say it was your fault. Everyone should be grateful that you saved our little brother, and if the lady says even one word,

I'll give her a piece of my mind," Rosa said, looking very stern.

Rosa put bandages on Katitzi and then Rosa and Lena helped each other put the trailer in order again. Katitzi sat rocking her little brother in her arms. After a while he fell asleep and she put him down on the bed she and Lena shared.

While Katitzi had been rocking the baby, Lena had stood watching her and she remembered that she had promised Katitzi a doll to replace the one the lady had taken away from her when she came from the orphanage.

"Rosa," Lena said, "do you have any scraps of cloth?"

"What do you want them for?" Rosa asked.

"Do you have any or don't you? Why does it matter what I want them for. If you have to know, I need them for a doll for Katitzi. I feel so sorry for her—why did she have to come home anyway? She was much better off where she was."

"Lena, I don't want to hear you talk like that. Katitzi is our sister and she should be with us. Don't you understand that? Even if it's hard for us many times, we must stay together. Come with me and I'll see if I have a bit of fabric somewhere."

Rosa rummaged through a bundle and found a piece of red fabric. Then she took some yellow silk ribbons and gave it all to Lena.

Lena went off to the nice lady on the farm and asked if she could have a piece of wood.

"What do you want with a piece of wood? You're welcome to pick twigs around here, but I can't give you any wood."

"Yes, but I don't want firewood. I'm not going to make a fire, I'm making a doll for Katitzi."

"Making a doll out of a piece of wood! I've never heard of such a thing. But go ahead and take a piece of wood. Why don't you take two in case something goes wrong with the first one."

She searched around eagerly and finally found a piece of wood that would make a good doll, one that was just the right breadth and length. She didn't need two pieces because she knew that with this one she just wouldn't make a mistake. Then she borrowed a knife and carved where she thought the head should be. She wrapped the piece of fabric around the wood, and she tied the yellow ribbons around the waist so that the dress wouldn't fall off. Where the head was, she painted a mouth, nose and eyes with a piece of coal. Then she put a little piece of the fabric around the head to make a scarf.

When Katitzi got the doll she was so happy and she kept it for many years.

Excerpted from *Katitzi*. Translated from the Swedish by Rose Marie Oster.

℟ Sigrid Undset

Sigrid Undset (1880–1949), the Nobel Prize winner who gained international fame for her trilogy, *Kristin Lavransdatter,* was forced to flee Norway when the Nazis invaded in 1940. She escaped to Sweden and from there traveled eastward, through Siberia to Japan where she sailed to San Francisco. She lived in New York City for the rest of the war years and it was there she wrote "Florida Water."

Undset's story is drawn from her childhood and recalls a time when summer vacation meant endless, lazy days in the country or by the seashore, activities with family and friends, but also time alone—to read, to sketch, to daydream. At thirteen, Sigrid is starting to think about her future. Will she paint? Will she have a sailor sweetheart who brings her gifts of perfume? Then one day she stumbles into someone else's dream world and is delighted with the role she is assigned.

Florida Water

I would never say that summer can't be as beautiful in other parts of the world as it is at home in Norway beside the sea, but it's impossible for it to be more beautiful. It is beautiful the whole way around the coast, but I especially think of the Oslo fjord, since that is what I have known since childhood. It was called the Christiania fjord then.

I remember blue and sunbaked summer days, with white mackerel clouds blown across the vault high above, and hazy fine-weather clouds billowing over the horizon. They grew and took on the shapes of hills and deep blue valleys, until a reddish gleam began to glow within the cloud bank: Oh, God forbid, is it going to thunder? Oh, what shall we do! There was nowhere to take shelter on the little islet where we had landed to go swimming from the beach, make coffee, and fry our whiting. There was only a rocky hill, reddish gray and polished, with a little clump of tough, sunburnt turf growing in the middle where it was lovely to lie down and stretch out—and then there was a thicket at the lower end of the dock, close-cropped by the wind. It was impossible to get through that tight tangle of briar and blackthorn and what we called "the bush the devil skinned a goat under"—I never heard another name for it when I was a child, but it is some kind of buckthorn. It was barely possible to crawl under the edge of the bushes to dress and undress in decent privacy, and that was more important in those days than it is now—remember, there was nothing called sunbathing back then. But we were perfectly content to be allowed to go out fishing among the islets with the grown-ups.

The thunderstorm came to nothing, and the sea glittered and glittered with soft little ripples, broke innocently and indifferently in little white streaks over the sunken rocks, and wove a border of shiny spray around the pink granite rock. Right across the sound was a small island. A few cows grazed on its hill, and a copse of alders grew where a little stream ran out to meet the tide. Underneath the trees was a well, with a pale blue wooden roof shaped like a tent. The woman from the house that stood farther up came with two shiny polished zinc pails on a yoke to fetch water.

The coast in front of it was not especially high, but quite steep, mostly naked reddish-gray cliffs. But wherever the rocks had formed a ledge the carline heather made a carpet, and a few short, tough fir-roots clung in the cracks. And in between were ravines filled with broad-leaf trees, dark and fertile. Gusts of summer wind carried with them a fragrance of flowering lime—the wild lime that clings to the mountainside and hangs its flower-laden branches out over the edge. And beyond the highest point was the coastal town.

The town, with the cutters at anchor in the bay, the steamship pier, and bath house. Alongside the country road that followed the river down from the uplands were all the big fashionable houses belonging to the ship owners and the doctors and the sea captains, and to the merchant's widow—the most powerful widow in the place. There were burly, domed maple trees and fruit trees with whitened trunks in beautiful gardens. On the lawn in front of the widow's veranda shone a large reflecting ball, looking like a globe of pure silver. The ship owner's roof was tiled with blue-glazed Dutch tiles, and how the sun could sparkle on those tiles!

Perched on the ledges and knolls of the mountain behind were smaller houses, painted red and ochre and light blue and white or light green, so tidy and well-kept that they were a joy to look at. Almost all of them had a bit of a garden—nasturtiums where there was a crack in the rocks, a flower-bed and a vegetable patch where people had built up a terrace and filled it with soil—some black loam that was brought from Holland as ballast, or so they said. The big yellow rosebushes that so many people grew were said to have come from Holland too. And there were houses beside the water; some people had their own little jetty built on poles, and boats were moored by the boom that stretched across it, and fishing nets were drying on the beach. Everything was well-kept, everything pretty, everything smilingly soft—in summer, at least.

In those days most of our merchant fleet was sailing ships. To have seen a three-masted vessel beating her way down the Christiania fjord in full sail was something to be grateful for for the rest of one's life. Yes, we knew the different sailing ships by their riggings—or at least we thought we did. We knew the steamships by their funnels and by their hoot, the Wilson boats and Tingvalla Line and Koch and Melchior, and all the little fjord boats that plowed back and forth between the city and towns and hamlets, with summer guests and mailbags and groceries and fathers and strangers on Saturday afternoons.

In all the homes, big and small, everyone had things that sailors had brought home with them—stylish English furniture, carpets, silverware, and china in the big houses. In the small cottages they had rocking chairs and American clocks—square, with a wooden frame around them just like pictures, and fronts of glass that had landscapes or flowers painted on them with a peephole so one could see the pendulum swinging inside. They had tea services of luster and dining services of old English faience that someone's grandfather had brought home for someone's grandmother. There were unusual and strange foreign color prints of horse-races and ladies in crinolines and folding parasols and children with lambs and kittens. And the women had silk shawls and foreign dress material and French leather shoes and gloves in their drawers and cabinets. But one thing that I think all sailors brought back to their girlfriends in those days was a bottle of Florida Water. Whenever our maids wanted to reward my sisters and me for good behavior they sprinkled Florida Water on our dresses. Mama disliked all kinds of scent, but she hated Florida Water most of all—perhaps because when one of the maids had had a visit from a sailor friend, our entire home became permeated with that odor.

But I adored Florida Water, and how I coveted a bottle! On the front was a picture of a garden with a fountain, and tied around the neck hung the cutest, tiniest little gilded corkscrew. I fervently hoped that when I was grown up I too would have a sailor friend who would give me bottles of Florida Water.

After the death of my father, the slogan of our home life had become "we cannot afford—." We could not afford any of the things we wanted to buy or do. And certainly not to go away to the country during the summer holidays. So when my mother came home one day the second summer after my father had died and told us that we were going to the country after all, we three little girls were quite wild with joy. Mama had met the artist Theodor Kittelsen's wife in town, and Mrs. Kittelsen had told her that their neighbor, Mrs. Hansen, wanted to lease her house to summer guests because her husband had gone to sea, and she and her mother-in-law always moved into the wash-house during the hot season—that was the custom where Mr. Hansen's mother had come from. Mrs. Hansen was asking only ten *kroner* for the whole summer, so my mother thought that even we could afford that.

It turned out to be the most glorious holiday I had ever had. The Hansens' house wasn't large—a sitting room, kitchen, and bedrooms—and we had no view of the sea, because the house was some way up the hill by the roadside. But we went down to swim every afternoon, and sometimes we were invited to go rowing or sailing with people we knew from the last time we had been there. And besides that there were plenty of places around the house where we children could make playhouses, and the Hansens's lot ran unfenced into the forest, right up to the hill. It was a beautiful forest, with tall, sighing spruce and thick mossy hillocks where blueberries had just begun to ripen, and the twinflower was still in bloom when we arrived. There Mama found a place where she liked to sit and read, and I ran around and drew sketches.

Our closest neighbors were the Kittelsens—we saw them almost every day. In those days I thought of nothing but becoming a painter when I grew up. I drew pictures day in and day out (even during school lessons), and I had been in love with Kittelsen's paintings for a long time—his two books of pictures from Lofoten were some of the loveliest I knew. I was actually just as excited about Krohg and Werenskiold up until the time I got to know Kittelsen personally, but then he became, in my eyes, the absolute Number One of all of Norway's artists. I ran in and out of his house, where his drawings and paintings were all over the walls—there, the whole fantastic world of enchanting and horrible and droll creatures that roam about in Norway's landscape, which have become a part of our legends and fairy tales from all corners of the land, came to life. Even on his furniture—much of which he had made and decorated himself—there were pictures of trolls and of sweet, serious girls standing in grass and flowers up to their waist—but if you looked carefully behind them you would discover a cow's tail, like a snake in the grass. All the windowsills were full of Mrs. Kittelsen's flowering plants in unusual hanging pots, and on pedestals that he had made out of old twisted roots and stones and shells from the beach. Theodor Kittelsen himself was one of the handsomest men I have ever met. He also had a beautiful voice, and in the evenings, when we sat in the dusk in his studio where the big painting of the water sprite, Nøkken, stood on the easel, he would sometimes sing for us—the song about Ole Velland, or a ballad from Valdres. I was thirteen years old and I adored Kittelsen and everything that belonged to him, including his wife—she was young, lovely, and an extremely good housekeeper—and their children,

Missy, who was five, and Little Man, who was three. But the sweetest of all was the baby, who was called Mollusk, because she was such a soft little thing that she seemed to have no bones at all in her tiny body.

I remember it as though it were sunny every day that summer, but it must have rained sometimes, because I also remember sitting up in the Kittelsens' nursery with the rain pounding on the window while I made paper dolls and paper castles with windows that opened and shut. Missy ran downstairs and showed them to her father, and Kittelsen came up and told me he thought they were both original and beautiful. At that, I plucked up enough courage to show him my sketchbook. "Yes, poor girl, you certainly have talent," he sighed, and shook his head. "I have often thought that I should start up some kind of Salvation Army and go through the streets with music and big banners saying: Do not become artists, dear young people; it is no fun to be an artist! It is to be never satisfied with what one has done; always to dream of doing something better; always moving towards things undone. And that's to say nothing of the humiliation, the poverty, the intrigue and the gossip! Oh, no, dear Sigrid, talent certainly is not a blessing, it is a curse." Of course I didn't believe a word of it except that I had talent, and I was blissfully happy.

At that time Dr. Olav Johan Olsen began a campaign to get people to take an interest in some of the mushrooms that were rotting away out in our forests. (People laughed at him and the papers made jokes about "Dr. Mushroom." One fine day he applied to have his name changed to Dr. Mushroom, in all seriousness!) Kittelsen got so fired up about it that we all got mushroom fever.

At least every other day we went to the woods with baskets and buckets and Dr. Olav Johan Olsen's mushroom books—Mr. and Mrs. Kittelsen, their children and their nursemaid, Mama, we three girls, and our maid Laura. Mollusk was carried out in the largest basket, and home in a kind of sling on her mother's back. She thrived on this gypsy life, became fat and brown and so hungry and sleepy that she never had time to cry, she only ate and slept. We brought a picnic basket and coffee pot with us, so we could stay out until late in the afternoon. When we got home Mama and Mrs. Kittelsen and our maids began to clean the mushrooms and make mushroom dishes. Even Mama, who hated housework and wasn't really a very good housekeeper, got caught up in the enthusiasm; she even preserved mushrooms in jars and threaded them on string so they could dry in the sun and wind and be stored for winter use.

Our young maid, Laura, had overcome the prejudice most Norwegians had against mushrooms surprisingly quickly. She sautéed chanterelles in butter and sour cream, and made a fricassee of polypons with celery and parsley. And it was Laura who figured out that we only needed to buy half as much ground meat on Fridays, when they sold ground meat in the shop: instead of making meatballs she would make a roulade filled with mushrooms and bacon, braised in a Dutch oven. I ate almost the same dish later in Paris, but Laura had discovered it quite on her own, and hers was one of the best I have ever tasted.

Mrs. Hansen utterly refused to taste any of our mushroom dishes; she threw up her hands and shrieked in terror when we tried to persuade her to eat some. And she expressed her relief every morning when she saw all five of us alive and unharmed; she had expected that we almost certainly would be dead from mushroom poisoning.

Then, one day towards evening, able seaman Jørgen Hansen came driving home. He and a few of his shipmates had caught the train from Christiania "for a little variety," and taken a cab from the station, and they were in very high spirits—not exactly drunk, but what the Swedes would call "over-refreshed." Hansen was overflowing with *joie de vivre* and goodwill toward the whole world. Mrs. Hansen ran back and forth between the wash house and us to show us everything he had brought for her and his mother. Then Mr. Hansen himself emerged—a block of a man, short and strong as a giant, his face so reddish-brown that his light red hair and eyelashes seemed almost white, and with kind, watery blue eyes. He was hoping that Professor Undset's wife would not be offended that he had brought a few trinkets home for the summer guests, but when his wife had written him about us, he had taken a fancy to doing so.

It was one of my mother's talents that she was able to receive whatever she was given as though it were exactly what she had wanted all her life. Her face glowed when she saw the enormous brass picture frame shaped like a shield with spears and halberds around the edge. Laura was given a lovely music box, and for each of the "dear young ladies" Hansen had brought with him a bottle of Florida Water—and they were not small bottles, either!

I couldn't resist prying open my bottle at once, and I mutilated the cork so badly that I had to make a new kind of stopper out of a twig wrapped around with a bit of paper. I splashed myself from the first bottle of perfume I had ever owned—I knew Mama wouldn't say anything out of consideration for Hansen. And she didn't, but she looked volumes.

But Kittelsen and Mrs. Kittelsen let out a scream when I burst in—we were expected there for supper, to eat mushroom hamburgers with Mrs. Kittelsen's rowanberry wine. It was touch and go whether I would be allowed to sit with the others at all—I had to sit by myself at the very end of the table. It was terribly humiliating. And they said that if I wanted to go mushroom-picking with them the next day, I had better not pour that detestable-smelling stuff over me.

All the same, I was so pleased with Hansen's present that when I put on my newly ironed cotton dress the next morning, I put the bottle of Florida Water in my pocket. (In those days women too had deep pockets inside their dresses, so little girls, like boys, could carry their most precious belongings with them.)

I remember the white summer dress with black flowers in a kind of garland pattern, because Kittelsen had said to Mama that he would like to draw us three girls in those dresses. Mama fell for something she called the Kate Greenaway style—with tiny little puffed sleeves, a high waist and a skirt that reached almost to the ankles. I had suffered a great deal at school because of the peculiar way my mother always dressed us, but I loved those Kate Greenaway dresses.

That day we went far into the woods. Butter-gold chanterelles sprouted in circles where the ground was carpeted with brown needles in the pine barrens. Along a gulch between steep rock cliffs where the limes hung over the edge we found the liver-colored ox tongue mushrooms, which are rare and grow only on the matted roots of old lime trees. And when we came to a little opening in the wood, the kind of little green clearing that Kittelsen called a fairy meadow, there were the milk fungi—which unfortunately were much too popular with all sorts of maggots too—and the wild champignons and the little white puffballs, which we used to call fishball mushrooms. Between times we picked raspberries for diversion, and we were wonderfully tired and hungry when we came to a beautiful little forest tarn, where Kittelsen thought we should build our fire and make coffee and rest for a while.

We ate and we rested, and afterward we resumed our mushroom-hunt. I had strayed away from the others because I was following up a brook that ran into the tarn. At the edge of an ant-hill I caught a glimpse of a cluster of "proud sealy," the dark gray agaric fungus that looks so unappetizing and yet has the best taste of them all. I jumped over the brook, fell flat on my face, and the stopper came out of my perfume bottle. The next moment even I had to admit that one can have too much of a good thing.

It had been so dreadful the day before, when my idol had commented so scathingly about the odor I had spread about me, that I didn't have the courage to go back to the others right away. I tried to rinse it out of my dress a little but it did not help much. I sat down on the moss near the brook and drifted off in thought. When I opened my eyes again I discovered that the sunshine had become a rich yellow and the shadows across the brook had lengthened considerably. I must have been napping, and I could neither see nor hear the others.

I called out, but only an echo answered. Then I picked up my basket and hurried back along the brook. There was the tarn and there were the ashes from our coffee making—black and doused with water. All around me was the solitude of the forest and the water and its marshy inlet.

How the others had managed to lose me like that I could not see. The landscape was so forbidding, with dense woods and little valleys between steep mountainsides, with massive rocks that had fallen off the mountain tops so long ago that they were now overgrown with moss. And we had fanned out while we were looking for mushrooms. I was not exactly scared; I was used to roaming around in the woods here by myself, though I had never been so far from home. But I didn't like to think how I would be greeted when I found my way back into the bosom of the family. Mama would be badly frightened by now, and I had long since learned that nothing makes parents more angry and upset than being really worried about you.

I began to run down what looked like the most likely path. Soon it vanished into nowhere. The forest was crisscrossed with cow paths and brooks and ravines. I knew I was lost and I didn't like it at all, since it was already rather late in the afternoon. Then I decided to follow the sun, south and west, path or no path, because that way I would eventually have to reach the road that led to the fjord.

All of a sudden I came to a fence, and beyond it was a field with the rye already yellow-white. Further away on a little hill I saw a beautiful big farm, with a white farmhouse and red outbuildings with fields and meadows around it. The evening sun was shining over it, warm and golden. I didn't know the place, but I thought perhaps they would have a telephone there—I could run up and ask them to call the Kittelsens.

Somebody touched my shoulder. "Is that you, Ingrid?"

The old woman standing behind and looking down at me was tall, erect and gray-haired. She was carrying a tin bucket. Then she sniffed and chuckled, "I see. So Hagbarth has seen you already—I smell it, my girl. Well, well. So now Hagbarth's come home, has he? So now he's home again."

I didn't know what she meant, but I thought it had something to do with the return of Mr. Hansen and his shipmates the previous day. So I nodded vigorously.

"Well, I don't blame him—that he went to see you first," she said softly, "but he'll be coming home tonight to see his mother, won't he? Perhaps he is on his way now?"

"Oh, yes, he should be here any minute now," I answered.

"But then we must go in right away and put the coffee on, so everything will be ready when Hagbarth gets home."

I didn't think I had any choice but to follow the old woman along the path through the grain. But it did not lead up to the farm, it led down to a little green patch by the foot of the hill. There was a shiny pond, and by the pond stood an old gray cottage nestled under two large apple trees.

It was rather dark inside, and the air was foul. The room looked dirty, and on a table by the window were unwashed cups and dishes. Clothes were lying about on the floor and draped over the unmade bed.

The woman said a little shyly, "It's my eyes, Ingrid—they are not as good as they used to be." I had guessed as much when I looked into her pail—she had been out picking blueberries, and there were just as many leaves and green berries there as ripe ones. "Well, you see, I'm getting old—I am old now, my girl. Thank God, Hagbarth is coming home at last!" She gave a long tremulous sigh.

"Well—but now he'll be here soon, you know." I didn't know what else to say. I had begun to realize that she was a bit odd, so I had to play the role of Ingrid, the girl she was talking to. So when she said, "Maybe you would be good enough to tidy up a bit while I put the kettle on," I found a basin, fetched some water from the tank on the stove—it was barely lukewarm—and began to wash the cups.

That seemed to please the woman. She wandered about prattling and clearly did not expect me to answer much. When I had finished the dishes I wiped off the table and began to tidy up the room, and the last thing I did was to straighten the bed a little and spread the cover neatly over it.

"And now we'll have to lay the table." She unlocked a cupboard. "We'll have the best set today, for Hagbarth's homecoming."

I peered into the cupboard. It was full of the loveliest things on all the shelves—a whole coffee set of Royal Copenhagen china, among other things, and jugs and sugar bowls and breadbaskets of silver or plate. The woman passed me a silver cream pitcher. "The cream—you will find that in the pantry."

I guessed that the door behind the stove must lead to the larder. The little room was filled with evening sunlight, but the shelves were nearly empty, apart from a lot of dead flies. Flies were buzzing and droning all over the place. The only other things there were a half a loaf of bread, hard and dry, and in a dish a piece of butter that was nearly melted. In another dish was an end of sausage and a bit of sweating yellow cheese, and in a third, a little cream, thick and sour and barely enough to hide the bottom of the cream pitcher.

"If I had only known he were coming today"—the woman had followed me—"I don't have much here now, but if I had known about it I would have taken care to have everything we needed." She suddenly took hold of a fold of my dress and lifted it close to her old dim eyes. "Why, you're in mourning, Ingrid! I think this looks like a mourning dress! Ingrid, Ingrid!—is there something you haven't told me? You haven't had bad news, have you, Ingrid?" Her voice was so full of fear and pain it went right through my heart.

I don't know how I managed to answer, calmly and merrily, "It is for my father, you know. Mama thought we ought to wear half-mourning for him this summer, too. You must not worry . . . mother-in-law," I whispered tentatively. I had become convinced that she mistook me for her son's sweetheart—I sensed there had to be something sad or tragic behind her strange behavior.

"Your father? Oh yes, of course, of course, your father." She laughed softly. "Hagbarth is home. I can smell that you have seen him . . . Florida Water—I do like that smell so much! Anton always brought me home Florida Water too. He will be here any moment now, don't you think, Ingrid?"

"Oh, sure."

She had laid the bare, unpainted surface of the table with Royal Copenhagen china, and in two silver baskets were a few cookies, mostly broken, and some milk biscuits. The sun must have gone down now; the room was full of gathering shadows.

"Is there anything more I can do for you, mother-in-law?" There was nothing I wanted more than to enter into the dream world of this poor creature. And I was flattered that she mistook me for a grown-up young woman who had a sweetheart and all. . . .

"You might bring in a few buckets of water—if you'd be kind enough. My back isn't so good these days."

I shouldered the yoke and hitched the two pails onto it. And feeling very important and grown-up I trod my way down toward the pond.

Behind the big farm the top of the spruce forest stood dark against the golden sky, and little pink and gold clouds reflected in the lovely eye of water. I stood on a small wooden bridge with tall reeds on either side, and a little water from the buckets I had filled trickled back into the pond and made ripples on the surface. A few small birds were singing over in the woods. Suddenly I felt myself outside of time and the world of my everyday life, and I knew that I would never forget this strange moment when I had become Ingrid, the sweetheart of a boy who had died long ago. Then I hooked up the pails and walked toward the cottage again—and all of a sudden, a young man— a farmhand, he looked like—appeared in front of me:

"Hey there—are you Mrs. Undset's girl that they are looking for high and low over half the township? What on earth are you doing here at Berte's? You had better come with me now. Well, well, I think you'll get it when you get home to your mother and the Kittelsens!"

The woman was dozing in the rocking chair when I came in with the water. She nodded and very sweetly replied good night when I said good night and thank you. Then I walked with the farmhand to the big farm and he drove me home. It was quite a long way and it was a lovely trip in the soft twilight; much of the road went through the forest, and I enjoyed it, despite everything. And I must say I *did* get it when I got home!

Yet the memory of my meeting with the woman in the cottage by the pond remained with me as something very strange, melancholy, and beautiful. I was never sorry that I had gotten lost that day, especially after Mr. and Mrs. Hansen told me her story. For some reason that even I didn't understand, I never mentioned one word of this experience to my mother or to the Kittelsens, but I told it to the Hansens, because I thought they might know who she was.

She was the daughter from the big farm, and when she became engaged to First Mate Anton Viken her mother did not like it at all—the last thing in the world she wanted was for the girl to marry a sailor, as so many of her relatives had been lost at sea. But Berte just laughed: the last time she had been in Christiania she had gone to the woman on Engensgate who could see the past and future in your palms and tell your future in cards, and the fortuneteller had said that there was one thing Berte could be sure of: none of her menfolk would ever die beneath the ocean blue. So Berte got married to her handsome young bridegroom and they lived in the white house with the rose hedge around it that Mrs. Grønneberg, the artist, has now. They had two children, a boy and a girl, and were very happy together. Mr. Viken had his own ship, and was home for several weeks before he had to sail. One Sunday they borrowed a horse and carriage, planning to take a trip around Lake Langdal, but when Captain Viken was harnessing the horse it kicked him so hard in the stomach that he died a few days later.

The widow mourned inconsolably. But she was rather well off, and she had the children to live for. Oh, she was a fine person, Mrs. Viken—so kind and able and handsome, and her children were so attractive and promising. The boy, Hagbarth, had always wanted to go to sea, so he went away as soon as he finished grammar school. He was already second mate when he got engaged to Ingrid Langseth, the daughter of the village shopkeeper up by the church—a sweet girl, and there was money there, too, so everything looked just as hopeful as one could wish. Then a telegram arrived saying that Hagbarth Viken had died in a hospital in Mobile, from yellow fever.

But the thing that finished Berte Viken was her daughter Helene's accident. She was in the maternity hospital, studying to become a midwife, and she was probably secretly engaged to a medical student, a nice young man from a fine family and everything. One Midsummer Eve they had all gone to Sarabraaten—Helene and her boyfriend and some other young people. They went out on the lake and the boat overturned. The boyfriend tried for an hour to bring her back to life after they got her out of the water, but to no avail. "You see, the wise woman had only promised that the menfolk would never die by drowning."

Berte owned the little cottage which once had been a tenant farm on the family's estate. She used to go out there with the children for a few days when the berries were ripe, or when there was good skiing in the countryside, and so forth. She now moved out there and refused to have anyone live with her; she wanted to be completely alone. Her nephew and his wife, who run the big farm now, look after her in their way, but they have enough on their hands already. So they would like her to move in with them. No, not for the sake of her money, for she has already willed it to the seamen's mission, but they are very decent people and are worried about having her go on living in that little cottage all alone, especially now that her eyesight isn't very good—and sometimes she's not quite right in the head, either. But the doctor says, yes, of course it's not impossible that some morning they'll find her lying dead in her bed, but let her live the way she wants to, poor soul. If they try to move her against her will then she probably will go quite mad.

"And what became of Ingrid?" I asked.

"But you know her: the baker's wife, Mrs. Andersen."

Plump, merry, middle-aged Mrs. Andersen! Mr. Hansen must have seen how shocked I was, as he roared with laughter. "Yes, poor girl, she mourned Hagbarth for four years, but when she was near the end of the fifth she married Andersen. Good heavens, she was so young, only a child. And life is a long business—at least for those who live safely on land."

CR

When I visited Florida in the spring two years ago, I asked in every drugstore I saw about Florida Water. There was no one who had even heard of it—no one until I got to Jacksonville. There I met a very old pharmacist.

"Florida Water! Oh, do you know about that?" He smiled, in a way the Americans call "wistfully." "Oh, yes, the Norwegian sailors, they used to buy a lot of it. It was really very nice." The fashionable Southern gentlemen used to use it to freshen their faces after shaving, he told me. "Yes, it really was a lovely perfume, indeed it was. But they don't make it any more."

Story from *Nordmannsforbundet*. Translated from the Norwegian by Sherrill Harbison and Benedikte Wilders.

ᐳᏃ Selma Lagerlöf

Nobel Prize recipient Selma Lagerlöf (1858–1940) is famous throughout the world as the creator of Nils Holgersson, the little boy who traveled the length and breadth of Sweden on the back of a goose. *The Wonderful Adventures of Nils* was specifically written for Swedish schoolchildren, but otherwise Lagerlöf wrote novels for adults. She did, however, write three books about her own childhood and "The Bird of Paradise" is taken from the first of these, *Mårbacka*.

Mårbacka is the name of the family manor in the region of Värmland, in western Sweden, where Lagerlöf was born and where she died. That Mårbacka was cherished by the entire family is made clear in the very first paragraph in the story below. It was a great sorrow when economic necessity forced the family to sell Mårbacka in 1890, but thanks to her success as a writer, Lagerlöf was gradually able to repurchase the entire estate.

In *Mårbacka*, Lagerlöf remembers her childhood home as harmonious and idyllic. She writes about herself in third person, underscoring the distance between author and subject. The illness which was temporarily crippling and left Selma with a permanent limp is the background for "The Bird of Paradise," but the focus of the story is on the power of the child's imagination.

The Bird Of Paradise

They lived in a tiny little house at the beginning of Karlsgatan, and they liked it so much that Lieutenant Lagerlöf and the children decided to call the place Little Mårbacka, surely the noblest distinction that a house in an unfamiliar city could ever have.

In front of the little house was a garden plot inside a picket fence, and under the green fullness of the garden's trees they ate their breakfasts and suppers, which were prepared at home. Behind the house was another little garden, big enough for two potato patches, and above them, pressed against the steep rock face, stood a cottage that wasn't much bigger than the cabin aboard the Uddeholm. In the cottage lived their hostess, Mrs. Strömberg, the wife of a sea captain.

They had learned that Mrs. Strömberg lived in the house during the winter, but in the summer she rented it out to resort guests and moved into the little cabin. There she sat, from morning until evening, surrounded by large flowering oleander trees, while all her tables and shelves were covered with curious things brought home from foreign countries by Captain Strömberg.

When Mrs. Lagerlöf and Aunt Lovisa went out to drink coffee at their friends' houses, and Lieutenant Lagerlöf was out fishing for mackerel, and Anna had gone to visit the confectioner's daughters, and Johan to see the crabs, Back-Kajsa picked up the youngest girl and carried her up to Mrs. Strömberg's cabin.

She was a very special friend. It was just as restful to sit with her under the oleander trees as to sit in grandmother's corner sofa at home at Mårbacka. Mrs. Strömberg wasn't a storyteller, but she had lots of interesting things to show them: big seashells, full of sound, which murmured when you put them to your ear; little Chinese men of porcelain with long pigtails and long mustaches; and two enormous shells, of which one had been the casing for a coconut and the other for an ostrich egg.

Back-Kajsa and Mrs. Strömberg mostly spoke of solemn and pious matters which the child didn't understand, but sometimes they spoke of more ordinary things. Mrs. Strömberg talked about her husband and his travels. They learned that he had a big beautiful ship named the *Jakob* and that he was just then sailing to Saint Ybes in Portugal to bring home a cargo of salt.

Back-Kajsa wondered how Mrs. Strömberg could possibly have peace in her soul when she knew that her husband was sailing the fearsome seas. But Mrs. Strömberg replied that she believed Someone was watching over her husband. She didn't worry any more about him when he was on board than when he was walking the streets at home in Strömstad.

The kind Mrs. Strömberg turned to the little girl then and said that she hoped her husband would come home soon, because there was something on the *Jakob* that the little girl would surely like to see: a bird of paradise.

The child immediately became enormously interested. "What is that?" she asked.

"It's a bird from paradise," Mrs. Strömberg said.

"Selma has heard her grandmother talk about paradise," Back-Kajsa said.

Yes, of course she remembered. Grandmother had told her about paradise, and she had imagined that it looked like the little rose arbor outside the western gable at Mårbacka. At the same time, she had a clear idea that paradise had something to do with God, and for whatever reason, she got the idea that the Someone who watched over Mrs. Strömberg's husband so that she felt equally at peace whether he was on board the *Jakob* or walking the streets at home in Strömstad, that Someone was none other than the bird of paradise.

She absolutely wanted to meet that bird. Perhaps it would be able to help her. Everyone pitied her parents because she wasn't getting well, and now they'd even undertaken this expensive trip for her sake!

She would very much have liked to ask Back-Kajsa and Mrs. Strömberg if they thought the bird of paradise could do something for her, but she was too shy. She thought they might laugh at her.

But she did not forget that conversation. Every day she wished that the *Jakob* would come, so that the bird of paradise could fly ashore.

Only a few days later she heard that the *Jakob* had indeed come in.

It gave her great joy, but she didn't tell anyone about it. There was something very solemn about the whole thing to her. She remembered how serious Grandmother had been when she had talked about Adam and Eve. She didn't want to tell Johan and Anna that there was a bird from paradise on board the *Jakob,* and that she wanted to ask it to heal her leg. No, she couldn't even tell Back-Kajsa.

It was odd that the bird of paradise hadn't appeared. Every time she went to see Mrs. Strömberg, she expected he would be sitting and singing in the oleander trees, but he was nowhere to be seen.

She asked Back-Kajsa about it, but Back-Kajsa thought he stayed on board the *Jakob.*

"But soon Selma will get to see him," she said. "The Lieutenant has said that tomorrow we can all go on board the *Jakob.*

And Back-Kajsa was right. Captain Strömberg had barely been home a day before he and Lieutenant Lagerlöf became fast friends. The Lieutenant had been out on the *Jakob* several times, and he felt quite at home there. Now the whole family was going out to see how pleasant it was.

When they left home, none of them had imagined what going on board the *Jakob* really meant. The little crippled girl, for one, thought that the ship would be docked at the wharf like the big steamers.

But of course it wasn't. It lay far out in the harbor, and they had to get into a little boat and row out to it. It was amazing to see how the *Jakob* grew taller the closer they got to it. Soon it towered above them like a mountain and it seemed impossible that they, sitting in the little rowboat, would be able to climb aboard.

Aunt Lovisa declared straight out that if it was that giant boat they were heading for, then she could not come along on board.

"Wait and see, Lovisa!" the Lieutenant said. "It'll be easier than you think."

But Aunt Lovisa declared that she might just as well try climbing up the flagpole on the point at Laholmen. She thought it would be best to turn around on the spot.

Both Mrs. Lagerlöf and Back-Kajsa agreed with her and voted to turn back.

But Lieutenant Lagerlöf was stubborn and stood his ground. They would be able to get on board, there was no doubt about that. This might be the only chance in their lives to see what it looked like on a merchant ship, and that wasn't an opportunity they should pass up.

"Well, if we make it on board, we'll never make it down again," Aunt Lovisa said.

Half way out, they encountered a boat loaded with sacks.

"Do you see that boat?" Lieutenant Lagerlöf said to his sister. "Do you know what is inside those sacks?"

"No, dear Gustav, how would I know that?" replied Aunt Lovisa.

"Well, my dear, those are sacks of salt from the *Jakob*," he explained. "They have neither arms nor legs, but if they have been able to make it down from the ship, then you certainly ought to be able to do it, too."

"Well, you ought to get dressed up in crinoline and long skirts, and see how brave you'd feel then," Aunt Lovisa said.

They kept up this bickering the whole way out. The little girl, who dearly hoped to see the bird of paradise, wished with all her heart that her father would be able to persuade Aunt Lovisa and the others to go on board, but she thought, as they did, that it looked impossible.

They put in under a swinging gangway at any rate, and a couple of sailors from the *Jakob* jumped down into the boat to help them climb up. The first person they helped was the little crippled girl. One of them lifted her up to his buddy, who carried her up the ladder, or whatever it was, and set her down on the *Jakob's* deck. He went back down to help the others, and left her standing there alone.

She was alarmed, because she had only a narrow strip of deck to stand on. A big, gaping hole opened up in front of her, and deep inside it she could see something white as snow being loaded into sacks.

She remained standing alone for quite some time. Some resistance must have been raised down in the boat towards boarding the ship. No one appeared, and when she had had a chance to collect herself, she started looking around for the bird of paradise.

She looked for it up in the rigging. She had imagined that it would be at least as big as a turkey, so it should have been easy to catch sight of it.

But when no bird was to be seen, she turned to Captain Strömberg's cabin boy, who was standing nearby, and asked him where she might find the bird of paradise.

"Come with me and I'll show him to you," he said. He gave her his hand so she wouldn't fall into the hold. Then he climbed down the cabin steps backwards, and she followed him.

It was very elegant down in the cabin. The mahogany of the furniture and walls gleamed, and there, indeed, stood the bird of paradise.

It was even more wonderful than she had imagined. It wasn't alive, but it stood there anyway, beautiful and complete with all its feathers.

She climbed up onto a chair and from there onto the table. She sat down next to the bird of paradise and examined its beauty. The cabin boy stood beside her and showed her the long, light, hanging feathers. Then he remarked, "See, you can tell that he comes from paradise. He doesn't have any feet."

This observation fit her idea of paradise perfectly: You didn't need to walk there, but could manage with just a pair of wings. She contemplated the bird with great devotion, and clasped her hands as she did when she said her evening prayers. She wondered very much whether the cabin boy knew that it was the bird that protected Captain Strömberg, but she didn't dare ask.

She could have sat there in wonder all day, but she was interrupted by loud shouts from the deck. It sounded as if they were calling her name: "Selma, Selma."

The next moment they all came rushing eagerly into the cabin: Lieutenant Lagerlöf and Back-Kajsa, Mrs. Lagerlöf and Aunt Lovisa, Captain Strömberg, Johan and Anna. They were so many that they filled the whole cabin.

"How did you get down here?" they asked, looking tremendously amazed and astonished.

All at once she realized that she had walked on the deck, walked down the steps, walked into the cabin, and that no one had carried her.

"Get down from the table," they said, "so we can see if you can walk."

She crept from the table to the chair and from the chair to the floor, and when she got down onto the floor, she was able to both stand and walk.

How delighted and happy they were! Now the whole goal of the trip had been achieved, the expensive venture had not been in vain. The little child would become a normal human being, not a helpless, unhappy cripple.

They stood with tears in their eyes, and said that it was the excellent baths in Strömstad that had effected the cure. They praised the air and the sea and the whole town and were so pleased that they had come.

The little girl had her own thoughts about it. She wondered very much whether the bird of paradise hadn't actually helped her. Had it been the little miracle with the quivering wings, that had come from a place where you didn't need any feet, that had taught her how to walk on this earth, where it was such a necessary skill?

Excerpted from *Mårbacka*. Translated from the Swedish by Anna Sonnerup.

⊕ Dea Trier Mørch

In 1976 Danish author Dea Trier Mørch (1941–) published a novel that was soon to resonate with readers all over the world. The book, *Winter's Child*, is about mothers giving birth, what they think and feel and how they share these emotions with each other on a hospital maternity ward. Children and parenting are also at the heart of *Chestnut Lane*, the novel from which "Grandma in the Painting Room" has been excerpted. Both these books have been illustrated by the author, who is also an accomplished artist.

Chestnut Lane recounts events from a summer and fall when three little children came to stay with their grandparents in the house on the street shaded by chestnut trees. Their father was ill with tuberculosis and their mother was working full-time in Copenhagen. The story below is about the special relationship that develops between Grandma and her six-year-old granddaughter, Maja. Along with her brothers, Maja is delighted with all the wonderful things their artist grandmother can make, and when Grandma starts telling her life story, Maja is enthralled.

Grandma in the Painting Room

Maja stands in the doorway to the painting room and sees Grandma sitting bent over her drawing table.

There is something like the taste of honey, something like a snail shell about Grandma.

She's always wearing one of her special linen dresses that she has made herself. They all have snug long-sleeved tops with lots of little buttons down the front, and a loose white collar. The skirt is big and wide and reaches down to the middle of her leg. The fabric is either checkered or striped in blue and white. Or in placid brown and yellow stripes. Or black and brown. Around her waist she has tied a soft apron.

These everyday clothes are worn and washed out, yet very sturdy, and the colors seem to have aged with beauty.

When she wants to get dressed up, she wears the same kind of dress, but in white linen that Mom has woven. Grandma has embroidered pink flowers and light and dark green leaves around the cuffs and on the front.

Around her neck she has a necklace of white shells that one of her grandchildren in Jutland made for her.

At home she is always bareheaded. Her hair is gray—not white like Grandpa's—and big hairpins hold it in place around a hair pad. But when she goes shopping or on a painting excursion, she puts on her old flat-crowned, wide-brimmed straw hat, with the black velvet band and the velvet rose. It casts soft shadows on her old wrinkled face.

Grandma's small solid plump body has a light scent of apples and ear wax to it. It's a scent from the old days, a bit musty, yet it's awfully nice.

There's something soft and rocking about Grandma. Her old breasts are still full, and it feels good to be pressed close against them, and whisper something in her ear.

Maja once heard Grandma say that if she hadn't been able to draw, she would have laid down and died. She draws almost every single day, and if the children can promise not to disturb her, they may stand around the drawing table and watch.

She sits on a black-lacquered, three-legged chair with an arched back that she had a carpenter make for her. She also designed her work table. She has actually designed lots of furniture during her life.

On her table are two clay jars with worn brushes of hog bristle sticking up. On some the hair is completely worn down to the metal, yet she can't bring herself to throw them away.

All her tools are old. You can tell that she has used the same things her entire life.

In a little green metal box, that used to be for Penguin Pipe Tobacco, she has a bunch of pencil stubs. Grandpa has sharpened them for her many many times, and now they simply cannot get any shorter. It also contains a small flesh-colored snail shell, a Gillette razor blade, a dirty eraser and a Norwegian coin.

She pulls out the big broad drawer in her work table and searches for a piece of blotting paper. On the board partition in the drawer she has written *The Installer is in complete lack of any work ethics* and *In 1933 the Hafnia Insurance Policy will be cashed* with a soft pencil. Next to this she has been trying out a purple stamp that says *Interior Designer.*

She sits with a big piece of white drawing paper in front of her. She has drawn a Virginia creeper with a soft pencil and is just about to color it with gray and gray-greenish aniline dyes.

It is as if she becomes a bit remote when she works, a tiny bit cold. If the children should happen to disturb her, she sends them a colorless and empty look and immediately they stand as quiet as mice, their hands by their sides.

Like the sound of a kettle, singing on the stove, she whistles a quiet melody between her teeth.

Then little Malthe cannot contain himself any longer:

"Won't you draw something for us, Grandma?" he whispers.

"Oh, please?"

Grandma pulls on the tip of her nose and looks at him for a moment, her eyes darkening slightly.

"Can't Maja do it?"

"Why do I always have to do it?"

"Oh, for Heaven's sake, so what should it be?"

"Uhm, uhm, a pilot," says Martin.

"No, I'm not very good at that. How about Noah's ark?"

"Oh yes, Grandma, please!"

She nods, takes her long wallpaper scissors, quickly cuts a piece of paper in long strips, and glues the strips together into a long length. At lightening speed she draws a round boat with ribs and a gangway and animals that come marching out of the boat two by two, straight legged. Two Icelandic ponies, two giraffes, two swans, two striped cats, two crocodiles, and two little fat pigs, each with a curly tail.

A paint brush clinks in the glass of water, Grandma is painting the picture in watercolor. The pigs turn pink, the crocodiles green. And above them a dove is flying on a blue sky with an olive twig in her beak.

Sometimes she makes coloring books for the children. She buys the cheapest unlined notebooks and fills the pages with motifs drawn with Indian ink or pencil.

But as soon as the children show the coloring books to their mom, she takes the books away from them. She says they are far too pretty to be painted in. They are to be kept in a hidden place until the children have grown up and can fully appreciate such things.

Which actually seems to make Grandma proud. Yet at the same time she's indifferent and gets on with another project for the children; a ship out of folded paper which she paints with poster paints. A picture lottery. Cut-out dolls with lots of shapeless clothes.

She simply knows how to do *everything.*

Almost. For there's one thing that Martin is disgruntled about: Grandma does not know how, or can't be bothered, to make jigsaw puzzles. Martin has a great interest in jigsaw puzzles. Grandma *has* tried to make him one. She once rushed up the loft stairs, tore a picture out of *The Family Journal,* and glued it on cardboard with flour paste. Then she grabbed her huge wallpaper scissors with the rust stains and cut-cut-cut the picture into equally sized squares, and then she was done.

That jigsaw puzzle turned out to be so easy to do that doing it felt completely foolish.

But Grandma has promised Martin that when he has grown up a little, he can have a look at the adult jigsaw puzzle, *The Black Ocean,* which she keeps in a shoe box in the bottom drawer of the chest.

Every now and then Grandma paints gigantic wallpapers. Then she runs around in the painting room in her stocking feet. She has huge pieces of butcher paper rolled out on the floor, and she's put chairs and things in the corners of the paper so that it won't roll up again.

Maja has seen Grandma make a wallpaper in six lengths! A bear claw was the motif. Grandma shaded it with coffee, and Maja was permitted to get down on her knees and draw wee tiny circles with a pencil on the edges of the paper.

The bear claws Grandma uses as her models are brought to her by Grandpa who gets them at a place she calls Värmland. Because it reminds her of Sweden, and Grandma loves Sweden. The Swedish forests, the Swedish painters and illustrators, the Swedish authors. Everything that's Swedish.

She sells her designs in Gothenburg where there's a factory that prints them. Grandma keeps sending the Director lots of sketches and ideas and proposals. Then suddenly one day she began to worry that it had become too much, that it might somehow annoy him. So she sent him a big envelope with a stamped envelope and two notes. On one of the notes she wrote "Stop," on the other "Keep going."

The Director returned the latter.

What she loves the most is to paint with oil. She has a paint box that she got from her father just before he died. When she was sixteen years old. She has always taken extremely good care of it and brings it on her painting excursions. It's small, yet there's room for lots in it. There's a folded palette in the lid. And in the bottom there's a metal container with many compartments. Here there are pencils and rags, little bottles with linseed oil and turpentine, and crumpled tubes of oil paint that are often impossible to open. Then Grandma strikes a match and holds it for a second under the cap so that she can twist it off.

The paint box is equipped with a broad leather strap so she can carry it across her stomach when she bikes.

If Grandma has been in her painting room finishing up a little picture, and still has some oil paint left on her brush, a *dangerous situa-*

tion arises. At least that's what Mom says, and Maja has seen it herself. Because then Grandma might decide to tiptoe through all the rooms, squinting intently at all the other painters' paintings—which the house is full of.

Suddenly she's seized by a desire to correct their paintings, just a tiny bit. Maja has seen her tiptoe over to her brother Fritz' big painting of Verjhøj, take a quick look to either side, and whisper:

"That cloud has always bothered me!"

And then she lifted her brush and made the cloud appear a bit rounder.

In Grandma's bedroom there is a copy of a very fine picture of her great-grandmother when she was young. Mom has seen her adjust that one slightly with a green crayon.

"We'll have to see if we can get that off with some lukewarm water and soap," said Mom. "After all, I'm the one who's going to inherit the picture."

Maja leans on Grandma who sits bent over her drawing table. Maja sees her wrinkled neck and the little necklace of white shells that have holes bored into them.

Grandma turns to her and pats the paint box gently.

"You shall inherit this when I die, little-Maja."

Maja felt a little shudder.

"I was born in 1877," begins Grandma. "My father was a Jew. He was baptized as an adult, converted to Christianity, and founded a Grundtvigian folk high school. It was a place where girls and boys from the countryside could come and get an education. I was the oldest of five children. My mother died in childbirth."

"From what?" asks Maja.

"It was something awful which happened in the old days. It was a fever women could get just after they had given birth. It was shortly before I turned six."

Maja holds her hand in front of her mouth and her eyes feel warm.

Grandma strokes her hair:

"My father died when I was sixteen. Oh, it was terrible! And then we were orphaned."

Maja hides her face against Grandma's shoulder. She can barely stand it. She dares not look at Grandma, because then she'd start crying.

"That same year your Grandpa and I got engaged. He was a carpenter's apprentice and had gone to the folk high school. My father was very fond of him."

Grandma pulls at her nose, which is hooked because she's half Jewish, which must not be confused with being half Jutlandic. Maja once made that mistake, and became the target of her older cousins' relentless ridicule.

"Later Grandpa traveled around as a journeyman. He was on the road in Europe. I attended a private art school in Copenhagen."

Malthe adjusts himself on Grandma's lap.

"We got married when I was twenty-two years old."

Maja can't take her eyes off a tiny blue spot on Grandma's lip that moves when she speaks. It looks like a louse. It jumps and dances.

"Grandpa worked as a master carpenter."

Martin pulls his hair. He also wants to be a master carpenter when he grows up. He's made up his mind.

"Over the next fifteen years we traveled from place to place wherever there was work. I was painting and drawing as much as I could, and had a child every other year. Eventually we had seven."

"Seven is a lot," says Maja.

"But when the seventh child was born—and that was your mother, Hanna, you know—I got a huge assignment. I knew a wealthy family from the old days. They had bought an estate, torn it down and built it up again. Now they asked me if I would design a number of large parlors for them—a parlor is a kind of room, almost a hall! I was supposed to design everything: doors, windows, floors, attics, furniture, and wall decorations."

Grandma brightens up:

"*Me*—an ordinary wife with seven children. Can you imagine what this meant?!"

Martin yawns right in Grandma's face, but Grandma has gotten her steam up now:

"I was to design all the parlors in different *styles*. One was to be Chinese, another Indian, a third Italian, and several as in the French castles."

"I want a piece of candy," Martin shouts, tugging at her apron. "Don't you have any?"

"Tell me more," says Maja. She's sitting on the drawing table. The boys are outside playing.

"Well, at one point I had eleven master artisans working for me at the estate. You probably can't even imagine that, little Maja! Eleven master artisans—and each had his own journeyman! And all of these people I was to keep busy."

Maja adjusts herself so that she can see Grandma's eyes and lips when they move with that little blue spot.

"I designed everything in full size. The drawings were huge! Oh, what a glorious time."

Grandma runs out to the middle of the room and shows Maja with her hands how enormous the drawings were:

"And Grandpa, he was the foreman of the works. That is, he was the one who made sure that all the artisans had their correct instructions, so he was *my* foreman. That did him in, to tell the truth."

She grabs one of the brushes from the table and scratches her hair with the handle.

"No, life wasn't easy for him during those years. Often I even wished that things had been the opposite: that he was the one in charge and I was *his* assistant. But what could we do? Can you tell me that, please? After four years the assignment was completed and all seven parlors were ready. And I can tell you, that ... "

She walks over to the window, looks out at the garden and suddenly turns around:

"I received great recognition for that work!"

She nods, pleased, her eyes shining. Grandma and Maja look proudly at each other.

When Grandma talks, her hands are moving all over, back and forth to her face, over to Maja, like two small animals, investigating everything.

"Suddenly one day your Grandpa was asked if he would be the foreman of the workshop at a brand new mental hospital. We got an official residence at the hospital, and once again the family was united. Then I had my eighth child, your aunt Inger. I was forty-one years old."

Maja can't help laughing when she sees Grandma's face.

"But what was most important was that your Grandpa was appointed to the manager position of the mental hospital in 1919. He was selected *out of 200 applicants!* From that moment your Grandpa was a new man. He got his dignity back. Now, that was a day of glory."

Grandma pauses:

"We stayed at the hospital from the first to the second World War. Then Tyge was pensioned off because of his age, and we moved to this place. Thank God for that pension," Grandma knocks on wood three times. "And our eight children are spread out all over Denmark, and we have twenty-five grandchildren. And I am seventy-one and Grandpa is seventy-five."

"Yup, and I am six-and-a-half," says Maja, proud.

Excerpted from *Kastaniealleen*. Translated from the Danish by Anne G. Sabo.

ᏚᏒ Suzanne Osten

Although Suzanne Osten (1944–) first became known for her controversial feminist plays in the 1970s, it is her achievements as a director of children's plays which have brought her fame and recognition in Sweden and abroad. In the 1980s she began to write scripts for films, including *The Mother*. Osten's mother also figures in her first children's book, *The Girl, the Mother and the Garbage*.

In this story, Ti lives alone with her mother who suffers from paranoid schizophrenia. The mother crowds their apartment with things and paper that she finds on the streets. Polter and Geist are her mother's imaginary supervisors; they tell her what to do and she follows their orders. Ti realizes her mother's condition and tries to accommodate to her needs. Yet in the end Ti must take creative action to rescue herself from the impossible situation.

The Girl, the Mother and the Garbage

It's Sunday and Mother wants them to change clothes. But why should Ti wear a checkered scarf on her head?

Well, once her mother had found a book of paintings by the Dutchman Vermeer. In the book was a picture with three figures in it, two women and a man. The younger one who's crouching has a red checkered cloth, like a kitchen towel, tied under her chin, and is resting her right hand on her cheek. The older woman stands holding a basket of bread in front of her. She has a scarf on her head, too.

If you ever go to Scotland you can see the original painting at the National Museum in Edinburgh.

Ti's mother thinks it's handy to wear a scarf.

"You don't have to worry about what your hair looks like and constantly run to the beauty shop."

Ever since Ti started school she's washed her hair in cold running water every morning. She doesn't wear a scarf on weekdays, but on Sundays they dress up as Martha and Mary, just like the painting by the artist from Delft.

115

There's a man sitting at the table by the women. That's Jesus, but Mother says the picture looks a lot like Mr. Polter.

Well, Ti doesn't really know, but she'd imagined Mr. Polter as a crooked, hunched-over little man. But he can reveal himself in many ways, says Mother.

Every Sunday Mother places green leaves in a big Bible she found in a waste-paper basket at the City Mission. She goes there regularly to drink coffee and hear the news now that the radio's broken. The green birch leaves she's used to mark the places she's read look like green arrows sticking out of the book.

"The words are turning green," she says to Ti. "Now listen, little rat, to these ancient words and syllables."

She reads a few lines of God's green words and Ti thinks they ring out in the night.

"And the first shall be the last." That means, Mother shouts out, "THAT ONE DAY EVERYONE WILL BOW TO THE GROUND before you, my PRINCESS, my little rat-darling."

Ti is called Ti because her favorite fairy tale is the one about Ta the rat. Mother tells it at night when they aren't talking about horses or Dalarna or the problems with Mr. Polter or Mr. Geist. Ta the rat has a lot of babies and each of them makes up its own name. The first one is called Ti.

One day Ti gets a new pink silk dress from Mother. It comes way down below her knees.

It's hard to clear a path, but Mother bravely pushes aside piles of newspapers and miraculously a mirror appears. It must have been hidden in a cupboard. Ti has never seen the mirror before.

Mirrors are something Mr. Polter has forbidden Mother to collect. But on birthdays Mother sometimes does as she pleases and tricks Mr. Polter and acts like a child, the way Ti does. She doesn't want to trick him, but she simply has to once in a while because Mr. Polter is so strict.

"Think for yourself! Don't always do what I say," Mother says to Ti.

So there—it's all right to think for yourself. And send messages and go behind people's backs. No matter what, you have to talk to friends.

"Mirrors make you sad," Mother says. "You see time and sorrow."

Ti thinks the mirror is a door to something other than sorrow. She likes looking into the mirror for a long time. She sees how she fills it up, it's just like seeing her reflection in the water. She looks into her eyes, one at a time. She closes her eyes and leans against the ice-cold glass. Mother catches sight of the foggy mirror and says, "You seem to have a fever."

They can't find the thermometer in all the piles of junk and Ti gets to open her present instead.

It's cold outside and it feels good to have a fever. Mother has bought Coca-Cola and plain hot dogs. Ti has climbed up in the window behind the piles of newspapers. Outside she sees boats. The evenings have grown brighter, but the water is dark and the lights of the boats shimmer like beacons.

Once Ti was on a ferry that met a big ship. It was late at night and darker than now. Ti stood at the rail with Mother. Over there on the other boat it looked so cozy through the stateroom windows. She felt drawn to them. She remembered that she'd wanted to be on the other boat instead, the one passing by. She'd thought this but hadn't said it out loud. You can't say everything—Mother could easily misunderstand.

Other people's homes, other people's kitchens, other people's sandwiches, other people's mothers.

I know Ti sometimes wanted to be someone else's daughter. And Mother should have been someone else's mother. But now, when Ti was sick on her birthday, Mother was almost another mother. An ordinary one?

The pink silk dress seems brand new. It's even inside a stiff, black and white striped box. Ti doesn't want to ask where it came from, but the

NK department store box doesn't have many stains and the dress really does smell new and the lining rustles under the starched and sticky petticoat. Ti is hot and flushed from the fever and struggles eagerly into the dress.

It has puffy princess sleeves and all sorts of crazy little bows and a long skirt. She spins in front of the mirror. That's when she sees the spot on the back of the skirt. A dark, oily spot. All of a sudden Ti shivers and her teeth chatter. That day she goes to bed in the dress.

She plays poker with Mother half the night, using matches as chips. Mother wraps her in a blanket when she shivers. The next day, which isn't her birthday, she gets chilled, sweet canned peaches when she wakes up. Her fever is gone. Ti decides to put a bow on the oil spot, and she resolves not to mention to Mother that the elegant department store NK has sold a dress with oily spots on it. Mother's heart would break and Mr. Polter would come and demand a sacrifice, and Ti decides to keep quiet about her disappointment but make a fuss next time instead.

Her fever is back. It comes in waves, some high, some low. It's wonderful to have a fever, it's wonderful to lie in a daze.

Mother has time off from Mr. Polter and comes home with a Phantom comic book and old-fashioned vanilla ice cream. Mother tidies a bit around Ti's bed. Mother sings rollicking sailors' songs. Being sick is like a vacation. Mr. Polter hates infections and Mr. Geist is afraid of germs, Mother says. But Mr. Polter phones and Ti hears Mother's voice turn hard as ice:

"Yes, I will. No, we didn't agree to that. . . the fifteenth, we said. . . yes, on the dot. It's gone up! I'll call my lawyer!"

But he doesn't phone very often while she's sick. Mother teaches Ti how to play Go Fish and Whist. Ti always wins.

Mother always wins at Pirate King. That's the game where you collect trump cards and just enough high ones that you can always outbid your opponent. Ti collects too many cards.

Mother discards.

"They're bad cards," she says, and even tosses out a seven of clubs.

"Don't ever keep the bad ones," says Mother gravely.

"Bad cards are still cards," says Ti, furious to have lost.

Then Mother laughs one of her infrequent laughs and all her teeth show again.

"The brown one is from the war," Mother says, but when Ti asks her to laugh again she just says that she and Mona Lisa have their reasons for keeping their mouths shut.

"Why is it brown?" Ti asks.

She can't help herself when Mother tells her not to nag—she has to ask another nagging question.

"It was rickets that ruined my teeth," says Mother, "but I'm going to get new ones so I can laugh all day long."

They both go to a dentist called Sjökrona. In his waiting room there's a picture of an octopus holding awful drills and tongs in all his arms. He's sticking them into the mouth of a screaming crab. Mother likes her dentist because he has bad teeth himself. That's why he's nice—he knows what it feels like, says Mother.

While Mother's teeth are being fixed, Ti can play with old dentists' drills in a display case in the waiting room. And she always gets a box full of advertisements for a new, candy-flavored toothpaste or a special soft toothbrush to take home with her. It smells nice at Mother's dentist, a faint whiff of hospital. It smells completely clean and a bit like anesthesia. The waiting room makes you feel calm. Ti would like to stay at Sjökrona for a long time looking more closely at his book about the unhappy lobster that gets all its teeth pulled out, but time goes quickly there.

Mother and Ti sit playing cards and it's warm in the bed and warm outside and an unpleasant smell comes from Mr. Polter's garbage and junk. Ti has been away from school for quite a while now. She's lost track of the time. Mother doesn't go out as much, either.

When they've played Pirate King six times and Ti has lost every time, she notices that Mother is starting to get nervous and drop cards.

"When is Mr. Polter coming?" she asks, even though she shouldn't.

You never know when he'll turn up. All of a sudden he'll just be standing there—there's a letter, he rings the doorbell or just sends a message. Or Mother sees him from the window.

Mother lights a cigarette.

"Is Mr. Polter like a landlord, or somebody who's mean to you at recess and tries to grab your cap or your book bag?" asks Ti. "Can you talk to him?"

"Talking to a man is like sticking peas to a wall," Mother replies.

That's a Russian proverb, she says later.

Mother takes out her smelly bag. Ti sinks down into the bed.

"I have to call my teacher."

"I already did," says Mother, "she knows you're home and sick of school."

"No, I'm not. I'm sick for real."

"Well, anyway, I said you won't be there for the rest of the term. You need to get some rest."

There's nothing Ti can say.

Mother doesn't notice that all the cards slide off the bed. It's as if the whole room grows dark.

When Mother has left, Ti lies there with her eyes closed. She wants to cry but no tears come. She gets up out of bed and climbs over all the mountains of stuff till she reaches the window. She takes the blanket along and leans her forehead against the windowpane and then sits there all evening looking out over the water. Along the embankment people are hurrying from work carrying packages and bags, on the way home to their families. Soon maybe she'll catch sight of Mother in the twilight, pulling her wheeled bag, bent over from the strain. The red turban is what she'll see first.

Today there are no waves at all; it's completely calm. Has the piece of paper asking for help been found? Has it reached someone who can read her secret writing? Who will come for Ti?

Ti wonders what they do in school when she's not there. She can barely imagine that school exists. It's there when she is. Then every day it's packed up until she returns. Now it's all packed up, waiting for fall and the end of summer vacation. Since Mother said she won't be going back this spring, that means there won't be any end-of-school ceremony either, and no one else will go and no one will see her new dress. That means the school building has been folded into a box and it won't be till August that the principal and the teacher will put it up again, like a tent. Everything has been packed away and put into boxes.

Actually, the whole world has been packed away and put into boxes with labels. The only thing left is the side toward the water, outside the window. Everything she can't see has been packed up and put away in storage cartons with tags.

Category One,
School yard with swings and jungle gym,
Teacher with white collar,
Principal with Siberian husky,
Bus depot with traffic circle,
Me at the hot dog stand,
Bus number 56 with purple graffiti: *I want to live—Thomas di Leva.*

The steps outside the door are gone and the whole front of the building. Vinell's Furniture is gone, maybe the hall and Mother's room. Only the big room facing north and the water are left. Soon maybe that will be packed up by Mr. Polter and Mr. Geist and sent far away, too.

First the alarm clock jangled. There was an awful noise in the house with yellow plaster. The demons Polter and Geist ran off with overflowing suitcases, leaving the light on.

A bell cuts through the silence. The sound of a doorbell that's escaped all the packing out there. A voice calls out, a voice that isn't packed away:

"Hello, are you there, Ti?"

And nobody but you really needs to know that I was the one who finally got involved and sent a message to the right person, to someone who could help anxious people. The Water King who came was wearing orange overalls just like the other one, and he did what I told him to. He opened the door and let Ti out.

When Mother comes home the Overall will bow submissively to her, introduce himself and explain that he's not dangerous—he's just there to help a little.

And when Mother gets scared and starts to cry—she's completely exhausted and she's terribly scared of surprises, she's actually scared of far too many things—then the man from the Water King's Emergency Service will explain that he hasn't taken anything, just cleared a little space in the middle of the living room so they can sit down. There's a floor underneath, it's just that they'd forgotten it was there. A star parquet floor that Mother was very fond of, once upon a time.

The neighbors with the car and the neighbors with the antique furniture have complained, demanding that they be evicted, and he'll say to Mother:

"You know what they're like, and you're really just as tired of all this as they are, aren't you?"

And later they'll clean for days,
and everything will be clean . . .
And everything will smell good . . .
And the floor will be shiny again.
Then summer vacation will come . . .

Excerpted from *Flickan, mamman och soparna*. Translated from the Swedish by Rochelle Wright.

Susanne Levin

Susanne Levin (1950–) is a high school teacher in Uppsala, just north of Stockholm. In *Life Goes On,* her first novel, she describes how it is to grow up Jewish in the city known for its cathedral and university. Levin has taken on the task of telling the story of her Hungarian mother who lost her whole family in Auschwitz and of her father who grew up in Uppsala in a Swedish-Jewish family. The novel tells how Leah struggles to fit in at home, at school and in her body.

Judaism in Sweden dates back to the end of the eighteenth century when Jews were allowed to enter the country without converting to the Swedish Protestant State Church. At that time only three cities (Stockholm, Gothenburg and Norrköping) accepted Jewish settlers. The nineteenth century was a time of emancipation, when restrictive laws were abolished to allow Jews equal rights in society. At the beginning of the twentieth century, about 7,000 Jews lived in Sweden. This number doubled after World War II when the rescue of the Danish Jews and the humanitarian actions of Raoul Wallenberg in Budapest and Count Bernadotte in Germany brought thousands of Jews to Sweden. Today there are about 17,000 Swedish Jews.

The excerpts below begin when Leah is seven years old and continue over several years. She has already learned how to keep the two different worlds of *goyim,* the non-Jews, and her own home apart.

Life Goes On

Leah is seven. They're lying in Dad's bed, she curled up against his back. Tomorrow is the first day of school, and he's testing her in arithmetic.

"One plus one?"

"Two!"

"Two plus two?"

"Four!"

"Three plus three?"

"Six!"

"Great, Pinchen! But what about four plus four?"

"Dunno . . ."

"Eight."

That's as far as they get. With her nose against his sweater, she inhales the typical Daddy-smell of pipe, sweat and hair tonic. It doesn't matter that the next day she won't know eight plus eight because they didn't get that far. She likes lying behind him like this, talking about all sorts of things.

The next day, when she's sitting in a large room with paper and pencil, drawing a house with a chimney and a flagpole in the yard, a lady comes up to her.

"Do you have your registration card?"

"What? I don't have a card." She squirms uncomfortably. She doesn't understand and wants to do the right thing.

"What's your name?"

The lady goes out through the yellow door to the mothers in the hallway. When she comes in again, she looks completely baffled. Now she's at Leah's desk.

"Did your mother come with you?"

"Yes."

"Yes, but she isn't here any more."

Her hands get sweaty and her throat starts burning when she hears the lady talking to somebody else up front. A teacher?

"The mother has disappeared and the girl doesn't have a card."

Disappeared. But where could she *be?* What's happened?

Finally Mother is there on the bench in the hallway, but instead of throwing herself into her arms Leah is watchful and holds back.

"Why didn't you wait?"

"I had to go home and cook for Tommy and Grandpa and Julius."

Her teacher wears a pale green suit and has round breasts. She smells like violet lozenges and during recess Leah holds her hand the minute a place at her side is free. The rest of the "birds" gather at the jungle gym, where they swing and climb around like one big happy swarm. The "birds" are the ones who belong with Mrs. Ethel Fogelberg, their teacher, who is strict and beautiful with her silver hair and green suit.

Everything about her is round: her nose, her lips, her breasts, her tummy, her bottom. She teaches them to read, write and do arithmetic, and they love her. But when she plays the organ, she sings out of tune.

"What can you use a meat grinder for?" she asks the first grade one day.

Right away Leah thinks of her father, his tongue sticking out of the corner of his mouth as he turns the handle with one hand and feeds in fish fillets, onion, and bread with the other. Mother stands next to him, telling him not to splatter the sticky ground fish all over the kitchen.

"Gefilte fish."

She squirms at her desk. Who said that? The teacher looks completely perplexed and now Mia repeats, "You can make gefilte fish with a meat grinder."

"Leah."

"Ground beef for meatballs."

"Very good."

At recess she goes up to Mia and asks the question that's been on the tip of her tongue ever since.

"Do you eat gefilte fish?"

"Yes."

"Are you . . . Jewish?"

"What?"

"You're not Jewish?"

"No." Mia looks bothered and runs off. But back home Leah tells Mother and Father and Grandpa about the girl in her class who's so dumb she answers "gefilte fish" in front of all the *goyim* in the class, who've never in their lives eaten fishballs with *chren*, red horseradish. How could she be so dumb she thought they'd understand? Leah herself knows exactly how to to keep her home world separate from the world of school, which words you use at home and not at school.

The next day Mia comes up to her.

"I asked my mother, and she says she and her mother and father are Jewish."

"Well, then you are, too."

"No, not me. My dad's Spanish."

"Well, but you're Jewish anyway. It comes from the mother."

"Not me."

Mia's nails are sharp as knives when she pinches her. She's the only one who calls Leah by a nickname. "Lollo," she says, and pinches her.

It's summer vacation the next year and her grades have come. C's, B's, and an A in music. A light rain falls on the grass on top of the root cellar. Way above, up high, out of reach from their children's fingers, are the green cherries. Right now she's sitting at the kitchen table by the window reading a letter from Mia.

"What does she write?" Mother wonders.

"Mostly about her grades and what she's doing this summer."

"How many A's did she get?" Dad interjects.

"Five."

"And you only had one! That's not good!"

Oh. She hadn't thought about that. Up till now, the letters hadn't meant anything to her. Not before now. So you're supposed to get A's.

"Remember, you can lose everything you own, but once you've learned something it's yours forever."

Mother's words are imprinted in her mind.

Dad himself didn't do particularly well in school, mainly because he'd always preferred sports. But now that she has the chance he wants her make up for what he squandered and for opportunities her mother never even had. That's why, from now on, they get together in the living room, he with a pipe in his mouth and with, for instance, her history book in his lap. She sits opposite him, ready for the questions that rain down quick as a whip.

"1066?"

"The Battle of Hastings."

They play this game for many years and both of them love it just as much.

His beaming face and his cheers confirm that by being good at school she can make him happy.

"Give it to them!" he urges her. "Let them see how smart you are. Remember, a Jew always has to be a little better than everyone else to be accepted."

"Oh, that's not the way it is," she says, annoyed. But even so, each year the standards she sets for herself are higher.

For two years she has the round, green teacher in the bright yellow school by the railroad. The teacher watches them exchange bookmarks and pictures of film stars, and she smiles at Leah when Jacob lets her take her turn at baseball.

Yes, that spring, Jacob, with his dark, silky curls and angelic cheeks, joins their class. The icy patches by the fence have melted when he suddenly appears. He brings with him the fragrances of her home world, unfamiliar to everyone except her.

"Jacob is a Jew, did you know that? A Jew! Weird, isn't it? Being a Jew, I mean."

Klas with the red hair draws a swastika on the bench.

"Why don't you tease me? I'm Jewish, too, you know."

"Oh, you . . . you're just like us."

"Yes, but still, I'm Jewish, just as much as he is. So you should tease me, too."

But she isn't new in the class like Jacob. Not now. She'll be new in the fall when she has to leave the "birds." Her family moves outside of town and her new school is made of gray stone. When she arrives summer is over and she has bandages on every finger. Under the bandages are open wounds, but nobody will ever find out that Astrid in second grade gave her warts. No matter how many questions they ask she won't tell what's under the bandages! Having warts is disgusting and shameful, she's realized.

The doctor had to prick her fingertips ten times before it smelled like burnt flesh. A good thing she didn't know then that every single wart would come back in the same place on top of the scars!

But now she's here, wearing bandages that are a deep, dark secret no one knows anything about.

Next to the gray stone school building is their barracks.

They're nine. Anna and she are both new in the class and expectantly join the other children.

And the teacher.

He's small and thin and his brown hair is combed down against his head. She wants to like him. She knows it's possible to like your teacher, and in a strange class in a strange school it's good to be able to like your teacher. It's so different here from what she's used to. She'd had no idea she wasn't good at jump-rope. Nothing she does is right.

"Arms straight up!"

"Attention!"

"At ease, sit down!"

The teacher drills them as if they were a group of soldiers and he the sergeant. He conducts lessons by issuing military commands. Everything is hard. The things that were easy and fun before are boring and hard now. In class her senses seem to have shut down. The only thing she can feel is that her stomach hurts. In bed at night she cries, wishing morning would never come.

And the cat dreams come every night.

When she grows up she'll drop out of school as soon as she can. School is the worst thing she can imagine. The teacher thinks she's a very poor student. She'll barely be able to pass. But Dad doesn't believe that.

"My daughter seems gifted to me," he contradicts the teacher over the phone.

"A stomach ache, right. Every problem is wrong—no doubt that's why you want to go home," says the teacher as she sits with her arithmetic in front of her and a big lump in her throat.

In December they find out that a new girl will be joining the class. The teacher laughs when he writes out her name, which he can't pronounce.

"She can't be from Sweden."

Deep inside she has an inkling of what he's writing, even though he confuses L and Z. It's her own name up there on the board, it's her name everyone is laughing at and no one can pronounce. Yes, that's right, the new girl is called Lujza and comes from Hungary. She'll start after Christmas. That's what they find out the next day, after he's made inquiries. But Leah Louise won't be in the class then.

When Mother takes her to the pediatrician he wants to hospitalize her for observation. She realizes something must be the matter with her since she can't go to school and has a stomach ache. She's on the children's floor for a week, though she's out of bed most of the time. She's not *really* sick, says one of the nurses. But before they're sure they stick funny curlers to her scalp and she has to look at a wavy TV screen. It's called an EEG and if there's something the matter inside your head it shows up on the test. But she's completely normal and gets to go home for Christmas.

After that she takes a bus into town and returns to her green, round, silver-gray teacher. All her classmates laugh and are glad to see her and say they missed her. It doesn't matter that she can't jump rope as well as the others since Helga and she write better essays than anyone else, and by fourth grade they're putting on plays during Show and Tell.

But in fourth grade their new teacher dies, the one they liked so much. He played boogie-woogie on the organ and sang and was almost always in a good mood.

The substitute is stiff and straight-backed and ignores the swastikas. The carefree quality of the yellow school with the big clock is gone forever.

She has so many secrets to keep.

The smell in the lunch room makes her queasy before she's even through the door. When she steps inside and gets in line she hears that the dish is called lung sausage. She's never had that before and the only thing she knows is that the smell makes her stomach turn. But all the children have to eat every day and you're never, ever allowed to leave anything. You can ask for just a little, but that doesn't mean for sure that the ladies who serve the food will give you a small portion. You're never allowed to serve yourself.

"Just a little," she begs in a pleading voice.

Then she sits all through lunch period with the plate in front of her. One of the lunch-line ladies in a white coat and cap has sat down next to her and shakes her head in concern about the child who refuses to eat.

"How will you get by? Going all day without food!"

She can tell by the lady's voice that she's considered a *problem*. It's awful to sit here causing trouble for others, but she can't bring herself even to touch the food. And it never occurs to her that she could tell them she's forbidden to eat this food since she's Jewish.

"What are we to do with the girl?"

Now the lady has turned to one of the others wearing a white coat. Both of them regard her somberly, shaking their heads. Soon she'll be in tears, she can feel them coming as she catches sight of the nasty custodian standing by the wall, the one who yells at them and rules over the long food lines and sees to it that you don't throw the food away. She's very scared, and now she's sure she doesn't belong here. Everybody else eats the food and recognizes it from home. At home she herself has never eaten any of the things they get here in school: blood pudding, kidney hash, sausage. . . She usually tries, holding her breath while she swallows, but today she just can't.

When lunch period is over she's allowed to leave. By then the room has been empty for ages. Her legs tremble when she walks.

It's not always easy to dare to be the person you are, especially when you don't really know who you are and why. She's different. Most of the time she manages to play both roles, at home and in school. Each term she gets better at keeping the two girls separate. There's more and more of the school girl and less and less of the Pinchen-girl, but still.

She's different and feels out of place wherever she goes.

When she's with the other children in the Jewish Association she's Swedish, when she's with her classmates she's Jewish. She doesn't really belong anyplace and wants to belong everywhere.

"Show-off" is what her classmates call her when she tries to be somebody else off-stage. But when she's Jacob's leading lady in the plays they put on during Show and Tell, then she belongs.

Just think if she could be someone else, someone with long hair and small breasts who wasn't so big and clumsy.

"Elephant baby," her mother calls her when she bumps into the furniture at home.

"Look, Leah's got breasts!"

By the time she's eight her gym suit reveals that she's the first one. No matter what she does she can't hide them. When hair starts to grow under her arms and down there, like Mother's, she feels like an abomination, a monster.

"Prematurely developed ... Only nine, and already ... "

She can hear her mother's worried conversation with the doctor. And she tries to avoid being stared at by her classmates after swimming, when you have to take a shower.

"Do you already have hair?"

"No, of course not!"

"I didn't mean ... "

But she has to play hooky from swimming until at least one of her classmates catches up. Meanwhile she refuses to accept what's happening to her body. Before she's ten her period starts.

"Well, sweetie, now you're grown up!"

Mother's voice is full of pity and soon Leah has cramps that make her nauseous and give her diarrhea. It's yet another secret to hide.

Something must be wrong with her. If only she could be someone else.

Leah's little doll with the dark corkscrew curls is a *late* developer.

❧

At the school by the railroad nobody has breasts as big as Bea and Leah. It's torture, since the guys chase them and try to snap their bras and compare whose are biggest.

Both of them feel like great big cows.

And they do their homework and try to outshine each other in class.

At first they're the tallest.

They're taller than Helga who takes posture classes. Her big blue eyes and transparent skin, her round, red lips and straight bangs annoy Bea. Helga's dad is from Austria, but he doesn't live with her mother anymore. Helga is different. Leah knows she's unique. On a shelf in her room are two dolls named Max and Moritz. With all her heart Leah wishes she had two dolls like that. She'd lie right next to them in bed and caress their freckled little faces and red hair. But the dolls belong to Helga. They were a present from her dad.

Leah knows that Helga is a precious stone in the gravel of the school yard. No one else knows. Not Bea, anyway, who one day wants the whole class to gang up on Helga and give her a licking. That makes Leah furious. She goes up to the group and tells them off in her nastiest voice. Then she turns on her heel. Bea doesn't take her eyes off her for a long time.

Leah is the only one who refuses to do what she says. Bea wants to boss everyone around and she does. There's something about her that wins the trust of the teachers. She's the one who's sent to get the books from the storage room. Once when Bea is sick Leah is supposed to bring back the box of extra reading material, but she can't open the door. She fiddles and fiddles with the lock until finally the flimsy key breaks. The teacher never entrusts her with an errand again. Leah isn't someone you can count on, but Bea is.

Her hair is like an angel's, light, long and wavy. When she lets it hang loose it reaches her waist. Sometimes it's Leah's turn to comb it.

Bea lives across the street; she can see the schoolhouse and the green clock from her door. Inside she lives with her mom and dad. She's an only child. She's the only one on earth they love. You can tell.

And Leah is envious. Nobody in the world loves *only* her best.

The school yard is full of slippery patches of ice. The two girls stand there quarreling with each other. Their knitted wool caps have slid down on their foreheads and their red tortoise-shell glasses are foggy from heavy breathing. Bea pushes Leah and now Leah grabs her and swings her to the ground. Her head hits the ice with a thud.

"Oh, dear—are you all right?"

"No problem."

But Bea stays put on the ground for a while. She's holding her head. And then she gets up and goes home.

The next day she's back in school. She lifts off her cap and shows Leah.

"Oh, dear—you don't have any hair left!"

"Do you see the stitches? Doesn't it look dumb?"

"Oh, Bea, I'm sorry! I didn't mean to!"

Leah bites her lip when she sees the stubble and the stitches on Bea's head. Just when it feels as if her heart will break, Bea takes her arm.

"Almost all my hair is left—just a little of it's gone. It was my own fault."

Now she lowers her voice. Hesitant, uncertain, she continues.

"You know, Leah, I want to tell you something. The others are scared of me. I can tell. You're the only one who dares go against me. I don't want the others to be so scared of me. Do you know what I mean? It's awful."

Leah nods.

"I'm not a bit scared of you!" she says. "But you could have *died!*"

"Nah."

Their arms around each other, they go inside.

Excerpted from *Leva vidare*. Translated from the Swedish by Rochelle Wright.

ᚬ Ellen Marie Vars

Ellen Marie Vars (1957–) lives on Finnmarksvidda, the high plateau country in Norway's extreme north, and she writes in Sámi, the language of Scandinavia's indigenous minority. The Sámi live in the Arctic regions of Norway, Sweden, Finland and Russia; they do not recognize national borders, however, and call their country *Sapmi*, a name signifying all of Samiland, from Norway in the west to Russia in the east.

Like Native Americans, the Sámi people have survived cultural oppression and forced assimilation. Their children were required to attend schools where the language of instruction was not their mother tongue and where their own history, religion and culture were ignored if not discredited. This policy was discontinued after the Second World War and the Sámi language has slowly been making a comeback. The Sámi did not have a written literature at that time—as in other traditional cultures, the Sámi had transmitted their legends, stories and epic poems orally. Sámi authors are now writing and publishing their work in their own language, thus helping to kindle and nurture a sense of ethnic pride. Ellen Marie Vars has the distinction of being the first woman to write a novel in the Sámi language! *Kátjá* was published in 1986 and "Boarding School" is a chapter taken from that novel.

Boarding School

The first day at school and the days that followed were all alike. Kátjá quickly learned what it was like to live at the boarding school and attend classes. She didn't understand why no one was supposed to talk about their parents or home, but that was the message she got on the very first evening, when she explained where she was from. The two girls who came over to her looked friendly.

"What's your name, and where are you from?" they asked. Kátjá was eager to answer. She told them about her family back home and about her grandmother.

"Do you have reindeer?" asked the girls.

"No, we don't. We have cows and sheep," Kátjá answered quietly.

The girls sneered. Then one of them kicked her and said, "Then

how come you walk around in a *gákti?** You're not Sámi if you don't
have reindeer. All Sámi kids have reindeer. You can't live at this boarding school, only Sámi kids get to live here!"

They struck at Kátjá and drove her out of the school. Crying, Kátjá
ran away, toward town. On the way she met some children on bicycles. They weren't wearing *gáktis.* One of them pointed at her and
yelled something insulting, but Kátjá didn't understand, because it
was in Norwegian.

The others laughed and mimicked the way the Sámi speak Norwegian. They pushed their bicycles threateningly at Kátjá, who became so frightened that she turned and ran back toward the school.
But they caught up with her, tore off her cap, and threw it in the
ditch.

She didn't dare retrieve it, she just ran away as fast as she could.
Scared to death, she looked desperately for a place to hide at the boarding school. She saw a cabinet in a corner, standing a bit away from the
wall. She squeezed herself behind it, closed her eyes tightly, and pressed
her hand over her mouth, so no one would hear her cry.

"If I close my eyes tightly enough, maybe I'll be with Grandma,"
she thought. Grandma! It was a long time before she dared move.
Finally, she couldn't stand to stay squeezed behind the cabinet any
longer. Cautiously she crept out, looked around, listened and waited.
The coast was clear. She quickly sneaked out to look for her cap. There
it lay, at the edge of the road, embedded with sticky clay. She dashed
back, found a bathroom in the school, and began to scrub her cap.
Most of the dirt disappeared, but the lump in her throat remained.

Days, evenings and nights were equally horrible. Kátjá was always
hungry, but she couldn't get herself to eat. She just cried. None of the
grownups, not even the teacher, asked her why she cried so much.
Nor did they concern themselves with the fact that the other children
hit her, even though they often saw it happen. The children hit and
kicked her and pulled her hair, but the adults didn't do a thing to stop

---

*Sámi traditional folk dress

them. Before long, Kátjá hated all the grownups and the migrant Sámi children, who picked on her the most. Picked on her because her parents didn't own reindeer.

"You're poor," they teased. "People who don't have reindeer are just poor trash."

She had no friends, but then she didn't feel like playing with anyone, anyway, because she was so homesick. Her body ached all the time, too, but it was the homesickness that hurt the most. The mere thought of Grandmother brought tears to her eyes, even in the classroom. But Grandmother was far away.

"If I only knew the way home, I'd run away now!" Kátjá often thought during class time.

The first snow fell, but it didn't cheer Kátjá up. Back home, this was always a big event. Grandmother used to wake her up early with a secretive whisper, "Look out the window, little helper!"

And Kátjá would run to the window before she was fully awake. Her sleepiness vanished when she saw the pure, white snow. It was always so nice! Afterwards, she would cozy up to Grandmother again.

But here, at the boarding school, there was no one who cared about Grandma or the new snow. One day, when the air was thick with snow, Biret came up to her and said that Father would come in two days to bring them home for Christmas.

Home! To Grandmother. Tears began to run down her cheeks and her heart pounded. Grandma!

When she arrived home, she threw herself onto Grandmother's lap and sobbed so that her entire little body shook. She clung to Grandmother. It was as though she no longer had any words, only tears.

Grandmother stroked her face and spoke to her lovingly.

Kátjá cried for the longest time, until she fell asleep in Grandmother's lap. Grandmother carried her to bed.

"Can school be good for Sámi children?" she sighed. Her eyes were full of sadness as she looked at her little helpmate, lying there asleep. "Poor little thing. I wonder what you have been through. And this is just the beginning!" She sat a long time beside the sleeping child.

She remembered the night when Kátjá was born during terrible weather. Was that a sign that hers would be a stormy life?

"Dear Lord, please give her the strength to make it through!"

The long, sad winter finally ended. The sun shone behind the pale clouds, and with the sun there was spring in the air.

But for Kátjá, it didn't feel like spring. She couldn't hear or smell spring's arrival while she was in school. She often thought about that as she stared out the window during the endless afternoons after classes.

"Why is the spring sun so strange and cold here? Back home it's so warm. I'll bet it has melted some of the snow already. At least enough so that Father can find dry ground for his campfire, and he can boil coffee when he's out duck hunting. I wonder if he has gotten many birds this year. What if my little brother is big enough now to run out and meet Father when he comes home from duck hunting? Maybe he's even learned the names for all the different kinds of birds. I wonder if Father misses me when I'm not around to ask what happened on his hunting trip. Mother probably doesn't have time to ask which birds have already arrived. And Grandma doesn't need to ask Father about anything. She already knows everything.

"Oh, how I wish I could watch when the ice breaks up! Go along with Mother and Father when they put the boat in the water. Row between the ice floes. That used to be so much fun!"

When the ice broke up, they went out and set the nets. Father always brought along the shotgun on trips like that. He could hear the ducks long before they came near. He would quickly fasten the net to the boat and get out his shotgun. Kátjá used to duck down in the front of the boat and wait anxiously. You could hear the longtails a mile away. They flew in flocks and made a big racket. The common scoters would show up suddenly, only two or three at a time. She had never really figured out how they made that pretty whistling sound when they flew. What if Father had gotten a wild goose! How she longed to be along on a duck hunting trip. Just think of coming home with all the birds Father had shot and proudly showing them to Grandma!

The food at the boarding school seemed even more unappetizing when she thought about fresh roast duck.

But spring brought summer, and Kátjá's first year at school finally came to an end.

It was strange to come back to the familiar tundra. As soon as the school bus pulled up, they could see Father sitting there, a short distance away, boiling coffee. Kátjá felt that she had come home.

She ran to him. Her feet felt so light. Father! Father!

He stood up and lifted her up onto his shoulders, saying, "Why, honey, you don't weigh a thing! How thin you've gotten. Here, first you have to eat some of this jerky, so you'll have the strength to walk home."

But Kátjá couldn't calm down enough to sit and eat. She had to run around, for she had suddenly become so light. It was almost as though she were flying.

The walk home was as in a dream. Kátjá walked ahead of the others along the crooked path, anxious to see whether they would be home soon. When Father stopped at their usual resting place, she didn't have the least interest in taking a break. It took the others, all of whom had things to carry, such a long time to eat and rest.

When they came closer to home, they began to trot. Even Biret, who had the most to carry. Kátjá saw Grandmother standing there, in the distance. She had come to meet them!

"Grandma!"

Kátjá set off running toward her. The path disappeared in a mist of tears, and she stumbled. She got up quickly and ran on. Grandmother almost toppled over when Kátjá threw herself around her neck.

"Grandma, you smell so good." Kátjá cried as she spoke.

"Little helper, how pale you are. Don't you eat anything at school?"

Kátjá didn't answer, she just kept her arms around Grandmother, afraid that the old woman might disappear if she let go. The others caught up, and they continued on toward the house. Grandmother told about everything that had happened while they were away. Kátjá's little brother was a big boy now, good at helping. The cat had had kittens, and in the barn were three new calves, and Father had bought a new boat and net. A big boat with plenty of room for fish.

Grandmother hadn't heard the cuckoo yet, which she thought was odd. Kátjá stopped. "Look, Grandmother, the trees here have already begun to turn green, but at school they are just dark and ugly."

Only when they had come inside, and Kátjá had eaten all she wanted, did she realize how tired out she was.

She asked Grandmother to lie down with her on the reindeer skin in the corner of the room and tell some more about everything that had happened while she had been away at school. Grandmother told about the spring flood and about all the fishing and hunting trips. She kept on talking, long after Kátjá had been lulled to sleep by her warm voice.

Kátjá opened her eyes, surprised. Was she still dreaming? She saw the little room at home and heard familiar voices! She quickly closed her eyes again, in order to hold onto her dream. She lay quite still. Slowly, a feeling of happiness came over her. She was home! Kátjá got up and ran to the kitchen. Gone were the school and all the hardships she had endured. She sat down on Mother's lap, ravenous once again. It was lovely to be home again, just like before, and to eat Mother's good food. Mother and Father asked about school, but Kátjá didn't answer. It was just too painful to think or talk about. She couldn't find words terrible enough to describe the school. Kátjá kept on eating in silence. Ate and ate, as though she hadn't tasted food in years! At last she felt full. She couldn't stand to sit inside any longer. She had to see absolutely everything! First, the new boat. Wow, so big! It has to be the biggest boat in the whole world. There must be room for hundreds and hundreds—no, thousands and thousands of fish!

She hopped and jumped across the meadow, filled with bubbly joy. It was so good to just run, free of pain and hardship, with no fear of being beaten up or teased!

Suddenly she stopped. There was the cuckoo! She stood completely still, listening. Then she began to run. She had to tell Grandma that the cuckoo had come! Grandma, who always says that summer is really on its way when the cuckoo calls.

Kátjá played with her little brother, Joavnna. She went and got pieces of wood from the shed to represent the teacher and the housemother.

"The housemother is a strange lady who always says that I'm dirty. She talks really funny, and she smells funny, too," Kátjá explained. Her little brother listened, round-eyed.

"The housemother never answers when I ask her anything, and she doesn't care when the big kids hit the little ones. She is really stupid." Kátjá hit the "housemother" log with a twig. Joavnna helped. They hit and pounded for all they were worth. It was fun to give the stupid housemother a good beating.

"The teacher is an idiot, too," said Kátjá. "She never says a word to the other kids when they make fun of me because I can't speak Norwegian. The teacher doesn't understand a thing, so she gets a beating, too!"

Kátjá and her little brother punished the housemother and teacher for quite a while. It was good for the stupid women to get a sound beating. They deserved to suffer, too. Joavnna heard all about the Norwegians; that it was people like that whom all children had to fear and obey, because if they didn't, they got their ears pinched and were sent to stand in the corner. "At school you're not allowed to talk about your family or home, and in the boarding house you have to fight all the time," Kátjá continued. "You have to watch out, otherwise you get a beating or your clothes get spoiled." Her little brother's eyes grew dark with indignation. "They laugh because Grandma can't speak a word of Norwegian, and because Mother and Father don't have reindeer, they just have *gáktis*."

They sat talking like this for a long time. Joavnna understood that the school was a bad place, and he promised that, when he started to go there, he would flatten the whole lot of them if they so much as came near Kátjá.

The summer went quickly, and the time for school to begin approached. All summer, Kátjá brooded over how she would manage to stand another year. She and her little brother came to the conclusion that a person had to be really mean in order to survive at the school. Kátjá decided that no one would get the chance to beat her up again. All summer, she and her little brother practiced fighting.

But she had a stomach ache for several days before school began, because she worried so much. On her last night at home, she clung to Grandmother. When morning arrived, she begged Grandmother to come along with her to school. But Grandmother couldn't, and Kátjá had to leave the warmth and safety of her grandmother and family. She followed reluctantly behind Father and the others.

The school year went all right, in a way. Each day was as dismal and long as the one before, with nothing to especially enjoy. Kátjá taught herself to be as hard as a rock, just in order to survive at the boarding school. Never again did she cry when others could see her; but not a single, long night went by without her pillow's being wet.

She would never depend on anyone again, either, never tell anyone about herself, never expose her feelings.

Here a person ate at mealtimes, even if they weren't hungry. When a person really was hungry, there was no food to be had between meals. Everything she had learned not to do at home, she had to do at school and in the boarding house.

Life at the school was the opposite of home. She had to force herself to put up with it all. She got to feel in earnest what it means to not be a migratory Sámi child.

"You are nothing," said the children of reindeer owners. "Don't think you are Sámi, because you aren't," she heard every day at the boarding house. At school she was made to see that she wasn't Norwegian, either, that she didn't have Norwegian clothes. The kids at church pestered her constantly.

Kátjá couldn't understand why it had to be this way, why they thought she was so different. She soon began to hate them because she couldn't understand. She was filled with hate toward everyone and everything that had anything to do with school. Her hatred made her unafraid, dangerous. She could fight; she no longer feared anyone. Even the biggest children grew wary of her when they discovered how diabolically naughty she had become. She was small but quick and strong, and she despised everyone. She couldn't care less about the housemother, stuck out her tongue and spoke nothing but Sámi, so the woman didn't understand a word. The other children approached her with caution, suddenly wanting to be friends with Kátjá, who was so good at fighting. But she didn't want to be anyone's friend. She just wanted to be left alone.

Kátjá stopped smiling. She kept to herself, and she was left alone. No one teased her, no one hurt her, and no one dared fight with her anymore.

Excerpted from *Kátjá*. Translated from the Norwegian by Edi Thorstensson.

ℛ Camilla Collett

Camilla Collett (1813–1895) is the grand old lady of Norwegian literature. In her first novel, *The District Governor's Daughters,* she portrays a spirited girl who resists conforming to the prescribed female role of securing her economic future through marriage to a husband chosen by her parents. The heroine in Collett's novel wants to study and learn, develop her talents and put them to good use.

That same spirit is evident in the little girl Collett depicted in her memoir, *During the Long Nights.* The title alludes to sleepless nights and the author introduces herself as a Scheherazade who will entertain those who, like herself, can't sleep at night with stories of her childhood. The book is divided into nights instead of chapters, and the following excerpt is taken from two "nights."

The first story describes a sea voyage the family took when they moved from Kristiansand to Eidsvoll, and Collett recalls the perfection of the summer evening on which her father rechristened her with the name, Camilla, that would bring her fame for generations to come.

The second story recounts the trials Camilla experienced at a boarding school far from home and how she won her first girl friend.

The Hunger Trial

The sea voyage to Christiania* lasted fourteen whole days—that was not uncommon in those days, although now it sounds almost like a fairy tale. Imagine fourteen days with five small children in a little boat. Mother told us often in later years about the difficulties and occasional dangers we had to face, but never really as if there had been anything unpleasant or upsetting about it. I think people had a different constitution in those days—they were stronger in both soul and body, they didn't complain as much. And what could be unbearable to a vigorous married couple, happy people who loved each other and saw life stretching ahead of them in a rosy haze. Poor Father and Mother! I dare say I must have had a confused impression of an eternal,

---

*Present day Oslo

143

endlessly rocking cradle, and that there was no longer firm ground to walk upon. I remember only that on a clear, still June evening we cast anchor on a little island a few miles from Christiania and that I believed we had arrived in Paradise. The whole shore seemed to be strewn with beautiful white bells of saxifrage and I sat in the midst of this billowing meadow in a state of quiet rapture. My little brothers climbed happily among the flat stones. Father stood near me, his then still trim figure and his fine pale face rosily illuminated by the evening sun. Inside the cabin Mother and the maid were busy making tea and cooking fish. Then she came to the door with my youngest brother in her arms and called to me, *"Bina! Bina!"* Father beckoned her down to him. "From now on she will not be called 'Bina,' we'll call her by her other christening name instead." Camilla—the name of the role Mother had played so brilliantly! This was said in his own characteristic way, in which there was no possibility of contradiction. I instantly felt a secret delight at the new name and never failed to remind people when they got it wrong. Whenever my brothers and sister wanted to annoy me, they called me "Bina," until the hated name finally died away. Well, people may have their own thoughts about this, but I think that the name one gets at one's christening is not without a secret, unconscious influence on the individual. *Noblesse oblige* they say, and I believe that about names as well, that they carry obligations with them; I am even convinced that a person who is called "Coelestine," must necessarily develop differently than someone called "Stine." Bettina Brentano[†] would hardly have written her earthshaking letters had she simply been called "Tina." Many a "Tina" or "Stina" has merited another name and will always feel a kind of disharmony, a gap between herself and her name that she cannot manage to fill. Conversely, a brilliant and demanding name can redound in a parodic way upon its owner. It's quite another matter if I personally have had reason to congratulate myself on my rechristening. Perhaps

---

[†]Bettina Brentano (1785-1859), a German writer who published her correspondence with Goethe.

I would have become a more useful, happier, more respected and fa-vored member of society if I had kept my modest, household, "Bina" name, which moreover has a venerable tradition in the family be-cause so many in my mother's line have held it. . . .

☙

From those years when I stood on the borderline of my childhood, I see a picture rise up which I can banish no longer. Often, for long periods, it lay buried, before awaking once again at quiet moments, equally fresh, delightful, and full of life—but I have never been tempted to drag it out of its hiding place and expose it to other people. The name that attaches itself to this picture, I have named through every step of a first passionate friendship; I have named it every day, every hour, in dreams, until suddenly one day my soul closed itself around this name and I have never, never spoken it since. It was the name of one of my school friends, and she was called Christiane Schoulz.

At the age of fourteen I was sent down to Christiansfeldt, where I was to stay until I reached my sixteenth birthday. I believe the idea for that was principally awakened by a dazzling, but utterly superficial description that a traveler, after only a single day's visit to the place, had written for the newspaper. There was so much that was good and decent underlying this establishment that one must beware of mis-judging; but what is true about this one, is true about all of its kind—it is not suited for everyone. It cannot manage, just as little as any other school in which education is a wholesale business, to provide each individuality, each soul, its unique provision. For many natures it could perhaps be a tranquil, highly beneficial transition to the life they would lead subsequently, and I have heard children raised in a worldly way praise the peaceful time in Christiansfeldt as the happi-est in their lives. For many unhappy children it was a blessed haven, where they could sometimes calm themselves for life. For me it was isolation, loneliness, only in another, more cloistered form than I had been used to. But the goal is really not that you be initiated into the life of a cloister but that you learn to make your way in the world afterwards. You should learn to know yourself and your talents and powers and whether they are equal to the battles that will inevitably come. . . .

But back to Christiane's first period in the academy. That I felt powerfully drawn to her, everyone can imagine. But there was also in her, as in her sister, a kind of dignified reserve, and she was also shy, but in a different way than I was. You understood that with all of her shyness, she was brought up in the world; she had confidence, dignity; she effortlessly discharged all the little daily duties which in an academy have to be performed to the minute, with a sheer perfection from which I unfortunately was far removed. So I never came any closer to her. I looked up at her adoringly; she was also half a head taller than me. How could I, who signified so little to the other children, hope to win her friendship? And still I was impelled by a powerful need to make myself understood by her, the first person in the world to whom I thought I had something to say. With all the eccentricity of my age, I desired an opportunity to show myself great, remarkable, to her. Chance is indeed every fool's guardian; so an opportunity was not long in coming.

I was in weakened health at that time and quite a pitiful little husk to look at, the consequence, I believe, of the rather sharp and dry climate at home, which has a debilitating effect on constitutions of a certain kind. But I developed in the same way as young turkeys, which are so difficult to keep alive in infancy; when we have reached a certain age, things even up and we get along fairly well. Among the other girls there was a quadroon from St. Thomas named Anna Friborg. This Anna was not one of the ferns;‡ she was utterly a product of her

‡In one of the early sections of Collette's memoir, she speaks of a group of older girls who bullied the younger students. Like ferns, they were common plants that spread and thrived, choking out the smaller, more worthy species.

own distant zone, a cactus with sudden, fiery-red blossoms, sharp thorns and bizarre leaves—to me, however, an impossibility, a perfect, exotic, mysterious being, just as I must have seemed to her. She was beautiful and gracious, even charming on occasion, but so curiously passionate and moody. For whole weeks she could be melancholy and withdrawn, then excessively merry again, as if possessed by a teasing demon. In the crazy gibberish she called English/German/Danish, her teasing most often only brought forth laughter. The fact that I, frail in health and pampered at home, had trouble tolerating the academy's early rising time and strict daily regimen gave her particular material for mockery.

One day Anna attacked me in this way while some of the other children and Christiane were in the vicinity. One word led to another, and to convince them once and for all that I didn't deserve their accusations of sensitivity and softness, I vowed I would undertake to live on four shillings a day for eight days and strictly eat nothing but what I could get for those four shillings. This was very amusing indeed, but the vow was received and sealed with all formalities, and we all agreed to take care that the teachers not discover it. That I was eating bread and milk while the others had tea could be explained on dietetic grounds. We ate in two dining rooms. If I wasn't in one, then I had to be in the other. It really was a terrible promise, more terrible than I had imagined. And it had to be kept. If you think about my relationship to those children who tortured and misunderstood me, to Christiane, whose friendship I wanted to win, whatever the cost, then you can understand that I had to keep it if it cost my life. Very seriously I prepared myself to begin the hunger trial. My dear listeners, shall I tell you how I did it? Yes, why not! I haven't promised anything other or more than what I have experienced myself, and if you fall asleep at my story—well, God bless you, that's the best thing that could happen to you!

The struggles of those days are strangely clear in my memory, to the smallest detail, as if they had happened last week. Saturday the trial was to begin and in the morning I bought two shillings worth of bread, a shilling's worth of milk, and one of fruit. It went tolerably that day, sliding on the coattails of the previous day. Even now I see the jug with the rosy red landscape, containing the white elixir of life, from which I took nearly a half-pint at a time. Sunday was worse. Going to church exhausted me, and it was more difficult than I had thought to be reverent when you had fasted for a day. In the evening we strolled around the beautiful Christineruhe, a park given to the village by a pious, deceased estate owner who had lived nearby. Within these establishments, you walked in pairs, everybody all together, you could only choose the person to walk with. In the woods the flock could be escaped and you played and mingled as you pleased. During the course of such a walk, you could run into boys with their herds—a half smile, quick sidelong glance, but quite mute as they wandered by. It was a lovely, warm September evening. On the path I stopped by a blackberry bush, intending to pick some berries; from that a dispute developed about whether it was permissible. Some of the more tenderhearted thought blackberries were not included in the prohibition. But the more legalistic heads reasserted what had been said: "what a person could buy for four shilling." These blackberries were not bought and it was thereby decided: blackberries were not allowed.

Monday was no worse. I bought the same ingredients, only a slightly more substantial bread. The evening, however, offered a difficult rock to get past. Following an old custom, something superior was served each Monday, a warm dish, for instance. *Gott, die Arme!* [§] I heard one of the children say when I was leaving the room. It helps to get a good night's sleep. But it was less pleasant to get up at quarter past five to clean two rooms. A young Swedish Baroness and I had to do it that week. Monday evening Christiane asked me if I would do her a favor; would I switch weeks with her because she wanted so much to be free the next week. Rather naively I believed this was the reason and I was doing her a great service.

[§] "God, the poor thing!"

Tuesday was bad, worse even than I imagined such a trial could be, and I still had three days left. To lose my grip would be the most miserable fiasco, so it was a matter of hanging on. In the evening while the others sat down for dinner I had just enough strength to bolt away into a side room and burst into violent tears; but because nobody must see this sign of weakness I went down to the orchard. The remainder of my scanty rations I had already consumed that afternoon with the ravenous hunger of a true fifteen-year-old. There was no more left for today.

The orchard abounded with fruit. However, there was an implicit point of honor among us older, nearly grown-up girls—that we wouldn't touch an apple even if it had fallen. That was something little children would do. And we held this rule so strictly that we would incur a self-contempt worse than that of others if we sinned against it. At this sharpened appeal to be stoical and not give way, I tried as well as I could to overcome my stomach's growling protests. And one is stoical when one is fifteen years old. I sat down in front of a pear tree and surrendered myself to my reflections, among others my thoughts flew away toward Eden's first days, and I cannot deny I thought about our celebrated Mother Eve with less friendly, less respectful feelings. Oh Eve, Eve, what a deficiency in strength of soul you showed. Not enough the general misery you have introduced into the world, but the shame you have brought upon your poor daughters! That load of prejudice and stereotyped accusation we must drag along for all eternity. Now every male person who shakes the tree of knowledge to his heart's content has permission to call us names—your daughters, Eve. And every schoolboy plundering the neighbor's plum tree follows their example. Oh, Eve, Eve, who didn't even have to live like I do on four shillings a day, but reveled in the gardens of Paradise. Perhaps you, on that very day, had eaten roast pheasant, peach compote, and strawberries with cream and God knows what, and still were going to lay hands on that unfortunate apple! If it had at least been a pear, of exactly the same kind as these hanging here—

Dear friends, are you asleep? Good. Then only a word before I go on. I lie when I say that I gave that speech while I sat in front of the pear tree that evening. No, I didn't give it there. The most I thought was that pears are greatly preferable to apples, although apples are also very delicious fruit. I confuse these reflections with others that I made on later occasions—and oh! there have been no lack of occasions. You laugh at my fancy of wanting to be stoical, you are scandalized perhaps, you call it affectation, fanaticism, madness. Oh, I think there is a deep, serious wisdom underlying it. These youthful trials of strength, some of which you yourselves surely remember having performed, are these unthinking games anything less than an ominous prelude to an entire existence? In Sparta, young people frequently practiced enduring pain. Hunger and flogging were subjects in school there—like geometry and feminine neatness are in ours—all to toughen them for their destiny: war. So should every single academy for female education set up some weekly trials of strength. I know and could suggest a number of ingenious ones. You never know how useful such exercises might be. What do you think of a hunger trial for the heart? The heart when it comes with its immoderate demands. It doesn't want to subsist, it wants to gorge in the Garden of Paradise and it only has four shillings to live on, and—no blackberries allowed.

The next day, Wednesday, I didn't feel well and in the morning got permission to go to bed. Milk and bread didn't taste right to me, which was indeed gratifying, it was so much more economical! I lay in a doze the greatest part of the day, but awoke to see Christiane kneeling beside the bed, her eyes streaming with tears, begging me to stop the trial, otherwise she was going to tell on me. That it hadn't happened already will perhaps seem unbelievable; it has often occurred to me how strange it was. In order that no self-reproach or lapse of memory should mislead me, I recently talked with a teacher from that period who lives here in town. She said it was the two dining rooms, and the fact that nobody could imagine the truth because a trick like that had no place in any of their experiences—that had kept it hidden. But back to Christiane. If she gave me away, I don't know, but somebody gave me away. Dr. M. came—he was nobody to trifle with; he interrogated me sharply, prescribed a cup of good tea and some strong drops, and in the evening this little tragicomedy ended, satisfactorily I believe for all parties concerned, and with that I'll end my story for tonight. . . .

Christiane's and my friendship was sealed by the hunger trial.

Excerpted from *I de lange Nætter.* Translated from the Norwegian by Judith Messick.

◎ Tove Nilsen

Tove Nilsen (1952–) is a contemporary Norwegian novelist with a strong feel for the rhythms of urban life. In her novel *Skyscraper Angels,* Nilsen uses her own experiences growing up in the '50s in the first highrise apartment complex built in Oslo.

The residents live and breathe the life of the apartment building:

> Day breaks and a gray apartment building is no
> longer so gray. A windowshade goes up on the
> third floor; on the first floor someone turns on
> a kitchen light; a comforter is hung out to air
> on the seventh, and on the balcony of the twelfth,
> a black silhouette appears. . . .
>
> Alarm clocks ring, pipes rattle, doors bang, shoes
> clatter through the hallways, down the stairs, the
> elevator hums up and down. The apartment is as
> alive as a teeming anthill, as a giant, well-ordered
> hive: a couple of hundred people are on the go
> again.

The highrise is like a vertical village where the child's world can easily intersect with the adult's—a stimulating environment for adventuresome and enterprising girls like Tove and her friend, Rita.

Raffle Tickets

"First we'll go to Mrs. Bruun," says Rita. "Old ladies always buy raffle tickets."

We've finally gotten hold of a book of raffle tickets in an attempt to make our always shaky finances go further. Mrs. Bruun is one of the few old people in our apartment building. She's over seventy and always goes around in a black coat that sweeps the floor, with a boa that drapes around her shoulders like a many-headed dragon with teeth and claws. Mrs. Bruun isn't your sweet kindly grandma type.

She is a big truck of a woman with a hawk nose and messy hair, who is usually muttering irritably to herself.

"Can't we try picking bouquets of white anemones instead?"

"You know what would happen then. We'd risk just getting a *thank you*. Don't you remember the time we dragged home all those bottles of milk for Goggen's mother and all we got for it was a dry old waffle each?"

"Sure, but what if she figures out it's a scam?" I object uneasily. "It must be a crime. Maybe we'll be expelled from school and have to pay a fine."

Rita has only to look at me to tell me what a pitiful coward I am.

We ring the doorbell of Mrs. Mimi Caspara Bruun. I hold the yellow raffle book. Rita has the notebook and pencil. First there's a series of explosions, as if someone is choking to death inside. That's the lap dog. Then Mrs. Bruun comes shuffling, shuffling, shuffling in felt slippers. She sticks her hawk nose out between the door and the security chain.

"Hello!" we curtsey in unison. "We wonder if you'd like to buy a raffle ticket?"

"What cause does it benefit?" asks Mrs. Bruun and squints suspiciously at us. The lap dog gurgles angrily between her slippers.

"Starving children in India and Africa," I say, my tongue as dry as blotting paper.

"What does it cost?"

"Fi . . ."

"One krone apiece," says Rita and curtseys deeply again.

"All right, you better come in then." Mrs. Bruun removes the chain. "If it had been for a marching band or some such spectacle, I would have said no. But starving children. Hector! It's only two sweet little girls!"

Rita pinches me triumphantly in the side and nudges me forward through the door into the entry. I lift my feet high and wait for the jaws of the lapdog to grip my ankle any second.

"My, my, starving children," mumbles Mrs. Bruun and shuffles into the dim interior while she coaxes the little dog in front of her.

All apartments have their smell. At Rita's it smells of the camphor wood chest her father brought back from the Orient. At Siri's it smells of wet diapers. At my house it doesn't smell of anything but home. Here it stinks of mothballs and the Norwegian Folk Museum.

"Come on into the living room, little girls."

"Go on!" whispers Rita and sticks her index finger like a pistol into my ribs while she shoves me through dusty velvet drapery with silk tassels.

The living room is full of dark furniture and potted plants. On the window sill is a Norwegian flag on a silver stand, along with the Stars and Stripes. Under the coffee table lies the dog with the whites of its eyes showing.

We seat ourselves on the edges of our chairs.

Mrs. Bruun shuffles out to the kitchen. "When is the drawing?"

Bewildered, we look at each other. It's embarrassing, but we hadn't thought about that.

"In the fall," calls Rita quickly.

"Really? That's a long time off."

"It's because it's such a big raffle, you see."

"Oh well, then. What can I win?"

"A piano for first prize, a fruit basket for the second prize and a comb, brush and mirror set for the third," Rita informs her without blinking.

From the kitchen comes the sound of clattering and rattling.

"What's she doing out there?" I whisper.

"How should I know?" Rita makes faces at the dog under the coffee table. It's worn itself out completely and lies there gasping asthmatically while its fat belly goes in and out like a pair of bellows.

"No, piano playing is something I won't have in the house. There are enough men knocking at my door. How about some juice, girls? And some little sandwiches?"

The old lady stands in the doorway with a plate and mugs.

I'd give anything to get out of here as fast as possible, but Rita smiles and nods obsequiously. Mrs. Bruun bends over so her house dress slips up. The brown stockings end in a roll over her knees; above them her thighs are pale and doughy with thick blue knots.

"I was married once to the Duke of Luxembourg, you know," says Mrs. Bruun and points toward a picture of an old guy with a handlebar mustache who's wearing a uniform.

"Were you?" It's the first time I've been presented to the Duke of Luxembourg. All I can say is that he's not handsome. It looks like he's been cut off at the chin and has his cheeks stuffed with warm potatoes.

"But *I'm* not someone to play second fiddle to anyone!"

A strange sound comes from Rita. Her face is bright red.

"I've never in my life played second fiddle. So when he took after Josefine Charlotte, I gave him back all his jewelry, emeralds, rubies, everything. And then I left for New York."

"You've been to New York!"

"I passed the best years of my life over there." With the gesture of a movie star, Mrs. Bruun pushes her disheveled hair back and reveals an unusually long and meaty earlobe with pearls. "The earrings are from over there. I wore them when I danced the polonaise with President Roosevelt. Of course that was before he became paralyzed. Now you little girls must eat as much as you like," smiles Mrs. Bruun, with a faraway look.

Finally. Our hands shoot out at the same time. Open-faced sandwiches with brown goat cheese. The cheese looks dry and splintered, but Rita and I are always hungry. I sink my teeth in and stiffen on my chair. Rita coughs unrestrainedly; the crumbs spew out.

"Eat up. And you'll get your dessert, Sweetie," Mrs. Bruun says to the dog and shambles out to the kitchen again.

I spit out my bite and look under the cheese. "She's put mustard instead of butter on these."

"I *know*," groans Rita. She sticks her tongue out and points at her head to show the old lady is nuts. "Maybe he'd also like a little food?" she asks hopefully and looks under the table.

"Oh, no, Hector only eats cocktail wieners and mocha chocolates." The pug snaps at the chocolate Mrs. Bruun holds out and growls at the hand with the bread and cheese.

"What a strange name he has," I say, taking a gulp of juice.

"Because of his daring. Only for that reason." Mrs. Bruun throws her hands out in that movie star way again. "It was Hector who slew Patroklos, you know. Son of Priamos, married to Andromache."

Nobody from our apartment building. I sweat and chew, the mustard stinging my tongue and the brown cheese clinging to the roof of my mouth. Damn that Rita; she's cruised through the mustard sandwiches, no sweat.

"In America everyone has his own bungalow," explains Mrs. Bruun, nodding towards the Stars and Stripes.

"We know that very well," answers Rita. "My father has been there many times."

"There, a lady is treated like a lady. It's not like here, where no one . . . " Mrs. Bruun's voice suddenly gets thick; she blinks, quick and odd like a hen, and stares at her lap.

Only the frankfurter under the table breaks the silence with his panting. I sneak the last bite of sandwich into my pants pocket and glance uneasily at Rita.

"I think we should . . . "

"In American everybody has his own car, too," sniffs Mrs. Bruun and looks reproachfully at us.

"We know that, but I think we have to go now," explains Rita. "We've just begun to make our rounds, and . . . "

"At the very least, one is *respected* there."

We get up.

Mrs. Bruun looks up with a sharp glance. "Do you have to go? As you wish! Hector and I are planning to take a nap anyway, so it suits us just fine."

Rita clears her throat. "Aren't you going to have a raffle ticket?"

"Raffle ticket? Oh the raffle. For the starving children." Mrs. Bruun gets on her feet. "How much did you say it cost?"

"A krone each."

"Then I'll take two, one for Hector and one for me. Normally we're not gamblers, but this time I'll make an exception."

Rita writes it down, untroubled, while my hands sweat as I tear off the raffle ticket.

"Now, the money." Mrs. Bruun shuffles out to the kitchen. "Come here, and I'll give it to you."

In passing, I glance at the picture of the Duke of Luxembourg. Next to him hangs a certificate, made out to Johan Bruun, thanking him for long and loyal service to the Norwegian Railroad, 1924–51.

Out in the kitchen we open our eyes wide. There stand boxes full of dirt with green sprouts; the boxes are everywhere, on the counters and tables and close together on the floor. There is only a narrow passage to get through.

"Wow! What's this?"

"What? Oh, they're my potatoes," says Mrs. Bruun and counts up small change from a bowl. "Cultivating potatoes is something more people should do. Then there would be less knocking on doors and begging for food."

I'm putting the money quickly in my pocket, ready to leave, when the old gal suddenly grabs my wrist. Like a wrinkled claw her hand grips mine hard. The skin is covered with brown spots, witch's spots. Help, we've been caught. Now comes the punishment for lying.

"Are you the ones who put out rumors that I'm chasing after truck drivers?" hisses Mrs. Bruun and sticks her hawk nose down in my face.

"No way!"

"Oh I hear well enough how they whisper and gossip. But I want you to know, I don't get mixed up with just anyone!"

"Come on, Tove!" Rita pulls at my arm so that the old gal has to let go. We hurry out through the entryway smelling of the folk museum. The felt slippers scuffle after us. The lap dog comes gurgling too. Open the door!

"I have plenty of offers, I'll have you know. I don't need to lie

down in the back of a truck," the witch-like voice calls after us.
" . . . And I don't want to be dealing with any piano crate."

We run down the hallway. Down the stairs. Our hearts are hammering; money burning in our pockets. Not until we're out on the
path do we stop and look at each other. Yikes! But we did it. We have
sold our first raffle ticket. Fingers pointing at our foreheads, we begin
to yell: "There's a hole in the fence at the loony-bin. There's a hole in
the fence at the loony bin, a hole in the fence at the loo-ooony bin.
And that's why we are here!"

In front of the newsstand is Silda, with a cardboard box between his
legs. Some big boys exchange something or other with him, before
they give a military salute and go their separate ways. We crowd curiously up to him. There are white mice in the box. It's full of them
creeping and crawling down there.

Silda put out a hand. "Two fifty for one, four for two."

"But where have you gotten all these from?" we ask, beside ourselves with excitement.

"My brother and I started with two each a few months ago. They
have babies all the time, the creepy little things just leap out, between
seven and ten in a row."

"Are you allowed to have so many mice?"

"Not by my mother, but she can't do anything, because she doesn't
dare touch them. My father says it's all right, as long as they make a
profit," Silda tells us with satisfaction.

"How much have you earned then?"

"Twenty-seven kroner so far. I started with forty-two mice a half-
hour ago. Now I have thirty-eight left."

Rita does a quick calculation. "Forty-two at two-fifty, that's a hundred and five kroner!"

Silda nods with an oily grin.

Meanwhile we've spent a half hour earning a krone each, and on
top of that being scolded and practically poisoned, too.

"You probably give a discount to people you know?" asks Rita sweetly.

"Are you stupid or what? I know at least half my customers. If I did that I'd go broke for sure. I don't throw money out of the window either." Silda shakes his head firmly and refuses any form of bargaining.

"Can we owe you half a krone then, so we have enough for one?"

"There's no sense in just having one. Don't you understand anything, Tove!" Rita gives me a warning nudge. "Listen, we're going around selling raffle tickets. They cost a krone apiece. We'll give you five raffle tickets free if we can have two mice."

Silda hesitates. "What would I win?"

"First prize is scuba-diving equipment. Second is an Indian tent, and third is a tool box. With five raffle tickets you have a good chance of winning, right?"

Silda looks down in the box. "All right then." He selects two mice. "Here's a boy and here's a girl. All you have to do is let them alone a while; you don't have to do anything. In a couple of weeks the babies will start streaming out," Silda assures us. "You can just sit on your ass and be rich as anything. By May 17th you'll have at least twenty of them."

Rita nods eagerly. She already has dollar signs in her eyes.

New customers arrive. We get in line for the newsstand, each of us holding a warm mouse in our hands. The little rodents have eyes like cod-liver-oil pills and squeak with a sound that comes from deep inside their stomachs. Their whiskers quiver and quiver.

"Where shall we keep them?" I ask, worried. After my hamster gnawed up half the carpet before he was killed, it's been forbidden to bring four-legged creatures home.

"I'll hide them in my room. Anyway I don't think my mother will make a stink about it." Rita sets the mouse on her shoulder. The long tail is like a pink worm in the hollow of her neck. "But don't you go talking to Siri about this. I don't want to share any of this with that drip."

"No way."

We grin at each other, delighted. Talk about lucky! Talk about financial know-how! Starting with absolutely zero, we've ended the day with two white mice, ten banana chocolates and four frozen juice bars.

Excerpted from *Skyskraperengler*. Translated from the Norwegian by Barbara Wilson.

🕮 Torborg Nedreaas

"Red Reflections" is one of many stories and books Torborg Nedreaas (1906–1987) has written about Herdis. In the earliest stories Herdis is a little girl, five or six years old, and in subsequent stories and novels Nedreaas traces her development through childhood and adolescence. Herdis is a perceptive and sensitive child who nonetheless possesses a fierce instinct to survive. In her portrayal of Herdis, Nedreaas has been both relentlessly honest and deeply compassionate.

"Red Reflections" is set in the city of Bergen, Norway during the second decade of the twentieth century. The world around Herdis is growing more and more unsettled, in her neighborhood and in a distant Europe, and she struggles to reconcile the horror and fear these events awaken with the reality of her own young life.

Red Reflections

The double doors to the street were still standing wide open, and they had not collected everything from the pavement. A broken kitchen lamp lay at the very edge of the pavement, and an ironing board and some kitchen utensils which were strung together stood against the wall of the house, together with a large wickerwork basket, which was held together by a piece of rope wound round it. A small Christmas tree in a pot stood beside it. The garland of Norwegian flags had come loose and was lying in the dirt of the muddy pavement, and a shiny paper angel, much too big for that little tree, was swinging to and fro in the wind. The windows gaped open, curtainless, in the apartment where Evelyn and her folks had lived.

Herdis had a dry, empty feeling inside her. She leant against the wall, just as she had done the previous night to watch the eviction, and saw it all again. Once before she had watched while someone was evicted, but that was a long time ago and it was different then. In those days there was a great commotion when people were evicted; they had stood round and jeered at the police and yelled "Ya-ha, ya-ha" and made a row.

But now it was done in silence. The kids would stand around not knowing what to do, watching as all the things gradually piled up on the pavement; some would help to load the hand-cart, but without looking at the people they were helping. The women from round about would stand silently against the house walls, and disappear like shadows when they had seen enough. Such evictions were not an uncommon occurrence any longer.

Demonstrations and disturbances in the streets were not uncommon either. Wild-cat strikes and protests against inflation blew up like sporadic hailstorms in various parts of the town; the kids from the back streets regarded it as a chance to have a bit of free fun, and trudged along, silent and hungry, after the workers down to the shipyards, looking forward to some brass-band music and perhaps a few scuffles if the police were waiting for them in Solheimsviken. But nothing more came of it. The storms passed over, a gray stillness descended on the area again. Even the steadily growing number of evictions aroused no excitement.

Herdis wandered homewards with her eyes on the pavement and her music case bumping against her thin legs. Jenny disappeared into her room the moment she had opened the door for her. As Herdis hung up her coat in the hall she noticed that her mother's and father's coats were both there. She listened—there was no sound from the living room. Nor were there any lights on. She warmed her hands by the stove in the dining room without putting the light on, and between the curtains through into the drawing room, which were drawn back, she could see the faint glimmer of the Christmas tree in the dark.

The night before, a small Christmas tree in a pot had been carried out from Evelyn's folks' and put down on the pavement, with garlands of Norwegian flags which had come loose and hung down into the mud on the pavement. She stood and let herself feel what it was like to be *home,* in warm, comfortable, and pleasant rooms. The piano keys smiled in a friendly way in the gaslight which shone through the window. Quietly, as if she were afraid of waking someone, she went into the drawing room and climbed into a chair, where she curled up. She hardly dared to breathe for fear of disturbing the almost painful stream of sensations which crowded in upon her.

From the bedroom she could hear her parents talking to each other. For a moment she listened—thank goodness. They were talking quietly, normally. Then she saw it in her mind's eye, one thing after another. Things were lifted and moved and carried out and down the stairs and left in the street. The piano. It stood freezing in the street, it was raining on it. The palms of her hands began to sweat, she took deep breaths. Things like that *did* happen to some people. It was difficult to believe when you were sitting in a good warm room. It was difficult to believe any of it when you were comfortably off yourself, difficult to believe it completely even if you knew it. You could not believe things until you felt them so deeply that you experienced them yourself. Herdis felt as if she were missing something when she was not able to grasp the experience, the times when she was passively contented or passively discontented, because she could not get hold of and be a part of the experiences of people she knew and people she did not know. Even though the experience itself filled her only with unease and fear.

She was continually preoccupied with the thought of war. But when she tried to imagine what it was like, she could not manage it. She discovered that she did not believe that people shot each other down, that human blood was shed. She could not manage to feel what it was like to have lost an arm or a leg, however much it said about it in the papers. And she knew that all the others were like her, that she was like all the others—they ate and drank, worried about inflation, wished for things and clothes and sweets, laughed and lived and slept. She and all the others were made in such a way that little children could be crushed and towns burnt down in other countries, without it becoming unbearable.

For what was war? It meant, for example, that Olsen's Bakery was no longer Olsen's Bakery, but had become Harder's Shipping. It now occupied two floors of Olsen's corner so that Elsi had her own room in English style and gave large parties.

War was strikes and discontent and the fact that the children from the back streets were skinnier and more ragged than before.

War was bread and drippings and hoarding away stores in the attic. The respectable little families down in Solverstad did without their breakfast eggs and cakes with their coffee, and scraped together enough to be able to buy a silk dress and a second-hand top hat, so that they could make a good impression on the more fortunate, who would one day arrive with riding horses and cars and champagne lunches. They hoarded flour and goat's cheese, so as to make sure of not going hungry when times got even worse.

War, that was about little things. War meant that the rats grew fat and dangerous.

Herdis realized that she was sitting bolt upright, in a most uncomfortable position, and gripping the arms of the chair tightly. The voices from the bedroom disturbed her, they were burning in the walls and made her skin shivery with anxiety.

Suddenly her lips grew cold; her father's voice was raised, loud and ominous, in the other room. Mother's low laughter flared up through father's hoarse, grating shouts—Herdis was up out of her chair in a flash and into the dining room where she switched on the light. Suddenly she was afraid of the dark.

The light frightened her even more. Something terrible was happening at this moment, something in the little house was being destroyed. The door to the entrance hall was standing half open. The bedroom door was jerked open, father rushed through the hall, mother was trying to hold him back. She was still laughing her little breathless laugh, her blouse was torn at the shoulder.

Everything happened in a sudden rush, just like the comic films Herdis sometimes saw at the cinema: father had a bunch of ten-kroner notes in his hand, he tore at them and crumpled them and threw them into the stove. The flames were devouring them hungrily even before father had shut the stove door.

Herdis could not feel her own body any longer. It was like in her dreams she herself did not exist, while terrible things were happening around her. She felt as if she were falling into the stove together with the notes and being burnt up with them. Money, money—just what they never had enough of! She heard his hurt, cracked voice but did not understand what he was shouting; the walls were burning, her home was burning. She heard mother say, "You're mad."

Herdis had hardly had time to take in the unbelievable thing father was doing with the money, when something even worse happened, something which was worst of all, now something happened which was unbearable. Father threw himself down on the chaise longue and burst into tears. They were terrible tears. Herdis never knew that men could cry. He sat hunched over, with his hands over his eyes, and sobbed aloud; it sounded like bitter laughter, a shuddering, tearing laughter, his shoulders heaved and his mouth twisted bitterly.

Mother stood rubbing her shoulder, where there was a blue mark. Her little laugh had become so helpless. She called his name softly and gently. Then he leapt up—"Go, just go! He can give you everything you want"—he sank down again in uncontrollable, shameless sobbing.

Herdis was unable to move a muscle, and just as in her dreams there was no one who noticed her presence. She saw herself throw herself down in front of her father and cling to him, kiss him and tell him she loved him. But she stood quite still. She shut her eyes and stood and died.

As so often before, it passed over. Yet it was not like before. The passionate atmosphere of reconciliation which she feared and hated because it made her lonely was not there this time. Her parents were polite to each other, even respectful. Herdis longed for them to kiss each other and embrace and forget her—sooner that.

Every now and then mother had a little cry on her own, but straight afterwards she sat down at the piano and sang operetta melodies with her soft and sparkling voice, her eyes dreamy with happiness.

Herdis froze between them. She froze all the time at home now, unless she had an exciting book to read. She wished she had a sister, and pretended to herself that the little girls she knew were her sisters—preferably those who were in some kind of difficulty—Evelyn who had had all her teeth pulled out and had moved to the slums, Julia who had gone to a cheerless children's home, Christi whom she had lied to when she said she had lost the magic glass. Her parents often had long, low-voiced conversations out of her hearing. She escaped into dreams of desperate, pleading hope.

The hope grew into a fearful joy when her mother one day asked if she would like to go to the cinema with her. It was a long time since she had been out with mother, and the cinema was an event and an occasion. She jumped up and down beside her mother with her hand under her arm, and felt a warm glow of affection and possessiveness. All the splintered anxiety she had felt recently was pushed so far to the back of her mind that she really felt a sudden desire for cakes as they walked past a café window. She asked cautiously whether they might go to the café after the cinema—mother was so warm and affectionate that it made her daring. And when the answer was a whole-hearted yes, she became completely happy, and thought that everything was going to be all right again, absolutely all right. She would ask if they could buy some cakes to take home for father too. If she had had money herself—yes, if she had had any money herself—it was quite unbelievable that anyone could put money in the stove and burn it, however angry they were with it—

When mother had bought the cinema tickets, Herdis suddenly saw that she was standing crying.

"But mummy—you've got tears on your cheeks—"

"It's so windy out. Oh dear, my eyes can't stand all that wind."

Mother was just going to shut her handbag, but she opened it again and took out a five-kroner note which she gave to Herdis. Herdis was struck dumb, she did not dare to believe straight away that it was true, she had never owned, never dreamt of owning so much money. Mother closed her hand over the note. It took some time to convince Herdis that she was allowed to spend it just as she wished.

The auditorium had gone dark. Then the green light streamed on to the screen, there was a sound like pouring rain in the auditorium, and a lady began to play a cheerful march on the untuned piano. Herdis felt her mother's arm hugging her warmly. Mother said, "You must enjoy yourself with it. Just be happy and glad and make sure you enjoy yourself." Then she paused for a moment, holding her breath.

"I'm going to leave," she said, in a hoarse voice. "Your father and I are going to separate."

And then the film began. Herdis did not see any of it. She tried dizzily to think about the five-kroner note, about everything she could buy with it. It all hurt too much.

Mother's eyes were red from crying behind her veil when they came out of the cinema. Herdis heard her talking—now she had to be a good, sensible little girl, she was so big and clever. She must try to understand Mummy.

The wind had increased; the gas-lights, which had just been lit, guttered. To Herdis it felt as if the ground was blowing away from under her. Everything was blowing away, mother and father were blowing away, and her home, everything. She clung desperately to her mother's arm, she shrieked and begged and cried—they *mustn't* separate, it wasn't true—she made herself wretched, worked herself into hysteria, big girl that she was. Mother's voice was calm and mild and terrible, "It has to be like this."

Herdis calmed down, she just froze. They forgot that they were going to the café, they let themselves be borne by the wind through the park, mother talked. Herdis would understand when she was older. Mother had fallen in love with someone else.

Herdis could feel the five-kroner note inside her mitten, like something wicked and shameful. She wanted to give it back to her mother, wanted to get rid of it, but was torn by a miserable desire to keep it instead. She had a vague feeling that she would perhaps regret it if she surrendered all the possibilities it offered. And she felt unhappy and wretched because she was incapable of giving it back again.

The feeling of homelessness was even worse at home than it was outside. The wind had turned into a storm, the window fasteners rattled. Inside Herdis's head some of the phrases from the merry tunes played at the cinema churned round and round, making her unbearably miserable. And her parents stifled her with a wall of friendliness.

Suddenly father leapt out on to the balcony. From below there came shouts and the sound of fire bells being rung, salvos of galloping horses' hoofs echoed through the streets.

"The whole town is on fire!"

Father shouted down to someone and was told that the fire had begun somewhere in Strandgaten. Mother's face went white. Father said: "I think I'll go down and see." He went out into the hall and came back with his hat and coat.

"I suppose you'll being going *there*. But—someone must stay at home with the child." There was a mixture of bitter scorn and questioning hope, and sorrow in his voice and glance. But the little flicker of hope which it contained leapt like a spark over to Herdis, it rushed through her mind—if Mummy stays at home with me, everything will be all right again. Mother looked down and said in a voice that was only a whisper, "Jenny is at home."

A little later the front door shut after Father, and a cold gray mist descended on Herdis.

Jenny came in from the balcony with her hair blown into a storm by the wind. "It's blowing away up Småstranen now, the wind's blowing it down to the market and Veiten. I can't understand what kind of lass you are, that don't want to go up to Sydneshaugen and have a look."

Herdis shook her head. She persuaded Jenny to go, she was not afraid of being left on her own. Sølverstad was not in any immediate danger. A red glow as if from a feverish sunset lay over the houses and pavements, while the storm tore at the slates and the window fastenings and howled round the corners.

Herdis was glad to be alone. She could see down in the street that people here and there were moving things out, getting ready to flee. Herdis stood and watched them without seeing anything, she stood bowed under the weight of her own pain. She had not known that sorrow could hurt so much, the pain raged and flamed within her. Now she knew that the man her mother—the one who—

He lived in Strandgaten. Strandgaten was on fire.

Dear God, let his house burn down. Let him be burned in it.

She ran frightened out of the dining room. When God looked down to see who it was who had whispered those terrible words, he would find the room empty. Restlessly she went into the bedroom and looked out of the window into the backyard. There was a humming from all the iron steps as if from a large double-bass when the wind came sweeping down over the sloping roofs; doors and windows creaked and groaned. Over the roofs the sky was quite red; every now and then a handful of sparks spurted over the chimney pots like fireworks, scattered like stars and went out. From the town came a noise of muffled thuds and a continual hiss of flames and fire hoses. The red light was reflected dimly in the dark bedroom. She wished Jenny had been there after all. Just there in the flat. Not that she could talk to her, she had nothing to say. Her own sick pain was lashed by a new, frightened excitement which seared and soothed at the same time. Now it was all burning up, now the flames were devouring everything which hurt her. It was an exhausting and agonizing feeling, but with flashes of exhilaration too, like forcing one's way through a storm or being out alone in a thunderstorm. A driving whirl of disjointed thoughts piled up inside her and urged her into a feverish intoxication of emotion.

The bedroom was oppressive. She ran up to the loft. It was cold up there, but she put a box under the sloping window and put her head out through the open window to cool her face. Now she could hear the noise of the fire clearly. There was a thundering and a crashing and a scraping of heavy metal plates; far away someone screamed. All this about her father and mother had suddenly become unreal, just as unreal as the fiery sky, as the flickering red light on the floor of the loft, as the fire which swept across the town. A wordless thought sprang up like a spurt of flames within her and caught the soreness in her like the stinging lash of a whip—Strandgaten. Mother—if Mother was in the middle of the blaze, if she—Herdis curled up and clutched herself as if the whiplash had struck her right in the stomach. Fear suffocated her. "Mummy," she moaned softly between her teeth.

All at once the pain parted with a violent surge, thoughts of her mother were smothered by the picture—*this* was a fear she was sharing with many, many people, maybe at this precise moment. The crashing, the hissing, and all the indeterminate gusts of sound from the burning town were suddenly very close to her, as if it were something in her which released them. Mothers went in fear for their children, children went in fear for their mothers, she felt their cries in her hammering temples, a dark and angry terror overcame her like a heavy giddiness, she felt as if she were going to be sick.

This was what it was like in war. The fear which threatened to crush her to pieces was the fear of living people here and now and the whole time, only much worse, and much more real. She had managed to get down from the box, and sat crouched in the corner with clenched fists; she sat and held her hands clasped tightly around a new knowledge, and felt that it was a terrible and agonizing treasure she had found.

Exhaustion made her feel calmer and cooler, though the thoughts did not cease piling up inside her head. One of the little girls in the street had vanished one evening a few years earlier; Herdis saw her as she ran round the corner, and she saw her now and wanted to shout to her and run after her and take her with her. It was only now that she realized how crazy it was that a living little girl should stop there and not exist any more. And the world was full of little girls who were full of mischief and did not want to go home and go to bed at night; in the countries where there was war there were also lots of them, and many many were just left lying there, burnt or smashed, and did not get any further.

Her thoughts came in pictures rather than words, and the pictures told a story like a brutal film. "Mummy," she whimpered involuntarily. She remembered where her mother was, and began to cry.

But the thoughts raged hatefully on, and her crying stopped bitterly.

Julia. She did not know where that children's home was. She longed for Julia. Julia, Julia. She had never been really nice to Julia. She hardly ever saw her any more.

She crept up on to the box again and clung to the window post. Shreds of sooty material were blowing about, floating between the sparks in the red, angry sky. It could be burning money. Ten-kroner notes. A splintering sound pierced through the noise from the town, the sound of glass smashing. And with the feeling that something was gripping her heart and squeezing it until she felt she would burst, she suddenly saw father again, relived it all over again—he sat hunched over on the chaise longue in the dining room whilst the reflection of the flames danced around the room and the fire tore at the walls— no, no—it was *now* it was burning. He just sobbed loudly and brokenly—

"Mummy," it came out as a whispered cry. She tried to make herself cry, but could not find any release from the pressure inside herself, no tears would come.

Suddenly she started to hunt urgently for something in an old doll's pram with three wheels and a ragged hood, which was standing there. She had hidden some things there.

She found the prism, and looked at it. Since Christi had come home she had not looked into it. Since the time she had told Christi that she had lost it she had not dared to look into it for fear of being found out. She stood feeling it with cold, clammy fingers. She put it to her eye and looked up.

She saw nothing. The red sky was splintered, pierced through by green flashes, there was yellow and there was mauve light which moved and changed, but it was all meaningless. *She saw nothing.* Feverishly she moved around, turned the piece of glass between her fingers so that new colors and forms sprang to life, but the experience was a dead one, and only made her feel disturbed. Her hand shook as she lowered the piece of glass. She half-closed her eyes as if she wanted to hold fast to what she had seen before with her eyelids, to relive the fairy tale of the magic glass, without the magic glass. *To see.*

She saw only her own racing thoughts. Mother and father are going to separate. Living people kill other living people. Mummy is going to leave me, Mummy is going to go away. There was only a name on a list which was left, there was only the name of Nikolai left when his boat was torpedoed. Mummy, Mummy—I never want to see that man. The town is burning down tonight, *the whole town is burning.*

She opened her eyes, reality was pressing down on her with a desperate weight; it hit her between the eyes with crushing force. Mummy, Mummy, help me.

She wished suddenly that Jenny had come back, that Jenny was down there waiting for her, she could not bear being so completely alone any longer.

Jenny had not come. No one had come. They had forgotten her, all of them. And the magic glass was not a magic glass any longer, she had to manage with her own eyes. She was filled with a bitter calm. Everything was bad, everything was pain, wherever she turned she found only pain. She took the five-*kroner* note out of the pocket of her pinafore in order to look at it and find a little comfort in all the brilliant possibilities it offered.

It looked back at her. It looked evilly at her. Payment for having the ground cut away from under her feet.

A cold terror ran down her spine when she had opened the door of the stove and dropped it in. Now it was curling up. First it went black, then it flamed up. Then there was no five-kroner note any longer. She tried with all the force of her will not to think of everything you could get for five *kroner.* But she failed. The corners of her mouth drooped, trembling, as she thought of it all with a great and lonely sorrow. And everything was still painful, still just as painful.

But yet she felt, falteringly, a kind of ground beneath her feet again.

Excerpted from *Trylleglasset.* Translated from the Norwegian by Janet Garton.

Eeva Kilpi

Eeva Kilpi (1928–) spent the first twelve years of her life in the eastern part of Finland in a region called Karelia, which bordered on the Soviet Union. In November 1939, wishing to expand their territory and military operations, the Soviet Union attacked Finland. For 100 days, Finnish forces successfully resisted the Soviet Army, but ultimately Finland had to concede defeat. As a result of the Winter War, Finland lost Karelia and thousands of Finnish families had to flee from their homes and relocate.

Eeva Kilpi has written about this dramatic period of her life in *The Time of the Winter War: Memories from Childhood*. There is an immediacy in her narrative as she recounts the scenes and events she witnessed. In the excerpt below Kilpi recalls the solemnity and mystery of the first wedding she ever attended.

The Time of the Winter War

My young aunt and the pastor were married the Sunday after Epiphany, on January 7, 1940. We had a new year. And there was still war. The bodies of four soldiers from Hiitola had been sent home to be buried in their native soil. They were probably not the very first, but nearly so. The first casualty had been announced on Independence Day, December 6. The young pastor was to commit these boys to eternal rest before his wedding ceremony. He had gotten leave partly for this reason.

I think that I only heard about this event, yet I can almost see before me the row of coffins in front of the altar of Hiitola church, behind them the young pastor in his ensign's uniform, and above them all the altar painting of Christ with his outstretched hands.

The next day he stood in the same place with my aunt, with his back to us, facing the old dean, and that time I was there. I sat next to Grandma, near the altar, on the side reserved for the bride's relatives— the two of us—and I was shivering, for the church was ice cold. Almost at eye level, the hem of Auntie's dark blue dress trembled, for she too was shivering from the cold even though she was wearing a woolen sweater. "Do you wish to take . . . ?" asked the priest. And both said yes. They gave an affirmative answer to whatever fate awaited them. Without anything extra being said, this feeling was palpable and even a child could sense it. You could never hold fate accountable; they had wanted it so themselves.

I remember their backs well, and especially their clothes. They were so completely different from everything I had imagined and seen of weddings. So you could get married even without a veil and a long white dress, even without a bridal bouquet, dressed in just a wool sweater. Of course Auntie was wearing one of her best dresses, even if it was of the simplest kind, and in choosing it she had made her first decision in the capacity of pastor's wife.

"Which one of these should I wear?" she had appealed to Grandma, in the room that had been put at our disposal in the Dean's house. I observed these preparations on Sunday morning, perched on the edge of the bed, my hands squeezed between my knees. My fingertips tended to turn white and cold with excitement, and now they were completely stiff and bloodless and not even Grandma had time to massage them.

Auntie first held up a dress that was very close fitting. The waist and entire bodice were trimmed with ruffled satin that was tight under the bust, showing off her figure. In the back it turned into a wide sash that was held together by many hooks and eyes under the shoulder blades. The dress was very stylish; I had seen it on Auntie myself and admired it. But. . . .

The other dress was less elegant. The skirt was a bit bell-shaped, not really wide, but not narrow either; something in between, neither one nor the other, like the clothes of pastors' wives often are. There was a narrow sash at the waist, just right for a pastor's wife, which didn't emphasize the waist or bust too much.

"This one is probably better," said Auntie. "Since I have to wear that wool sweater over it. And woolen underwear. That other one probably wouldn't even button properly—I've gained weight from the volunteers' endless pea soup."

And so she chose the uglier dress, which I also thought was more suitable for the occasion, but somehow it felt sad just the same. And as a final touch, she decided to fasten a couple of white, flat flowers made of piqué at the front of the collar, just as a little accent, and with that she changed her own, former style so decisively that my childish heart almost clutched with pain. And those piqué flowers, completely different from anything that she had worn before, were impressed on my memory so deeply that I could sketch them even now.

So it was the hem of the uglier dress that was quivering before the altar a few moments later, next to the smart officer's trousers and polished boots. The sleeve of the woolen sweater shyly drew toward the army gray, which a broad leather belt and shoulder strap seemed to restrain from any premature display of emotion.

"I declare you man and wife," said the dean.

And at that moment it truly seemed as if a miracle took place (this *was* the time of miracles!).

My aunt and the pastor began to look like man and wife. They looked as if they had already known each other for a long time, from the beginning of time, had been meant for each other ever since the fates were decided and had even experienced their fates, had begun to resemble each other in their expressions and gestures, the way that couples do after a long life together. They looked as if all this was just a game, a special kind of playful ceremony, through which they wanted to re-experience the first moments of their youth and love. When they turned toward us few onlookers, everyone forgot the woolen sweaters and military boots, and saw only their faces. They glowed, though not from joy alone, for they were serious at the same time. My aunt had tears in her eyes, though her mouth was smiling. The young pastor's lips trembled, but his eyes were joyful.

The groom's mother hadn't had time to obtain the necessary travel pass and had been unable to leave Savo, so no one was present from the pastor's family. Grandma and I were the first to congratulate the couple.

I threw my arms around Auntie's waist and hugged her. She was only ten years older than I. She would turn twenty-two at the end of January. I would be twelve in February. When we looked each other in the eyes, we remembered in silent understanding the excitements of the Easter holiday, and how we had climbed on Linnavuori in the summer, as if these were already but pale memories of a time before this fulfillment. Even Jesus, who stood behind us on the Mount, with outstretched hands, seemed to understand our feelings perfectly. I probably just stretched out my hand to Uncle Pastor and curtsied when I congratulated him. If I had hugged him too, I'm sure I would remember it.

I had played out my role as chaperone as well as I could, and now it was time to step aside. They had found each other, just as in the fairy tales. I might even have considered myself extremely successful, if I had been able to understand it. Maybe that was why I had been included at the wedding.

Although I have no memory of the Christmas Eve dinner in Jyvävaara, I clearly remember the meal we ate at the Dean's house a while after the wedding. Above all I remember that my aunt blushed several times at the table, for no apparent reason. She blushed when someone mentioned her name, or when the pastor said something to the dean or his wife, or when Grandma began telling us about something that everyone already knew, and once Auntie even said to Grandma, "Please, don't tell them about everything."

I sat next to Grandma on one side of the table. The pastor and Auntie sat facing us and the dean and his wife sat at either end. The pastor was like a son in this house. This had been said often and it was now said once again at the table. It was a joy and a blessing to be able to lead him into the haven of matrimony, even in these tragic times. It was a great gift from God to be blessed in marriage by one's own dean and his motherly wife.

Both the dean and his wife were already white-haired and they looked as fine and elegant as the characters in an old illustrated Bible. I had never seen such people before at such close range, and it felt strange to think that they put food in their mouths just like everyone else, or even that they needed food like ordinary people. And that they chatted and even smiled.

The dean's wife leaned toward the couple, quietly jovial, and said:

"One thing that wasn't said in this marriage ceremony was that the man is the wife's head. When we were married, that was said to me."

She glanced almost shyly at her husband. As he sat there at the head of the table it was easy to believe that he had indeed carried out the task assigned to him by the marriage vows with tenderness, dignity and fortitude.

"Isn't it true," mused the pastor, "that the man is the woman's head and the wife is the neck that makes it turn?"

Auntie blushed again and everyone laughed. Just think how clever our pastor is! "Proverbs make good responses to Bible sayings," said the pastor modestly, without taking any credit himself, like an honest servant of the word.

I understood that this was the best society I had ever experienced, and surely also the most elegant occasion, not counting my birth or perhaps my christening, when this same dean had christened me and Grandma had carried me to the altar. I was so excited that I felt as if my breath alone could have made the heavy knives and forks rattle on the table in front of me. There they lay, together with a big spoon, on a tablecloth that was stiff and dazzlingly white. How could anyone ever manage to eat without staining it with food? On top of everything yet another stiff, white cloth was spread out over my knees; that too had to be treated carefully. The dean, to be sure, tucked his napkin under his chin and Grandma wanted to do the same with mine, but I pulled back in my chair and firmly refused. Under my chin it was sure to get stained.

At some point grace was said. It may have been some more elegant version of "Bless our daily bread" which we used to say in school, but the idea was the same anyway. When we sat down at the table, we still didn't know what kind of food would be served; there was a soup dish at each of our places. Fine folk are able to fill out such empty moments so that they don't become embarrassing, I noticed. In fact, it is probably a sign of real society, and we were now in such society. This was far from the kind of "ladies and gents" that Grandma used to joke about. "Ladies and gents, please be served." "Kindly have a seat, ladies and gents." "Step in, step in, ladies and gents" or "How are the ladies and gents today?" How on earth could you swallow anything, even if you were able to get something all the way to your mouth with these utensils? How on earth could people eat at weddings at all—and even at funerals, people supposedly eat? And when had the dean's wife prepared the food, since she sat there so calm and cool at the head of the table? Until now, I had seen only the terrible haste and commotion before guests arrived; sweaty and flushed faces, the banging of dishes and rattling of lids, and mother's transformation at the very last minute into a smiling hostess—a metamorphosis that I had never grown used to.

But then a servant stepped into the room, maybe even dressed in a black dress and white apron, and began ladling a green soup out of a serving dish. A smooth, green soup without any potato or even any clumps at all, just a thin broth. I also got a ladle-full in my bowl. When everyone had been served some soup, we were served some tiny, irregularly shaped pieces of rye toast covered with a sprinkle of grated cheese. They were placed next to the soup bowls on special little plates, and you were supposed to nibble at them now and then, like a sandwich, but delicately. I understood that there was a food shortage and that this was part of the reason why the pieces of bread were so small, but at the same time I couldn't help feeling that it was a way to make us all feel elegant, in spite of rationing. The soup was supposed to be thin, the bread slices extra small and without any butter, and they were supposed to be cut just like this.

It was a long time before I realized what the soup was made of. What is this familiar taste, I wondered and tried to remember. I've tasted it somewhere before. What can it be? Then it suddenly dawned on me. This is pea soup! It's just that the peas have been strained out!

For a long time, the minimal slices of toasted bread covered with grated cheese and the clear pea soup were the most wonderful foods I could imagine. I dreamed that one day, I would prepare such a meal myself and serve it to delighted and appreciative guests. I had to wait a long time before my first opportunity presented itself, and even though it belongs to another time and another age, I can't help letting it intrude into my story, as it wells up irresistibly from the timeless storage of memory.

Father and Mother had been out cutting hay—that is, many years after this event—and in the evening they returned home (to the home that awaited us in the future)—tired and hungry. My task that day was to cook for them and I had made clear pea broth and small lopsided pieces of toast topped with grated cheese. I can still remember how Father asked,

"What's for dinner?"

And I answered, "Pea soup and toasted bread squares."

I realized right away that everything had gone wrong. The unheard of happened: Father got furious. He went to the pantry door and looked inside.

"Aren't there any leftovers from yesterday?"

There were. He scraped out some leftover gravy from a bowl into the pan and warmed it up himself on the stove. He didn't say anything until he had finished eating. Then he said, "That's a little better."

I didn't dare say a single word to explain what a remarkable and memorable meal he could have had.

To Mother's credit, I have to say that she politely tasted the soup— she herself was a good cook and could make even the simplest everyday meal taste good. I remember that she tried to say something positive about the food, but it wasn't anything that stuck in my memory.

⌘

I don't remember what was served as main course at the dean's house, nor do I remember the dessert. This, my most memorable dinner, is completely dominated by the pea soup and the cheese-covered pieces of bread. As far as I remember I didn't spill anything on the table-cloth, not even milk. I noticed that you weren't supposed to put the big spoon completely in your mouth, not even point it directly to the mouth, but rather you were supposed to tip it against your lips so the soup floated into your mouth from the long side, and at that moment, of course, you couldn't let any slurping sound be heard. You weren't supposed to blow on the soup, nor should the spoon clank against the bowl. You were supposed to swallow soundlessly. Your mouth was supposed to be closed when you chewed, and talking was forbidden then, in addition to being impossible. Still, people talked all the time at the table and the plates were emptied. When you scooped up the last drops, you weren't supposed to tip the dish toward your-self, but in the opposite direction. Still, the most elegant of all was to leave the last drops unscooped, even if it was wartime and there wasn't much food. Maybe they let the cat lick the bowls, which was good, of course.

Evening fell and Grandma and I retreated to the room that had been made up for us. We slept next to each other in the same bed, which had high iron gables; I lay on the inside by the wall. For some reason I felt that I had to stay turned toward the wall all the time, even before I fell asleep, because my aunt was also in the room. I didn't know what to say to her anymore, now that I had congratu-lated her in church, nor had she said anything to me after that. Some-thing unexplained had now opened up between us, and for the first time, I distinctly felt that she was grown up and I was a child. And that something awaited her this evening, something that perhaps awaited me too, although only after a long time. I heard her wash up and exchange a few words with Grandma in a low voice. It probably wasn't anything important, since people never say anything important at the most important moments, because then there's no need for words. But I still had the feeling that they exchanged some kind of women's secrets, the kind that I too would soon have the right to know about. I strongly felt the presence of something in the atmosphere, something that bound women together one generation after another, at the same time that it bound them to the men who waited for them somewhere, behind the wall or beyond a stretch of years. The fact that you never talked about it made it a mystery. Something inside me told me that that was how it was supposed to be. Love and its consummation was supposed to be a mystery, and woe to the one who tried to pry it open prematurely or to draw it out into the daylight with explanations. Still, something deep inside me was burning to know. And it wasn't simply curiosity.

I wanted to turn around and look at Auntie, now that she was going to go and sleep next to that person whom she until now had longed for only from afar. What did she look like now, how did she move? What if her stomach began to growl, for example, like that time when we sat on the front row bench in church at Easter?

But I felt that I wasn't supposed to turn around, not look nor ask. I shut my eyes tight, pulled the blanket over my ears and pressed myself against the wall, to leave room for Grandma.

Excerpted from *Talvisodan aika: lapsuusmuistelma*. Translated from the Finnish by Sonia Wichmann.

✦ Agnes Henningsen

Stepping Lightly is the evocative title of Agnes Henningsen's (1868–1962) first volume of memoirs, published in 1941. Henningsen begins her story in the 1870s when she was a small child living on the island of Fyn in Denmark on a manor which her father managed. Her mother died after a brief illness, leaving her husband with three little girls. Agnes' father remarried and increased his family by four more daughters, and then he too died. Agnes was fourteen years old at her father's death, and neither she nor her sisters had had any formal education. There had been governesses, but at the time it was assumed girls would follow in their mothers' footsteps and didn't need book learning in order to raise a family and help run an estate.

The father's youngest brother, Ferdinand, came to live with the family and oversee the manor until more permanent arrangements could be made. Agnes had idolized her uncle as long as she could remember, and he had returned her affection. But now Ferdinand's affection for his niece became infatuation, so powerful that he broke off his engagement only weeks before the wedding. Aunts and uncles cried scandal and sent Agnes and her two sisters away to a boarding school on the island of Sjælland. This is the point at which the chapter excerpted below begins.

Stepping Lightly

The first of May was blustery; we were flung across the Storebælt* and arrived at our destination pale and bewildered. Mimi and I in our black dresses looked far older than our years when we were not twittering like happy birds. And we had finished with that at Skovridergården. Even Tut looked like her wings were clipped; she insisted that, judging from the way Uncle Lymann had talked about Antvorskov, and even from the school's own catalog, it was not an abbey we were going to but a prison.

Antvorskov was attractively set at the end of a drive. Even the vestibule presented an air of affluence, as affluent, it was said, as the homes

---

*The waterway between the islands of Sjælland and Fyn.

of the students. My chest tightened as we children and Aunt Mathilde were shown in to see the director; it was a bad start, having our own mother's sister glare at us, and glare she did.

But the director, Miss Bryndum, had eyes full of wisdom. She put me at ease with her friendly manner. Dignified. There was something just a little strict about her, but this was surely because there was so much she was in charge of.

The two young teachers who came in and greeted us seemed equally encouraging. The beautiful Miss Aschlund. And Miss Harries. So maybe her one eye was crossed and her foot was a little twisted, she was charming nevertheless—quite charming. I was so captivated by all three of them that I felt as though my wings had already begun to grow out.

Miss Aschlund told us that there was nothing left of the old abbey but monks' stones and monks' bones. We could find them out on the slope beyond the hedge. She showed us the way through the students' lounge, and I hoped she would join us. But when she left us, Tut exclaimed, "Oh, we get to take a walk in the garden by ourselves."

It would have been a park, if not for the enormous cherry tree that dominated the view of the lawn and overshadowed the tall plane tree behind it. Of course, nothing so large had any business being so close to the house, but we forgave this indulgence and walked enraptured under its canopy. Outside the *pyrrhus japonica* glimmered light and dark red. White petals drifted down over us, and we felt ourselves consecrated. "Here it is spring at last," said Mimi softly. And I thought, here I can finally be young.

The garden extended down a hillside. The path descended so steeply that it was impossible to walk; the momentum was irresistible. Below, we glimpsed fruit trees in blossom, dozens, a whole orchard. "Everything here makes you giddy," I shouted. "Tut, let's race. From here till where it flattens out."

"Stop." Mimi assured herself that we could not be seen from the house and measured off in deliberate steps a distance farther down the hill. "You are older and a better runner, so Tut gets a thirty-foot head start." She prophesied ceremoniously: "The winner will wed most happily," and shouted, "Go!"

I stumbled just before the finish line. Good. I wanted Tut to win. I wanted them all to win. I would have my turn some day. I wanted my success to begin here at Antvorskov: "Did you see how large the classroom was?" I asked. "We will sit at that table with seventeen others and fill what father called our empty vessels. Just think how they will be filled."

"I've been away from my reading for much too long," sighed Mimi. And Tut sighed, "I'm much too little for the two of you." Then I had to sigh also, for how could my German help these two?

Exhilarated, we explored the garden further. We found the monks' stones, then we remembered that we were supposed to go and look at our room, so we ran up, red-cheeked and hopeful.

In the hallway, Miss Bryndum came rushing up to us and handed Mimi a letter. "From Langeland." Now her tone was sharp: "Who is it from? Open it."

So Aunt Mathilde had told her that I was engaged and made her aware that there might be a letter from him! The blood rushed to my head.

Mimi looked at the handwriting: "It's from my girlfriend in Fårevejle."

"Open it."

Two young girls from the capital who clearly knew their way around came past us on the way to their rooms. Their surprise made clear that they did not have their letters monitored.

Mimi, ashamed, obeyed: "It's from my girlfriend in Fårevejle," she repeated.

Miss Bryndum nevertheless investigated the signature. So Aunt Mathilde had also told her that we were liars!

Our room had three white beds—three of everything—and a dormer window looking out over the garden. It was no doubt a splendid bedroom, but we now felt it resembled a cell.

Tut shuddered a little: "This is a prison; you two wouldn't believe me, but it's a prison."

She looked so small and lost that we had to do something at once. "Mimi, let's show them that we won't stand for this sort of thing," I pleaded.

But she was ready to rush off: "Aunt Mathilde is still here, in with the director, and she's leaving soon. We have to go down and get ready to say good-bye to her."

"Let's go in there while they're together and ask them not to treat us like criminals just because we don't have a father," I said.

"You know very well that has nothing to do with it. Aunt Mathilde is only doing what she has to do. We've got to go downstairs. We've got to thank her for everything and for accompanying us here."

"And for tattling on us."

"How can you say Aunt Mathilde is a tattle-tale?" Mimi came toward me menacingly. "If you accuse Aunt Mathilde of tattling, then you'll have a fight on your hands."

It would have been a relief for me to fight now, so I stood my ground: "She brought us here so she could tattle on us. None of the other girls have their families along. No—because they have their parents. Parents don't tattle, only aunts do that."

This time Tut did not go out of her way to avoid conflict; she stepped in between us and looked resolutely up at Mimi. "Uncle Lymann's family is only so furious with us because we love Uncle Ferdinand, whether he's engaged or not. And we do."

Mimi grabbed her hand: "You are coming downstairs with me to say good-bye. It would be hard enough for the two of us to have the whole family against us. But for a little girl like her it would be completely impossible." She forgot her anger and looked at me pleadingly: "Don't go ruining it for Tut also."

Also? I thought. Well, she was right; Ferdinand and I were to blame for her losing everyone she admired.

"Do you think it's fun to travel from Glorup to Antvorskov and back in one day?" she continued. "Do you think Aunt Mathilde would make that sacrifice for anybody but us? She did it because she hopes that if we are treated strictly, we will act more sensibly in the future."

"I'm sure she does," I mumbled; even I could not think of any other reason.

So I trooped along behind her, received a chilly farewell from Aunt Mathilde, and moved my lips by way of saying thanks.

At six o'clock all the girls were together for dinner: nine from last year and eleven starting today. In their light wool dresses they looked like rosebuds that had just begun to color. In my enthusiasm I spoke flower language to myself, and I called the two shy ones wild pansies because they had such intelligent faces. I wanted the one to be my friend because she had the same melancholy eyes as the little one at home.

We were not allowed to visit each other in our rooms at bedtime. One of the rosebuds, a light colored one who was almost in blossom, slipped in and introduced herself: "Klara, from Copenhagen, with a K. Don't be afraid of the tests tomorrow. They're just being given by the young teachers. Miss Aschlund is not much older than we are, even though she's studied in Paris for a year. Miss Harries has had a love affair, so she's cheerful. Sleep well, little Langelanders."

She was gone before we could tell her we were from Fyn. But her friendliness remained in the room and helped us to sleep well.

We were to be tested one at a time. I was pleased with that. People are always kinder to each other when they are face to face.

In spite of my incompetence in French, I was happy meeting with Miss Aschlund. She was completely different from the day before, without a smile either on her lips or in her eyes; she asked her questions abruptly. So she also knew that we were liars!

Miss Harries was just as serious. Not even my German made an impression on her. When I left, she gave me a sympathetic little smile. She also knew about it. Well of course—she had been engaged herself.

As expected, we scored at the bottom. But we certainly had not expected that we would be quite alone at the bottom. It was just us three on our level, which made it not much better than at home.

But just when I thought everything was hopeless, good fortune smiled on me. Miss Harries reported that I would skip two grades in German. I would join Klara and three others from last year. I was ashamed on Mimi's behalf; she needed something to be happy about much more than I did. I crept into the small classroom and wrote a thank-you note to my teacher, Dagmar.

Shortly before we were to have the first joint history class with the director, with all twenty of us participating, she sent a note saying that she wished to speak with me. Just me? What had I done now? Was I not allowed to write a letter about my life here? Was I not allowed to write any letters at all?

We had placed at the bottom; it was certainly our own fault. But we found ourselves in an exceptional and unpleasant situation, which we did not deserve. I decided that I would brook no further unjust treatment without protest—no longer remain silent during my trial. I strode into Miss Bryndum's office with my head held high.

She stood selecting books for class. "How can it be that you are so advanced in German when you are so far behind in everything else?"

"We got a new teacher in November," I answered. "She thought that there wasn't time to pursue more than one subject if I didn't want to be considered feeble-minded when I got here."

"Feeble-minded? Is that the word she used? You may find it irksome, since you have worked so hard at your German, but I would prefer that you take English instead."

"Isn't a student allowed to choose between the two languages, as it says in the catalog?"

"Your situation is different. I have my reasons."

An exceptional situation. I wanted to look her in the eyes and have a talk about this situation, but my gaze was deferential as it met her calm authority. "I have my reasons too," I said softly.

"For having a particular interest in German?"

"Yes. And mostly so that I can be in class with the interesting girls."

"I'm pleased that you can tell me frankly." She nevertheless wrinkled her fair eyebrows. "But you are of course not here primarily for your amusement. And it is natural that you should stay together with your sisters."

"I've been together with them from the time I was born. But I've never sat and learned anything sitting next to outsiders—never had anyone to compete with. And Miss Bryndum, I've never had a friend or a playmate."

She clapped her books shut with an expression that said, this is settled. "If you work hard, you can take all three languages after six months. There is a great deal to do here if you three are to be ready for the university entrance examinations in two years. But the tests proved that despite all your disadvantages you have exceptional abilities." She turned toward the door and looked at me sharply. "I use that word deliberately. You have exceptional abilities. Use them."

I followed after her as in a dream. I hoped that a fire would break out so that I could run through it and rescue her. Exceptional abilities? Oh, if only Father were alive to hear that.

Klara with a K was practically dying of laughter when she met me alone. "Ha, ha, it's too ridiculous. Do you know why you can't be in our class? Because when I was fourteen, I dated a boy and told mother and father that it was my own business. They're afraid that it's contagious."

"Ooh, are you one of those girls with a past?" I stared at her fascinated. "Then I'd be happy to spend time with 'difficult young girls from affluent homes.'"

"Ha, ha, you have such an droll way of putting things. If we had time, we could be friends. But God knows we don't have time. Not when we're watched walking down the street and watched doing our homework. And the two of us will never belong to the elite, who get permission to walk home alone from music lessons in Slagelse."

⁑

We did not know what we were going to do for Pentecost break. Just a few days before, Miss Bryndum told us that she had received a letter from Mrs. Lymann, and all three aunts who would have hosted us for the holiday had agreed that we should not leave for eight days when we had so recently arrived.

"It's terrible for the people who have to stay here because of us," Mimi exclaimed.

When we returned to our room, she hid the things she had been getting ready for the trip, as though she could not stand to look at them. I was sorry that once again she was being punished because of me. Nor was it very pleasant that the school would have to stay open because we were so difficult that no one would have us. But it was always her way to sweep misfortune under the rug. I minded my own business and set about writing new vocabulary words from my last class onto flash cards.

Then she burst out, "Ferdinand? What about everything I promised him for Pentecost? And now I won't even be able to talk to him."

"No, well, we can't do anything about that."

"And we never hear a word about him. The maid must have found out that her letters don't go through. Tut asks about him. Tut talks about him. You just sit and read. You sneak up to the window and read when you think the rest of us are asleep—of course I can see it. Yes, yes, yes, of course I know that it's best that you forget each other. But it's so tragic for him because he was serious. What will become of him?"

"No, well, we can't do anything about that," I repeated and mumbled distractedly the word on my first flash card: "Idiosyncrasy."

She tore it from my hands and hurled it to the floor. "I'm getting an idiosyncrasy from your reading and your vanity. So if you want to get angry, be my guest."

"No, I'm touched that you and Tut have so much affection for him. But has it ever occurred to you that my reading and my vanity are helping me?" I picked up the card and continued writing.

During Pentecost we were like guests at a manor house. Miss

Aschlund volunteered a day to take us to Sorø. Perhaps because she was so young she put rather too much emphasis on the grandeur of the locale; she was at too great a remove to get us interested in the Academy, especially when all the boys were gone, and least of all in the reminiscences of Ingemann.[†] I felt homesick for Antvorskov and my books.

Every fourth week was chore week; it was like a vacation. We could have heart-to-hearts and make friends. Four of us at a time were transformed from students to servant girls, stirring pots and sweeping up. Mimi and I were assigned to work with the very two I had hoped for: the wild pansy, Nana, with her beautiful, hungry eyes, and the lovely rosebud, Alice, so gruff that she lashed out at anyone who tried to help her. I was determined that I would win her friendship.

One perfect summer evening, Nana asked me to take a walk. She was nearly mad with longing, she said, but she would not say why. "Let's go pick cherries," I suggested.

From the veranda we heard the old tree rustling and groaning, heavy with fruit. No—it was Alice way up in the top. No one had been to the top of that tree in our lifetime. She stuck her head out from between the thin branches and waved. Red cap on her chestnut curls, red mouth from cherries, red cheeks from the rapture of being up so dangerously high.

We walked on. Although I was myself a daredevil, a shudder of fear went through me, making me run back and demand that she get down to where it was safe. She shook her head. Then I threatened her with calling the adults in. "You irritating idiot," she snarled and started descending.

But the momentary delay had worsened Nana's mood. "She's the daughter of a gentleman, but she talks like a sailor. She's contrary

---

[†]Ingemann (1789-1862) was one of Denmark's most beloved poets who had lived at Sorø.

with everyone. She doesn't even care if she learns anything. Yet she's the one you're always mooning over."

"Yes." I smiled at hearing it spoken aloud. "She's so above it all."

We walked into the labyrinth, the only place where I could run without being seen. High privet hedges turned around and around, ending at a gazebo. I would run back and forth through the spiral passageway until I had run myself out.

As soon as we had entered, Nana leaned up against the hedge and closed her eyes. "I wish I were as beautiful as you, so that someone could moon over me."

"I wish I were as clever as you," I answered. "I wish I had your interesting eyes. Open them up."

She squeezed them tighter. "It's my brother's fault, the one who's two years older than me, that I'm unhappy so much of the time," she whispered. "When we were little, he insisted on cuddling up to me and caressing me."

"But that was sweet."

"As little as I was, I knew that it was wrong. It was before we got dressed; we were just out of bed. He promised me his allowance, and imagine, I took it. And he kept his word every time."

"Wasn't that nice of him."

She opened her eyes and looked at me evenly. "You just don't understand, do you? I have my mother's medical book here. I will show you where you need to read so that you won't be so ignorant about the human body."

"No thanks, I have quite enough to read if I'm ever going to catch up to you."

She whispered again, "Since then I've felt so strange. And sad. Everything you really want to do is a sin. You have no idea what I'm really like."

So it was something about boys. On that subject I could certainly surpass everyone here at Antvorskov Abbey. I mimicked her without realizing it, casting my eyes down and whispering, "You have no idea what I'm really like. I have sat rocking on a tree branch, kissing my own father's brother."

"Are you making fun of me?" she exclaimed and burst into tears.

"Hey there," we heard, soft and quite nearby. "Who's bawling away in the labyrinth this time?"

It was the two girls from Århus, whom I had thought were from Copenhagen that day in the hallway when Mimi had to open her letter. Ingeborg, so sturdy in her policeman-blue dress. And Thyra, quiet as her shadow.

"What have they done to you in this confounded institution?" asked Ingeborg.

"She misunderstood me," I said. "You misunderstood me, Nana, as sure as I'm standing here."

Nana's face at once assumed its little-teacher expression. "We don't think that Antvorskov is an institution, and it is not in the least confounded."

"Not you either?" asked Ingeborg and fixed her burning gaze on me. "I'll never forget your sister standing there in the hallway, all grown up and smartly dressed, letting herself be treated like that. What kind of fool is she?"

"She is as she should be. She loves her country and her family and obeys blindly, while I'm a born rebel," I answered. "Mimi and I agree only on one thing: that our situation here is wonderful."

"Including when the tyrant investigates your letters as soon as she sees handwriting she doesn't recognize?"

"I may have done something to justify that. Or my family may have requested it."

"Some rebel you are. No—you have the soul of a slave, which makes this place all the more intolerable for the freeborn among us. Now I'm going to tell you something else: this afternoon on a walk with Miss Aschlund, Thyra and I registered a protest against the school's rules. A couple of handsome workmen waved to us, I'm sure mostly to tease the teacher. And we waved back, mostly to show that we are not children, nor do we feel the inclination to become nuns."

"Don't shout so," said Nana. "When we came past the cherry tree it was buzzing with girls."

"No, there isn't anyone but Alice, and she's too stupid to worry about."

"That's not so," I rejoined on Alice's behalf. "She would have been much too smart to wave at workmen when she was walking with a group from a girls' school, where there are rules for everything. It's no wonder that the teachers are strict when they have so many spoiled, coddled 'daughters of affluent homes' to take care of."

"Hear the sparrow twitter," cried Ingeborg. "Well, you sure aren't from a coddled home, that much is clear. But your humility has bolstered my strength. We're expecting to be called in for a real blowout; now I'm finally ready to take the tyrant on."

There was a rustling in the passage. Miss Bryndum's face appeared, looking more pale than usual. It was from anger; she did not take the time to say a word to any of us. She just signaled to Ingeborg and Thyra for them to follow her.

Nana and I slunk after, as though we were the guilty parties. "It's like we're traitors," I whispered.

When we emerged onto the garden path, Alice jumped down from the tree. She was wearing her pants from gym class, and she sauntered up to me, hands in her pockets. "It took me a while to get down from that height; I had to endure the whole deplorable episode. The day I came here, I thought, the little one in black has some fire in her. Good night."

It was too much to take all at once. I tore the cap off her head and threw it in her face. "You must be reading some awful kind of romance books if you think I'm going to play the defiant heroine, when I'm happy to be here." I was so angry that I shrieked and ran up to my room.

But after that evening there were no more opened letters, so Miss Bryndum must have heard every word we said in the labyrinth. We became such good friends that I was alternately proud and embarrassed, for it suggested I was far more virtuous than I was. She made sure that we got clothes that suited us—light and colorful. Mimi won her over by being so considerate of others and by always coming prepared to history class. And she described us to our three aunts in such a way that we were well received each in our own location during summer break.

The only sad thing was Ferdinand. At Skovridergården I missed him and missed going out driving with Bella.

Mimi returned without once having heard his name; he was not discussed at Strandgården. He avoided his relatives from Langeland. There was no trace of him.

But the activity at Antvorskov made me forget it. All my progress made me forget it.

The music teacher, who was married to a doctor in Slagelse, liked to have as many pupils as possible meet at her house, and I became one of the elect. When Mimi heard about it, she thought that I, like Griffenfeldt,[‡] had risen too quickly and prophesied that these trips would be my downfall. I had a nasty way of attracting attention, she said—the way I walked said, look, here I come. If I did not want to ruin everything for all three of us, I should stop gliding along with my nose in the air, not looking to the right or to the left.

One day in November, it was already dark as I came home from my lesson. I missed Alice, who now liked me nearly as I much as I liked her, and I missed studying by lamplight. But I walked as I had promised Mimi—I had even hit my leg in gym class so that it was completely impossible to glide.

The street was empty. It sounded like a man was following me. Surely not in this little town. I remembered Alice's story, told in her deliberate Jutland accent. A very proper seaman had pursued her one lonesome night on the jetty in Fredrikshavn. It was a pleasure simply

[‡] Griffenfeldt's (1635-99) brilliant career started when he was a student and excelled in his studies. He rose from his middle class origins to a position of great wealth and influence, becoming one of the King's closest advisors. He fell out of the King's favor, however, was arrested and spent the last 23 years of his life in prison.

to speak with such a refined creature, he had said, and he continued on variations of that theme until she began having thoughts about him that ill-befitted her. So she spun around directly in front of him: "Shut up, for Christ's sake!" He froze right in place, completely stunned.

There *was* a man coming after me! And now we were on the lonesome avenue. Had Mimi had been right after all?

I would do what Alice did. But I carried it out so abruptly that I collided with my pursuer. The words rushing out of my mouth sounded pitiful: "Oh, won't you leave me alone. So much is at stake for me and my sisters."

He laughed nervously and introduced himself: "My name is Frenchel. My wife stood on the balcony after your lesson and thought that you were walking stiffly and holding your head as though you were dizzy. Are you afraid to be walking home by yourself?"

"I'm not afraid of anything in the world except whatever has to do with men." I laughed with relief. "Forgive me, Dr. Frenchel, I only mean that I am afraid of anything that is against the rules, since we are so happy to be there. Please say hello to Mrs. Frenchel and thank her for her concern."

I continued at my own pace, relieved, kicking at the new-fallen leaves.

Then I began to think about Ingeborg and Thyra. It really did not take much to get thrown out. Those two had been forgiven in June, but by October, Miss Bryndum had lost all patience with them. Thyra's somber-faced father had come and collected them both. It all looked so tragic.

My heart began hammering in my chest at the thought. Or was it because I again heard a man's steps behind me? Well, other people have the right to walk on this street.

It really was a man's strong, decisive steps. Would a pursuer not walk more softly? No, no, it was clear that it was me he was intent on. I could not stand to wait for the attack. If he was innocent like Dr. Frenchel, he could always say so. I spun around.

It was Ferdinand. The worst person it could possibly be, the greatest crime.

We stood staring at each other, as though it was impossible that we were both here. I thought I heard him murmur that he had not been sure it was me until I turned my face.

He held his hat in his hand—I saw the dark curls on top of his head, his burning eyes. He no longer looked like a draught horse—he was slender, lithe. And elegant. And wonderful. He must be getting much more attention now. "How did you get here?" I murmured.

He reached out his hand for me. I retreated behind a bare tree; its trunk provided a little cover. "How did you get here?"

He followed me slowly, smiling broadly and showing his beautiful, straight teeth. "Mimi mentioned your music lessons at Strandgården when my brother Axel was visiting. The next morning he told me about it when he visited me, and I didn't waste any time following him to the steamer. Unfortunately, Mimi didn't specify the time. I have spent several hours outside Dr. Frenchel's door. And then you slipped away from me."

He turned me to face him. "You've changed. You've became even lovelier. And so grown-up. Such a stroke of luck that it is almost your birthday." He removed something from a package, entwining it gently around my throat. "It's Mother's gold necklace."

"They trust me here," I stammered. "I'm one of the only ones who has permission to come to Slagelse alone, the elite; I can't let them down."

"If we're discovered, I will accompany you to the director," he replied. "I'll be speaking with her soon in any case."

"No, no, you mustn't come unannounced," I pleaded.

"Very well, so I'll send her a letter. I'll arrange it so that we can write to each other as soon as you turn sixteen."

"Love letters? I'll be thrown out if I get properly engaged."

"You're as frightened as a little pig at slaughtering time," he laughed and lay his arm around my shoulders.

It helped. I felt the courage to tell him about school: "I have friends here—one who's beautiful, but she doesn't care about that, and one who's smart—it's completely impossible for me to catch up to her. The teachers are wonderful. The history classes are better than novels—the way Miss Bryndum describes things the people come to life—acting, suffering, finding happiness. In two years we'll have learned as much as the regular students."

"Two years," he exclaimed, releasing me. "You promised me one year that day in the old garden."

"But the curriculum is two years. I would only sit there with you thinking, now they're having French, now they're having English, how far has Nana gotten, is Alice coming along? Miss Harries has already brought me so far that I'm translating *A Tale of Two Cities;* she says that I have exceptional abilities in that area."

"But you don't want to.... Are you one of those modern girls who wants to *become* something?"

"Never. She also asked me about that, and I answered, 'Nothing but marriage.' She smiled at that so nicely, because she has been engaged herself. I want to get married and have batches of children ... " I stopped, horrified.

"Have they told you that we're too closely related?"

"Yes."

"That's just nonsense. You're so different from me, and we're both so healthy that it will go splendidly. I have this from a doctor—he told me himself. One who knows you, too. Aga, I'll wait those two years. But we must stay in contact. Otherwise you'll forget me. I promise to bring it off so discreetly that no one can take anything away from you."

"Thanks. But. . . . Now I should be at my desk studying. They'll start to notice that I'm not back yet."

"I'm going, my dear, I'm going. I just want to hear one thing out of your sweet little mouth. You love your friends and you love your teachers—and me too, don't you?"

I looked around. I heard steps rustling in the fallen leaves. "Of course, of course. But not here."

"You scaredy-cat, that's nothing but the wind. I've put up a swing for you on the hill. And what a swing it is. The maid uses it once in a while and positively shouts with joy."

"Thank you—but now someone's coming."

"Well good-bye, my darling. Shall I say hello to Bella? Shall I say hello to the maid? We talk about you all the time." He bent over and gave me a kiss. "So run along, scaredy-cat."

"Good-bye, thank you." I shot off like a dog that has slipped his leash.

But then I realized that it was he, that he had traveled here after six months of loneliness, and that the whole way home he would sit and brood over how afraid I had been to lose my privileges. I rushed back, burrowing deep into him and kissed him with all my might.

And then I remembered something that would make him really happy. "You won't be getting some know-nothing farmer's wife. Even Mimi is amazed that I know how all the food was prepared at home. And at the way I can use my hands now—they aren't all red anymore."

"My blessed little child," he whispered.

He did not kiss me forcefully, as I had done. He kissed slowly and tenderly, and I would have been delighted if I had not known that they were there wondering: what has happened to her? He kissed too slowly—all my fears returned. But I stood fast. He must go home satisfied. I endured it, until he pushed me away himself and whispered, "Go."

Excerpted from *Let gang på jorden*. Translated from the Danish by Paul Sandvold Baxter.

ᘓ Moa Martinson

Born to a working-class woman in Norrköpping, Sweden, Moa Martinson (1890–1964) grew up when Sweden was changing from a rural to an industrial society. As a young woman she followed the pattern of all women in her class: she married a working-class man and gave birth to five sons. But starting in the 1920s Moa Martinson became a public figure who wrote articles and books and gave lectures all over Sweden. She wrote and spoke about what she had experienced first-hand, the situation of the working-class woman, mother and wife.

"The New Teacher" is excerpted from *Mother Gets Married*, the first book in a trilogy about a girl called Mia. The trilogy is set at the turn of the century and is to a large degree autobiographical. The relationship between daughter and mother is at the heart of this work and in "The New Teacher" we see how the girl's first infatuation affects the way she perceives her mother.

The New Teacher

I arrived in Holmstad in the middle of the term with no expectations whatsoever, but at the same time not a bit worried about how I would get along with the mean teacher. The kids came up, then withdrew to talk me over; they had a hard time placing me. I was straightforward and fearless and knew their slang, but to most of them I seemed too well-dressed.

My mother always saw to it that I was neat and clean. The only thing missing was the embroidered purse from Dalarna that would have placed me among the really well-dressed. But Mother never bought me a purse. She couldn't abide showing off. The fact that my hair was so long and thick for my age was enough to make me stand out. In the outskirts of town, a girl with a long, thick braid was always accepted.

The new teacher was about forty and tall and slim, with curly brown hair cut short like a man's and a snow-white center part in the middle. Was she ugly or beautiful? I think she was very beautiful. To me she was the most beautiful creature I'd ever seen. The room was large, but so run-down and blackened by smoke it made my previous school seem nice in comparison. Big chunks of plaster were peeling from the walls. When I was standing by the map of Jerusalem and Nazareth that taught geography to beginners the pointer wanted to keep moving across the cracks in the plaster on the wall to other towns of Christ's Passion—the entire wall looked like a map.

I sat at a desk by myself. Here the desks were for two, and sitting alone was no privilege—it was easy to tell that by the way they all wanted to sit next to their special friends so no one would be tempted to sit by the new girl.

I'd heard there was another newcomer but didn't know whether it was a boy or a girl.

I didn't really mind sitting alone nor did I mind sitting with a boy. The previous teacher had made this a punishment. If a girl misbehaved (it had to be a minor offense) she'd be moved to a boy's desk.

But a boy never had to move to a girl's.

Why it was a punishment to sit by a boy I could never figure out. During my brief time with that teacher it happened to me twice. I thought it was a pleasant change of pace, especially since I ended up right by the window and could look out. Apparently she noticed that this punishment was more like a pleasure for me, so toward the end, as I mentioned before, I had to stand in front of her desk instead when I'd misbehaved.

I soon figured out why it was shameful to sit by yourself in this new school. The ones who had lice had to sit by themselves till the teacher could disinfect them.

It sounds cruel, but her method worked. What could she do when so many kids came to school with lice? Both body lice and head lice. The teacher set to work at once when she saw someone was infested, dousing their hair with sabadilla vinegar and giving them a change of clothes she'd somehow gotten hold of. No matter how many poor little kids with lice she took down to the wash house and scrubbed, they all got clean underwear or shirts, and the old clothes were put in boiling water. And of course there was a note to the parents or the matron at the poorhouse, or the farmers with foster children, to please not send children to school with lice, so the story got out that she was mean.

I sat watching my new teacher while she sat quietly waiting for the class to come to order. For the first time in my life I noticed a woman, an unfamiliar woman. My feelings were chaotic and confused.

I'd clearly fallen in love with this dark, serious woman, and that seemed like a potential betrayal of my mother. When I called to mind her hollow little face with the thick crown of light hair, she seemed so utterly dull and ordinary compared to this vision. I sat clutching the note Mother had sent with me, a grimy note in poor handwriting. Up till now I'd had more faith in Mother's actions than in those attributed to God, but now all of a sudden I felt I couldn't turn in this note. It seemed so paltry that I slipped it into the desk. At the same time tears came to my eyes as I remembered once when Mother had been crying.

I'd seen her cry many times, but this particular time came to me now. She'd been sitting at the table with her face down on her arms, strands of hair falling down her neck and her bun to one side, and when she heard me come in and lifted up her head, her face was so strangely contorted by anguish that I let out a scream. At this moment I could see Mother's anguished expression so clearly that I thought I could hear her sobs. Looking shyly at the new teacher, I nearly started crying myself. My mother's poor contorted face as it had appeared a couple of years ago won out, for the moment, over my new love. I took the note out of the desk again and went up to the teacher. It only said that my mother was away doing laundry and couldn't come with me. Then I handed the teacher the report from my previous school, which just stated flatly that I'd attended for five months. She read the report as well as Mother's grimy note while I stood staring as if bewitched at her short, curly hair with the white part. I instantly decided not to give Mother a moment's peace until she'd cut off my hair.

The teacher welcomed me, took me by the hand and looked searchingly at me with a serious gaze. I shivered with bliss. I would have done whatever she asked on the spot, but she merely asked me to go sit down. I stared at her the whole time from my desk. Just think, next morning I could come back, and then the next and the next.

All of a sudden the trouble I'd had with my previous teacher didn't matter at all. Instantly Mother was just my servant who worked, made my sack lunch, and starched and ironed my pinafores. There were three of them. Unfortunately I wasn't wearing the nicest one now on my first day. It was dirty. Mother usually took them along in a little bundle and washed them when she did other people's laundry, but for today she apparently hadn't. I sat thinking about this and became very annoyed at Mother. She should have seen to it that I looked as nice as possible now that I was starting at a new school.

"There's supposed to be another new pupil," said the teacher in her soothing, perfect voice—because if you love someone, everything about them is perfect.

"Are you there, Hanna?" she called out into the hallway through the open door of the classroom.

A tiny figure stepped into the doorway.

Little Hanna. I've never forgotten you. You arrived just as my feeling of unselfish love blossomed for the first time. (Loving your mother is always selfish. Mothers are a necessary part of everyday life, and at this moment my mother was merely a washerwoman, a washerwoman whose eyes were red from crying, who had strands of hair falling out of her bun down her neck, while my new love had a snow-white part and brown, curly hair.) That evening I prayed fervently to God for curly hair. Hanna! A tiny figure stepped across the threshold and stopped just inside the door, staring at the floor. I hadn't noticed her before at all; she'd probably been hiding the whole time before the teacher came downstairs.

Her hair was nearly white and so tightly braided that it formed a little tail that stuck straight out from her neck. Her face was white as a flower in the sun, a flower that soon will turn pink. It was shining, that face, that small, thin face. She was wearing one of those jackets that fastens in front with about thirty hooks, fifteen for the lining and the rest for the jacket on top. A skirt that reached nearly all the way down to her feet, much longer in back than in front.

Her bare feet stuck out, small and white under the hem of the skirt. It was the end of May, warm as summer in the middle of the day but nippy the moment the sun went down. None of the other children were barefoot, and this was Hanna's first day. Her hands were clenched tight in front of what would have been her stomach if there had been any sign of one beneath the tight skirt. I remember her knuckles were white, that's how hard she was clenching her hands. She was maybe three feet tall.

"Step forward, Hanna, you have a new friend to sit with."

But Hanna didn't dare budge from the spot. The other children leaned toward each other and started whispering. They knew who she was. She was from the poorhouse at Vilbergen. Broom-Mina's Hanna, who used to trudge along to the square and deliver brooms to houses where the wives were so elegant they didn't want to carry them home themselves.

I sat looking at Hanna while the kids whispered and the teacher sat waiting for her. Then I got up as if in a trance. I think I must have been convinced she was a pretty little troll-woman without wrinkles (I already read everything I could lay hands on, and what I'd encountered was rather quirky). I went up to her and took the hand she reluctantly gave me, laughing and talking the whole time as if I weren't in a school room with an unfamiliar teacher and unfamiliar children but alone with her. I took her along to my desk, whispering to her when I saw the teacher's smile; she was watching us both and smiling.

"You have to show your report card. Do you have a note from your mother?"

"No," whispered Hanna.

"But your mother should have written a note," I said reproachfully.

"I guess she can't write," Hanna got out, her lip trembling, since I'd probably looked stern.

"Come along," I said, and the tiny barefoot figure in the thirty-hook jacket made of leftover yarn trudged up to the teacher, her hand in mine.

The other children looked a bit pale. This was a highly unusual break in the routine; they were supposed to have started Bible study fifteen minutes ago. A pupil who talked without asking permission was beyond their experience. This would come to a terrible end.

In front at the teacher's desk I whispered, "Hanna's mother can't write and Hanna doesn't have a report card. Please, teacher, let her stay anyway."

"Of course," said the teacher. "Don't worry. She can stay." And she stroked Hanna's tightly braided hair.

I wished the teacher had cut off my hand or my foot instead.

We went back to our desk and then Bible study started. I have no idea how Hanna had found out the assignment, but she knew it. Standing there with her hands tightly clenched, a tiny figure three feet tall in a long skirt and warm jacket with puffed sleeves, in a single breath she rattled off, "Abraham dwelt in the plain of Mamre . . . "

I was in an emotional state all day. During the lessons I sat there secretly pinching my arms, nearly putting my fingers out of joint to see how much pain I could take. Some instinct told me you had to be able to tolerate pain without blinking or crying out when you loved someone who was as perfect as my new teacher. For a long time afterward there were bruises on my arms. My first day in that school was a great success, but I myself didn't notice just how successful it was. A deep groundswell of emotion had surfaced. For a long time after that, outward achievements and attention seemed worthless. You don't demand attention from someone you don't care about. That evening I lay awake late, counting the row of wooden acorns on the frame of my settee and pinching my underarms till the tears came.

"What are you doing? Say your prayers and go to sleep now," said Mother in irritation as she sat staring, lost in thought.

"I've said them."

"Well, go to sleep, then."

Just like that, on command. But my eyes felt full of sand and I pinched my arms even harder. I mortified my flesh and counted rosary beads like a Catholic, though I'd never even heard of the Pope. When love has come into the world, no church is needed. Love leads to both mortification and confession.

No one, not even a child, can fall asleep on command.

Like many others who've just fallen in love, I lay awake all night the first night after the miracle. I was so tired in the morning I nearly had to stay home from school.

It was probably a good thing for me that Hanna was there to deflect some of my violent infatuation for the teacher—otherwise it might have ended badly. For a few days I was a complete egotist anyway. I got a whipping from my mother, which brought me part-way back to normal. It hurt enough to make me stop torturing myself. Out of the blue one afternoon I'd started asking her all sorts of questions. For instance, why didn't she put alder cones in the vases any longer? Why was there just a strip of cloth across the only window of our room? Why was everything always a mess at home?

"And you haven't washed my best pinafore. I have to go around looking like a . . . "

"Like what?" Mother asked in an ominous tone. "What are you carrying on about? Are you starting to be like 'him'? You should be ashamed of yourself! Is that what they teach you in school, to come home and be nasty to your mother?"

Now Mother was really mad. She couldn't put up long curtains here because the window was so small. Besides, the stove smoked, and she couldn't make this room as nice as the one on our old street. No one could have felt less at home in this room than she herself did, and that made my criticism sting more. But I'd imagined having coffee in a nice room with long, starched curtains and a white tablecloth and had dreamed of seeing my beautiful teacher sitting in this room on the acorn settee, which was beginning to look the worse for wear.

"What did the teacher say?" Mother suddenly asked. "Did **you give** her the note?"

"The teacher is so pretty—she has short, curly hair and she looks like the Queen on Grandma's picture" (that was Crown Princess Victoria).

Mother said nothing for a while.

"Couldn't you make things look nicer here, too?" I finally ventured. "And couldn't I have a Dalarna purse? I have to go around looking like a . . ."

"Here's what you get for that," said Mother, giving me a couple of hard swats on the behind on top of my clothes. "Be happy with what you have. You should be ashamed of yourself! Here I slave day in and day out washing people's filthy clothes, just so you can have enough to eat."

Ah, so that was it! Enough to eat, was that so important?

The spanking hadn't made much difference. I sat there sulking for a while.

"You could have found another man, one who supported us," I said after a bit. I'd heard my aunt say that once to another of Mother's sisters.

"That's enough out of you," said Mother, and in the silence that followed I got birched.

Hanna became the conduit for all my love for the teacher.

It was quite strange. The other children had a dreadful respect for the teacher. No beatings or punishments of any kind were needed here. That wasn't the sort of method she used; the children obeyed her anyway. But I don't think anyone loved her more than I did.

From now on, since one of the boys no longer volunteered, Hanna and I took over bringing in the wood. Hanna couldn't carry much, but I was sturdy and strong as could be. What wouldn't I have done for the teacher's sake, anyway? Every day that we brought in wood she gave Hanna dinner. I was never included. Once she offered me coffee, but I was in such a state about being alone with her in her nice, airy room that I started to cry, which I very rarely did.

"Dear child," was all she said, stroking my cheek. "Dear child, don't cry. Today you may recite 'Spring has arrived.'"

I left without drinking the coffee, and she didn't insist.

I was often asked to recite:

Spring has arrived. Its flowering garlands
The meadows adorn; the heavens are blue.
Fringes of gold bedeck the young willows.
Hiding in grass tufts, elves frolic anew.

The poem was like a fairy tale, and when the teacher's dark eyes rested on me, just as attentive each time I recited it, everything seemed to become a fairy tale.

Excerpted from *Mor gifter sig*. Translated from the Swedish by Rochelle Wright.

⊘ℜ *Laila Stien*

"Here I Come!" is the title story in a collection that Laila Stien (1946–) wrote about growing up in a small community in North Norway, near Mo i Rana. The time is the 1950s and Stien tells, with humor and warmth, about life at school and at play. The stories recall childhood as a time that was happy and secure, a time when you could find guidance and support through disappointment and small crises.

The story below takes place during the winter. Winters are long and snowy so far north and skiing is a favorite pastime for everyone, young and old, girls and boys. Ski jumping, however, has traditionally been a male sport. The girls in "Here I Come!", an active and high-spirited bunch of ten year olds, cheer the older boys on as they come hurtling down the ski jump. Until one day one of the more daring girls decides she'd like to try it too.

Here I Come!

Wintertime—everything was great. We always knew just what to do. We spent all our time around Håkstad Hill and Floodlight Hill. That is, when we weren't in school or home eating.

Around Floodlight Hill we could keep going right up till supper, since it was light. There were lights on tall poles running from the ski jump all the way down the hill. That's why it was called Floodlight Hill. My brother and a few of the other big boys had jumped over twenty meters on that slope.

We girls—nine, ten, eleven years old—mainly stuck to the small slopes nearby. We packed down the snow and made smooth tracks. We made little ski jumps too. Then we had competitions and awarded judges' marks. Our marks were generous. Everyone got nineteen. May Brit got nineteen and a half because she was the best.

You could give marks for the funniest jump, too. We kicked our legs out, squinted our eyes and flapped our arms. Then anyone could get nineteen and a half.

When it got too dark, we skied over to Floodlight Hill itself to watch the boys. They walked around carrying heavy jump skis on their shoulders and spit in the snow, saying, "Here goes nothin.'" Then they climbed to the top of the jump and pushed off. We held them in awe.

We stayed well to the side of the hill so we wouldn't be in the way. "Get off the hill," they shouted if we got too close. We stood shivering at the edge of the scrub forest and heard them shout, "Here I come!"

Then they came hurtling down. Their ski pants flapped in the wind over the knoll, at the crest of the landing slope. The best of them leaned way over, their arms relaxed, bowing out from their bodies.

We stood and stamped our feet, watching them shoot out from the jump, one after the other. They jumped with a cry: a high, quavering AHH! They all tried to copy a skier named Recknagel, a foreigner who jumped like a dream.

"Here comes Recknagel!"we shouted from the forest edge when someone set off.

"Here comes Slåttvik!" we might also shout.

Slåttvik was the most famous ski jumper in Norway and in the whole world practically. He won the gold medal in Nordic combined at the Oslo Olympics in 1952 even though he had lived in Bjerka for a while, working at the power plant like a perfectly ordinary man.

They liked us shouting. When they came down on the outrun we would shout, "Nineteen and a half! Hurrah, Simon Slåttvik!"

When we gave them high marks and called them such distinguished names, they might even treat us to a "Hi" as they passed by on their way back up the hill.

Sometimes we got up the courage to go up to the knoll. Stood there leaning on our poles looking up at the jump. It was built of criss-crossing timbers and boards and was terribly high. It was a miracle that anyone had the courage to fly off from the end out into empty space. It was terrifying to see the jump so close at hand. I got all dizzy. It didn't look nearly that scary from down below. May Brit didn't think it looked that scary at all. May Brit went up to the knoll a lot. She liked to ski down from there. She bent her knees, held her poles back and rushed down. None of the boys shouted, "Get off the hill" to May Brit. She was one girl who didn't tumble down and make holes in the landing slope. But it wasn't as though they never made any holes themselves. Some of them came off the jump looking like crows. They kicked and flapped their arms and cried out before they hit the ground. Then we were allowed to run out from the edge of the forest and pack down the snow. We tramped around until it was nice and even, then we backed up to the loose snow.

"All clear?" came the voice from up above.

"Clear," came the answer.

If we were lucky, another crow would come along. Then we got to tramp around some more, which kept us warm.

We kept warm all winter, for the most part. We were well dressed in our ski pants, wool sweaters, and anoraks. Little balls of ice and snow formed on our black and white wool mittens; they were handy to suck on when we got thirsty.

Floodlight Hill drew us with its light and excitement. We hurried there right after school, so that we would get a couple hours to ourselves before the ski jumpers started drifting in.

We all practiced on the landing slope. Side-stepped up from the outrun, starting out higher and higher each time.

After a while I couldn't let people see me starting from the middle of the slope any more. May Brit had been going from the knoll for at least a year—maybe two. Vigdis was starting off from the top now too. And Snøfte, small as she was.

It was my turn. There was no way out.

I side-stepped up. All the way up. Stood under the ski jump, slid-ing my skis back and forth a little on the hard-packed snow. Tried to feel if the undersides had gotten clumped with snow and ice. They hadn't.

The outrun spread before me like an abyss far, far below. I shud-dered. That's where I was headed. I'd end up there if I just pushed off and skied down. I'd end up there on my feet, on my face, or on my behind. I might fall and have blood spurt out my nose. I might get a concussion and tear up my ski pants. I might break both my arms and my feet and my collarbones. I might lose control and crash sideways into a tree trunk or into one of the light poles. I might die.

"Whatcha doin' up there?" they shouted up to me from the outrun.

There they stood. There stood all the others who had risked it. They were giddy and happy. Vigdis had taken her skis off and stood there waxing them. She stood rubbing and buffing with a piece of paraffin, or maybe it was graphite wax. She wanted better glide. They stood chattering, shuffling their feet. Johan had arrived. Johan with his black curly hair had come all the way from Mo. Now he was standing on the outrun watching as Vigdis waxed her skis so that she could go even faster the next time she skied down the entire landing slope.

I stood under the ski jump and knew that there was no way that I could side-step down now. Not with Johan standing there, with his stocking cap pushed back and his Mediterranean good looks, talking with Vigdis and the others.

"'God, who holds small children dear, please grant the prayer of your child here,'" I prayed and pushed off.

It went by so fast. I nearly managed not to think. Managed to think only one single thought: STAY UP!—Stay up, stay up, stay up, I said to myself as the wind lashed my face. Tears welled up in my eyes, misting them over. I blinked them away. Down I plummeted.

I stayed up!

The momentum carried me past the knot of kids. Past them and out on the outrun. I didn't snowplow. I went on and on—way out to where the snow softened and the tracks trailed off. I sailed as far as I could go, my face wet, my body weightless, and happy—deliriously happy.

The next day it wasn't nearly so scary. But I had butterflies in my stomach. Especially at the start. And as I reached the outrun. There the butterflies were so bad that it almost hurt. But it was only for a little bit. Then it passed.

The winters were quite long. They lasted until Easter and often beyond. We got braver and braver on the slopes each day. Soon we took the landing slope at Floodlight Hill completely in stride. "Nothin' to it," we thought, full of confidence. We got up the courage to come further out from the deep snow and scrub pines when the boys were jumping. We skied out on the outrun and started talking to some of the daredevils.

"Jeez, you almost jumped all the way to the outrun!" we said, buttering them up.

They really liked that.

"What kind of wax ya usin'?"

"*Fyklakk*,"* they answered.

"Red or yellow?" we asked and knew what we were talking about.

"Yellow," they mostly said.

Then they spit in the snow because it was expected, shouldered their skis, and no longer had time to stand on the outrun chatting. They had to practice. They planned to jump Fagerås Hill someday and places even more dangerous. Most dangerous of all was Gråkall Hill in Trondheim. The best went there. My brother had been there and knocked himself silly several times.

"Doesn't it look fun?" said May Brit one day while we stood watching beside the knoll.

"Whaddaya mean?" we wanted to know.

"Jumping, whaddaya think?"

May Brit looked up, following with her eyes the next pair of blue ski pants that came flapping through the air.

"Fun? No way," I said and shuddered.

---

*A preparation the boys applied to their skis to attain maximal speed down the ski jump.

"I really wanna try it," sighed May Brit, looking positively entranced.

"Are you serious?"

"Hey, I'm sure there's nothin' to it. That guy Kjell Arne did a jump and he's younger than we are."

"But still I. . . "

Before we could say any more, May Brit hoisted her skis on her shoulder and started climbing up.

"May Brit! Don't do it!" we shouted with trembling voices, thinking that it would lead to disaster.

But May Brit completely ignored us. She was already past the knoll and on her way up to the tower.

"She's nuts," said Liv and meant it.

"She's got ice water in her veins," said Snøfte with admiration in her voice.

"She's out of her mind," I added.

Vigdis didn't say anything. She stood up on her toes watching May Brit's narrow back as she scrambled up to the top with her Splitkein skis bobbing on her shoulder.

The boys on the outrun and on the knoll and everywhere all stopped and stood, just watching. No one shouted. It wouldn't have done any good. She had made up her mind.

In a moment she turned. She crouched down and bellowed:

"All cleeear?"

"Clear," came the answer from the outrun below.

Those of us who stood among the scrub pines stamping our feet didn't shout anything. We had lost the power of speech.

"Here I come!"

May Brit's voice was high and thin, but still it carried a long way.

Now she was pushing off.

Now she was coming down.

A skinny girl's body heading toward the abyss. We couldn't do anything about it. It was going to happen whether we liked it or not.

She shot off the ski jump with her mouth wide open and her hands over her head. She was standing straight up and down in the air, looking terror-stricken. There was a smack and a clatter and a groan. We stood stock still and stared.

She stayed up!

May Brit had jumped over the knoll and stayed up. Now she sailed along down the slope and out on the outrun. Her ski pants flapped in the wind. She glided onward like a queen in a flowing gown and accepted our applause and cheers and shouts of hurray.

"You did great!"

The boys were full of shouts and compliments. We could hear it all the way up where we were standing in the scrub forest. There was no end of extravagant praise. As for us, we still hadn't regained the power of speech. We had grunted a few times when the tension was at its peak, but now we were mute. We just gaped. Until Vigdis said:

"I wanna try too."

"Aren't you scared?" the rest of us gasped.

"Well . . . I'm sure it's no big deal."

With that, Vigdis also slung her skis over her shoulder, turned her back, and was on her way up.

Snøfte giggled. "This is exciting," she said. I didn't feel entirely well. Liv shook her head and laughed.

Vigdis pulled her cap firmly down over her ears with one hand. She gripped her skis tightly with the other.

"Whaddaya think you're doin," Arnfinn shouted impatiently from the knoll when Vigdis came trudging past him. "This is gettin' outta hand."

"Yep," panted Vigdis, laughing, and kept climbing.

Snøfte and Liv were all worked up. They shouted and carried on about how terribly exciting it all was. I didn't say much. My heart was beating in my throat. And I was cold. Especially my feet.

Vigdis was up at the top. She had bent over to fasten her bindings. She had nice tight *Kandahar* bindings. Now she snapped them into place. She stood up and pulled her stocking cap down firmly. Stood like that for a moment. We waited. Everyone waited. Including May

Brit. She had stopped down on the outrun and stood watching.

"All cleeear?" Vigdis shouted, her voice strong.

"Clear," shouted Arnfinn ceremoniously, his forehead wrinkling. "Here I come!"

Vigdis' voice sounded less familiar now. Shrill and slightly wavering.

Now she started. Crouched over to jump. Quick and silent down the track. Approaching the jump. At the edge. She grunted perfectly and went into her tuck. Stretched out her hands, hurtling forward. She landed with a smack. Waved her arms to keep her balance.

She stayed up! She kept going all the way to the bottom of the landing slope. Then she just sat down on her behind to stop. Must have thought that was far enough.

"Four meters!" Arnfinn smirked.

"Five!" I shouted.

"Six!" growled Snøfte, irritated.

Arnfinn hoisted his jump skis on his broad shoulder, grinned, and went up, banging out a twenty-meter jump that made the scrub trees tremble. But no one yelled "Slåttvik" or "Nineteen and a half." Everyone was still focused on May Britt and Vigdis. Johan came up and clapped them on the back. In a few minutes they came side-stepping up the landing slope to where we were standing. There they stood, out of breath, laughing and chattering on about how incredibly fun it had been, what a blast, the coolest thing they had ever done in their whole lives, not dangerous at all, not one bit, no worse than skiing down the landing slope, really. They carried on so much about how much fun they'd had that the rest of us could hardly get a word in. Then suddenly Snøfte broke in and announced:

"Heck, I'm gonna go up and try too!"

Well, now things really were getting out of hand. This didn't bode well. My feet were getting colder and colder. Not only that, but now I felt a little nauseous, too. I knew what was coming next. Felt it in my gut and all over. Yep—here it came: May Brit said it first. Smiling:

"You too, Laila!"

I gulped. I looked away. Sniffed indifferently.

"Yeah, you've gotta go up and jump, you really do!" Vigdis chimed in, surely meaning to be nice.

"Do you wanna go before me?" Snøfte asked sweetly and stepped aside.

"No . . . no, you go ahead," I stammered.

Snøfte started on her way up.

Everything was buzzing all around me: "Of course you're gonna go up." "It's your turn next." "Sure Laila's gonna. Definitely."

I knew what they were thinking. Knew all too well and it caught in my throat. They were thinking about my brother. The great jumper. They were thinking that since I was his sister, I . . .

"What about you, Liv?"

May Brit was all excited and as sweet as ever.

Liv smiled beautifully and said that it would never occur to her even in her wildest dreams. So they didn't bug her about it any more.

Snøfte was on her way. Tiny little Snøfte sped like a bullet toward the edge of the jump. Over the edge. Quicker than lightning. It happened *too* quickly. I couldn't take it in properly. Couldn't see it clearly. Saw only a white cloud and one lone ski shooting out between the bushes. Snøfte was inside the cloud. Snøfte was a bundle bristling with arms and legs. The bundle rolled down the hard-packed landing slope, faster and faster and faster. The boys rushed over to the base of the slope where the bundle finally stopped.

"Didja hurt yourself?"

"Are you OK?"

"Didja break your neck?"

"Are you bleeding?"

They peppered her with questions. Snøfte lay still and didn't make a sound. Then Vigdis turned around, pushed off, and raced down the slope; she stopped short on the flat and skied over to the lifeless bundle.

"Synøve!" she shouted, using her birth name. "Synøve . . . , are you hurt?"

The rest of us stood stiff and tense, waiting up at the top.

"No way," laughed Snøfte, jumping up. She brushed herself off in a flurry of snow.

The boys stared openmouthed. "She's tough!" somebody said.

Snøfte was laughing and laughing.

Vigdis was laughing too.

"Next," shouted Vigdis, turning up toward the knoll.

"Yeah, now it's your turn," smiled May Brit.

"Get up there and jump!" shouted the boys from down on the outrun, waving their arms at me.

I stiffened. I couldn't move. My feet were nailed fast. My whole body was cold and stiff. Down below, they were shouting and hollering. They were a clump of waving arms and wide-open mouths, flailing and cajoling and shouting. They said my brother's name several times. Said it to each other and said that now we'd see some action because now the sister of the great jumper himself was going to go.

"What's the matter with you? Didja use *klister* wax?!"

They were stamping and grinning.

"Come on!" shouted Snøfte, sounding healthy and unhurt and perfectly normal.

Vigdis and May Brit were both jabbering at once, but I didn't hear what they were saying. There was something pounding, pounding in my ears. Something that hammered and banged and filled me completely. Everything became hazy. Inside the fog I saw my brother in a blue ski sweater, the start number on his chest, with a trophy and a big smile. But the smile soured more and more and became an embarrassed grimace because there I stood, scared to death, bringing shame on him and our whole family. It was unbearable.

Then I became aware of Liv, who stood stamping and shivering right beside me. She had a red nose and white cheeks. I realized how happy I was that she was there. I managed to move my feet, turn around.

"Do you wanna . . . do you wanna go home?" I stammered out, sending her a silent and heart-felt plea with my eyes.

"Yeah, sure," she answered, her teeth chattering.

I had one single clear thought in my head: Go. Get away.

"Come on. Take your jump first."

Vigdis and May Brit were getting impatient.

"What's the matter? Isn't she goin'?" Arnfinn bellowed and started up from the outrun.

Soon everyone else started up.

I gathered myself and cleared my throat, making my voice as relaxed as I could:

"No, I'm not up to it. I'm too cold. . . I gotta go home."

I noticed that my voice shook. That it felt as though it was going to break off in the middle.

"Ehh—you're scared to!" somebody shouted.

"She's scared to?"

"Isn't she gonna jump?"

They buzzed and droned. It was me they were buzzing about. I had to get out of there now. Fast. Fast as lightning before they all came up from the outrun in a bunch. I fumbled with my mittens, got them into the loops on my poles, struggled to get my skis into a track that sloped gently through the scrub forest, down toward the flat land. My heart pounded and my knees shook, but I was moving forward. Liv followed after in the same track, steady and close. We were both frozen solid. The grips on our poles were stiff. We went as fast as we could. Got closer to Håkstad Hill. It was slow going: long and steep. We heaved our way forward, kicking out our legs to make herringbone tracks. We climbed side by side, panting. My throat stung. I didn't dare to stop or look back. It was as though someone were tailing me and would grab hold of me if I stopped. Grab hold of me and take me back there—back there and up onto the jump tower. I hung on my poles. My arms ached. I lifted my heavy feet with all my strength and pressed on, higher, higher. My chest whistled. Liv groaned. She was there. Right beside me like a friendly good fairy in the middle of all my misery.

Up at the top we could rest and ski down alongside the road.

"See ya," we gasped and parted.

⊘

Inside it was light and warm. It smelled of *fyklakk,* as it did so often. My brother was preparing his skis for the weekend and the competition at Fagerås. Now he was standing in the kitchen, fumbling with a pair of ski pants; he winked, flashed a smile, and told me he'd give me a *krone* if I would press them for him. I smiled back weakly and told him he didn't need to give me anything. I would do it for free. Then I got out a damp cloth and the steam iron and pressed and pressed, and knew I could never do a good enough job for my wonderful brother whose reputation was now perhaps totally ruined. Soon everyone would be talking about his pathetic, miserable sister who was afraid to jump at Floodlight Hill like all the other little girls were doing.

I pressed the crease until it was as sharp as a knife. I pressed it until stinging tears welled up in my eyes.

"Here you go," my brother said and gave me one *krone* fifty.

I thought about Lohengrin chocolates with the custard center; my mouth started watering and I took it.

After that, I lay down on the sofa with warmed-up wool socks on my feet and hot chocolate. The wood stove crackled and popped. I had dug out our book of Hans Christian Andersen. I settled in and read the tale of the wild swans. It was about eleven young princes who had been driven from their home and transformed into swans by their evil stepmother. They were able to fly about as long as the sun was up in the sky, but as soon as the sun sank down into the water, they became princes again. Once a year they got to return to their homeland to visit. They flew over land and sea, over forests and towns, over Fata Morgana's dazzling palace, but they always had to make sure to land before the sun went down and they became human again. Otherwise they might tumble down and get hurt. Every morning at sunrise they rose up and flew—farther, always farther on their long journey home.

The fairy tale about the wild swans was the most beautiful one I knew. I lay and thought about it for a long time. Thought about how wonderful it must be to lie down to sleep at night and wake up the next day and be transformed: transformed into a big, brave ski jumper.

Excerpted from *I farta!* Translated from the Norwegian by Paul Sandvold Baxter.

Martha Sandwall-Bergström

Many Swedish girls, especially those born in the 1940s, grew up with Kulla-Gulla as a role model. Martha Sandwall-Bergström (1913–) made her debut as an author of children's literature with peers such as Astrid Lindgren and Tove Jansson. Her series of books about Kulla-Gulla, the orphaned girl who lived with poor estate workers, introduced working-class ethics and conditions into the genre of children's literature. In the 1990s, her books were acclaimed by yet another generation.

The excerpt below is from the first book in the series, *Kulla-Gulla*. Gulla (which is a nickname for Gunilla while Kulla refers to the site of her new family's home) is twelve years old and has settled in as a maid in a family that works for the manor of the region. The mother is ailing, and the grandmother has just died, so Gulla cares for the house, the five children and the animals, and helps with the harvest for the patron. At school and on the fields she protects Johannis, the oldest son, from the bullies. Her integrity, calmness and self-confident appearance influence all around her.

Kulla-Gulla

A week or two after the harvest, orders came from the manor calling everyone to the potato fields, and the next few days they worked just as hard and as fast as earlier during harvest time. There had already been some frosty nights, and all the root vegetables now had to be brought in before they froze in the ground. There were people in every field, on all fours, digging potatoes. School was closed once more and the children were given time off to help. Eight-to-ten-year-olds hoed easily, and the very youngest children who weren't strong enough yet to dig, ran ahead of the diggers and pulled the withered potato plants out of their way.

Gulla and Johannis were working side by side in one of the manor's potato fields. On either side of them were rows of maids and farmhands, crofters and day-workers bending their backs to their hoes. There was a rhythm to be kept, and if anyone fell behind, the foreman quickly caught them, shouting and ordering. He might even box the ears of some young man, or lash at him with a switch he tore off a bush from the edge of the field.

Gulla worked away at her own serene, systematic pace. Now and then she would lean over to the row where Johannis was working and give him a hand when his energy seemed to be flagging. He was paler and thinner than ever after this hard-working autumn, and his red hair hung tousled and sweaty on his forehead.

"Don't take such short strokes with your hoe, Johannis, take fewer and longer ones ... like this ... deeper and slower. You'll get less tired, feel less miserable, and you'll get at least as much done, too. ... "

She dug her hoe into his row once or twice, and pink and white potatoes rolled right up out of the moist soil.

"Isn't that sweet!" a couple of the older farm hands working alongside them teased, "Just look at little Johannis. Does he have a nursemaid now? Hasn't he learnt how to hoe a row of potatoes?"

"Johannis hasn't ever done this kind of day work before," Gulla informed them placidly, "and hoeing potatoes is an art to be mastered like any other."

She turned to the farmhands and gave a little smile, not wanting any trouble in the fields. That day, she wanted everyone to be her friend. It was such a fine day—the sun was shining and she was full of energy and good humor. As children do, she had already put her grief about Grandma behind her, and yesterday she had been to school and spoken with Big Kalle. His nose was neither broken nor disfigured, just bruised and swollen, and once she knew that, a millstone fell from her shoulders. Of course Big Kalle had tattled to schoolmaster Bromander about their fight, claiming that Gulla had assaulted him on the way home. Bromander looked upset when he reached for his cane and called the two of them up front. But when Gulla and Big Kalle were standing at his desk, he suddenly lost his strict manner and burst out laughing, asking the rest of the class what Biblical figures came to mind when they saw Gulla from Kulla and Big Kalle standing next to each other. Everyone had answered in chorus:

"David and Goliath."

Bromander had laughed once more, so hard that his spectacles slipped down. He poked Big Kalle with the cane.

"Back to your seat, young man," he instructed. "I'm sure you did something to deserve that swollen nose of yours, knowing you, Kalle."

Then he turned to Gulla and looked gravely at her. She met his gaze, clearly and openly, looking him right in the eye, as she always did.

"Did you hit him?" he asked. And Gulla told the truth, saying she had.

"Why?"

She hesitated for one moment, not wanting to tell on Big Kalle. She felt that the matter was over and done with, since she had given Big Kalle a beating and an ugly nose as a punishment.

Instead of telling the whole story, she looked their teacher in the eye and said, solemnly, "It is important to talk to people in a language they'll understand."

Bromander seemed more than satisfied with this answer to his question. He even ran his hand gently over her hair. All the other children gasped with surprise; their eyes seemed to be popping out of their heads. Nothing like this had ever happened in Bromander's classroom before. At recess several girls abandoned Linnea that day and crowded around Gulla, chatting as if they were old friends, as if she were one of the crowd.

So today, Gulla felt that life was grand, and didn't want a fuss about anything. When one of the farmhands went on bullying Johannis, she gently asked him to lay off.

"A person who's not grown-up or very strong has to concentrate completely on the work at hand," she explained, "or he'll fall behind and lose the rhythm. He can't possibly talk and work at the same time, you see."

Just then the foreman strode up the row in his tall, black boots, shouting at them to get moving. Each back bent deeper, each hoe moved faster, and the insults of the farmhands ceased for the moment.

But Johannis still couldn't keep up. He moaned softly over his hoe.

"If only I could straighten up for a minute," he whispered. "I think my back's breaking, Gulla."

"Oh no, it only feels that way," Gulla whispered back. "Grit your teeth, Johannis, don't feel anything, don't think any thoughts . . . just keep working . . . calmly and rhythmically . . . one . . . two . . . one . . . two. . . . "

Johannis clenched his teeth so his lips bled. He was bent nearly double over his hoe. His freckles glistened like bright golden drops on his pale cheeks.

"Get going over there," the foreman yelled, swinging a switch over his head threateningly. "The master won't pay a full day's wages if you don't do a full day's work."

Johannis bent more and more deeply to the ground. He looked like the ox back home, pulling a heavy load uphill with a yoke around its neck.

Once more the farmhands working the next row started to snicker, and the minute the foreman turned his back, one of them gave Johannis a smack on the behind with his hoe. That was all Johannis needed to land flat on his face in the soil.

"Oh my Lord, Johannis," whispered Gulla, "get up. . . . "

The farmhands were exploding with laughter when Johannis rose on all fours, his face brown as a mole's.

"Come along, good people, get your job done," the foreman shouted across the field. His voice had suddenly turned sympathetic and friendly, but that wasn't what made the workers suddenly redouble their efforts. Instead, everyone had noticed the elegant horse with the master on its back that had halted at the edge of the field. The master was elderly, but he sat tall. He examined the workers in the field. The eyes under his stern brow rested on the workers in the field and each and every one who felt his gaze hoed with great determination to show what a good worker he or she was.

Gulla alone had failed to notice the master, because her eyes were glued to the back of the farmhand who had made Johannis fall flat on his face. He had managed to get slightly ahead of her, and Gulla was working to catch up. Slowly she gained ground, and when she was right alongside him, her hoe shot out and deftly caught his leg.

The farmhand tipped right over, just like Johannis had before him, and Gulla smiled.

"What are you lying there smelling the ground for?" she wondered innocently.

At that very moment she caught sight of the rider at the edge of the field and curtsied deeply. She saw instantly that he was the very man who had been sitting in the carriage at the manor when she was there once before, and knew he must be Master Sylvester.

"Come over here, you," he said, pointing at Gulla with his riding crop.

Gulla's knees almost buckled under her, but she managed to walk calmly over to the edge of the field.

He looked at her, and his eyes were stern.

"Shame on you," he said solemnly. "I don' tolerate playing and mischief at work." And he lifted his crop and dealt her a smarting blow across her legs. Gulla started but stood still.

"Pardon me, Master," she said, "but I was not playing."

She raised her face and looked openly into his eyes. Her braid had come undone and her hair hung in disorderly curls around her head. Her tiny face with its dark blue eyes, narrowing towards the temples, contained neither fear nor disobedience, simply great gravity.

"What's that . . . ?" the Master asked, staring back. Seldom did anyone dare to talk back to him or to stand so erect in front of him, but that wasn't what made him stare so hard. He inspected the frail little body in clogs and a patched dress, his eyes finally returning to her face.

"Who are you?" he demanded, sounding rough and upset. "Hey, foreman, who in heaven's name is this little girl . . . ?"

Gulla replied herself, "I belong to Karlberg's from Kulla." And the foreman scurried over to confirm it.

"That's right," he said, "she's from Kulla. Begging your pardon, Master, but they have so many kids at the crofts around here one can never learn all their names."

"No, one certainly can't," the master mumbled, wiping his brow.

He turned on his horse, thinking to depart, but changing his mind he called out to Gulla, "Come back over here, child."

Gulla obeyed hesitantly, wondering whether he intended to strike her another stinging blow across the legs. The master fumbled a coin from his vest pocket. It was two-kronor coin. He pressed it into her hand and rode off.

The workers slowly straightened their backs, staring curiously. "What was that?" they asked. "What did he say? What did you get?"

Gulla held up the big, shiny silver coin triumphantly. It was no small sum, more than a grown man would make in two full days' work. She waved the coin slowly back and forth in the air so that everyone, including the foreman, would see how it twinkled in the sun.

"The master asked me to tell everyone, that this was for Johannis," she said loudly and openly.

"Johannis?" exclaimed the two farmhands at once. "Is that the latest fashion, to give the greatest reward to the worst worker . . . ?"

"The master is a good man, and he knows more than you two," said Gulla. "Here's what he told me: 'I've been sitting here watching all of you working from astride my horse. I've noticed that some of you are stronger and some weaker than others, all in accordance with the endowments of our Lord. I find it natural for the weaker to be able to do less than the stronger. Still, I can see that some of you work unwillingly while others work gladly and wholeheartedly, and that is what really counts. Please give this coin to that lank lad over there, whose heart is the most willing of them all.' Yes, that's what the master had to say to me."

Gulla caught her breath, stepped right across the furrows and solemnly presented Johannis with the coin.

"This is for you from the master."

"Thanks." Johannis took the coin between his muddy fingers and tied it into a corner of his hanky, never for a moment dropping his questioning eyes from Gulla's. She looked away and was quick to take up her hoe.

And that day, the farmhands teased Johannis no more and when the foreman addressed him his voice was less harsh.

That evening, walking home, they were silent for a long time. The moon was pale over the fir trees, it was already twilight and sure to be a frosty night. Gulla exhaled into her cold hands, sneaking a glance at Johannis. She was embarrassed, knowing that Johannis must have seen through her story about the master and the two-kronor coin.

"Are you angry with me Johannis?" she finally asked.

She felt his rough boy's hand seeking hers, and heard a sound in the darkness that sounded like a sob.

"I'm so very fond of you, sweet Gulla, that it hurts like a heartache," he whispered.

Excerpted from *Kulla-Gulla*. Translated from the Swedish by Linda Schenck.

ᴂ Minna Canth

The legacy of Minna Canth (1844–1897) is that of courage and accomplishment. Against all odds, she took up her pen as a means of supporting herself and her seven children after her husband died. Today Canth is known as Finland's first woman dramatist, a forefunner for women's social equality and the rights of the working class.

"The Nursemaid" is a short story written during Canth's most political period at the end of the 1880s and it points to the inhuman work situation of young women in the cities. By using Swedish in the text Canth also underscores the social injustice between the Finnish-speaking working class and the Swedish-speaking population that had more education and power in society. Finland had been ruled by Sweden until 1809 when Sweden lost it to Russia. During the following years the Finnish people strove to develop their own language and culture. They became independent in 1917, after the Russian Revolution.

The Nursemaid

"Emmi, hey, get up, don't you hear the bell, the lady wants you! Emmi! Bless the girl, will nothing wake her? Emmi, Emmi!"

At last, Silja got her to show some signs of life. Emmi sat up, mumbled something and rubbed her eyes. She still felt dreadfully sleepy.

"What time is it?"

"Almost five."

Five? She had had three hours in bed. It had been half-past one before she finished the washing-up: there had been visitors that evening, as usual, and for two nights before that she had had to stay up because of the child; the lady had gone off to a wedding, and baby Lilli had refused to content herself with her sugar-dummy. Was it any wonder that Emmi wanted to sleep?

She was only thirteen. And in the mornings her legs always ached so badly that for while it was very hard to stand up. Silja, who slept in the same bed, said it was because she was growing. She ought to have them bled, in Silja's opinion, but Emmi was afraid it might hurt. They were thin enough already, without having blood taken from them. They never ached while she was asleep, but the moment she woke up they started again. If she managed to get to sleep again, the aching stopped at once.

Now, as she sat up in bed, they were painful all over, from her knees right down to her heels. She felt the weight of her head pulling her down towards the bed again: try as she might, she could not lift it. Would she ever, in this life, be granted a single morning when she could sleep happily as long as she needed?

Emmi rubbed her legs. Her head had fallen forward, her chin touching her chest; her eyes would not stay open. In next to no time, she was asleep again.

The bell rang a second time. Silja dug her in the ribs with her elbow.

"For pity's sake, why can't the little hussy do as she's told? Up with you!"

She gave Emmi another shove with her sharp elbow, and it hurt so much that the girl cried out.

"How many more times do you have to be told, before you'll get up?"

Emmi clambered out of bed. She felt dizzy, and almost fell.

"Splash some cold water over your eyes, it'll help to clear your head," was Silja's advice.

But Emmi had no time to do this, for the bell was ringing yet again. She quickly pulled on her petticoat and skirt, smoothed back her hair with both hands, and hurried in.

"I have rung three times," said the lady.

Emmi said nothing, but simply lifted Lilli from the lady's side and held her in her arms.

"Change her wet things and then put her in the cradle. She won't go to sleep again anyway, if she comes back beside me."

The lady turned on to her other side and closed her eyes. The cradle was in the adjoining room, into which Emmi now carried the baby. She changed its diaper, and then began to rock the cradle and sing. Every now and then some thought or other would come to her. Not a very big or complicated thought, but it was enough to interrupt her singing.

"Sh, sh, sh. Ah, ah, ah. Sleep little one sleep. Rock-a-bye-baby, on the tree top. When the wind blows, the cradle will rock. Oh, lord, how sleepy I feel. Bye, baby bunting, daddy's gone a-hunting. Silja's still in bed, asleep, lucky devil. Daddy's gone a-hunting. Sh, sh, ah, ah . . . "

Lilli dozed off. Emmi lay down on the floor beside the cradle, put one arm under her head, and was soon fast asleep. Unknown to her, Lilli had woken again almost at once, and was now rubbing her nose and gazing round her in puzzlement, as there seemed to be no one with her. The child tried to sit up, but could not manage it; instead, she turned over on her side and got her head over the edge of the cradle. Seeing Emmi, she chuckled delightedly and reached out to touch her. Over went the cradle, and out tumbled Lilli, striking her forehead on the base of the cradle as she fell.

A piercing yell had everyone awake in seconds.

"Jesus bless us!"

Emmi, finding the baby on the floor beside her, went as white as a sheet. She snatched her up, cuddled her, showed her the fire, and rocked her in her arms, all the time horrified by the thought that the lady must have heard. And in her panic she did not think of looking to see whether the child had been injured, or was just crying from shock.

The lady opened the door. Emmi felt faint, the whole world went black before her eyes.

"What's happened to her?"

"Nothing."

Emmi did not know what answer she was giving. Instinctively she stammered out words, any words that might save her.

"Why is she crying like that, then? There must be some reason."

Emmi made desperate attempts to make the baby quiet.

"Give her to me," said the lady. "Oh, my poor baby, my darling one, what's the matter? Good heavens, there's a great bruise on her forehead."

She looked at Emmi, who just stood there helplessly.

"How did that bruise get there? Tell me, I want to know. Are you dumb?"

"I don't know ..."

"You dropped her, that's obvious. Out of the cradle, was it?"

Emmi said nothing, and stared down at the floor.

"You see, you can't deny it any longer. What a useless, careless creature you are. First you drop the baby and then you lie to me. I'm sorry I ever took you on. Well, I'm telling you now, you're not staying on here next year. Get yourself another job, if anyone will have you. I've had enough of you, I'd rather do without a nursemaid altogether ... Sh, sh, my darling, mamma's own sweet one, yes ... Mamma will get you a better nurse next year, don't cry, don't cry."

Lilli stopped crying, as she found the nipple and began to suck; and after a little while she was smiling contentedly, though teardrops still sparkled in her eyes.

"There, there, my precious, are you giving Mamma a lovely smile, then? My own dear child, how sweet she is. What a nasty horrid bruise on her forehead!"

Lilli did not cry again that day; she was just as happy as before, perhaps even a little happier; she smiled at Emmi, put her finger into Emmi's mouth and pulled at her hair. Emmi let the child's delicate little hand wipe her own wet cheeks, down which teardrops as big as cranberries kept trickling all day long. And when she thought that in six weeks' time she would no longer be able to hold this soft, delightful child in her arms, or even to see her, except perhaps for an occasional glimpse through the window as she passed down the street, a rejected outcast—when she had these thoughts, or rather these feelings, the tears flowed so fast that they became a stream, and made a little puddle on the table.

"Oh dear, just look at that," she said to Lilli, who at once began to mop it up with the palm of her hand.

Later that morning the lady had visitors. Mrs. Vinter the doctor's wife and Mrs. Sivén, whose husband was the headmaster, very grand and elegant, both of them, though not nearly so grand as our own lady, said Silja, and Emmi was inclined to agree.

When Silja took in the coffee, the lady sent her with a message to Emmi, to bring Lilli in to be shown to the visitors. Emmi dressed her in her prettiest bonnet, and a brand new hand-embroidered bib. The child looked so beautiful in these that Emmi had to call Silja to have a look, before she carried her in.

How those ladies cooed with admiration, the moment they appeared at the door!

"*O, så söt!*"*

And eagerly they took turns to hold Lilli in their arms, kissing her and squeezing her, and laughing delightedly.

"*Så söt, så söt!*"

Emmi stood in the background, smiling quietly. She did not really know the meaning of all this "*så söt, så söt*" but evidently it was high praise indeed.

But suddenly they became very serious. The lady was telling the visitors about something; Emmi did not know what, as it was all in Swedish. But she guessed what it was when she saw the horror on their faces.

"*Herre gud, herre gud, nej, men tänk, stackars barn.*"†

Three pairs of eyes, full of pity and concern, turned simultaneously to look at the bruise on Lilli's forehead, and then, with shocked disapproval, at Emmi.

"*Ett sådant stycke!*"‡

Emmi stared at the carpet on the floor, and wished that something would fall from the ceiling on to her head, crushing her to pieces and at the same time burying her deep beneath the earth. Surely she was the wickedest, wretchedest person who had ever lived. She did

*"Oh, so sweet!"
†"Oh, heavens, no! Just fancy! The poor child!"
‡"What a wretch!"

not dare to look up, but she knew, and felt in every toe and fingertip, that their eyes were still upon her. Those grand, elegant ladies, who never, never, did anything wrong themselves. How could they, when they were so wise and clever, and so far above other, ordinary people?

"You may take Lilli away," she heard her employer say.

Emmi's arms had suddenly become so limp that she feared she might drop the child if she picked her up.

"Did you hear?"

"Där ser ni nu, hurudan hon är." §

Emmi lurched forward and somehow managed the few steps to where the lady was sitting. The desire to get out of sight and back into the nursery gave her just sufficient strength to go through with her task. Or was it just out of long habit that her arms now obeyed her and fulfilled their function as before?

She lowered Lilli into the cradle and sat down on a stool close by to show her a toy. But Lilli had raised both legs in the air and was holding on to them with her hands. This game she found so amusing that she laughed out loud. Emmi would have laughed too, but for the distress that gripped her throat and made laughter impossible.

Sitting there, she thought with surprise that she had not, that morning, remembered the trick she had so often used in the past to combat sleepiness: pricking and scraping herself with a needle. And just because of that, all this had happened; this great, irremediable calamity, that had now ruined her life.

Late in the evening, when everyone else had gone to bed, Emmi went out into the yard. All was gray in the fading light, but overhead the stars were shining. She sat down on the bottom step to think about her present and future situation. Not that thinking about it made it any clearer; it remained as dim as gray as the evening itself.

Casting her own cares to one side for the moment, she looked up into the blue-gray sky, where heaven's candles were burning so brightly. What happy souls, she wondered, were up there with the stars? And

---

§"There you are, you see what she's like."

of the people now living, who would go there? Would there be any nursemaids there? she asked herself doubtfully. But the gentry—they would be there, of course, all of them. Obviously, since they were so immeasurably better, even here. She wondered, too, who had to light those candles each evening, the angels or the people? Or did the people all turn into angels when they got there? And what about little children who died young? Who nursed them and looked after them? But perhaps they didn't need looking after any longer, once they were in heaven.

Silja opened the door and hustled her inside.

"What the devil are you sitting out here for, in the cold?"

As she undressed, Emmi turned to Silja and said, "Why is it we're so wicked, we servant girls?"

"Don't you know?"

"No."

"I'll tell you, then: it's because we have to stay awake so much of the time. We have time to commit more sins, half as many again as other folk. Look, the gentry can sleep on in the morning, till nine or ten o'clock; there's not so much time left for them to do bad things."

Well, perhaps that was it. If she had been able to sleep a little longer that morning, Lilli would not have fallen out of her cradle, all because of her.

The following Sunday was the third Hiring Day. Emmi was given her employment book and sent down to the church.

Outside the church there were lots of people: would-be employers and would-be employees. They stood about in large groups; all of them seemed to have friends and acquaintances everywhere, and to be in league with each other.

Emmi felt forlorn and lonely. Who would want to employ a frail little creature like herself?

She stood by the churchyard wall with her employment-book, and waited. Ladies and gentlemen walked past her, to and fro, but none of them ever glanced at her.

There was a group of youths sitting by the church steps.

"Come over here, girl," one of them called. The others laughed and whispered together.

"Come on, come on, what are you waiting for? Come and sit here with us."

Emmi blushed and moved further away. Just then a lady and gentleman came up to where she was. Well, not exactly gentlefolk, perhaps: the lady was wearing a head-scarf and the gentleman's clothes were very shabby.

"What about this one?" said the gentleman, pointing at Emmi with his stick. "At least she doesn't look as if she'll demand much in the way of wages. Eh?"

"Whatever you like to pay me," said Emmi quietly. "I'd be content with that."

A shy hope sprang up within her.

"What good would she be? She could hardly manage to carry a tub full of water."

"Oh, I could."

"And could you do the washing?"

"I've done that too."

"Let's have her, she seems quiet and clean," said the gentleman.

But the lady still had her doubts.

"She looks sickly to me. See how thin she is."

Emmi thought of her legs, but dared not mention them. If she did, they would certainly turn her down.

"Are you sickly?" the gentleman asked, glancing through Emmi's employment book, which he had snatched from her hand.

"No," Emmi whispered.

She made up her mind that, however much her legs ached, she would never complain.

Putting the book in his pocket, the gentleman gave her two marks as hiring-money, and the matter was settled.

"Come to the Karvonen farm on All Saints' Day, in the evening, and ask for Mr. and Mrs. Hartonen," said the lady. "On All Saints' Day, remember."

Emmi went home.

"That's a bad place you're going to," said Silja, who knew the Hartonens; living conditions were mean and squalid, and the lady such a shrew that no servant ever stayed a full year. And the food, she had heard, strictly rationed and pretty small rations at that.

Emmi flushed, but quickly recovered and replied: "Well, those good jobs are hard to come by, there aren't enough of them for everybody to have one. Some people have to be content with the worse ones, and thank their good fortune that they're not out on the street."

She took Lilli into her arms and pressed her face against the child's warm body. Lilli seized hold of her hair with both hands and chuckled "Ta, ta, ta."

Short story, "Lapsenpiika" (1887). Translated from the Finnish by David Barrett.

❧ Gerd Brantenberg

Readers all over the world have been challenged and entertained by *Egalia's Daughters,* Gerd Brantenberg's (1941–) delightful satire on gender roles. Soon after its publication in 1977, Brantenberg's novel had become an international best seller. Her next literary project was a trilogy about Inger, a semi-autobiographical character. The title of the first book, *The Song of St. Croix,* alludes to the school Inger and her friends attended in Fredrikstad, a small town on the Oslofjord in southeast Norway. "Sixth Grade Girls Learn to Cook Cod" is a chapter from that novel.

In the third and final novel, *The Four Winds,* Inger leaves her hometown, working first as an au pair in Scotland and then starting her studies at the University of Oslo. Questions about sexuality and sexual identity, central to *The Four Winds,* are just beginning to interest the girls in Inger's sixth grade class. In her characteristic style, Brantenberg grapples with serious issues, but always with a good measure of hilarious humor.

Sixth Grade Girls Learn To Cook Cod

Fredrikstad, September 15, 1953

> *Dear Inger!*
> *When hill and dale us part*
> *and me you do not see,*
> *remember it was Marthe*
> *who wrote these lines to thee.*
> *Love Marthe Rud, 11 ¹/₂ years old*

By now everyone had written in everyone else's scribble books—the albums where they put in red and blue-flowered borders and their photos—or just a fancy frame ("Picture later/ When I'm greater"). They put Norwegian flags in the books, a drawing of its owner and her future husband, princesses, picture cut-outs, all the kids at the skating rink and a little lamb. Until they ran out of ideas.

In sixth grade they started with the question books. They asked about everything imaginable and passed them around to everybody during class. First: What's your name? Where do you live? How old are you? Address and telephone number, if you have a phone. What's your favorite color? What's your favorite food? Do you have a crush on anyone? Who do you like best in the class? Do you have a best friend? What do you think about our teacher, Anna? What's your greatest wish? What are you going to be? Who is your favorite person? a) male b) female. Who's the greatest cowboy in the West? Who's the dumbest person you know? Do you believe in Jesus? Have you done it? Have you had your you-know-what yet? Do you have hair down there? They giggled and wrote. Nobody's questions were exactly the same, but they copied each other. If one of them thought of something funny to ask about, it soon spread to the other question books. It was exciting. It was exciting to answer and see how the others had answered. The question books spread like an epidemic throughout the class, during every subject and all the recesses for at least two months, displacing the scribble books and albums and the little colored rings from pigeons and chickens they'd been collecting.

Jorunn's favorite person was Rita Hayworth, because she had brown, wavy hair and Jorunn's mouth was slightly full, so they looked alike. Nobody could have the same one, so Fanny had Susan Hayward and was going to be a missionary. Her least favorite was Sølvi Andersen. Marthe Rud had just split up with Sonja Eriksen; now she was best friends with Inger, and had a crush on Mr. Bihmeland (fat chance). Lillian was best friends with Vivi after she and Inger split up, and now they had been best friends for two months. Liv Mo's favorite food was canned fish cakes. Astrid Evensen had a crush on Kai Hansen, and was going to be a stewardess. Everyone believed in Jesus, except Marthe, who wrote, "You'll have to ask him!" You'll have to ask him, imagine that! Everyone laughed at Marthe's answer. Ingeborg Fengerstad's favorite color was dusty rose and Elsie Olsen was the dumbest person she could think of. Jorunn had hair down there. As far as the greatest cowboy went, the class was divided between Hopalong Cassidy and Roy Rogers. It was impossible to like both of them at the same time. Either Hopalong was the best and Roy Rogers blah, or the other way around. Nina thought that their teacher Anna was an old hag with crocheted underwear and an umbrella, and a hat that looked like a bird's nest from above. Inger Kari Gullichsen lived down on Storgata, but she was going to move to Oslo soon, because her father had a new job. She wrote with her neat handwriting in Inger's question book. "Question 10: What is your greatest wish? Answer: To not have to move."

One day Miss Wahlstrøm confiscated Nina's question book in English class. Oh no! Now she'll see all of Nina's crazy questions. Do you think that Anna and Mr. Bihmeland have screwed? Do you think Miss Wahlstrøm has red hair down there? A week later Nina got her question book back. The teacher didn't say a word about it. But the question books were banned.

School was the same old, boring thing. The sixth grade girls, group one, dawdled their way over to the wooden building for their cooking class with Rakel Jonassen. They were having fish today, and first she was going to lecture. She was the only one at the school who talked about lecturing. Luckily the period had already started. They moved at a snail's pace across the road, and when they got into the cloak room, they fiddled around putting on their aprons, which they had made in fifth grade, and the silly little caps they were supposed to wear on their heads so that they didn't get hair in the food.

Finally they came out into the kitchen where Rakel Jonassen was standing with the fish ready and waiting on a board. It was a large, grumpy codfish, and now Rakel Jonassen held it up between her sharp fingernails and pointed and explained. Fish contains complete proteins, fat and minerals, she said. Inger was bored. How dull. She didn't know why, but as soon as anyone started talking about protein and carbohydrates, her brain dozed off.

There was a particular smell in the school kitchen. She didn't know what it came from, but it was a cold, clean smell. Everything was spic and span when they arrived, and it had to be spic and span when they left. And Rakel Jonassen came with her long nails and let her fingers glide along the side of their sinks to see if they'd left a ring. Gross.

The only bright spot was that when you were a 3 or a 4 you could go to the laundry room. There were four girls at each table, and each of them had a number that changed each time. Being a 1 was the worst. They had to cook. The 2s had to do the dishes and peel the potatoes, but the 3s and the 4s were supposed to wash the towels in the laundry room or set the table and put things away in the cupboards. It was safest to be a 4. Then you only had to do what you were told all the time, and the only thing you had to dread was eating the food.

That was the smell in the school kitchen. The smell of gross food that you had to cook first and then eat and wash up after, so that it didn't smell. Rakel Jonassen had picked up the codfish by the tail between her red-polished nails and started lecturing about its internal organs, which they would see in a moment. She was the only teacher they had with red fingernails. Anne Marie Gjende, whom they'd just had for math, didn't wear nail polish, even though she was younger than Rakel Jonassen. Lots. Miss Gjende was from Grimstad, and she had the southern accent people from there had. She was sweet. Maybe cooking class wouldn't have been so boring if they'd had her. But it was hard to see how cooking class could be anything but boring.

"What did I say, Inger?"

The question flashed into Inger's head; she was gazing out at a woman walking across St. Croix Square with two big bags and great big fat legs.

"Well, what did you say?" Inger said.

The class laughed. Miss Jonassen slammed the flat of her hand on the table. "Pay attention. From 100 grams of cod we get 53 grams of waste."

Inger's thoughts drifted out the window again. She couldn't help herself. The lady had made it almost all the way across the square now. In her bags she probably had codfish, potatoes and carrots, and now she was going home to make dinner for her husband who was coming home from work. Her thoughts drifted away, even though Inger knew Miss Jonassen could grab them at any moment, and hold them tightly. But only as long as she talked directly to her and tortured her. She had twelve others to watch, too. Therefore Inger took a chance not thinking about codfish.

The lady had stopped, for she'd met another lady walking in the opposite direction. They could stand there for at least half an hour, Inger knew. It was incredible how these pantomimed conversations could last so long. She sat looking at them, thinking, without actually thinking about them. But in order to think she had to look at them. They had something to do with her thoughts. The thoughts began with them, but drifted onward. There was something about these people in Fredrikstad. First they acted silly and went out on the town. And afterwards they turned out like those two ladies. How could that happen? First they wore high-heeled shoes and lipstick and stuck their rear ends out with swinging skirts. Every time they saw a mirror they combed their hair. Their eye-shadow made them look stuck up and they chewed gum. The gum traveled around in their mouths and was part of the Fredrikstad dialect. "What'cha talkin' 'bout, huh?" But the only thing they could think about was getting a boyfriend. And they did. Suddenly one day they were hanging out next to some hot dog-slurping guy over by Randi's stand. The kind with a flat hat and a coat with a split in the back and thick-soled tractor-tread shoes. They could stand like that for hours, gabbing. One Saturday evening after another. Inger could see them from her window at home. It was something that just happened. She didn't understand how. But it just happened—at one point or another—that one of those couples got together. "Now they're going steady," people would say. Inger wondered how what started out as talking at the hot dog stand could turn into going steady. What happened? Was it some deal they made? Was it that one day they were just standing there and one of them said to the other, "Hey, let's just say we're going steady." No. She didn't believe that. It had to be something else. Something strange that nobody saw.

And then they went home and did it.

But how did they decide to do it? Was it just that after he'd been standing there a while eating hot dogs and gabbing and saying something that she laughed at, that the guy said, "Hey. Let's go back to my place and do it." No. Inger didn't believe that either. But in a way she could imagine that. And she couldn't imagine it any other way.

Maybe it just happened. At any rate it always ended up that way, and it had to happen one way or another.

Inger had been watching people in Fredrikstad for a long time. It was odd to think that all human beings had done it. They didn't look like it when they were just walking around. Cato Ålberg, the lawyer, who walked by her house every day with his topcoat and briefcase, and tipped his hat to everyone he met, had done it. He had two little daughters. And the man who collected tickets at The Blue Grotto movie theater had done it. And Mrs. Wilse-Abrahamsen, who always wore a black leather coat, and had a little dog that looked just like her, had done it. She had a grown-up daughter in a light-colored leather coat. For a long time when she was little, Inger had wondered how people had children just from getting married. She didn't understand it, but that's how it was. When she found out that was wrong, she told Lillian on the way to school. "Everyone who has children has done it," she said. "My parents and your parents, too." But Lillian didn't believe her. She believed there were a lot of people who had done it, but not her parents.

They didn't know what it was then, and in a way Inger didn't know now either. There was something with a naked lady and a naked man and that he lay on top of her and that he was supposed to put his thing inside somewhere, but she didn't really get it. It was hard to imagine. It was something that was in a kind of mystical light. Because at the same time they were supposed to love each other, and that was why they did that stuff. That was what Inger couldn't understand. How was it possible that two people who really loved each other could act like that? No, it wasn't possible. There had to be more there that Inger didn't understand.

One day when Mama and Papa were having their after-dinner nap she had walked right in without knocking like she usually did. Papa had his shirt tails hanging out and his bare behind and Mama lay on her back under him, looking up in the air with a sad expression. She wasn't doing anything. "Oh damn!" Papa said, and rolled over on his side with the blanket when he discovered Inger. Inger just left. It was the dumbest thing she had ever seen. Mama looked really stupid. Imagine just lying there, staring up at the ceiling. And what was he doing with his bare behind and shirttails?

She didn't understand it, and that wasn't fair. How could they be doing something that she didn't know about? Silliness. But she didn't dare ask them. That same evening when she came into the living room and Mama and her friend, Rita, were talking together, she heard Rita say, "Poor Inger!" They stopped talking when they saw her in the doorway. It was annoying. She didn't understand what it was, and they didn't want her to understand it.

At any rate it happened everywhere, with Mama and Papa, and with the couple at Randi's hot dog stand. And one day, after they had been carrying on like that for a while, they got married. Then they stopped combing their hair and didn't stand by the hot dog stand anymore. They didn't wear high-heeled shoes so their skirts swung out behind them, and they didn't wear lipstick or chew gum. Their hair got ugly and they wore faded old coats and looked fat. Why did they get like that? It was like the whole business was just a trick.

Fredrikstad people were strange; Inger was sure it wasn't like that in Oslo. In Oslo they talked nicely and didn't smear on the lipstick or chew gum just because they weren't married. She didn't believe that people in Oslo did it either. At least not like folks in Fredrikstad. In Oslo they went for walks in the woods in Nordmarka and held hands when the blue anemones were in bloom. Just like in Evi Bøgenæs' romance novel *Secret Destiny*. In Oslo they went for walks up Slemdalsveien while the lilacs hung heavy with blossoms over the picket fences and wrought iron gates. He was tall and blond and wore knickers and his name was Erik. He loved the mountains, but had traveled to many places. Now he had come back and wanted to stay in Norway. And she had been thinking about him the whole time, and known about him, and now—when he saw her again—he knew that she was the one he had loved the whole time. Then he took her in his arms and looked at her with his kind, gray-blue eyes, and he gave her a long kiss. Oh, give me an Evi Bøgenæs man! A man who comes smiling out of a fairy tale and loves only me! A man who carries me away from Rakel Jonassen's cooking class and hot dog stands and people who chew gum with a Fredrikstad dialect inside it, holds me tightly and carries me off into love.

That's how they made love in Oslo. Inger looked at the two ladies. They had said good-bye fifteen times. The two ladies had done it, too. And that's how they had ended up. Inger wondered if Rakel Jonassen had done it. She looked at her. By now Rakel had cut up the codfish and removed the head, which now lay grumpily by itself in a little pool of blood. The body was cut into pieces, and the entrails lay in little piles spread out over the counter so that everyone could see what had been inside it, and now they were supposed to get busy and make a codfish dinner. Miss Jonassen clapped her hands. Yes, Inger was sure she had done it. There was something about that nail polish.

Inger stood in the laundry room laughing with Marthe Rud. They were supposed to be washing towels in the big laundry tubs and that was incredibly comical. They hung over their wash boards, laughing. "And then we'll take a little baking soda!" They took a little in their hands from a container on the counter and imitated Miss Jonassen's movements and voice. Collapsed in laughter on the floor. "Was it baking soda we're supposed to use?" "I haven't a clue!" They poured handfuls of soda into the tubs and scrubbed. Inger got a splash of water in her face. Splashed back. Marthe went and got a dipper. Filled it up and looked meaningfully at Inger. "No!" "Yes!" "No." "Yes, you started it!" Inger laughed and got half a dipperful over her. "Now we're going to have some fun." Inger fetched the scrub bucket and started filling it up. Marthe splashed her from her tub the whole time. Like a cloud-burst. "You better watch out! One, two, whee!" Inger flung the contents of the scrub bucket over Marthe. Marthe got sopping wet. Her long, thick hair was plastered to her head. Her clothes and cooking class apron were dripping wet. God! What were they going to say to Miss Jonassen now? Inger got a dry towel and started wiping her off. Marthe laughed into the towel. She looked like a troll. She said that her boobs are freezing. "Come and warm me up!" It was cold in the laundry room in the wooden building at St. Croix School. Not exactly a cozy place. Marthe stood on her toes, laughing. "Like this. Now I'm your boyfriend," she said. She said she knew how they kissed, she learned it from her sister, who was seven years older. "They stand like this," said Marthe, and sort of put her knee between Inger's legs. Her mouth got closer. They laughed. "Cut that out now. They're completely serious when they kiss. Now I'm going to give you a hickey!" Marthe put her mouth against her neck and sucked. It tickled and felt warm.

"Are you sure it's like that?" Inger said.

"Yeah, sure. And afterwards they screw." Marthe laughed.

Then Astrid Evensen appeared in the doorway, snickering with her hoarse laugh. "You're crazy," she said enthusiastically. "Raka is ticked off. You're gonna catch it."

They giggled. The smell of codfish permeated the hallways. Liv Mo had cooked her codfish to pieces at Table B, and that was where Rakel Jonassen was supposed to eat today. They laughed. Astrid and Inger and Marthe trooped into the kitchen and over to Liv Mo and laughed. Ha, ha, ha. And Liv Mo laughed with them. "Well, we're having little baby fish today, Miss Jonassen," she said.

And up at the teacher's desk Rakel Jonassen stood with one hand planted on her hip, sipping potato water from a coffee cup. "It's slenderizing," she said. But for next time Liv Mo must learn that fish should be poached. She was in a good mood, Rakel Jonassen, for the day was almost over, and she had other things to think about than teaching a bunch of giggly sixth-graders to cook cod. She pretended not to notice that Marthe Rud had taken off her cooking class apron and was sitting with Inger's jacket on. "Well, let's sit down and eat, girls!"

But on the way home Inger asked Lillian if she thought Rakel Jonassen had done it. No, Lillian didn't think so. Did Inger think so? "Sure thing," Inger said. Now that Lillian asked the question, she was positive. Lillian was in doubt. But deep inside she wanted to believe it, too.

Excerpted from *Sangen om St. Croix*. Translated from the Norwegian by Margaret Hayford O'Leary.

☙ *Annika Thor*

Annika Thor's (1950–) novel, *Truth or Consequence,* first appeared as a film which was lauded for its frank portrayal of pressure and conflicts among teenagers. *Truth or Consequence,* from which this excerpt is taken, addresses the complex ethics of friendship, deceit and the courage to take responsibility in a contemporary school setting. When Sabina and her new friends begin a campaign against Karin, an outsider in their class, it's up to Nora to decide where her conscience should lead her.

Truth or Consequence

The girls in our class were playing against a sixth-grade class from Högalid School on the Zinkensdamm field. It was our last match in the South Stockholm Cup, the soccer tournament among the schools in the South End area. We have a good team. Fanny is strong and tough and not afraid to take anyone on. Maja is a great goalkeeper. And I'm quick and pretty good at scoring goals.

In fact, I was the one who made the first goal of the game. The boys in our class and all of 6A sat on the bleachers and cheered. Even Gunilla shouted, "Go Nora!"

It felt good, like coming out into the sunshine on a summer morning. On this September day there wasn't any sun; it was cloudy and gray and pretty cold. The spectators sitting on the bleachers were wearing warm jackets.

The other girls on the team hugged me. Everyone except Fanny, who had to re-tie her shoes. And Karin, who stood at the edge of the field and watched. She always does that. She just wasn't participating, but the other team also had a few players who were hopeless, so it didn't matter too much.

There were a few minutes left until half-time and Fanny had the ball. I was open where I stood near the other team's goal. I could have made a shot, if I had had the ball.

But I didn't get it. Fanny made a shot herself—from an impossible position. There was no way that it could get through the goal posts.

And it didn't.

The referee whistled and it was half-time.

Sabina, Fanny and I sat together during the break. Fanny massaged her legs and Sabina turned around and waved at Tobbe on the bleachers.

"Too bad you didn't make that goal," I said to Fanny, because I wanted to hear what she was thinking when she made the shot herself instead of passing the ball to me.

She flared up immediately.

"Yes, isn't it too bad that everyone isn't as good as you!" she fired back.

"Don't make a scene," Sabina coaxed. "Who cares?"

"And you," said Fanny, "you just stand there staring at Tobbe instead of playing!"

"I do not! You take everything so seriously."

Fanny stood up. I saw that she was really angry, not just in a bad mood.

"I'm glad! Isn't it great that you don't!"

Then she went and sat down next to Maja.

The Högalid girls scored in the beginning of the second half, and then not much happened for a while. I began to think that the game would end in a 1-1 tie, when Fanny got hold of the ball and made her way deep into their side of the field without anyone being able to stop her. She was almost in goal position when their left back tackled her. The ball rolled out toward the edge.

There stood Karin. She looked at the ball that came toward her as if she didn't know what it was, but she stopped it with her foot anyway.

"Here! Pass!" screamed Fanny, who was still in a good position.

Karin kicked the ball. It ended up right at the feet of Högalid's left back, who passed it further and then it was on our side of the field again. Their best kicker got it and Maja was a tenth of a second too late.

"Goal!" they shouted. "Goal!"

Fanny went up to Karin and got right next to her.

"What the hell are you doing, you stupid loser!" she said. "Go sit down, damn it."

Lotta, our gym teacher, saw it at once. She's good that way, doesn't let anyone make fun of the kids who don't play as well.

"Back off, Fanny," Sabina whispered when she saw Lotta coming.

"Fanny!" said Lotta. "If I hear any more from you you'll have to sit on the bench for the rest of the game."

"If anyone should get out it's her," said Fanny defiantly. "She just ruins everything!"

But Lotta was hard as stone.

"This is the last time I'll warn you. One more word and you're out. Understand?"

Fanny shrugged her shoulders.

When there were just a few minutes left in the match I got the ball again, a couple of meters from their goal. Two of their players were between me and the goal. I saw the opening and kicked. The goalie threw herself at the ball, but it flew by her outstretched hands.

"GOAL!"

The whole team screamed and hugged me. The guys and everyone from 6A came running down from the bleachers. Everyone wanted to pat me on the back. Even Tobbe, who usually barely sees me, came up and thumped me on the back.

"Nice goal," he said.

Then Sabina got a dark look on her face. Fanny took her by the arm and led her off the field. I saw Fanny whisper something to her, but I didn't hear what she said.

When I think about what happened next, I almost wish I hadn't scored those goals. Actually it doesn't really matter who wins a soccer game. Anyway there are things that are more important than being good at scoring goals. Like having the guts to say "Stop!" when something that shouldn't happen happens. Like not caring what people think about you. Like being able to see who your real friends are.

Sorry if I sound like some kind of lecture on bullying, but I've come to this conclusion myself. Since Friday. Since Fanny's party.

All the fuss after the last goal made me be the last one in the locker room after the game. The others had already started changing. Sabina had showered and was drying herself with a pink towel. The water dripped from her black hair.

Fanny came out of the shower with a towel wrapped around her body. The locker room was almost full, so I had to stay near the door.

I looked at them secretly. Sabina's breasts are small and pointy. They look bigger when she's dressed, because then she wears one of those bras that push the breasts upward and together. Now they looked like a pair of white eggs against the tanned skin of the rest of her body. She was even whiter where she had worn a bikini bottom in the summer. There was a dark shadow in the whiteness, and I realized that she had started to grow hair down there.

Fanny had too, I saw when she took off her towel and started rubbing herself with body lotion. Though hers wasn't black, but light brown.

I don't have any hair there, and not under my arms either. If you look from the side you can see that my nipples stick out a little, but around them it's flat.

Sabina brushed her hair so that the water droplets flew.

"Can you put some lotion on my back?" she asked Fanny.

She lifted her hair so Fanny could reach. It looked pretty when she did that. She looked like a mermaid.

After I got my clothes off I took my towel and went to the shower room. Karin was getting dressed in a corner. She has a special way of changing in gym class. She never undresses completely, but takes off one piece of clothing at a time and then quickly puts on another. She doesn't want to show herself even in her underwear, she's that ashamed of her body.

"Karin?" I heard from Fanny's direction.

"Yes?"

"Don't you ever shower?"

Fanny knew, of course, that Karin never showers at school.

"Yes, I . . . ," Karin mumbled softly.

"What did you say, I can't hear," Fanny mocked.

She went closer to Karin, holding her nose.

"Yes, at home . . . "

I didn't want to hear any more. I went out to the shower room and hung my towel on a hook. From the locker room I heard Fanny's voice:

"How disgusting! Not showering after a game. And I bet you'll wear the same clothes tomorrow and sit in the classroom smelling bad."

That wasn't fair. Karin doesn't smell bad. On the contrary, she smells like soap and freshly washed clothes. It really doesn't matter that she doesn't shower after gym, because she never runs around and doesn't get sweaty like the rest of us.

I got into the shower, turned on the faucet and started soaping up. The sound of the water drowned out the voices from the locker room for a while. Then I saw, from the corner of my eye, that Fanny and Sabina were coming back out to the shower with their towels wrapped around them. They were whispering and doing something with the hose that's used for cleaning the shower. I didn't understand what they were up to, and didn't want to either.

"Karin!" yelled Fanny. "Come here a second!"

"Why?" I heard Karin answer from the locker room.

"We want to show you something," said Fanny.

I turned around and saw Maja at the door between the shower room and locker room. She nodded to Fanny, who was standing in the middle of the floor with the hose pointing toward the door, and Fanny nodded back.

Sabina was standing by the wall where the hose is attached. She held her hand on the faucet.

"Come on!" Fanny shouted again.

Karin showed up in the doorway, fully dressed.

"What is it?" she asked.

Everything happened so fast. Maja closed the door behind Karin from the outside. Fanny pointed the hose at Karin. Sabina turned on the faucet.

Ice cold water sprayed over Karin.

I was forced to look. I didn't want to, but I had to.

The water streamed over her head and body. Her hair stuck to her cheeks and her clothes were already soaked through. Karin shivered and cried, but she didn't try to get away.

"Stop!" said a thin little voice. I realized that it was mine.

No one heard it.

I don't know how long they kept it up. It felt like an eternity, but maybe it was just half a minute. Finally Fanny said,

"That's enough."

Sabina turned off the water and Maja opened the door to the locker room. Karin rushed out, and a moment later the door slammed behind her.

❧

What makes some people unable to defend themselves? Why do they just give up? They were three against one, but if I had been Karin I would have tried, anyway. I would have kicked their legs and bit them and tried to grab them by the hair.

In that way I've always been able to defend myself. I'm small, but I'm strong and not afraid of people who are bigger than I am.

But against the thing that was about to happen to me now, I was almost as defenseless as Karin.

When I came back out to the locker room, there was a wet spot on the floor where Karin had been. Most of the girls had left, but Sabina and Fanny were still there. Fanny got her gym clothes together and Sabina put on her Walkman headphones.

"Are you waiting for me?" I said.

They looked at each other. It was the kind of look that means you've agreed on something.

"No, we're not going home," said Fanny. "We're going downtown to shop for clothes. We're taking the subway."

"See you tomorrow," said Sabina. "Bye."

There was a gust of cold air from outside when they disappeared through the door. I was the only one left in the locker room. I threw on my clothes as fast as I could and left.

The 54 came just as I was on my way to the bus stop. I saw that there were a lot of people waiting at the shelter. If I ran, maybe I could make it while they were getting on.

I sped up, but I had to cross Ringvägen and there was a red light for pedestrians and a lot of cars were turning right from Hornsgatan. The bus had already stopped at the bus stop and everyone boarded. The last to get on were Sabina and Fanny.

They had lied. They weren't going to take the subway downtown. They were going home, but they didn't want me with them.

The bus driver closed the door. He must have seen me in the rear-view mirror, but I guess he thought there were enough kids on the bus.

There was no point in running now. I walked slowly the last bit of the way to the bus stop. Then I saw that someone was sitting on the bench in the shelter, way back in the corner.

Karin. With dripping wet clothes and her wet hair matted down.

"What are you sitting here for? Why didn't you take the bus?"

She didn't answer, just looked down at her sopping wet clothes.

"So, go home and change!" I said and felt irritated at her. Why did she have to be so helpless?

"Just say that we played in the shower. That you happened to get wet."

Karin shook her head.

I took off my jacket and held it out to her.

"Here," I said. "You can borrow it."

She just looked at me. It was almost as if she didn't understand what I was saying. She was all pale. Her voice was so weak I almost didn't hear it:

"Everyone hates me. Except you."

It felt as if someone had strapped a backpack on me that was so heavy I almost fell backwards. Like that time two years ago when Dad, Anton and I were going hiking in the mountains and Dad thought I should be able to carry my own things.

It was too heavy. I couldn't accept it.

"Come on," I said. "Take the jacket. We'll take the next bus."

I sat next to her on the bus even though everyone stared at us, and I offered to let her keep the jacket until the next day, but she didn't want to. But I didn't get off at her stop; I continued home.

Mom had set up her easel in the living room and was painting. She started painting after she lost her job. Or, started again, she says. When she was young she wanted to be an artist. But then she had Anton and me and then she thought it would be more secure to be a recreation teacher.

More secure—right! She's been unemployed for almost a year now. I think she paints well. Kind of strange paintings, but good.

"Mom," I said in the doorway.

She turned around with her finger on her lips.

"Shh, Kalle's sleeping."

Kalle was sick again. An ear infection this time.

"Come in and close the door," said Mom.

I cleared some newspapers away and sat down on the sofa. Cookie jumped up next to me and put her head in my lap. Mom went on painting. No one said anything. It felt good to just sit there.

After a while Mom put away her brush and sat down next to me. "What is it?" she asked. "Do you want to tell me?"

I thought about it. Often it's good to tell Mom about things. She doesn't interrupt but listens until you're done. Then maybe she'll ask something that makes you think about what happened in a different way.

But now I didn't really know where to begin. With the game? Or with what happened in the shower room? Or with how Sabina and Fanny had lied and went off without me?

That thing about Karin in the shower felt hard to talk about. It was as if I was ashamed of it, even though I hadn't done anything.

I wondered if anyone but me felt ashamed. Anyone but me and Karin.

Before I had time to say anything the phone rang. Mom looked at me with raised eyebrows, which meant, "Is it for you? Do you want to answer it yourself?"

I shook my head. She went and picked up.

"Lena Berglund."

That was her businesslike voice, the one that she used if someone was calling to ask her to fill in for a couple of days at the recreation center, or if someone wanted to sell her laundry detergent.

The next minute she had a completely different voice, lower and deeper and with a kind of vibration under the words.

"Oh, it's you! Where are you? . . . When? . . . Can't you come earlier? I miss you!"

I went out into the kitchen and made some hot chocolate. I closed the kitchen door, because I couldn't stand listening to her.

Excerpted from *Sanning eller konsekvens.* Translated from the Swedish by Sonia Wichmann.

Jette Drewsen

The excerpt below comes from the opening pages of a novel by Jette Drewsen (1943–) titled *The Little Disciple*. The time period of Drewsen's novel is the 1950s and the setting is a folk high school. A uniquely Danish phenomenon, the folk high school grew out of a popular movement in the nineteenth century based on the sermons, songs and hymns of Nikolaj Frederik Grundtvig (1783–1872). The folk high schools were established in rural locations, do not give degrees and emphasize basic learning. Today we would call them alternative schools.

Ella, the narrator of *The Little Disciple*, lives at the folk high school with her sister, mother and father, who is the principal there. The narrative begins when she is a five year old, curious, rebellious and fascinated by sounds and words. Ella doesn't always understand what the words mean, but she knows they can be useful, even powerful, and that is perhaps the reason she calls herself "we"—to give herself an ally in her quest for a separate identity. At the end of the book when Ella is a teenager about to leave her parents, she has just started using the pronoun "I."

The Little Disciple

Pow-wow tchikita-ita
Pow-wow tchikita-ita
Pow-wow tchikita-ita

We dance.
Illona doesn't like that we dance.

Pow-wow tchikita-ita

Well, that's Illona's business.

That's what we tell ourselves, but we don't tell her. We pretend that we've made a major decision though we haven't. But that's a big secret. It annoys Illona and the principal that we evidently have a strong will. That's their business.

Pang
Pow-wow tchikita-ita
That's their business.

No doubt, we've come from someone's loins, and we have certain difficulties with those whose loins we've come from. We want a whole lot of stuff, like hair clips with pretty flowers, for instance. And we have a feeling that raspberry pudding might actually taste a little better than the one we get. Ella, that's our name. Ella is a pretty name, and we're named after someone by that name. That's reassuring, because we have met that Ella, and she talks funny, in a singing way. She smells like perfume and makes us believe in the future. When we've been talking with her, we have great expectations for the future—that there will be hair clips with pretty flowers.

The nice thing about that is that we aren't disturbed in our dreams. Oh, it's so lovely, so lovely. To dream without disturbance is what we love the most. But we also wish for a little more reality, the kind of reality that has a beat. Clogs are real. We have clogs, click-clack, because when we were in town with Illona to buy sandals, the click-clack shoemaker had click-clacks, click-clack. Click-clack.

We are very happy with the click-clacks.

The worst thing is that Illona let us know that Jesus Christ did not speak Danish while he was wandering about here on earth. Naturally, we know very well that he is not among us any longer, that "he has long since ascended into heaven and sitteth on the right hand of God, the Father Almighty, from whence he shall come to judge the quick and the dead." Illona says that we're not to go around telling people that we believe Jesus Christ spoke Danish while here on earth. She and the principal have heard a colleague of the principal say that Jesus might have visited India some time. But Denmark and Danish? What on earth were we thinking?

We practice speaking in a singing voice, just like that Ella whom we're named after, and deep in our heart, for the heart we have in common, we cling to our faith that Jesus Christ, God's only Son, spoke Danish, for we *know* that he spoke to the people and let the little children come to Him, and therefore we also know that he couldn't have spoken in that gobbledygook we hear on the radio when we turn the knob. There's no use trying to explain it to Illona. We have told our big sister. She says it's irritating that we believe in such stuff. We have told the principal also, and he seems to understand what we're saying. But it's always so hard to tell whether he's actually listening or not.

In all secrecy we dream of having a teddy bear whose fur is softer than the one we have. The one we have has so much nylon in it that our teeth hurt when we put an ear or a paw in our mouth. That makes it hard to feel truly thankful for it. But we do love it, and it has a French name. His name is Jakves; it is actually spelled with different letters than those we have seen. We got the name from one of the principal's students, she had found it in a story in a magazine, *The Family Journal*. One day, out on the playground, she told us that it only rarely happens that the stories in *The Family Journal* are set in France. They are, on the other hand, often set in the United States of America, so if we wanted a pretty girl's name for the teddy bear, she had one, and that was Cynthia. We thought about it, but a teddy bear is after all a boy, and he might just as well be a boy from France. But one thing we were certain about: Jesus Christ could never have spoken in French, for how could such a super-holy man have decided to speak in a language in which a boy, whose real name is Jakves, is called Jock by the natives? We knew from the principal that the boy's name in French is Jock.

"Jock," we told Illona and our big sister, "that sounds like a bunch of guys."

We say our prayers before we put some of the teddy bear in our mouth. We learned the Lord's Prayer by heart a long time ago, and we have a hard time understanding the part about "forgive us our trespasses, as we forgive those who trespass against us." We think it must mean that God Almighty forgives someone who's been bad in the same way as a person might forgive another person who's been bad. And you can't accept that, not after everything we've heard about God Almighty. If he doesn't forgive those who've done something bad more than most people do, then all that eternal grace which we have been so much looking forward to, is not nearly as glorious as we have heard. It is difficult to explain these thoughts to others, but we think a lot about it. We have heard about monks and nuns, and as far as we can tell, neither Grundtvig nor Luther cared for things like that. We've seen a picture of Jesus Christ when he ascended into heaven. He flew straight up from the earth. We know the difference between vertical and horizontal. Horizontal is when you bend your hand all the way back toward your arm, and vertical is when you straighten your fingers completely and reach your hand up in the air. We've seen in a huge illustrated Bible that Jesus Christ left the earth in this way. He didn't take off slowly from the ground, like the pilot we saw during one of our outings. We've asked the principal if there are any planes that take off in the same way as Jesus Christ did, and the principal said that helicopters do.

Our big sister says that we mock God and Jesus when we say that Jesus is the only man who has ever flown like a helicopter, so we don't say that to anyone anymore. We never wanted to mock anyone up there.

It's exciting to hear about the nuns who are sort of married to God. This is difficult for us to understand. We'd find it easier if they were married to Jesus. After all, he looks more like a regular man. We might actually consider marrying him ourselves some day, if he ever were to return to earth while we are still alive. We know quite well that if you were to marry such a man, you would always have to live above something else, and that you'd have to learn how to fly straight up and down, to and from your home.

In the principal's office there are panels on the ceiling, and the ceiling is very high. We imagine that one of the panels could be made into a trapdoor, and then we could live above the room together with

Jesus Christ, if we were ever to be so lucky as to meet him some day. We picture ourselves in a pink, transparent dress, but with an opaque slip under it, flying up and down from the ceiling in the principal's office, usually holding Jakves in one arm. We don't know why we always include him in our daydreams, since we do, after all, find it rather difficult to be truly thankful for him. But we do picture it, looking down on Illona and the principal when they're sitting in the office before we fly up again to a great joy upstairs under the roof. For there awaits Jesus Christ, and he is always so pleased with us.

Every now and then our grown-up namesake comes to visit. They say that people haven't gotten accustomed to long journeys yet, though the war's been over for quite a while now, but we always look forward to her visits, and we are always sorry when she leaves, for she never pays much attention to us. Then we rub Jakves against our cheeks, it scratches a bit, someone might think that we'd been crying.

It's not so easy to say our prayers after such a day, because it is difficult to forgive Grown-Ella for not having paid more attention to us than she did. And so we feel a little twinge when we get to the sentence "and forgive us our trespasses, as we forgive those who trespass against us." We personally want much more forgiveness than what we are capable of giving Grown-Ella. But we continue as if nothing had happened, so God Almighty won't get any suspicions, "and lead us not into temptation, but deliver us from evil. For thine is the kingdom, and the power, and the glory, for ever and ever. Amen."

That part about the kingdom being his is also hard to understand. We have often joined in the singing of the hymn "In all the kingdoms and countries," so we know that there are many kingdoms and countries. But we haven't asked about it, for that can easily lead to trouble. They might easily get annoyed if there is too much we don't understand. For instance, we don't understand what the Holy Spirit is about at all, and one day the idea that we'd been baptized in the name of the Father, and the Son, and the Holy Spirit made us absolutely furious.

We stood in the doorway to the principal's office and said that we wanted to be rebaptized. That we wanted to be baptized in the name of the Father and the Son, but not the Holy Spirit's as we couldn't understand it. Not with that sausage factory.

"What sausage factory?" said the principal looking up over his glasses.

That's when we knew we were in trouble. We'd heard a story from one of the students, but we didn't understand it.

"What sausage factory?" he asked again, and we heard that he was getting angry.

Illona had crossed the hallway and now she was there, listening— the principal had raised his voice.

We did not answer.

Pow-wow tchikita-ita
Pow-wow tchikita-ita

We danced in the doorway, danced, pow-wow, we had heard it on the radio in one of the students' rooms.

"You must answer when Father asks you a question," said Illona. "What is all this nonsense about a sausage factory? I'd like to know what it is you go around listening to, Ella."

We sensed danger, for even though we hadn't understood the story, we'd understood that it was naughty.

Pow-wow tchikita-ita
Pow-wow tchikita-ita

Pow-wow, pow-wow, pow, ouch, Illona took us by the arm and stopped the dance.

"What's this all about, Ella?" said the principal. "Can you tell Mother what it is you go around listening to?"

"Pow, wow, ouch,"

The principal got up from his chair and came over to us and Illona.

"Neither Mother nor I want to hit you," he said, "but you have to tell us what bad things you are talking about."

Illona was still holding us by the arm.

We wished that we could have gotten those hair clips with the pretty flowers, then we could have gone upstairs right away and danced in front of the mirror on Illona's closet, danced and looked at ourselves with the pretty flowers, two on each side, four pretty flowers in our hair. The Holy Spirit couldn't possibly mind that.

That day we didn't even have Jakves with us, our arm hurt, we looked up at the panels in the ceiling and thought about our dreams, flying straight up like a helicopter together with Jesus Christ, straight up above the principal's office, soaring to heaven, like a helicopter, straight up, and we'd be smiling, "with a wreath of bright beams," straight up, just like when you don't bend your hand all the way back.

"Ella," they were both speaking to us now.

"There was a story," we said, "about a sausage factory which exploded during the war, it was the Germans."

"And how does the Holy Spirit fit into this?" asked the principal.

"Well, there is that sausage that lands at the Gates of Heaven, and Saint Peter who doesn't understand a thing. He has never seen red sausages."

We paused, for we were just about to start crying, and that was never any good. Illona and the principal looked at us, there was no escape, though Illona had loosened her grip.

"You can see that your father is busy," she said, "and I have to get started with dinner. Now, tell the rest of it, so we can finish this off."

Pow-wow tchikita-ita

Then we told them that Saint Peter had asked the Virgin Mary when she came by, if she knew anything about the red sausage.

"What—the Virgin Mary?" said the principal.

He is always suspicious when there is any talk of monks and nuns and the Virgin Mary, he doesn't like Catholics. We thought that we could leave it at that since he'd interrupted, but they showed no mercy.

"You haven't finished the story," said Illona, "you haven't mentioned the Holy Spirit one single time, and that was how this all began, right?"

She looked questioningly at the principal who nodded back to her.

"Saint Peter was showing the Virgin Mary the sausage, no I've already said that . . . "

"Get on with it," said the principal impatiently.

"If it weren't tied up at both ends, I'd have thought it was the Holy Spirit," said the Virgin Mary.

To tie up a spirit, what a strange thought. Spirit is air, it cannot be tied up, pow-wow, ouch. Illona was shaking our arm. We stood there completely still. We did not look at any of the grownups. We are standing in the doorway between our parents, we look from one to the other, back and forth between those loins that we have chosen to go through and come out from.

"You are big enough to understand," said the principal, "that only bad girls tell stories like that."

"This is, this is just like listening to a hussy," said Illona.

"To say the least," said the principal.

He speaks directly to us, staring at us from deep within the sockets of his eyes. He is a little older than Illona. "Mother and I know exactly where that story comes from, we know where you got it, you see."

He sits down behind his desk again.

Illona is soft to press close to, and if we had had the courage, we would have. But Illona is not available to us, not today, not really. We do not cry, for then one easily becomes the object of ridicule. Illona has told us so several times. We have come to understand that there is a difference between when we are crying and when Illona and the principal get tears in their eyes when they are moved.

We understand very well that no one is moved by the explosion of a sausage factory, and that is not why we feel like crying. We know that if we begin to cry now, then it'll be that kind of crying which will make us appear like a fool.

The principal knows that we dream a lot. We think that he dreams a lot also, and that there are many things he hides too. We know that his first wife died, and that Illona did not make her way into the picture until he had mourned deeply for a couple of years. A couple of years means two years, and that's a long time to imagine. The principal often says that time flies by so quickly these days. We don't understand what he means, but we've decided to ask, as soon as it feels right. First we must get some distance from the sausage factory, and we will probably never be rebaptized.

Excerpted from *Lillegudsord*. Translated from the Danish by Anne G. Sabo.

ℛ Hagar Olsson

During the 1920s and '30s Hagar Olsson (1893–1978) was a prominent voice in avant garde circles in Helsinki, Finland. In her capacity as journalist, literary critic and creative writer she was one of the leading exponents of modernism, a movement affecting not only Finnish, but all Scandinavian literature.

In 1933 Olsson published a novel she called *Chitambo;* the book's title refers to the place in Africa where David Livingstone died. In the spirit of Livingstone, *Chitambo* is a novel of exploration and discovery where the explorer and the explored are identical: a woman who begins her voyage of self-discovery at the time of her birth. "My Soul Is Troubled by Conflicting Names" is the second chapter in *Chitambo*.

The selection below brings to mind the words of Camilla Collett: "I think that the name one gets at one's christening is not without a secret, unconscious influence on the individual." The baby's father wants to name her after Fridtjof Nansen's polar ship *Fram* (an adverb meaning "onward" in Norwegian), and her mother wants to christen her Maria, a name recalling the Virgin Mary and a destiny of a very different nature. The destiny of *Chitambo's* protagonist was to follow "an unknown and dangerous course" where she risked occasional loneliness, but was rewarded with "a wider, deeper, more all-encompassing fellowship."

My Soul Is Troubled by Conflicting Names

Naturally, I was born in the year 1893. As we all know, that year is the proudest in the history of Nordic polar exploration. It was in 1893 that Fridtjof Nansen began his world-famous North Pole expedition aboard the ship *Fram.* Mr. Downheart considered this fact to be a personal distinction and a sign that fate had at last cast its eye upon him. He assumed that I was born to great things, and he managed to skillfully foster the same delusion in me.

His marriage had threatened to have just as disappointing an outcome as his other enterprises: it had remained childless for many years. Not that Mr. Downheart particularly desired to have children, but he felt that if one takes the trouble to get married, there should be some results as well, otherwise it would be a fiasco. He had, to be sure, no reason to reproach himself in this case, since he himself had not lifted a finger to make the marriage come about. All he had done was merely to notice the dreamy girl at Mr. Hurtig's, the carpenter in Nystad. She was so dainty and trim and reserved, and her big wistful eyes made Mr. Downheart melt inside. He himself didn't understand how it happened, but one day he paid a visit to the girl, with a bouquet of flowers. And alas, that was enough. There sat the father and there sat the mother, and Mr. Downheart, tormented by embarrassment, handed the girl his flowers. By the time he left they were engaged. He was quite surprised, but at the same time relieved: this whole marriage business had always hung over him like something one had to prepare for and consider and seriously decide to do. It was a good omen that this too, like everything else, simply happened by itself. So it was all the more regrettable when no children appeared; children, after all, were a part of the whole affair.

But when I let out my first cry in late autumn, 1893, he understood at once why it had taken so long. It would not befit a man like him to have his first child born in just any year, the way other people had their offspring. That year he had immersed himself completely in Nansen's expedition. He had followed all the preparations, rejoiced over King Oscar's generosity ("There's a real king for you!")—and at Midsummer, when the *Fram* weighed anchor, he went around posturing as if he were the one steering northward toward an unknown destination, over seas that no ship had ever crossed before. He changed noticeably, grew manly and gruff and adopted a harsh tone of command, such as might be heard on deck in stormy weather.

But Nansen was away for a long time. Nothing was heard from him and fate did not give Mr. Downheart any hint as to what deed he himself might be called upon to do. He had the painful feeling that everything once again threatened to remain the same. His business would stay the same, a little better one day, a little worse the next, and Mr. Downheart would remain Mr. Downheart, a little bolder one day, more subdued the next. Just as his high spirits began to flag, the baby

girl arrived in October! It was not long before Mr. Downheart declared that something extraordinary was on the way. Not only was
the child born in that remarkable year, it also saw the light of day on
the thirteenth. Now, as everyone knows, thirteen is a number connected with remarkable events, and in the year 1893 the number was
even more remarkable than usual, since the number of participants
in Nansen's expedition was thirteen, neither more nor less. For some
unfathomable reason Mr. Downheart connected my arrival with his
own visions of greatness, and he was by no means slow to implant
them in my soul. From the very first day that I lay in my cradle, the
mysterious aura of powerful forces swirled above my head. A face
grinning with delight, lively and surprising, was constantly bent over
me. Gestures, grimaces, and amazing expressions intruded themselves
into my dreams and drew my wakening soul into the enchanted circle
of great expectations, even before it had had time to separate itself
fully from the darkness out of which it had come.

Mr. Downheart devoted himself heart and soul to my upbring-
ing. In fact my arrival gave him a welcome opportunity to change
things here and there. The room where I had my abode was transformed beyond recognition. No piece of furniture was allowed to stand
where it had stood before, the rugs were rearranged, and a special
nook was set up for me with a little desk, a little chair, a little book-
shelf and a little globe, long before I—a wriggling bundle—had the
least use for any of these things. Under Mr. Downheart's guidance a
life's direction began to take shape, long before its owner had any
part in it. He had imagination, Mr. Downheart, but a somewhat unusual one. To my mother's horror and the amusement of their acquaintances, he decorated the wall above my white crib with pictures
so unsuitable for a child that they could only be considered offensive.
These wild and stirring images have etched themselves into my mind
forever. Surely they have influenced me and become my own to a far
greater degree than the obligatory guardian angels and fairy princesses who delight other small children.

Most beautiful of them all were the ships. They have inhabited my fantasy from my earliest years, and I know that they will always slumber deep inside me—those beautiful, anxious birds, spirits of adventure, waiting for the wind to fill their sails. These were not just any ships, the ones with which Mr. Downheart decorated my wall. They were ships of Destiny, heroic ships, conquerors' ships. One could see immediately that they were headed toward something vast, powerful, terrifying. I remember in particular a three-masted vessel with magnificently filled sails that was landing on a barren Antarctic coast. At its keel, coldly glimmering water, all around it expanses of ice and snow, the slender rig against a gray limitless sky. What gave the picture its eerily hypnotic effect was the enigmatic, ominous way in which the ship was tilting. In the middle of the frozen, impenetrable vastness, this passionate tilt, this expression of the will to move forward in spite of the resistance of the elements and the gods! In my mind I always placed this scene among the most disturbing of those on the wall. In the background a sky-high cliff, dark as night, rose with startling contours, surrounded by restlessly flapping birds, while on the ground below one could see three little mounds of earth of a faintly ludicrous shape. In spite of their ridiculous shape—like three brooding ducks—they infused me with an unspeakable horror. "The Three Graves on Beechey Island," it said underneath the picture. The word "graves" meant nothing to me, but still I knew from the picture what it referred to, and didn't ask anyone what it meant. It is indeed terrible to consider how much a little child knows.

On the other hand, it was a real joy to immerse myself in the beautiful engraving that represented "The Death of Captain Cook on the 14th of February, 1779." In it was life, movement, a wild rhythm. A swaying palm, a stormy sky, and on the ground a mob of excited savages rushing forward wildly, as they ambush the solitary white man in military uniform. I loved such pictures passionately. Even before I consciously understood what they represented, I was inflamed by the fervent rhythm of the gestures, by the horrible, savage facial expressions, by the high-pitched and volatile mood of the scene. Sometimes Mr. Downheart would take down one of the pictures and show it to me at close range. Then I would shriek aloud with delight.

But there was one picture of a completely different nature, a very quiet picture, which was closer to my heart than any of the others and which imbued my earliest years on this earth with its shrouded, lofty majesty. It hung right above my pillow, just where the guardian angel should have had his rightful place. In a strange hut with half-finished walls, a man sat on the floor with his legs crossed in front of him. A fat book lay opened on his knee. In his right hand, which rested on the book's open page, he held a pen. He sat in a stiff upright posture, staring straight ahead. Outside the hut stood two turban-clad, bearded figures in long robes. They leaned their heads together furtively and looked at the solitary man inside the hut. "Dr. Livingstone Writes in his Diary," the picture was called. The man's strange, stiff posture, the meaningful looks of the secretive strangers, and above all, Livingstone's eyes that gazed steadily into space and the fixed, ecstatic expression on his white face, made an irresistible and haunting impression on me. The poor, solitary figure projected an aura of profound nobility that no shimmering angel-wings or fairy-tale prince's crown could produce. From this image, long before I knew anything about Dr. Livingstone's deeds or even could spell out the difficult words in the ABC-book, the recognition of the sovereignty of the human spirit flooded along hidden channels into my soul, and became a compelling force in my fantasy life. To this very moment I retain the insignificant and clumsily drawn illustration as a precious memory from that time when Mr. Downheart, so merry and foolish, introduced me, in his own way, to the society of noble spirits. The ragged edge of the page suggests that the illustration was torn out of a book—perhaps from an expensive edition, who knows — and this touches me more than anything else, for it tells me that Mr. Downheart shunned no sacrifice when it came to surrounding the newcomer with symbols that might awaken her spirit's desire for the great and the sublime.

I am inclined to think that this image has been one of my life's most potent symbols. The indelible impression it had made upon me in my earliest childhood later caused me to look up—after I had undergone the confusions and disappointments of youth—just what this Dr. Livingstone had said in his diary. I came to know the spirit who had written about himself: "Inspired by the glowing love of Christianity, I decided to devote my life to easing the burdens of mankind." I cannot deny that such sentiments fanned a flame that already burned in my soul. A flame that had never been satisfied! In moments of deep sadness and despair I tell myself that the problem with my life is that my aspirations have, from the very beginning, been directed toward goals that are much too high for a spirit of insignificant measure and insubstantial character. But there are moments when all this is forgiven me — my weakness, ineptitude and pride—and like an echo from deep, shadowy forests my childhood answers me:

"Man must desire the great and the good! All else depends on circumstance."

I had imprinted this motto, by none other than Alexander von Humboldt, in large bright letters above my little writing desk, where I pored over the mysteries of my ABC book and other learned texts. And I must say that it appealed to me much more than the gloomy Bible verses and religious doggerel (to my mind, the unbearable "Thank You for Everything" is a prime example) that I saw in my playmates' homes. The relationship between cause and effect is always, I suppose, impossible to unravel, but it is certain that at those times when I feel most comfortable and most at one with the rhythm of my own destiny, I like to return, in my mind's eye, to the room that Mr. Downheart had redecorated so thoroughly in my honor. I linger there, refreshed, as if in my soul's rightful home. If I gaze around me at the walls I find the same symbolic writing that I know to be inscribed in my own heart. I see those arousing pictures, the passionate illusions of fantasy; I see the fascinating jagged outlines of unexplored coasts, and as an accompaniment to all this I can hear my father's stories about men who defied death in the virgin jungles and on the oceans of the world in order to be able to map out and name a single little dot on the surface of our earth, men who had penetrated into

Arctic regions where the cold extinguishes all forms of life except the hottest: human thought.

The direction that Mr. Downheart gave me for the great voyage of discovery could not fail to arouse my mother's deepest disapproval; especially since I was, after all, a girl. To implant such ideas and imaginings in a girl could lead to nothing but unhappiness and ruin. That much she knew. But Mr. Downheart did not care about such petty matters. Girl or boy, that meant nothing to him—it was enough that I was born under an adventurous star. I was in any case a living being who brought in my wake changes, plans, hopes—a new actor upon whom he could place his fantasies and his overwrought expectations.

Already with the holy rite of baptism, a chain of conflicts began between my father and my mother—the conflicts that would fill my early years with so much tension and divide my childhood world into two enemy camps. My father had decided that in commemoration of my remarkable birth year, and as a token of my special position in life, I would receive at my baptism the admittedly unconventional, but all the more symbolic, name Fram. Naturally, my mother was in despair. At first she kept silent, devoting herself instead to enlisting allies for the anticipated battle. In the usual irrational way of women, she ran to all the neighbors and complained. They listened, both amused and scandalized. The most well-meaning of them tried to convince her that it was just one of Mr. Downheart's jokes, while the spiteful ones did their best to egg her on. Mr. Downheart grinned with sly satisfaction and thought: "Let the women chatter away, but the girl shall be named *Fram!*" He wholeheartedly enjoyed being able to annoy my mother and her devout friends in this way. The more scandalized they became, the more keenly he felt his own superiority in their company.

On the day the holy rite was to take place, the storm broke loose. My mother cried and begged and wrung her hands, but to no avail. Mr. Downheart would not be budged.

Weeping, my mother carried me to the baptismal font. She quietly told the godparents that in the name of God the girl would be called Maria Eleonora, a Christian and thoroughly respectable name. Everyone breathed more easily; they thought that Mr. Downheart had given in. He bustled around, smiling and greeting everyone in a friendly manner. But when the pastor came, Mr. Downheart raised his voice and stated that the girl would be called simply Fram. With dignified mien and bearing, he laid out in a lengthy speech the points of view that had caused him, the girl's secular representative, to come to this decision. After the speech there arose a general feeling of dismay. The pastor and the godfathers were cowardly by nature and just gave each other sidelong glances. But one of the godmothers, our closest neighbor Miss Jonsson, who as it happened was a great favorite of Mr. Downheart, stepped forward resolutely and said that she considered Fram a heathen name and that she would take no part in such an affront to the female sex. Mr. Downheart hopped with rage and asked whether the girl was his or Miss Jonsson's. The whole business was heading toward a full-blown scandal. In view of my later life, I find it especially significant that I managed to cause a scandal at my very first ceremonial entrance into the cultural community of Christians.

Finally, the pastor found it necessary to step in as mediator. He tried desperately to think of a name that would be more appropriate for a girl child and yet at the same time satisfy Mr. Downheart's principal aim. People often get brilliant ideas when put in an uncomfortable situation; so now the pastor. Like a lightning bolt from heaven, the name Vega suddenly flashed before him. Wasn't the *Vega* as worthy a Nordic sailing ship as *Fram*, indeed even more glorious! After all, no one knew yet what would happen to *Fram*. One fine day we might hear that the ship had run aground and the entire crew gone down with her. That was something Mr. Downheart had not thought of. He grew thoughtful and long in the face. No, *Fram* was nothing to cheer about yet, the pastor continued, but lo, Nordenskiöld's *Vega*— now *that* was a name worth its salt. With such a name, one could well sail away into the storms of life. And besides, Nordenskiöld was a countryman, an illustrious son of Finland.

The pastor did not need to say more. With this, he had already touched the most tender chord in my father's heart. Moved, Mr. Downheart thanked the eloquent pastor for having pointed out these symbolic connections. Thereupon he uttered:

"Let the girl be called Vega."

For a moment, there was breathless quiet in the room. But Mr. Downheart was too consumed by the new idea to be able to let it glide away in silence. On the spot, he improvised a glowing speech in the *Vega's* honor. He depicted her voyage around Asia and Europe; described the hazards of the Northeast Passage to those present; let them glimpse Spitsbergen, Novaya Semlya, the Kara Sea and Cape Tschelyuskin somewhere above my downy head; sketched in swift strokes scenes from the life of the Tschuktschians, with herdsmen gathered around a lamp; lingered lovingly at a Samoyedic knife with a finely worked shaft of walrus tooth; and finished with a description of the shimmering festival of lights with which Stockholm had celebrated the return of the *Vega*. When he paused for breath the pastor took the opportunity to baptize the girl. Mr. Downheart was seeing such brilliant visions and enjoying so intensely the flight of his own fantasy that he didn't even notice that the pastor, without further ado, also took the names suggested by my mother and baptized the girl Vega Maria Eleonora.

When Mr. Downheart later discovered the betrayal, he immediately set about declaring the extra names invalid. With great dignity he arranged a ceremony in which he as father and guardian solemnly withdrew the names Maria Eleonora, with the natural result that it became my mother's consuming ambition to preserve them. She never called me anything but Maria. My father called me Vega. The cat (who, incidentally, had been the only witness at the solemn revocation ceremony) simply said "meow"; he was the only one whose neutrality I could fully depend on. Our acquaintances, of course, were put in an awkward position. At first they tried to laugh it all away, but soon enough they learned that the name war at the Downhearts was no joking matter. Out of respect for Mr. Downheart, his companions accepted the name Vega, while my mother's friends held fast to Maria. Some avoided calling me by name entirely.

For me, the situation became tragic. I dimly sensed that a battle was being waged over my soul and that the two names were symbols of unknown forces that seemed to want to tear apart my emerging, anguished self, which did not yet know its own foundation or essence. At an unnaturally early age, I grew aware of a tense inner conflict that probably rages within all human beings and perhaps provides the innermost driving force in the individual's struggle to develop, but which is seldom thrust forward so brutally at such a defenseless age. And my life has indeed turned out to be unusually discordant. I have never been able to enjoy peace, or a calm co-existence with others. I have lived my days out of balance, prone to abrupt changes in my emotional life, like a sailor in unsteady weather. I have been stung by rebelliousness, as soon as a reconciliation with the world and with others has come within my reach, and I have barely had time to pluck the fruits of my work or my intimate relationships, before they have turned bitter. The spirit of contention that wafted above my innocent head at my baptism has pursued me in all things, large and small, and has driven me to destroy what I have built up myself and to deny what I myself have called sacred. It seems to me that Vega, my father's blasphemous child, has won the contest with Maria, my mother's well-mannered and considerate daughter.

I do not know which name to curse. I have never been able to overcome my longing for Maria's cozy, secure, enclosed world—a world so near the earth that all its fortifications are solid and no cosmic rocking can be felt within. When I see those fortunate people who have "their own little nook in the world," where invisible walls of love and understanding shield them from the sharpest winds, I tell myself: "You too could have had all this, if only you had known how to keep hold of fortune when she offered herself. Instead you now have the self-reproaches and nauseating melancholy of your solitary nights." But then, when I look deeper into their joy and see the price at which it is bought, see the hard indifference to all suffering and loneliness that does not reach inside their protective walls, I think: "Alas, this is not what the human heart is made for." A wider, deeper, more all-encompassing fellowship stands before my inner vision, a fellowship that is not based upon excluding others. And like a gust of wind, the realization sweeps through my soul that such a fellowship can only be won through dangerous risk-taking and great losses. From this I conclude that in my innermost nature I am a Vega-being, and that my father hit the mark when he consecrated me to an unknown and dangerous course beyond the bounds of the near and familiar.

Long before this had become clear to me, and before I had any hope of understanding the fateful words "the die is cast," I instinctively made my choice. At my entrance into primary school, the first milestone on my conscious road to learning, I firmly chose—after a wrenching, emotional trial—the name Vega.

Excerpted from *Chitambo*. Translated from the Finnish by Sonia Wichmann.

About the Authors

Gerd Brantenberg (1941–)
Norwegian author
An outspoken feminist with a good sense of humor and sharp wit, Gerd Brantenberg has written several novels that have received international acclaim. Her first book, *Opp alle jordens homofile* (1973; *What Comes Naturally,* 1986), is a humorous attack on homophobic attitudes and prejudices. *Egalias døtre* (1977; *Egalia's Daughters,* 1985), her most successful book to date, is a parody on sex roles. Another novel, *Favntak* (1983; Embrace), has been excerpted in *Contemporary Norwegian Women's Writing* (1995). Brantenberg has written about her childhood in a trilogy: *Sangen om St. Croix* (1979; The Song of St Croix), *Ved Fergestedet* (1985; The Ferry Landing) and *For alle vinder* (1989; *The Four Winds,* 1996).

Minna Canth (1844–1897)
Finnish author
Little of Minna Canth's extensive production has yet been translated into English. The short story in this volume appeared in the journal *Books of Finland 2* (1994). Her most important play, *Anna-Liisa* (1895), about infanticide, is included in S.E. Wilmer's anthology *Portraits of Courage: Plays by Finnish Women* (1997).

Camilla Collett (1813–1895)
Norwegian author
Camilla Collett is an important figure in the history of Norwegian literature. Her novel *Amtmandens Døttre* (1854-1855; *The District Governor's Daughters,* 1991) was Norway's first realistic novel. A critical portrayal of contemporary society and an attack on the institution of marriage, Collett's book was also the first feminist novel in Norwegian literature. Another excerpt from Collett's memoir *I de lange Nætter* (1863; During the Long Nights) is included in the anthology *An Everyday Story: Norwegian Women's Fiction* (1995).

Tove Ditlevsen (1918–1976)
Danish author
Tove Ditlevsen is one of Denmark's most beloved poets whose popularity started with her first book, a collection of poems titled *Pigesind* (1939; A

Titles that are not italicized within parentheses have been translated by the editors. The works are currently not available in English.

Young Girl's Thoughts). To English readers she is best known as a writer of prose, however. Her short stories have been anthologized in *Contemporary Danish Prose* (1958) and *The Devil's Instruments and Other Danish Stories* (1971), and one collection of Ditlevsen's short stories has been translated in its entirety: *Den fulde frihed* (1944; *Complete Freedom and Other Stories,* 1982). Also available in English are her hauntingly beautiful memoirs from childhood through adolescence, *Det tidlige forår* (1976; *Early Spring,* 1985) and a searing account of a woman's struggle against madness, *Ansigterne* (1968; *The Faces,* 1991).

Jette Drewsen (1943–)
Danish author
If Agnes Henningsen's memoirs are emblematic of the women's liberation movements in the 1880s, Jette Drewsen is a spokeswoman for women in Denmark after the social upheavals of the 1960s. Her characters are women from all paths of life, including artists, journalists and housewives. *Lillegudsord* (1992; The Little Disciple) is the first part of a trilogy about the young girl Ella whose maturation into an independent nineteen-year-old woman evolves through complex word games in the following two novels: *Jubeljomfru* (1993; Maiden of Celebration) and *Filihunkat* (1994; Fili She-Cat).

Maria Gripe (1923–)
Swedish author
Maria Gripe has received many awards, at home and abroad, for her children's books. Some of her best-known works have been made into films, such as *Hugo och Josephine; Agnes Cecilia, Elvis,* and *The Glassblower's Children.* Gripe's books have been translated into many languages. The English translations include: *Josefin* (1961; *Josephine,* 1970); *Hugo och Josefin* (1962; *Hugo and Josephine,* 1969); *Agnes Cecilia: En sällsam historia* (1981; *Agnes Cecilia,* 1990); *Elvis! Elvis!* (1973; *Elvis and His Friends,* 1976); *Elvis Karlsson* (*Elvis and His Secret,* 1976); *Glasblåsarns barn* (1964; *The Glassblower's Children,* 1973).

Agnes Henningsen (1868–1962)
Danish author
Agnes Henningsen embraced the most radical ideas of her time and insisted on sexual and social equality in her life and in her writing. The eight volumes of her memoirs (published between 1941 and 1955) represent the largest work of memoirs in Danish literature. Here she conveys, with much humor and frankness, the price she paid to live according to her ideals. Henningsen supported herself and her children by producing a steady flow of short stories, novels and plays. An excerpt from her novel *Kærlighedens Aarstider* (1927; Love's Seasons) is included in *Contemporary Danish Prose*

(1958), and the second volume of her memoirs, *Letsindighetens Gave* (1943; The Gift of the Carefree), has been excerpted in *Scandinavian Women Writers: An Anthology from the 1880s to the 1980s* (1989).

Tove Jansson (1914–)
Finland-Swedish author and illustrator
The stories about the Moomin family have brought Tove Jansson international fame since her debut in 1945. Some of the titles in this series are: *Kometjakten* (1946; *Comet in Moominland*, 1950); *Trollvinter* (1958; *Moominland Midwinter*, 1962); *Det osynliga barnet* (1962; *Tales from Moominvalley*, 1973); and *Sent i november* (1970; *Moominvalley in November*, 1971). While most of her children's stories are enjoyed both by children and adults, she has also written novels intended for adults, such as: *Sommarboken* (1972; *The Summer Book*, 1977), and *Solstaden* (1974; *Sun City*, 1977). In her autobiographical work, *Bildhuggarens dotter* (1968; *Sculptor's Daughter*, 1969), she tells stories about her family, especially her father, Victor Jansson.

Eeva Kilpi (1928–)
Finnish author
Eeva Kilpi made her debut with a collection of short stories in 1959 and rose to fame as a radical feminist with her novel *Tamara* (1972; *Tamara*, 1978), and the poetry collection *Laulu rakkaudesta* (1972; Song About Love). While her writings in the 1970s strove to liberate particularly women from social conventions and norms, her works have since focused on memories from her childhood, and the pains of the Winter War (1939-40) as in the trilogy *Talvisodan aika* (1989; The Winter War), *Välirauha, ikävöinnin aika* (1990; Time of Longing: Interim Peace), and *Jatkosodan aika* (1993; Time of the Continuation War). Another excerpt from the *The Winter War* is included in *A Way to Measure Time: Contemporary Finnish Literature* (1992).

Selma Lagerlöf (1858–1940)
Swedish author
One of Sweden's most beloved authors, Selma Lagerlöf won the hearts of readers around the world with her enchanting tale about Nils: *Nils Holgerssons underbara resa genom Sverige* (1906-1907; *The Wonderful Adventures of Nils*, 1907, and *Further Adventures of Nils*, 1911). Lagerlöf drew extensively on historical as well as popular legends in novels such as *Gösta Berlings saga* (1891; *The Story of Gösta Berling*, 1898. New translations in 1918 and 1982), and *Löwensköldska ringen* (1925; *The Löwenskiold Ring*, 1928. New translation in 1991). She wrote three books about her childhood and youth: *Mårbacka* (1922; *Mårbacka*, 1925), *Ett barns memoarer, Mårbacka 2* (1930;

A Child's Memoirs, 1934) and *Dagbok för Selma Ottilia Lovisa Lagerlöf, Mårbacka 3* (1932; *The Diary of Selma Lagerlöf*, 1936). In 1909 Selma Lagerlöf was the first woman to receive the Nobel Prize for Literature.

Susanne Levin (1950–)
Swedish author
Leva vidare (1994; Life Goes On) is Susanne Levin's first novel. It was praised by critics for its depictions of Jewish identity and acculturation problems as experienced by the young girl Leah (Levin's own Hebrew name). It was followed by *Som min egen* (1996; Like My Own) and *Suggan i dômen* (1998; The Sow in the Cathedral). The latter intertwines tales of the Levin family at the turn of the century with the author's experiences of racism in the Uppsala school system where she is a teacher.

Irmelin Sandman Lilius (1936–)
Finland-Swedish author
The milieu of Irmelin Sandman Lilius's books resembles that of Tove Jansson's; each depicts life on the Finnish coast. Sandman Lilius is best-known for the triology about Fru Sola (The Sola trilogy): *Gullkrona gränd* (1976; *Gold Crown Lane*, 1980); *Gripanderska gården* (1977; *Goldmaker's House*, 1980), and *Gångande grå* (1979; *Horses of the Night*, 1980). Some of her stories have been adapted for children's theater, like *Petters valp* (1994; Peter's Pup).

Astrid Lindgren (1907–)
Swedish author
Astrid Lindgren has received numerous awards for her books for children and youth. Almost all of Lindgren's books have been translated into English. A selection of these includes: *Pippi Långstrump* (1945; *Pippi Longstocking*, 1950); *Pippi Långstrump går ombord* (1946; *Pippi Goes on Board*, 1957); *Pippi Långstrump i Söderhavet* (1948; *Pippi in the South Seas*, 1959); *Alla vi barn i Bullerbyn* (1947; *The Children of Noisy Village*, 1962); *Emil i Lönneberga* (1963; *Emil in the Soup Tureen*, 1970); *Bröderna Lejonhjärta* (1973; *The Brothers Lionheart*, 1975); *Ronja Rövardotter* (1981; *Ronia, the Robber's Daughter*, 1983).

Moa Martinson (1890–1964)
Swedish author
Moa Martinson launched her literary career writing articles in socialist papers and women's magazines. A strong believer in the Swedish socialist movement of the 1920s and '30s, she wanted to help change society. Her books include the autobiographical trilogy about Mia: *Mor gifter sig* (1936; *My*

Mother Gets Married, 1975), *Kyrkbröllop* (1937, Church Wedding), and *Kungens rosor* (1939; The King's Roses), as well as *Kvinnor och äppelträd* (1933; *Women and Appletrees,* 1975), her first novel.

Karen Michaëlis (1872–1950)
Danish author

Karen Michaëlis was a prolific writer and her work enjoyed a high level of popularity during her lifetime, both at home and abroad. She is best known for *Den farlige Alder. Breve og Dagbogsoptegnelser* (1910), a novel depicting a woman's mid-life crisis; the English translation, *The Dangerous Age: Letters and Fragments from a Woman's Diary,* was reissued in 1991. A short story by Michaëlis is included in the anthology *Contemporary Danish Prose* (1958). Among her books for children is a series about Bibi, an unconventional girl living a vagabond life. Two of these books were translated into English (*Bibi, a Little Danish Girl,* 1927; and *Bibi Goes Travelling,* 1934). *Little Troll,* a book of memoirs, was first published in English in 1946.

Dea Trier Mørch (1941–)
Danish author

Dea Trier Mørch had a very successful career as a graphic artist before she started writing fiction in the 1970s, so it is with good reason that all of Mørch's books have been illustrated by the author. Her first book *Vinterbørn* (1976; *Winter's Child,* 1986), became a bestseller, was translated into thirteen languages and made into a film. *Winter's Child* is about pregnancy, birth and parenting, subject matter Mørch returns to in several of her subsequent novels: *Kastaniealleen* (1978; Chestnut Lane), *Den indre by* (1980; The Inner City), *Morgengaven* (1984; The Morning Gift). An excerpt from "The Morning Gift" appears in *No Man's Land: An Anthology of Modern Danish Women's Literature* (1987).

Torborg Nedreaas (1906–1987)
Norwegian author

The cornerstone of Torborg Nedreaas's production is her series of four books about Herdis, a little girl living in Bergen, Norway in the early part of the twentieth century. One of these, *Musikk fra en blå brønn* (1960), has been translated into English, *Music from a Blue Well* (1988). Several of Nedreaas's short stories appear in anthologies: *Slaves of Love and Other Norwegian Short Stories* (1982), *An Everyday Story: Norwegian Women's Fiction* (1995), *Scandinavian Women Writers. An Anthology from the 1880s to the 1980s* (1989). A powerful novel about illegal abortion has also been translated into English, *Av måneskinn gror det ingenting* (1947; *Nothing Grows by Moonlight,* 1987).

Tove Nilsen (1952–)
Norwegian author
Tove Nilsen has been writing novels, short stories and children's books since 1974 to popular and critical acclaim. Her trilogy about growing up in a suburb on Oslo's eastside in the late 1950s and early '60s has become a modern classic: *Skyskraperengler* (1982; Skyscraper Angels), *Skyskrapersommer* (1996; Skyscraper Summer) and *G for Georg* (1997; G for George). One of Nilsen's short stories has been anthologized in *An Everyday Story: Norwegian Women's Fiction* (1995).

Hagar Olsson (1893–1978)
Finnish journalist, critic and author
Hagar Olsson was a prolific literary critic who helped launch Finnish Modernism in the early twentieth century. Many of her essays were published in the collections *Ny generation* (1925; New Generation) and *Arbetare i natten* (1935; Workers in the Night). Known as an astute journalist and critic, Olsson also wrote novels, such as *Träsnidaren och döden* (1940; *The Woodcarver and Death*, 1965), which often incorporate themes from fairy tales and Finnish folklore. The autobiographical novel *Chitambo* (1933) is perhaps her best-known work today. A short story, "The Motorcycle," appears in *Scandinavian Women Writers: An Anthology from the 1880s to the 1980s* (1989).

Suzanne Osten (1944–)
Swedish theater and film director
As the director of the Unga Klara Stadsteatern since 1971, Suzanne Osten has been the driving force behind the development of children's theater in Sweden. In the early 1980s, she also turned to film as her medium and she is now one of the most important female film directors in Scandinavia. *Bröderna Mozart* (1986; The Mozart Brothers), *Skyddsängeln* (1990; The Guardian Angel) and *Bara du och jag* (1994; Only You and I) are a few of her films. The autobiographical book *Flickan, mamman och soporna* (1998; The Girl, the Mother and the Garbage) was preceded by *Papperspappan* (1994; The Paper Dad) and the non-fiction book *Barndom, feminism och galenskap: Osten om Osten* (1990; Childhood, Feminism and Madness: Osten on Osten.)

Cora Sandel (1880–1974)
Norwegian author
Few Norwegian authors have been translated into English as extensively as Cora Sandel. Her trilogy about Alberta is a classic in feminist literature: *Alberte og Jakob* (1926; *Alberta and Jacob*, 1984); *Alberte og friheten* (1931; *Alberta and Freedom*, 1984) and *Bare Alberte* (1939; *Alberta Alone*, 1984). Her two other novels have also been published in English translation: *Kranes*

konditori (1945; *Krane's Café: An Interior with Figures,* 1986) and *Kjøp ikke Dondi* (1958; *The Leech,* 1986). Sandel was a masterful short story writer and two collections of her short stories have appeared in English: *Cora Sandel: Selected Short Stories* (1985) and *The Silken Thread. Stories and Sketches* (1987).

Martha Sandwall-Bergström (1913–)
Swedish author

Translated into nine languages, Martha Sandwall-Bergström's novels about Kulla-Gulla are the Swedish equivalent of L.M. Montgomery's books about Anne of Green Gables. The first volume, *Kulla-Gulla* (1945), introduces the orphaned twelve-year-old child as an industrious and self-assured girl with much integrity and compassion. The score of books that followed depict Kulla-Gulla's journey from childhood to adult life, from stark poverty to prosperity. *Kulla-Gulla håller sitt löfte* (1946; *Anna Keeps Her Promise,* 1978), *Kulla-Gulla på herrgården* (1946; *Anna at the Manor House,* 1979) and *Kulla-Gulla vinner en seger* (1950; *Anna Wins Through,* 1979) are a few of the titles available in English.

Laila Stien (1946–)
Norwegian author

Laila Stien is from Northern Norway and she depicts the everyday world of the people living in that region in her short stories and novels. Stien writes fiction for adults, youth and children and her talent and accomplishments in all those areas have been recognized with several prizes. Regarded as one of Norway's foremost short story writers, she has published five collections of stories to date including *Sånt som skjer* (1988; Things Happen Like That) and, most recently, *Gjennom Glass* (1999; Through Glass). Two of Stien's short stories from *Fuglan veit* (1984; Only the Birds Know) are included in *An Everyday Story: Norwegian Women's Fiction* (1995).

Katarina Taikon (1932–1995)
Swedish Author

During the 1970s and the '80s, Katarina Taikon was the spokesperson for Gypsies in Sweden. Within a decade she wrote twenty books about the life of Katitzi and her family, offering insights into the *Rom* culture as well as the discrimination and superstition that accompany Gypsies in their daily life. Her books have been translated into other Scandinavian languages and into French and German. The story begins with *Katitzi* (1969). A few other titles are *Katitzi rymmer* (1971; Katitzi Runs Away); *Katitzi i skolan* (1975; Katitzi at School, and *Katitzi kommer hem* (1981; Katitzi Comes Home).

Annika Thor (1950–)
Swedish author
Annika Thor, like Susanne Levin, has a Swedish-Jewish background. She made her literary debut in 1996 with the book *En ö i havet* (An Island in the Ocean), which depicts two Jewish girls who are sent to Sweden from Vienna during World War II. Their story is continued in *Näckrosdammen* (1997; The Pond of Water Lilies) and *Havets djup* (1998; The Depth of the Ocean). *Sanning eller konsekvens* (1997; Truth or Consequence) was awarded the August Prize for the Best Book for Children and Youth in 1997.

Ellen Marie Vars (1957–)
Sámi author
Ellen Marie Vars is both journalist (editor for a Sámi newspaper) and author of books for children and young readers. Most of her work has not yet been translated from the Sámi language. The excerpt from her novel *Kátjá* (1986) included in this anthology first appeared in *In the Shadow of the Midnight Sun: Contemporary Sámi Prose and Poetry* (1996).

Sigrid Undset (1882–1948)
Norwegian author
Sigrid Undset won international acclaim with her medieval trilogy *Kristin Lavransdatter* (1920-22; *Kristin Lavransdatter*, 1923-27. New translation in 1997-2000). She immediately went on to write another medieval epic, the four volume *Olav Audunssøn i Hestviken* (1925-27; *The Master of Hestviken*, 1928-30). An earlier work set in the Middle Ages, *Fortællingen om Viga-Ljot og Vigdis* (1910; *Gunnar's Daughter*, 1936), was reissued in 1998. Undset also wrote fiction with a contemporary setting, e.g., the novel *Jenny* (1911; *Jenny*, 1921), and the short story "Omkring sædelighetsballet" (1912; "The Charity Ball" included in *An Everyday Story: Norwegian Women's Fiction*, 1995). Sigrid Undset was awarded the Nobel Prize for Literature in 1928.

Dikken Zwilgmeyer (1853–1913)
Norwegian author
Between 1890 and 1911 Dikken Zwilgmeyer published twelve books about Inger Johanne and the spunky thirteen-year-old has remained a favorite of Norwegian children throughout the twentieth century. Some of Zwilgmeyer's books for children were translated into English. These include *Visiting Grandfather and Eleven Other Stories* (1900); *What Happened to Inger Johanne* (1919); *Inger Johanne's Lively Doings* (1926), and may still be found in libraries. Zwilgmeyer also wrote adult fiction and one of her short stories is the title story in *An Everyday Story: Norwegian Women's Fiction* (1995).

About the Editors

IA DŪBOIS is Swedish by birth and received her Ph.D. in contemporary Swedish literature from the University of Washington, Seattle. Her postdoctoral research has focused on expressions of ethnic identity in Swedish literature. She is a lecturer at the Department of Scandinavian Studies at the University of Washington and teaches Swedish and Scandinavian culture and literature.

KATHERINE HANSON has taught Norwegian language and Scandinavian literature at a number of colleges and universities, most recently at Pacific Lutheran University. She is the editor of *An Everyday Story: Norwegian Women's Fiction*, a collection of short stories that spans two centuries and includes many of the Norwegian writers in *Echo*. She has also translated *Ask the Sun*, stories about the Cultural Revolution by the Chinese writer He Dong, who now lives in Norway. In collaboration with Judith Messick, Katherine Hanson has translated three novels by the nineteenth century writer Amalie Skram: *Constance Ring, Professor Hieronimus* and *St. Jørgen's* the latter two published in one volume titled *Under Observation.* She lives in Seattle.

Permissions Acknowledgements

Excerpt from *Josephine* by Maria Gripe. English translation copyright © 1970. Reprinted with the permission of TransBooks AB.

"The Golden Calf" from *Sculptor's Daughter* by Tove Jansson. English translation copyright © 1969 by Tove Jansson. Reprinted with the permission of Schildts.

Excerpt from *Early Spring* by Tove Ditlevsen. English translation copyright © 1985 by Seal Press. Reprinted with the permission of Seal Press.

"The Cave" by Irmelin Sandman Lilius. Copyright © 1986 by Irmelin Sandman Lilius. Published for the first time in English translation with the permission of Schildts.

Excerpt from *Ronja, the Robber's Daughter* by Astrid Lindgren. English translation copyright © 1981 by Astrid Lindgren. Reprinted with the permission of the author.

"The Child Who Loved Roads" by Cora Sandel. English translation copyright © 1984 by the Seal Press. Reprinted with the permission of Seal Press.

Excerpt from *Little Troll* by Karen Michaëlis. Copyright © 1946 by Karen Michaëlis with the collaboration of Lenore Sorsby.

Excerpt from *Katitzi* by Katarina Taikon. Copyright © 1977. Published for the first time in English translation with the permission of Mikael Langhammer.

Excerpt from *Mårbacka* by Selma Lagerlöf. Copyright ©1922. Published in a new English translation with the permission of The Swedish Writers Union.

Excerpt from *Chestnut Alley* by Dea Trier Mørch. Copyright ©1978 by Dea Trier Mørch. Published for the first time in English translation with the permission of the author and Gyldendal Dansk Forlag.

Excerpt from *The Girl, the Mother and the Garbage*. Copyright © 1998 by Susanne Osten. Published for the first time in English translation with the permission of Brombergs Bokförlage.

Excerpt from *Life Goes On* by Suzanne Levin. Copyright © 1994 by Suzanne Levin. Published for the first time in English translation with the permission of Bokförlaget Natur och Kultur.

Excerpt from *Kátjá* by Ellen Marie Vars. English translation copyright © 1996 by Ellen Marie Vars. Reprinted with the permission of the author.

Welcome to the World of International Women's Writing

Allskin and Other Tales by Contemporary Czech Women, edited by Alexandra Büchler. $14.95. ISBN: 1-879679-11-6. The first anthology of stories and novel excerpts by the leading women writers of the Czech Republic.

Ask the Sun by He Dong. $12.95. ISBN: 1-879679-10-8. Short stories about the Cultural Revolution from the perspective of a child by a Chinese writer who now lives in Norway.

Aurora by Giancarla de Quieroga. $12.95. ISBN: 1-879679-12-4. A passionate love story and political exploration of power and class, this is the first novel by a Bolivian woman to appear in English translation.

An Everyday Story: Norwegian Women's Fiction, edited by Katherine Hanson. $14.95. ISBN: 1-879679-07-8. Norway's tradition of storytelling comes alive in this enthralling anthology. The new expanded edition includes stories by contemporary writers.

The Four Winds by Gerd Brantenberg. $12.95. ISBN: 1-879679-05-1. Gerd Brantenberg is one of Norway's cultural treasures, and a lesbian author with a huge international following. This is her hilarious and moving novel of coming out in the sixties at the University of Oslo.

Nothing Happened by Ebba Haslund. $12.95. ISBN: 1-879679-13-2. A novel set in Norway just before the German Occupation in 1939 which explores love and friendship between women.

Two Women in One by Nawal el-Saadawi. $9.95. ISBN: 1-879679-01-9. One of this Egyptian feminist's most important novels, *Two Women in One* tells the story of Bahiah Shaheen, a well-behaved Cairo medical student—and her other side: rebellious, political and artistic.

Unmapped Territories: New Women's Fiction from Japan edited by Yukiko Tanaka. $10.95. ISBN: 1-879679-00-0. These stunning new stories by well-known and emerging writers chart a world of vanishing social and physical landmarks in a Japan both strange and familiar. With an insightful introduction by Tanaka on the literature and culture of the "era of women" in Japan.

Under Observation by Amalie Skram. With an introduction by Elaine Showalter. $15.95. ISBN: 1-879679-03-5. This riveting story of a woman painter confined against her will in a Copenhagen asylum is a classic of nineteenth century Norwegian literature by the author of *Constance Ring* and *Betrayed.*

Unnatural Mothers by Renate Dorrestein. $11.95. ISBN: 1-879679-06-X. One of the most original novels to appear from Holland in years, this compelling story of an archeologist and his eleven-year-old daughter's attempts to build a family is by turns satiric and heartbreaking.

Wayfarer: New Fiction by Korean Women, edited and translated by Bruce and Ju-Chan Fulton. $14.95. ISBN: 1-879679-09-4. A fresh and powerful collection of short stories by eight of Korea's top women writers.

WOMEN IN TRANSLATION is a nonprofit publishing company, dedicated to making women's fiction from around the world available in English translation. The books above may be ordered from us at 523 N. 84th St, Seattle, WA 98103. (Please include $3.00 postage and handling for the first book and 50¢ for each additional book.) Write to us for a free catalog or visit us at our Website: http://www.drizzle.com/~wit/